Fair Winds
and
Following Seas
Part One

By

Melissa Good

FLASHPOINT
PUBLICATIONS

ISBN 978-1-61929-476-9

Cover Design by AcornGraphics

Editors Verda Foster and Mary Hettel

Publisher's Note:

Books by Melissa Good

Dar and Kerry Series

Tropical Storm
Hurricane Watch
Eye of the Storm
Red Sky At Morning
Thicker Than Water
Terrors of the High Seas
Tropical Convergence
Storm Surge (Books 1 & 2)
Stormy Waters
Moving Target
Winds of Change (Book 1 & 2)
Southern Stars
Fair Winds and Following Seas
(Part 1 & 2)

Jess and Dev Series

Partners (Book 1 & 2)
Of Sea and Stars

Chapter One

The parking lot in front of the doughnut shop was unusually packed for this early on a Monday morning. Every spot was taken, and there was a line out the door along with a stream of people emerging with stacks of boxes.

In a spot near the door a sport truck was parked, engine idling, a short, blonde, woman seated inside keeping an eye on the rearview mirror. Inside, the radio played a weather report on a local station. In the cab of the truck two large Labrador retrievers sat upright with alert ears.

A battered flatbed truck pulled in and double parked. A man in a white tank top jumped out and got in line. "Oh, that's gonna be a fight," the blonde woman said and shook her head. "C'mon Dar, hurry up before they have to call the cops."

The cream-colored lab barked gruffly.

"I know, Cheebles." The woman reached back and gave the dog a pat, as the second dog agreeably licked her arm. "Almost done." She straightened the cuff on her cotton T-shirt, and then folded her hands in her denim covered lap. "We have to get some treats for the staff. Just had no idea everyone else was going to do the same thing."

Both dogs cocked their heads, ears perking on hearing the word treats.

"No, not for you." The door behind her swung open and she smiled. She rolled down the window on her side of the truck as Dar emerged, carrying a stack of doughnut boxes, several bags, and two cups balanced on top of everything. She swerved to avoid the people in line as she made her way over.

"Here." Dar handed a steaming cup of coffee to her. "Crazy in there." She put the stack of boxes and bags into a cabinet in the back of the truck and closed it, then went around to the driver's side and eased her tall frame into the seat. "This is nuts," she said, and shoved a pair of sunglasses over her eyes. "Since when did Dunkin Donuts become emergency supplies?"

Like her partner, Dar was dressed in jeans and a T-shirt, her dark hair pulled back into a ponytail. She boosted the air-conditioning a little, as Kerry rolled the window shut and blocked out the steamy late summer air.

She put her own cup into the holder on her side of the cab. "Look at that jackass." She indicated the double-parked truck. "He's going to get his ass kicked by the squad of angry grandmas in there picking up their doughnut holes."

Kerry took a sip of her coffee, set the cup into a holder in the center console, then hiked one boot up and set it on her knee. "Thanks for going in there on our behalf," she said. "I'm sure the staff are going to appreciate the thought."

"Gonna be a long day." Dar put the truck in gear and carefully pulled out, crossing several lanes of traffic to a left-turn lane with fluid grace. "Damned hurricane."

"Aw." Kerry regarded the swaying tree branches with a brief grin. "I'm kinda fond of them. I'll never forget my first one." She glanced sideways at Dar's profile. "Even if that was only a tropical storm."

Dar smiled and looked both ways before turning, despite the green turn arrow. "It's a pain in the ass because we've got so damn much going on," she said. "We were supposed to meet that commercial real estate agent this afternoon to see the building he found us."

"I checked it online. Not sure it'd done us much good. Looks like a run-down tire shop." Kerry sighed. "We're going to have to start putting people in hotel rooms at this rate." She sipped her coffee. "Or start turning down contracts. Do we want to do that?"

"Not for that reason," Dar said, as they turned down the street the office was on. "Let's have Maria call some of the long stay hotels near here, see if we can get a three-month deal." She slowed to avoid a scurrying chicken. "I can put up a point-to-point bridge if it's line of sight."

"Could be worse problems than having more work than space or people." Kerry said.

"Could be worse." Dar parked the truck in the lot. "Looks like everyone's here already. Glad we got lots of doughnuts."

She got out and opened the cab door. Both dogs jumped out and shook themselves, then followed them as they walked up the path toward the building.

****

Dar stood in the reception area by the admin, Zoe's desk, her arms folded over her chest. "Listen, putting shutters on this place is not my damned responsibility," she said, in a loud bark aimed at the speakerphone on the desk. "I don't give a damn if he's in Cozumel. Get someone over here or it's going to be your damn building getting wiped out and my lawyer filing a lawsuit!"

Zoe sat quietly nearby, her head nodding a little in emphasis at Dar's words. On the desk in front of her was a plate with a few crumbs on it, and she licked a little bit of sugar off her thumb as Dar hung up the phone in irritation. "They will not help us." She said, softly.

"Has no clue what to do," Dar said in disgust. "Must be his boyfriend of the month he picked up off the beach running the shop." She reached up and pinched the bridge of her nose. "No point in trying to find someone in the area they're all booked up doing it."

"Yes," Zoe agreed. "Would you like a coffee, Ms. Dar? Or a milk?"

"Not right now." Dar drummed her long fingers on her arm for a moment, then hit the speaker button on the phone again and dialed. "Let me try something else." It rang twice, then was picked up.

"Lo," a deep, gruff voice answered. "That you, Dardar?" The voice had a thick as molasses Southern accent.

"Hey, Dad," Dar said. "Got the boats all tied up?"

"Yeap," Andrew Roberts said. "How's it your side there?"

"Sucks," Dar said. "You know of anyone around who wants to make a few bucks putting up plywood on this place?" She asked. "The idiot landlord is on vacation and the guy subbing for him has the brains of a hamster."

Andy pondered in silence for a bit. "Ah might know some fellers," he said. "Lemme call round and we'll see."

"Thanks, Dad. I'm going to keep on their asses but any help would be great. Later." She hung up the phone. "Cross your fingers," she told Zoe. "He'll either show up with a few old buddies, or a construction battalion. If you hear a tank pull up, yell. We'll need to move our cars."

Zoe took this in calmly. "Yes I will, Ms. Dar. Would you like a milk now?"

"Sure," Dar said. "Bring it over to Ker's office." She circled the desk and went over to the right-hand side door, opening it and going inside.

Kerry stood at her desk with Mayte, going over a paper checklist. She glanced up as Dar entered. "Any luck? I heard you yelling."

"Gave up. Called Dad," Dar said, succinctly. "Told Zoe to yell if anyone rappels into the courtyard." She went over to the desk and perched on the end of it. "I don't think moving the gear into the hall is going to do jack squat if he can't find us some wood and guys who know what to do with it."

"Well, hon, if anyone can, it's him," Kerry said.

Mark Polenti, their operations director, entered and closed the door behind him. "Backups are done," he said. "Col's got all the payments out, and we just transmitted the AP invoices." He sat down in one of Kerry's visitor chairs. "So that's all right, but the problem is—"

"The problem is, if this place takes a direct hit, we're out of commission until it's sorted and that'll kill us," Kerry said. "None of us expected we'd end up as successful as we did and we outgrew ourselves. I know."

"And I have a compile due to be transferred to the DOD by the end of the day," Dar said. "We should have found a bunker."

"We shoulda, but we didn't, yet." Mark made a face. "The support guys...Dar, I can throw up a VPN to the telecom system and we can put them on a bus up to Melbourne. We've got the secure storage facility up there."

Dar nodded. "They'd end up with more space probably. They're crammed in there like sardines. Start calling around for a bus. Make sure it's got a rig for wheelchairs."

"Got it." Mark got up and pulled his phone out. "At least this is tourist central. Bus shouldn't be a problem." He walked out and closed the door behind him.

"Ugh," Kerry said. "Let me get this buttoned up, Dar. You go compile." She gave her a nudge. "Let's get as much done as we can before things start going to hell."

"Start?" Dar got up and headed for the connecting door between their offices. "Let's hope we don't end up working out of shipping containers."

****

Dar propped her head up on her hand and studied her screen, idly moving her trackball in a circle with her thumb. The large, high-resolution monitor displayed an intricate diagram, and she selected, then zoomed in on a section to review it.

A spatter of rain hit the window and she glanced over her shoulder, looking over the foliage dense neighborhood where branches were tossing in the wind.

After a minute, it faded, and the motion slowed, the clouds overhead visibly in motion as they moved aside and a bit of sun came through.

Squall. Dar shook her head and went back to her screen, made an adjustment, and then saved the file, compressing it, and added it to a folder sitting on her desktop. Squall, and a rain band.

Hurricanes were peculiar things. The center of the tropical cyclone was still far offshore. It sucked heat energy from the warm waters of the Atlantic and putting a twist in the atmosphere that gathered bands of low pressure around it.

Those bands extended out far from the center and swirled over water and land, bringing bursts of rain and wind and then dying off as though no storm was out there at all. It made preparing for one frustrating and occasionally dangerous when gusts of wind took panels and wood out of your hands.

This one, right now, had ninety mile per hour winds and a Category two status. But all the weather stations and NOAA were saying it was going to strengthen, and by the time it hit the nearby Gulf Stream current it could be a Category five, with 150 mile per hour winds and very dangerous.

Very dangerous Hurricane Bob, with his cheerful, friendly name.

The problem with hurricanes though, was that they were predictably unpredictable. Everyone said it could strengthen, could hit the Miami area, could cause hideous damage and it very well might do just that.

Dar glanced at the ticker running at the bottom of her monitor as a flashing icon indicated it was time for the two p.m. update from the National Weather Service. She sat back to wait for the scrawl, with its anticipated bad news.

Or it well might do nothing of the kind.

It could hit the Gulf Stream and veer off. It could fall apart because it sucked dry air into itself. It could stop and just spin offshore, dumping rain over the area for a week, bringing a flood threat more than wind. An eyewall replacement cycle could take it from a Category five, to a Category two again overnight and end up just being annoying.

You really never knew. It was tempting to take the chance, and not go through the effort to prepare for the worst, but every once in a while, the worst did happen.

Dar got up and hopped up and down a few times. She shook out her arms and then wandered over to the window to look out. On the streets nearby, she saw trucks and cars with plywood strapped to their roofs, storefronts with hurricane panels being put on their windows, and people carrying cases of water.

Water, cans of evaporated milk, tins of Vienna sausages, spam, and SpaghettiOs. Small camp stoves to boil water. Batteries, and battery powered fans. Like taking part in a bug out event in slow motion as everyone stopped everything and watched the big buzz saw approach.

She was more than a little frustrated. She could hear, even through the glass, the sound of hammers in the distance, and the faint whirring scream of a drill. "Damn it!"

Kerry entered from the door between their offices. "You say something, hon? Maria just made coffee." She put a cup down on Dar's desk and came over to the window and reached out to give Dar a light scratch on the back as she joined her.

"I said, damn it," Dar repeated. "As in, damn it, I hate having to depend on someone to get something done and they don't do it!" She slapped both hands against the sills on either side of the window. "Really pisses me off."

Kerry half turned and sat down on the windowsill, which had a thick base and a cushion designed specifically for that purpose. "I know," she said. "We talked about buying the building, remember?" She put a hand on Dar's leg, feeling the powerful muscles jump under her touch.

"We did." Dar turned and sat next to her, her back to the weather. "But we said we're outgrowing it, so did it make sense?"

"At the time, it didn't," Kerry agreed. "Then we found out there really isn't any open office space around here that works for us. And building your own office building takes a hell of a lot of time."

Dar made a face. "Grrrrrr."

"No one expected this little venture of ours to go like it did, honey." Kerry patted her arm, then leaned over and put her head on Dar's shoulder. "I mean, we planned the whole thing over drinks and coconut shrimp. I figured it'd be you, me, and a half dozen other people and we could work out of our boat if we had to."

Dar's tall body shook a little as she laughed silently.

"Was not expecting to be talking to you about buying office buildings in their entirety just yet."

"No, I know." Dar put her arms around Kerry and gave her a kiss on the top of her head. "I wasn't either. This just caught us by surprise."

There was a light tap on the outer door. "C'mon in," Dar called out.

Neither moved as the door opened, their relationship taken for granted by all, and certainly by Maria who entered and smiled at them. "I have I think some good news."

"Awesome," Kerry responded. "We could use some."

Maria came over to the window. She had a clipboard with papers on it. "I have heard from Manuel," she said. "He has two things he wants to come to show, even with the storm." She displayed the clipboard to them, turning so the light from the window fell on the pages. "You see?"

Kerry took the board and reviewed it. "Oh," she said. "Is this... what is this?"

"It is a house, here." Maria pointed. "He says, it will need a fix. But it is separate, you see here the wall? And it has the thing here for the boat."

Dar craned her head to look at it. "Ah. That's Hunter's Point." She looked at the sketchy diagram. "It's that kind of corner lot, near the park." She regarded it with interest. "It's for sale?"

"Si." Maria handed her the paper. "Manuel said he also was very surprised. And he also found this, not so good I think." She handed Kerry the other paper. "It is the property next door."

"Next door to... "Kerry took the paper. "Oh!" She glanced to her right in reflex. "The lot next door? That run down... whatever it was?" She got up and went to the other window, looking out. "We don't want to buy that, do we?"

"Manuel thinks it would not be good, no," Maria admitted. "But he sent it because it was here."

A thick hedge separated the land their office building was on with the lot next door. There were two buildings on it, overgrown and long unused, at least part of it used by the homeless population as a shelter. "Well..." She half turned as Maria joined her. "I guess we can ask what they want for it anyway."

"There is a lot of work," Maria added. "It will need to be built up as a new thing. Manuel will come here, but I have told him I do not think we will have time to look at this today."

Dar got up and went to her desk and brought up her screen. "I'm done with this," she said. "I'll go over and look at this place." She held up the paper, then put it down on the desk. "It's probably in worse shape than the place next door, but I'd like to see it."

"You know it, Dar?" Kerry asked.

"Of it, yeah." Dar addressed the package and sent it over their secure mail system. "It's a nice size piece of land, not like most of the places off the water." She straightened up and folded the paper and stuck it into the back pocket of her jeans. "Surprised it's on the market to be honest."

"Well, hon," Kerry said, "we could buy both and hope the storm wipes everything clear for us to start over again with them. Would be our luck."

Dar chuckled. "It would be."

****

Mayte popped her head into Maria's office. "Mama, there is a truck here. I think it is Dar's papa."

Maria bolted around her desk and trotted over to join Mayte. They went to the bay window overlooking the front of the building.

As Mayte had said, a large panel truck was parked now in front, somewhat blocking the street outside. A half dozen men were jumping out of it, all dressed in coveralls. A moment later, Andrew Roberts appeared from around the corner. He held a roll of paper in one big hand.

"This is good," Maria said in a satisfied tone.

There was a load of wood in the back of the truck, and along the sides were lashed two extension ladders. As the two women watched, the new arrivals started unloading the material onto the lawn. One of them paused to speak to Andy, who stood with his arms folded over his broad chest, a ball cap covering his grizzled dark crew cut.

He was in faded jeans and a short-sleeved cotton shirt, and like the six men wore heavy, worn combat boots.

Dar emerged from the front door and came over to them, and even at this distance, the family resemblance between her and Andrew was evident as they stood side by side settled into the same stance.

"Dar's papa is so nice," Mayte said, after a silent moment.

Maria smiled. "Si, he is a very nice man, and now he is taking care of this problem for us. So, we must now go and finish the preparations." She turned and shooed her daughter. "Vamanos."

They went back into the hallway where there were now folding tables set up on the inside walls covered in plastic bags. Technicians pushed rolling carts off the elevator at the end of the passage and piled computers and gear onto the tables.

"Get everything up here onto the second floor." Mark called out. "We need more bags!"

"I got em." A wheelchair sped down the hall with a tow-headed man in it, his legs missing below the knee. He wore a blue polo with the company logo on the chest, tied off khaki carpenter pants, and tools emerging from all the pockets.

There was a large box of outdoor garbage bags on his lap.

"Thanks, Scotty." Mark grabbed the box as he wheeled by and set it on a nearby table. He ripped the top open and pulled out the black bags. "Soon as we get this done, we can get you guys on the bus and upstate."

"No problem," Scott said. "Chuck is in the demark, putting bags over the punch downs."

"One sweet thing about not owning no home is not having to deal with all this crap."

Mark snorted. "No kidding. My wife's running around looking for a hose to empty the pool with right now."

Scott turned in his chair and unhooked a sack hanging from the back of it, lifting it up over his head and setting it down in his lap. He opened the top and removed a stack of boxes. "Got all the little NAS off the dudes downstairs."

"They still working?"

Scott nodded. "Got something they gotta do they said."

"They do." Mark moved along the tables, ripping bags out of the box and draping them. "Project deadline's COB today for that sim framework. They don't give a crap about hurricanes."

"No, my dear, banks don't either." Colleen swept by with a cart loaded with document storage boxes. "Never a dull moment around here, let me just say!"

The sound of a hammer drill suddenly thundered, loud and very nearby. "Sweet," Mark said. "Now we're getting somewhere." He headed for the stairs. "Wish the damned generator install hadn't been late."

"Fuckers probably sold it to a higher bidder," Scott called after him.

****

Dar got out of her truck, pausing to lean against it to wait for their real estate agent to park and join her. She studied the wall in front of the truck, old and weather worn, and she suspected made of coral. It was higher than she was tall, and there was a set of wrought iron gates in it, locked with a thick wrapped chain and lock.

Manuel arrived at her side and twitched his linen jacket straight. "Buenos Dias, senora," he said. "Thank you for meeting me today, I know it's hectic."

"Buenos Dias," Dar responded amiably. "Yeah, it's a mess. I was surprised to hear this was on the market, so it piqued my interest."

Diaz nodded. "And I as well. I was really surprised to see the listing. My secretary saw it, and brought it to my attention this morning when we got in." He gestured to the side of the gate, where a smaller entry stood. "I met with the selling agent and got the key."

"Old place." Dar followed him to the smaller gate and stood while he unlocked it and pulled it open with some effort. "Someone living here?"

"No, no." Manuel went through and held the gate open, then let it swing shut behind them. "Not for some months they have said." He paused and regarded the open space before them. "At least they keep a gardener to work it seems."

There was a long, deep lawn in front of them, the wall stretching on either side and then down the property line until it disappeared into a thick line of trees. "Could play soccer on this damn thing," Dar commented.

"You could put in tennis courts, a little golf course... sure," Manuel said. "Plenty of space. You could even build another house on it."

"Mm."

They walked down the driveway, a surface made of paver stones that were old, and dirty gray black, partially obscured by dirt. They might once have been white, Dar considered, glancing to either side as they neared the tree line. "Plenty private."

"Of that, it's certain," Diaz agreed. "It's a little point, not too common around here. Most of the other houses are side by side."

They followed the path as it entered the trees, and now the pavers turned a stained deep brown as the canopy closed over them, a band of mature trunks and thickly leaved branches with a scattering of broken and tumbled stone benches underneath them.

They passed a collapsed pagoda, and a wrought iron table covered in green moss, then the driveway bent to the left and they emerged into another cleared space, this one far less empty.

"Huh." Dar stopped, and put her hands on her hips, regarding the view.

Manuel eyed her with wary hope. "Interesting, isn't it?"

The house on the lot was a three-story structure, with a porch on the lower level extending all around it and steps up to the door facing them. There were windows on the second level with shutters over them, and the third seemed to have just portholes that were covered now with dirty wood.

It had an old-fashioned air about the architecture, but the structure seemed relatively sound, and the posts holding up the porch roof were straight and all present. "Could be worse," Dar said. "At least it's standing."

"Well, it needs a lot of updating," Manuel acknowledged. "The agent said they did a bit of work before they listed it, but he said he knew it was a fixer-upper."

"No kidding."

They climbed up onto the porch and he unlocked the front door, opening it and standing back to let her enter. "I mean, the structure is okay, but there's nothing modern in it," he said. "Needs electrical, air-conditioning, plumbing. Nothing's to code, you understand?"

Dar paused inside the front door and looked around. The house was utterly empty but smelled faintly of old wood and a bit of new paint. "Yeah, I get it," she said. There was a staircase going up on either side of the entry, and the ceiling was high giving a general air of space.

It was dim inside, and very stuffy. "No power?" Dar guessed.

"No." Manuel shook his head. "The power, water, all of that's shut down for a long time. I told them they'd need to be certified for mold and spores. You will need a twenty-ton unit to cool this structure, and there's no insulation anywhere."

"Lot of work," Dar said. "Permitting'll take forever."

"No kidding," Manuel replied. "This is gonna make a general contractor a happy, rich man." He looked around the inside. "But there's some good structure here. It's very open. Not like some of the little boxes in boxes they build today."

"That's true."

Past the entry there were doors and they were open. They walked through them into a large room that filled the width of the house, with another set of double doors in the back that led into another room the same size.

At the back of that were floor to ceiling windows and those looked out onto the water, overlooking a multilevel pool area, with a large, battered, very empty pool.

Dar walked to the windows and looked out. The edge of the property was uneven and jagged, a seawall made of rocks surrounded the edge and a long stone dock extended out into Biscayne Bay.

Most of the grounds were overgrown with weeds and the deck itself was cracked and worn. There were double doors that opened out and she pushed them open, grimacing a little at the creak of the worn and warped wood as it scraped over the stone.

A breeze ruffled the waters and blew against her and she walked out onto the deck, past the empty pool, and then turned around to look at the house.

Manuel, following at her heels and watched her attentively. "You like this," he said confidently.

"I do," Dar admitted, with a faint smile. "Damn it's a mess. It'd be cheaper to build it from scratch probably, and the last thing I need in my life right now is a renovation project. But I do like it." She turned back around and took in a breath of the sea air.

"Not a good time to look at this type of property," Manuel said a touch mournfully, as a ragged line of clouds started moving overhead in another squall. "But I can say, this will not be on the market long. I think someone will buy it quickly, and make a guest house, or a hotel out of it. Could pay nicely for that."

"Well, not until the hurricane's over. You can't close with insurance under an active watch or warning," Dar said, in a practical tone. "And this is gonna need a big windstorm rider."

"That is so." Manuel edged back toward the doors as it started raining. "How about we go inside and I can show you what they're asking?"

Dar took out her cellphone and took some pictures of the outside, then ducked inside as the rain started coming down in a sheet. "No harm in looking." She took some pictures of the dining room, then went to a door on one side and pushed it open to reveal a hallway into a very large kitchen. "Talks cheap, right?"

Manuel smiled, following her into the space and removing a folder from underneath one arm.

****

Kerry perched on the edge of the folding table, raising a hand to wipe a sheen of perspiration off her face and push her hair back out of her eyes.

"Whoow." She looked down the hallway, now lit with the overhead fluo-rescents as half the windows were covered in plywood.

The tables were full, packed with gear, and swathed in heavy black plastic. Underneath the tables were waterproof crates full of personal effects and supplies. She watched Scott wheel out of the elevator, his arms shoving the rims of his chair powerfully as he pulled a laden cart behind him.

The once homeless veteran, now a senior in the tech support depart-ment, had turned out to be one of their best workers. He was good on the phone with customers, was a tenacious troubleshooter, and his quirky atti-tude and humor kept things lively in the support bullpen.

Kerry gave a tip of her mental hat to Dar, who'd hired him. "That the last load, Scott?"

"Freakin hope so." Scott twisted in the chair and unhooked the cart, then pivoted around to start stacking the contents in a yet uncovered water-tight case.

His wheelchair had been hacked. Kerry considered that was the best description of it.

There were no handles to push it from behind, instead, a metal grid was fastened to it with hooks and bungy cords for carrying gear, and the wheels themselves looked more like bicycle tires, turned by rims with nubs, and hand brakes so Scott could stop and turn, lift up onto the rear wheels and spin in a circle.

He lived in an equally hacked motor home parked in the parking lot of the gym just down the block, where he spent his free time working out and doing some IT favors for the management there in exchange for them let-ting him plug in his RV to an outside outlet.

His salary could have easily gotten him into an apartment, but he had no interest, retreating to his compact, disability friendly haven with its sat-ellite TV and no one to bother him. His old friends had moved on, and Kerry didn't know if he'd found new ones, but he seemed content, and the other techs all liked him.

Zoe appeared at her elbow. "Miss Kerry? The bus has come outside."

Kerry hoisted herself up off the table and went to the window, spotting a big blue passenger bus now parked on the side of the building. The driver opened the lower storage for it, and Mark had gone out to talk to him. "Did we get hotel rooms?"

"Yes." Zoe came over next to her and regarded the bus. "Ms. Maria has made it so there will be a meal waiting when they get there also."

"Great." Kerry went to the stairs and dropped down them two at a time, moving past the receptionists' desk and into the lower hallway. She walked across to the far side and then down the long side hallway until she came to the support desk bullpen. "Hey, guys."

There were two dozen techs inside, both male and female, and they turned as she entered and straightened to focus on her. They were all dressed in company polos and jeans, most were finishing up wrapping cables and putting headsets in plastic bags.

"The bus is here," Kerry announced. "So, grab your bags and get them loaded up. We've got hotel rooms and dinner waiting for you up there in Melbourne."

"Hot damn." Keela hoisted her backpack onto her back. "Jimmy, you got this?"

Jimmy was on the phone, and he half turned, giving her a thumbs up. Then he went back to his call, his eyes flicking over the screen of the PC in front of him. "They're going to have to wait tonight until we get the rig up."

Mark came in behind her. "Jesus, we need more people."

Kerry regarded him wryly. "If the Melbourne thing works out, maybe we can keep a group up there permanently. You think we can do some recruiting while we're in the area?"

"Mmm... good idea." Mark disappeared out of the room.

"Where is... ah there you are." Ceci Roberts appeared, dodging the stream of outgoing techs and joined Kerry near the back of the room. "Now I remembered all over again why I never really cared for this whole hurricane situation."

Kerry smiled at her mother-in-law. "Yeah, I used to read about those hurricane parties and thought wow, that might be kind of fun."

"It's not fun."

"It's not fun," Kerry echoed. "It's a lot of work, and it's causing us a lot of trouble."

Ceci nodded. She and Kerry were roughly the same height, and they both had pale hair, and slim builds. Most people who met them assumed they were related by blood rather than marriage. "Where's my kid?"

"House hunting." Kerry inspected the phone queue, gave Jimmy a pat on the back, and then she led the way back out into the hallway. "Want some tea?"

"House hunting in the middle of a hurricane warning. Nice." Ceci followed her. "I'd love some tea. I was about to go find some pizza for Andy and the boys."

They went to the first-floor kitchen, where there were now stacks of water in bottles against the wall along with packages of toilet paper. Kerry went to the hot water dispenser and retrieved two cups, adding some tea bags. "He saved our asses. The landlord is out of the country and whoever he had filling in for him is worth about as much as these tea bags once we're done with them."

Ceci pulled her cell phone out of her pocket to dial a number. "Since our prep consisted of parking the boat," she said, "and the shutters at your place out there are electric, I think he was feeling a little left out of all the getting ready nonsense to be honest."

"Thank goodness." Kerry handed her one of the cups. "We have so much in flight, it's crazy. Dar just finished one project and sent it off, and we've got two more due by the end of the week. If we get a hit here, I've got no idea how we're going to make those deadlines."

"Too successful for your own good," Ceci replied, watching her with a wry grin. "It's sort of hilarious."

"That could be true," Kerry admitted. "But at least, with those closed contracts it puts enough in the bank for us to expand." She glanced to her right. "That plot of land next door's open."

Ceci's pale eyebrows hiked up. "That swamp? Kerry it would take five years to clear that land and redo it."

Kerry nodded. "I know. But it's the only reasonably sized lot in the area. Otherwise, we need to move out of the city, either way south, or way north."

"Ew."

"Yeah," Kerry said. "I like it here." She exhaled. "What a mess. When we signed the contract on this place, we figured we'd have growth space for a couple years."

Ceci chuckled.

"And with all our government contracts, we have to work with secure space. It's not like I can just put people anywhere." Kerry took a sip of her tea. "They're really excited about that new rig Dar's designing, but I think she's going to end up finishing the programming in some bunker in the hills."

"Big?"

"Massive," Kerry said. "She did a demo for them three weeks ago and I swear they nearly pissed their starched uniform pants." She glanced around and lowered her voice. "I had to come up with a lot of vague, weird language to file our patent on it."

"That's pretty damn exciting actually," Ceci said. She followed Kerry as they went out into the hallway, the sound of drills and hammers easily heard from outside. "Let me get this pizza ordered," Ceci said. "Where's Dar out looking, by the way? Nearby?"

"Some place called Hunter's Point," Kerry said. "I was going to Google it."

Ceci paused in mid dial. "Huh? I can't believe the old man put that up for sale. He even told a bunch of those big money boys who wanted to buy it to kiss his ass."

"Now I really want to Google it." Kerry led the way up to her office. "Let's add enough pizza for everyone." She suggested. "You can even share yours with Scott."

"Yes, nice having another vegetarian around."

****

Dar sat in her truck, both doors open to let a cross breeze through the cab as Manuel sorted through a folder of papers. "So, wait, old man Hunter died?"

Manuel nodded. "Si, yes. Perhaps six months ago? They took some time to sort out the will and his granddaughter inherited this place." He handed her a sheet. "She very much wants to sell it."

Dar nodded. "That explains it. I know he was holding onto this place like a tick." She regarded the piece of paper, full of dense typing. "Developers tried to buy it off him for years... that's why I was surprised it was on the market. He was notorious for telling everyone to drop dead."

Manuel nodded. "That is what I also heard. He was a very harsh man, they said. But this property was paid off totally, no one could affect it." He glanced around. "We have the exclusive listing. My uncle did some paperwork for the gentleman in the past."

"All profit then. Good deal for the grandkid." She lifted her head and regarded the property and its stone wall. "Soon as someone hears this is on the market it's going to be a bidding war."

"Si."

Dar smiled briefly. "Tell the kid I'll pay what she's asking, in cash, soon as the title can close, as is."

Manuel frowned. "Ms. Roberts, that is not a good deal. There is a lot of work that is needed here." He gestured vaguely at the property. "The codes have changed; it needs a new electrical service..."

"Pointless unless we can close on it," Dar said. "See if the kid really wants to sell it as fast as she said. She may not, may wait to see if someone ups it." She handed the paper back. "I know what this piece of land's worth to a guesthouse developer. Give it a try. We don't grab it now, it'll be out of my range as soon as everyone else figures out it's available."

Manuel nodded. "Bueno, I will. I will call her right now, and let's see what it is she has to say to me." He got out of the truck and walked over to the gates, took out his phone and turned his back to Dar.

Dar leaned back in her seat and pulled out her phone, opening up her texting app and typing a quick message to Kerry. She sent it, then paused and expectantly watched the screen.

A moment later it lit up. "Hey." She answered it and propped one booted foot up against the door jamb. "Figured you'd call me."

"Honey, do you really want to make that decision today?" Kerry's tone, though, was humorous. "I know you hate to sleep on things, but Jesus."

"I like it," Dar said. "You will too," she added confidently. "But the deal is, if it gets around that this is on the market Marriott'll drive the price past anything we can do."

"Ah, a now or never thing."

"Something like that, yeah. The old guy who owned this thing was a jackass. Sounds like the kid that inherited wants no part of that." Dar watched as Manuel paced back and forth, one hand on the phone, one waving in a typical Latin motion.

"Got room for a garden?" Kerry asked.

Dar regarded the gates. "Got room for you to plant a crop of wheat and add a flock of sheep to keep the grass short. Probably have to rebuild the house from the ground up, hasn't been touched since the 40s," she said. "No power, no AC..."

"Flush toilets?"

Dar pondered. "I didn't check that. But I also didn't see any out-houses."

Kerry chuckled. "Okay, well, hon, I've got the bus being loaded here and a pizza truck just drove up so let me know what happens, okay?"

Dar smiled. "I'll get back there in a few minutes," she promised. "Want me to grab you some sushi?"

"Mm."

"Got it," Dar said. "See ya." She hung up and slid the phone back into her pocket as Manuel got into the passenger side of the truck and ran his fingers through his thick, black hair. "And?"

"It is very interesting," Manuel said. "The young lady, Ms. Gardner, did not want to speak to me at the beginning. She did not like my voice."

Dar regarded him with a slight frown. "Didn't like your voice?" She repeated.

"But I did get to say your offer," Manuel went on, holding a hand up. "So, there is no problem there. In fact, she found that very interesting and she is coming here right now to meet you." He glanced at her. "I hope that is all right. I know it is a very busy day."

"Well..." Dar pondered. It was more or less what she'd hoped, best case, would happen and therefore somewhat stunning to her that it had. "If she didn't like your voice without meeting you, I'm gonna guess this is going to be fast, one way or the other." She glanced at her watch. "Hope she's close. I've got sushi to acquire."

"She said ten minutes." Manuel sat back in the seat and mopped the sweat off his brow with a handkerchief as Dar boosted the AC a little. "But yes, my wife is right now at Sedanos. It is no doubt a loco day."

****

Kerry leaned over the phone on her desk, trying to block out the sound of the hammer drill behind her, "Sorry, John. They're putting up shutters," she said. "It's a little crazy here today."

"No kidding!" The voice on the other end of the phone said. "You're the only one who answered your damn phone down there. It's nuts! How can you expect to get business done?"

"Well," Kerry pressed the receiver against her ear, "you know, hurri-canes are a thing. No one enjoys them but you can't pretend they're not there." She glanced toward the door to her office where Zoe and Mayte were conversing. "Pain in the behind, actually."

"So move," John suggested. "Nobody says you have to park your office down there. Customers don't care about what you all have to deal with. We just want results."

"We talked about it." Kerry kept her tone even. "But most places have something they have to worry about. Tornados, floods, earthquakes or whatnot. The difference with hurricanes is you see them coming."

"And they take a hell of a lot more time away from doing business," John said firmly. "I'm telling you, Kerry—don't get me wrong. I like you. I like Dar. I like what you've done for us, but now you're telling me I might not have my build by Friday because you might be closed?"

"The problem is, John, we don't know. This thing could veer off and do nothing," Kerry said. "We're moving some of our teams out of the area, and Mark's working on standing up a cloud instance of our code base so we can have the programmers work remotely. We could have no impact at all, but we also could have the building blown apart if we take a direct hit here, and I thought it was only responsible of me to let you know the whole story."

There was a brief silence. "Yeah, no I get it," John said, in a grumpy tone. "And I do appreciate the transparency, Kerry. I just need to make my checkpoints. This is a big deal for us."

"John, I give you my word we will do everything we can to keep you on schedule. It's a big deal for us, too."

John grunted softly. "Fair enough. Good luck, huh? I usually don't pay attention to that tropical stuff, but I signed up for the alerts this time. Crossing my fingers it goes and hits Cuba."

"Crossing my fingers it just blows apart and goes nowhere," Kerry said. "Thanks, John. I'll be in touch."

She hung up the phone and sat back, reaching up with one hand to push the thick, pale hair out of her eyes. "What's the news, ladies?" She called out to Mayte and Zoe. "Bus take off?"

Mayte came forward with her clipboard, and Zoe trailed after her. It was now dark in the office, the windows covered with plywood. Kerry leaned over to turn on the desk lamp.

"The bus has left, yes," Mayte said. "The accounting people have finished their work, and Ms. Colleen has let them go home to prepare for themselves. Mr. Mark has not come back from the other building yet."

"He's competing with everyone trying to find space I guess." Kerry sighed. "Okay, whoever is done with their prep here, including you two, "She eyed them, "go on home and get your stuff done. Did we set up the phone dial-in system?"

Zoe nodded. "We have the code," she said, in her soft voice. "We can put in the message, and everybody knows to call and find out."

"Okay." Kerry stood up behind her desk and stretched. "Let me go call Dar and find out where the hell she is, and then we can wrap this up." She walked to the door of the office with them and looked up and down the hallway.

It was much quieter inside now, the doors to the individual offices were closed, the tables in the hall were covered in their plastic tarps.

Andrew Roberts was standing at the far end of the passage, his arms folded over his chest, two of the men he'd brought with him positioning a large sheet of plywood over the window at the end. He spotted Kerry and headed her way, his T-shirt covered in wood shavings and dark with sweat.

Kerry met him halfway. "We owe you big, Dad."

"Well." Andrew looked around with a dubious expression. "Ain't the best. But it's what could be done. This here place should have them shutters like ovah on the island does."

"It's true," Kerry said. "Landlord didn't want to spend the money. Now I'm going to write that into our lease renewal and whatever it cost for you to do this I'm deducting from our rent this month." She put her hands on her hips. "Should have done it the first time, but who knew?"

Andrew chuckled.

"I mean, who knew this was going to take off like it did? We were just worried about having a few desks to sit at to make sales calls the first few months."

"Need more space now," he agreed. "Ain't much room round here."

Kerry turned as she heard familiar steps on the stairs. "Ah." She smiled as Dar appeared at the top of the landing, a paper bag in her hand. "There you are."

"Here I am," Dar said. "Hi, Dad."

"Hey, rugrat," Andrew greeted her amiably.

"How'd the property thing go?" Kerry asked and reached for the bag. "Good?"

"Interesting," Dar said.

"Uh oh." Kerry bumped her toward the kitchen. "Tell me while I chow."

****

It was a mango tango roll. Kerry chewed a piece of it while she watched Dar assemble herself a cup of coffee and sit down across from her at one of the small tables in the break room. "So?"

Dar called up the pictures she'd taken and handed her phone over. Kerry thumbed through them. "Holy freaking crap," she blurted, putting down the chopsticks. "That's bigger than my parent's house."

"Probably," Dar agreed. "Definitely more property."

"Woah." Kerry looked up. "How old is it?"

"Nineteen forties, I guess," Dar said. "Like I said, no AC, no power right now... it's a crap ton of redo."

Kerry looked at the next picture, taken from the back of the house looking out over the water. "Nice view." She reviewed the panorama. "And a dock for the boat."

"Uh huh."

"Dog's'll love it."

"Without a doubt," Dar agreed. "Like I said, you could plant acres of wheat there, and a flock of sheep."

"Unbelievable amount of land... how in the hell did they hold onto it that long? You could park a whole Sandals on that corner." Kerry shook her head. "Okay, I get why you bit." She handed the phone back and picked up her chopsticks, expertly selecting another section of sushi and putting it between her teeth. "I like it."

"I knew you would." Dar set the phone down and sat back, cradling her coffee cup in her hands. "The old man who owned it was a notorious asshole. His great, great something was an original settler in the area back in the day when it was mostly mangrove and scrub, and Henry Flagler was building his railroad to bring all his rich friends south for the winter."

"Uh huh."

"He wouldn't sell the land just because he didn't want to. He just sat on it all these years," Dar went on. "Drove the county crazy. You know how much taxes they could have made on that land if it was commercially developed?"

Kerry chortled softly under her breath. "Oh yeah, I can imagine."

"Anyway, he's gone," Dar said. "Died a few months back. His grand-daughter inherited the place. "Twenty something kid. Can't sell it fast enough."

Kerry chewed and swallowed, studying Dar's face. "That's bad?" She watched Dar's eyes narrow. "You talk to her?"

Dar nodded.

"You don't like her," Kerry said, in a tone of certainty.

"I don't like her," Dar said. "She lives in California."

Kerry consumed another piece of sushi. "Well, a lot of people do, Dar. It's not a crime, at least last I heard."

"She's an arrogant bitch," Dar said. "She's in the entertainment business or something along those lines out there."

Kerry sucked on the tip of her chopstick. "Family?" She guessed and watched Dar definitively shake her head back and forth.

"Total breeder," Dar said, succinctly. "And a complete racist anti-immigrant asshole." She added, unexpectedly.

In the midst of taking another bite of her food, Kerry stopped in mid motion, the sushi halfway to her mouth, her light green eyes opening wide in surprise. "The kid?" she said, in some astonishment. "From California?"

"The kid, from California," Dar confirmed. "Apparently that's why she can't stand South Florida. Can't deal with all the people from other places."

Kerry's blonde eyebrows knit together, her face contracting in puzzlement. "Dar," she said. "I've been to California. It used to be part of Mexico. There's a lot of people there from other places."

Dar shrugged and took a sip of her coffee. "Kicked Manuel out of my truck. Had a complete flagpole up her ass until I started talking and she realized I wasn't Latin myself." She regarded Kerry dourly. "Which she, I guess, assumed because my agent is Latin, and I've got a tan."

"Holy bananas." Kerry put the sushi down. "Did you withdraw your offer?" She asked. "Or... I mean, I'm sure she backed out when she realized you were gay." She paused. "You told her that, right? Just to piss her off? I would have."

"I did. Didn't care." Dar shook her head. "All she cared about after that was did I have the cash and the fact I wasn't...wasn't from someplace else." She swallowed some coffee. "Said I was the first person who'd made an offer who wasn't a Latin man and she wanted nothing more than to screw them all by selling it to me."

Kerry blinked. "Wow," she finally said. "Isn't that a little young to be so... um..."

"Hate filled? You'd think," Dar said. "I wanted to kick her ass right into Biscayne Bay." She exhaled. "Matter of fact, when she found out I was married to another woman she thought that was awesomely hilarious."

"Awesomely hilarious," Kerry repeated, propping her chin on her fist and she gazed across the table at Dar. "So, we're buying it?" She ventured. "Or are you going to front the offer to some lawyer for Hilton named Juan? Because in the asshole Olympics I've seen you score gold, hon. Chickee from Malibu is not in your class, y'know?"

Dar smiled, finally, and chuckled a little. "Yeah, I don't know. She just ... maybe it was all the stuff going on today she rubbed me the wrong way with all that crap." She shrugged a little. "I told her we'd go forward with it. Hell, I sent it all to Richard. For all I know the stupid bitch doesn't even have clear title."

"Well," Kerry mused. "She should like him at least. He sounds as midwestern as I do."

"And, since we're under a hurricane watch... or is it warning already?" Dar asked. "It's got to wait for insurance clearance anyway. So who knows." She nodded at the plate. "Finish your lunch. I'm gonna go see what else I can wrap up before all hell breaks loose here." She stood up. "Bus gone?"

Kerry nodded. "Mark's still looking for secure server space," she said, before picking up a piece of the sushi roll. "I've been pushing off a call from Washington all day."

"Great."

"We decided to only code that local, hon," Kerry reminded her. "Twenty-twenty hindsight..."

"Twenty-twenty hindsight, we needed Seeing Eye dogs," Dar said. "So let me go find ours and see what I can do to help get us out of this mess."

****

By evening the winds picked up and the staff was winding down. Kerry walked through the lower floor and stuck her head into all the offices to make sure no one was left, the rooms as buttoned up as they could be, windows covered in plywood and everything off the floor.

Hurricanes were tricky things. The winds were dangerous, sure, but even more so if the storm came over the bay it would generate a storm surge that would pick up the waters not far from where they were and push what amounted to a slow-motion tidal wave over the land.

Flooding caused more damage than wind, sometimes with them and where they were just off the bay, meant it was quite possible the building would suffer both and they would have one hell of a mess to deal with.

She got to the server room and walked inside, the sound of the water chilled racks and stacks of equipment providing a ferocious low-pitched hum.

Dar was inside, arms folded, talking to Mark. Neither looked happy.

"Not a damn thing," Mark said. "They couldn't even spare two racks." He looked sweaty and there were smudges of dirt across his skin and his face. "I don't see any way of keeping this stuff up, Dar. I say our best bet is to move it to the very top of the racks and hope for the best."

"Or take it home," Dar said. "That place I live in's built like a brick shithouse."

Kerry joined them. "It is," she said. "And now that the island's got generators, there's a chance you could actually run these things." She regarded the racks. "But, hon, we're not going to get chilled brine cooling there in a day."

"No," Dar mused. "But if the power's out here, it's not going to matter." She looked up at the ceiling. "We can't send copies of the code home with the programmers. It's secure." She shook her head. "We're going to have to shut down the system and just secure it here, I think."

Mark nodded. "Figured that." He exhaled. "Once this is over, we can see about secured space... maybe one of the government centers?"

Dar shook her head. "No. I don't want to give up control over the code until we hand it over. Call me crazy."

"Never do that." Mark grinned briefly. "That new AI stuff you're doing is freakazoid coolness."

Kerry spoke up. "Yeah. Which is why leaving it here worries me. Maybe we should take it to our place, Dar. At least you'd have your hands on it there."

"Mm."

Carlos popped inside, turning a little sideways to let his big frame clear the door. "I jiggled around the inputs, and I got this whole level up on the UPS circuit," he said. "For the cams, I mean, and it'll keep the link up for maybe 48 hours."

"Good job," Mark said. "Least we'll be able to see what's going on here."

"Yeah, but we can't do much if someone breaks in," Carlos said. "And for sure the cops won't. They won't dispatch during the storm." He cleared his throat. "So, I thought… listen, how those guys boarded this place up, it's a hell of a lot safer than my apartment. I can stay here."

Dar drew breath as though to protest, then paused thoughtfully. "On the second level you mean?" She clarified.

Carlos nodded. "Yeah, in the corner there. I figured if we close all the doors, it'd be okay. We got enough supplies… we got water here, and I've got enough protein powder to last me a week." He grinned briefly. "Two of my buddies wanted to hang out too. They're east and had to evac. It's better here than one of those shelters."

He looked around at their faces. "What do ya think?"

Kerry glanced at Dar in silent deferral.

"Not a bad idea is what I think," Dar said, after a long pause. "Since you volunteered." She added. "I wouldn't have asked anyone to."

Carlos smiled. "Figured I should before you did." He gave her a sideways look, as Mark started to laugh and then a moment later they all did.

"Busted," Dar admitted, sticking her hands in her jeans pockets. "That secure code base has me spooked. I won't lie. It'll make me feel a lot better to have someone here."

Her security director gave her a thumbs up. "We got you covered, boss," Carlos assured her. "I'll go text my buds to bring over our camping gear. If we couldn't talk you into this, we were going to stay in the gym but their roof's kinda iffy."

Dar smiled in acknowledgment and looked over at Mark. "How's the five p.m.?"

"Hundred and ten," Mark said. "Going through an eyewall replacement cycle, so that means it's going to boof up overnight." He glanced around. "I might talk Barb into coming over here. Those military buds of Big A did not mess around."

"They never do," Kerry said. "I've gotten a whole new appreciation for the military since I've known Dar."

Mayte entered the room, carrying several small waterproof cases in her hands. "Here we go." She set them down on the worktable in the server room. "I have gotten satellite telephones so we can talk to each other if the regular phones have a problem." She regarded the boxes. "Like last time."

"Good job, Mayte." Kerry went over to examine the boxes. "This is great. I hadn't even thought of that. I forgot the last time we lost power and cell towers were down all over the place."

"Awesome sauce!" Carlos said. "I can keep one here, so I can let you know what's going on after it's done."

They sorted out the boxes. "I think we're as ready as we're gonna be," Mark said. "I've gotta stop for some evaporated milk on the way home. Barb couldn't find any." He looked over at Dar and Kerry. "You going home?"

Dar hesitated, then nodded. "Yeah, you're right. We've done all we can. Did the bus get to where it was going?"

"They're up and running," Mark said, briskly. "They've got calls online, and it's all good for now." He paused. "Unless the hurricane decides to jack up north. That would kinda suck."

"It could," Dar said. "Sometimes these things are just Mother Nature's middle finger, y'know?"

"Oh, I know," Mark agreed. "But I also know the more prepared you are, the less you need to be. I told the bus company to stay with em. If it looks like it does a hockey stick we just bring em back down the west coast."

"Good plan," Kerry said.

They walked out of the server room and locked the door behind them, stifling the hum as they made one last pass around the lower floor. The receptionist's desk had been packed up and set on top of the conference table in the conference room, and as they came to the foot of the stairs, two Labradors came trotting down to greet them.

"You ready to go home, guys?" Kerry sat down on the stairs as the two animals climbed all over her, smacking her with their tails. "Oof."

"Hey," Carlos said suddenly. "What about Scott's buggy? It's in the back of the lot by the gym... against those trees so I guess it's got some shelter, but my buds just texted me about it." He held up his phone. "Want to know if we wanted to do anything about it."

Kerry looked at Mark, "Did he say anything before he left?"

"He said screw it. If it gets blown apart he'll just get another one," Mark said. "He didn't seem like he cared too much, but you know Scott. He's pretty random."

"Yeah he's pretty live in the moment," Kerry mused. "I guess that's understandable."

"That was a lot of work though," Dar said. "How about I pull it into the middle area with my truck. It's more sheltered than the parking lot." She pointed to the center of the square building that served as a picnic area for lunch. The small tables scattered around had now been brought inside. "I can back it in through the loading dock."

Mark glanced at his watch. "That'd work. And it won't take much time."

"Won't take long at all," Carlos said. "I'll go run down there and get it ready to go if you pull around." He put his satellite phone down on the conference table and opened the front door, holding it against the gusting wind. "Yeah, it's time."

Dar got her keys out. "Ker..."

"I'll stay here with the kids," Kerry said. "And get the back gates open. It's a good idea. I know he said he didn't care, but if we can make it any safer, we should, and protect his stuff too."

"We should," Mark agreed. "Glad you brought it up, C."

****

"We just made it," Kerry said. She leaned back in the passenger seat of the truck as Dar turned off the engine, a wash of rain coming over the deck of the ferry they were parked on. "Holy crap that would have been a mess if we hadn't."

Dar shrugged. "We would have ended up staying in the office," she said. "But I'm glad we got to the ferry in time."

Kerry idly stroked Chino's head, which was sticking out between the seats. "I think I'm going to like not being reliant on a boat to get home," she said as the ferry undocked and started the slow churn toward the island they lived on. "Aside from the rest of it."

"Mm." Dar grunted agreement. "Yeah."

"No neighbors. No condo association," Kerry mused. "The more I think about it, the more I'm liking the idea." She stifled a yawn. "Crossing my fingers your gamble pays off."

Dar reached over and took Kerry's hand in hers, squeezing it gently. "Do my best to make it happen." She promised. "But let's get past this damn storm first."

Kerry chuckled wryly. "Fair."

The cut was full of ruffled white waves, and as the ferry approached the island dock, they saw the trees moving in fitful bends, the ground already showing evidence of downed fronds. Palms were designed for that, though. The branches were meant to give with the wind, and the trunk was smooth to let the force of it pass unrestricted.

Coconuts, though... a gardener in a maintenance cart was moving quickly along the line of the trees, picking up fallen branches and nuts, and stopping to use a pole with a hook to pull down those that looked perilous.

The other two ferries were already in their maintenance bays, with lines securing them, and the ramp had been stripped of its usual lines and guides, the landing looking very bare as this last ferry slowly nosed into place.

"Looks like it's really starting up," Kerry said, as Dar started the trucks engine. "Is that thing moving faster?"

"Let's check the eight-o clock intermediary," Dar said. "The outer bands were pretty spread out. But if it's moving faster that's maybe not good either."

"Faster is bad?" Kerry asked. "I thought the weather guy was saying the other day faster was better?"

"Well, Andrew was a speedy little buzz saw, but it came with embedded tornadoes that laid waste to most of South Miami," Dar said. "Two or three more recent ones weren't as powerful, but they just sat there offshore in weak steering and spun and spun and dumped rain and storm surge across all three counties."

"Bad either way," Kerry said.

"Bad either way," Dar agreed. "Depends on the steering currents too and that stalled front. Could pick it up and haul it north and end up slamming into the Outer Banks, or hell, New York."

"All around pain in the ass," Kerry concluded. "How did I ever think tropical storms were fun?" She glanced at Dar, with a faintly impish grin. "Oh. Right. I got stuck with you in my first."

Dar smiled easily. "I can see where that would skew your viewpoint," she said. "Back in that day it wasn't such a stressball though. Had more options. Miami was just one of many."

"Mm." Kerry waved casually at the dockhands as they moved from the ferry deck onto the shore, just as a squall came over and nearly whited out the truck's windshield before Dar got the wipers on high. "After hearing it a half dozen times today from customers... would we consider relocating the company, Dar?"

"No." Dar turned onto the perimeter road and felt the wind push against the sides of the vehicle. She glanced at Kerry, who watched her with hiked eyebrows. "We'll find a more redundant, foolproof way to run operations," Dar clarified. "I've got a list the length of my arm of all the crap I should have done when we started taking on clients and didn't."

"We didn't," Kerry protested mildly. "I was there."

"Okay, we didn't," Dar said. "We were too busy getting to our vacation. And that's fine, because we both agreed to all of that. I remember myself saying I didn't give a crap I was going rafting."

Kerry nodded. "I know. But we're paying for it now."

"I know you know." Dar sighed. "I just feel idiotic for not seeing where it was all going."

"We could have not done it," Kerry said. "We could have just stopped, then, and taken a few months, take our vacation and actually planned this company instead of going headfirst down into it. But we didn't." She shrugged slightly. "Hon, we are who we are, we did what we did, and we're in it. No point in kicking yourself. It's done"

"Yeah it is." Dar pulled into the parking garage attached to the building their condo was in, and parked next to Kerry's SUV. "Dad said he parked his truck down by the marina and he and mom are down there just making sure everything's secured."

"Slip comes with a spot," Kerry said. "C'mon, kids." She clucked her tongue and opened the door to let the two dogs out of the cab. "Let's get you all settled before it really starts to be weather."

They went up the steps to the entrance, where the windows were already covered with mechanized shutters, only the door itself left unencumbered by them. Dar keyed the lock and pushed the door open and the dogs rushed inside with their usual enthusiasm.

Inside the condo was atypically dark, the windows covered and the air with an extra sting of chill. Stacked near the opening to the kitchen were cases of water and pet food.

The dogs went to the kitchen door and looked over their shoulders at Kerry expectantly, as she came in behind them and opened it to let them out into the walled garden. She peered outside as they bounded down the steps and watched the whitecaps building offshore.

Curtains of rain were sweeping across the surface and she saw waves already coming up to wash against the seawall that bounded the beach, sloshing over it and spattering the coral walk that bordered the edge. The wind was gusting, and it disordered her hair as she watched the dogs explore their little domain, oblivious to the rain.

Behind her she heard the television come on, already tuned to the Weather Channel. She ducked back inside and regarded the kitchen, which unlike its usual state had supplies and oddities stacked up on the counters much like the office had.

Cans of sterno in case the gas line—fueling the stove and oven, along with the hot water heater—went out to ensure the all-important morning coffee. Powdered creamer for same. Packets of hot cereal and cold cereal, cans of beans and franks, a large cooler standing open waiting for a load of ice.

All in case the generators failed. Kerry remembered the steamy mugginess without the AC and hoped they didn't. She felt a little embarrassed at the thought, knowing herself to be one of the very privileged when others were huddled in shelters.

Dar appeared in the doorway. "Everything looks pretty squared away," she said. "I'm going to shower off all this gunk from the storage room." She regarded the smudges on her arms. "But before I do, we got anything in the fridge, or should I go scavenge?"

Kerry pondered the question. "I've got those chicken breasts I should use and some pasta. I'll do chicken parm, it won't take long."

"Sure?" Dar came over and bumped her a little. "Been a long ass day."

"Rather that then you having to fight the rest of the island for whatever avocados are left or sandwiches from the café." Kerry smiled. "Let's go shower off, and then chill." She hooked her index finger into one of Dar's belt loops and started out of the kitchen, tugging her along.

Dar went willingly, following her out and through the living room across into the large bedroom suite that held their waterbed. Kerry flipped on the lamp as she released her.

Dar sat on the bench in front of the bed and took off her hiking boots, then pulled off her socks and stuffed them inside. Then she stood and unbuckled her worn leather belt and pulled her shirt out from the waistband of her jeans.

Kerry had gone into the bathroom and Dar heard the shower start up. She could already feel the faint sting of the water pressure against her skin. She removed her jeans and walked over to the closet and tossed them into the laundry basket inside, followed by the rest of her clothes.

Then she went into the bathroom and opened the glass door, releasing a gust of steam. "Ahh."

"Ahh," Kerry repeated as she joined her inside. "Damn this feels good." Kerry handed her a scrubbie and took one for herself, squeezing out a glob of apricot scented gel on it. "Did you ever hear from the landlord?"

"Nope," Dar said. "But he told me he was going rafting in Costa Rica, and we know what that's like." She took some shampoo and started washing Kerry's hair. "He's probably going to get out of whatever river he's on and his phone's going to explode."

"We know what that's like," Kerry echoed. She scrubbed at a stain on Dar's skin across her ribcage along one side. "How in the hell did you get ink under your shirt?"

"Carrying a printer sideways," Dar said absently. "Don't ever do that."

"Ah... so that's what that big blotch on the floor was."

"Yeah. Lucky it was an inkjet not a laser. That toner never comes out."

Kerry chuckled a little, as she watched the shower carry slightly raspberry tinted suds toward the drain in the stone tiled floor. "We have the most romantic conversations, you know that?"

Dar didn't miss a beat. "Hey, we could be talking about those asics in the new AI controller. I think that might really turn out interesting." She finished washing her own hair, as Kerry rinsed herself off. "I got a call from someone who wants to talk to me about the framework."

"Hmm." Kerry put the scrubbie on its hook. "How'd they know?"

"Patent filing," Dar said. "At least, that's what they claimed."

Kerry turned off the water and pushed the door open. "They from some big company you think? They might just be fishing."

"Could be." Dar wrapped a bath sheet around herself and handed one to Kerry. "But I don't know. I think I kind of would want one of the big guys to buy the licensing for it. I don't know that I want to touch retail."

Kerry shook her head. "We don't. I'm totally on the page with you there." She ran a brush through her short hair and watched as Dar combed out her longer locks. "But if they're big enough, I want to be sure you get royalties on the patent, Dar."

"We get royalties," Dar said. "Half my brain belongs to you remember."

Kerry leaned over and kissed her shoulder. "Well, as you said before, let's get past the storm and its aftermath first, and our other customers screaming at us. Then we can worry about making money off your brain."

She gave Dar a pat on the behind, before she emerged back into their bedroom and traded her towel for a T-shirt and shorts. She walked barefoot back through the living room and spared a glance at the television, with its now familiar buzz saw shaped satellite view as the track and cone now seemed centered pretty much on downtown Miami.

She grimaced. "Ew. This is not going to be good." She went into the kitchen and removed the chicken from the refrigerator. She placed it on the counter, and then retrieved her pans and utensils. "Not good at all."

Chapter Two

Dar sprawled in one of the easy chairs, one leg slung over the arm, a diving magazine propped up on her knee as she browsed the pages.

She could hear the squalls lashing against the shutters, the wind coming and going, blowing gusts that spattered against the surface before going quiet again.

Hurricanes were large, spinning disks, and the squalls were the outer arms of them, extending hundreds of miles from the center, or eye, of the storm. They were freaks of meteorological nature. Low pressure centers that acquired rotation, like tornados on a grand scale that sucked up energy from warm water, hence why summer was their general season.

As the central pressure of the storm dropped, the wind speed increased around the eye and what you ended up with was a giant circle of ratty weather with a middle that could blow buildings apart. Even with the storm still a hundred miles out to sea, disruptive winds would shut down airports and make driving large vehicles difficult.

Dar glanced up at the television, where the buzz saw, now shown in infrared, was inching closer. "St. Thomas is getting slammed."

"Are they?" Kerry came in with two large cups and handed Dar one. "Wow that looks nasty."

"Hundred and fifteen," Dar said. "And the eye hasn't hit the Gulf Stream yet."

Kerry watched the screen. "Dar, why do weather people do that? Stand out in the rain, I mean? Look at that guy in Key West."

It was dark in the picture, and the man was standing right near the well-known marker that showed the southernmost point in the continental United States, in case his audience weren't aware of where Key West was. Occasionally the camera would pan up to a palm tree that swayed in the wind.

Dar laughed. "Why do they do that? Because weather events that take days and provide this much anticipation and entertainment are a godsend to the cable news industry, Kerrison." She regarded the screen with wry fondness. "They never made that big a deal of them before Andrew, and everyone was really just kind of meh."

"Meh?"

"Hadn't been a storm in South Florida for like twenty years before that," Dar explained. "No one paid any attention. I remember—what was his name—Brian Norcross running around screaming like a damn banshee trying to convince everyone this thing was going to be a monster and no one listened."

Kerry was surprised. "Oh, crap."

"Finally, everyone realized and by then it was too late. Wasn't any plywood or supplies left and people ended up surviving in their bathtubs under their mattresses as their windows blew in and their roofs blew off."

Kerry sat there, cup in hand forgotten, her eyes wide open as she stared at Dar.

"They'd allowed the codes to degrade, all kinds of shenanigans. That's why a lot of those areas in South Miami got blown apart," Dar continued. "So, the next time they didn't make that mistake again. Now, we have tax holidays for hurricane supplies and when we hear there's something brewing everyone makes a mad dash to top up their stores."

Kerry glanced at the kitchen. "And buy water and Vienna sausages."

Dar nodded. "Uh huh. It's why the supplies are so damn random. You never know with these things." She went back to flipping the pages of her magazine. "Here's one. Two week all included liveaboard dive vacation, Truk Lagoon. What do you think?"

"We'll be boarded by two headed pirates from the lost city of Atlantis," Kerry replied. "And cause an international scandal by finding and domesticating a giant sea squid who turns out to speak Dutch." She took a sip of her hot chocolate and wiggled her eyebrows.

Dar chuckled and toasted her with her own cup.

****

Kerry folded her arms and looked out the small window in the door that opened up to the garden. They had left the shutters off it so they could see outside but at this hour, before dawn there really wasn't much to see.

Behind her, she heard Dar crunching her morning cereal. "Are we in for a whole day of this?" She indicated the window.

"Uh huh," Dar mumbled. "If it keeps on this track, we'll be on the dirty side."

Kerry turned and looked at her.

"Right hand side of the forward motion," Dar clarified, lifting her bowl and drinking from the side of it. "I should call down to the marina and find out when my folks are going to head up here." She went over to the sink and rinsed the bowl out, along with the spoon she'd used.

"Guess I'll get some work done while I can then." Kerry sighed. "Let me go throw some clothes on and see if I can finish those contracts before I start getting calls." She added. "Mayte forwarded my desk phone and yours."

"Yay." Dar wiped the milk moustache off her lips with a paper towel. She went over to the landline phone on the small credenza near the door, picked up the receiver and dialed the number of the slip Ceci and Andy's boat was docked in.

Kerry went through the living room, dodging the two dogs who were tussling over a tug toy and trotted up the stairs to the condo's second level. There was an office there that was hers, a guest bedroom, and the second master suite where she'd once stored her things when she'd first moved in with Dar.

That was long past. She still occasionally sat on the second level patio to read or have a cup of tea, but their possessions were mingled in the big walk-in closet downstairs and now the upstairs suite only held the overnight bags belonging to Dar's parents.

The laundry room was there though, and she went in and opened the dryer, pulling out a pair of cargo pants and a T-shirt to trade her nightshirt for. She tossed the shirt into the hamper near the washing machine and went into her office.

Like their bedroom downstairs, this was at the front of the condo. Kerry sat down behind her desk and gave her trackball a whirl, bringing up the screen. Despite the early hour, her mail was already dark with new entries.

"Here we go." Kerry grimaced, as she opened the first of them. "C'mon people, I know this storms' on CNN. Give me a break here."

"Ker?"

"Yes?" Kerry lifted her voice as she heard Dar's hail from downstairs.

"Want another cup of coffee?"

"I love you," Kerry responded.

"On the way," Dar called back, her voice retreating as she went back to the kitchen.

Kerry returned her attention to the mail and started a reply to it.

Good morning, Erin. Our offices are closed today due to the hurricane, but we have some staff on duty, so the calls are being covered by a team up in Melbourne, Florida. If your staff is getting long wait times, let me look into it and see what I can do.

Kerry R.

"I can only imagine what Dar's inbox looks like." Kerry picked up her phone and opened a text message to Mark.

Hey, Technodyne is complaining they're waiting forever for the desk to pick up. I know it's early—what's the status up there?"

A moment later, the text came back.

Hey, Kerry. Let me buzz them and find out.

Kerry put her phone down and went back to her inbox, scanning the headers quickly to identify what burning fires she needed to look at first. On an ordinary day she might have one or two, but she'd also shut down early the previous day to help finish buttoning up the office.

Her phone buzzed and she glanced down at it. Then she shook her head and went back to her original email, opening a second reply.

Hey, Erin – just got off the line with that team and they asked me to ask your group to hold off calling them for weather status. It's what's jamming the lines up. I think maybe they don't realize they're upstate now and know pretty much the same as the Weather Channel.

Thanks – Kerry.

People were so weird.

Kerry put her mail aside for a minute, then she half turned and set up her wall mounted monitor to show the metrics screen Dar had written for them. It showed the status of the systems in the office, their cloud-based phones, project progress, and had a ticker on the bottom that now held the hurricane updates, but most often carried tech news.

Since all the storm had brought was rain, and a little wind, everything looked relatively normal except for the high call rate into the support desk, and the low number of calls to the rest of their departments because no one, save Carlos, was in the office.

There wasn't really that much to monitor, yet, but Dar had built the program anyway, amusing herself by creating a screen that also measured the health of everything inside their building and linked to the security cameras.

Occasionally, Gopher Dar would appear, and ramble through the metrics, tapping on graphs and chittering before disappearing out the other side of the screen.

"Okay." Kerry looked up as she heard steps on the stairs and paused as Dar entered with a large mug and two dogs at her heels. "Ahhh... thank you."

"Airport's closed." Dar set the cup down. "Ports are closed. Anything blowing up?" The dogs climbed up onto the couch against the wall and lay down, tails idly thumping.

"Not really, not yet," Kerry said. "Phones are hot, because everyone is calling support to ask about the damn storm."

Dar stared at her in bewilderment. "What?"

"I think they just know where we're located." Kerry chuckled. "And it's the out-of-towners. At least our local clients aren't bothering us." She cradled the cup in her hands, savoring the contrast of the warmth of it against the chill of the air-conditioning.

Dar's dark brows knit together. "People are weird." She echoed Kerry's previous thought. "I'll be downstairs working on the sim control matrix. I promised Scott we'd have a cleanup revision out to him by today." She turned and went back out.

Kerry glanced at the couch, as the two dogs lifted their heads and watched her retreat. Then they both turned to look at her. "Go on," she told them. "I know damn well whose dogs you are." She adored both of their pets and enjoyed interacting with them, but there was no doubt who they regarded as their pack leader.

The two Labs seemed to consider for a moment, then Mocha hopped down off the couch and trotted out after Dar, while Chino put her head down on the couch arm and settled her paws comfortably crossed, issuing an almost human sigh.

Kerry rested her chin on her fist, wondering as she had a few times before just how intelligent the animals were. Did they communicate with each other? Was there a dog language, perhaps in a sound level she couldn't hear? Did they discuss the daily happenings at the condo, and decide things like which one should go sleep where, and who should watch the back patio to bark at the birds?

Did they critique their meals?

Her email binged softly as another message came in, and she reluctantly left off imagining the thought bubble world of her pets and went back to her screen, finding a list of orders in progress whose delivery was now put in doubt. "Ah crap."

Chino opened one eye and regarded her, then twitched her nose and closed her eye again.

****

Dar had just finished setting up the screens the way she liked them when her phone rang. She glanced at it, didn't recognize the caller ID, and debated letting it go to voice mail. Then reluctantly she answered it. "Hello?"

There was a long moment of silence, then a man's voice emerged. "Ah... can I speak please to Dar Roberts?"

"Speaking."

"Ah, yes, hello. This is Michael Hengraves. I left you a message the other day? About your patent," he said. "Do you have a minute to talk? I know it's early."

Dar considered the question. "A few minutes. It's a busy day," she finally said. "You spend your day watching patent filings?" She asked.

"I don't. My staff does," Hengrave said, in a mild tone. "I represent a group of clients who invest in new technology. They provide funding to bring revolutionary products to market. So we watch patent filings to see if there's something out there that could be of interest to them."

Dar leaned back in her chair. "A lot of patents never go anywhere. They're just filed to protect ideas."

"We know," Hengrave said. "We've been doing this for a while and we've had a few successes, and some failures, and some... "He paused, and she heard the faint shrug in his tone. "Some that are just treading water."

"So, what's interesting about mine?" Dar asked.

"One of the lines in it, one of the descriptions," he answered promptly. "But I'm not really qualified to talk about the technical side of it. I have a partner who is, I just wanted to know if you were interested in, at least, having a discussion about potential commercial uses for it."

Dar considered. "Any of those investors actually produced anything?"

Hengrave chuckled a little. "If you mean, did they build the widgets, the answer is no. They acquire the intellectual property, so to speak, the idea, and they broker it to companies who can."

"For instance?"

He hesitated. "Not sure I understand the question."

"Give me an example of one of your successes," Dar said, keeping her tone very mild. "I've been in the tech industry a while. Something I may have heard of?"

"Oh. Ah. Hold on a moment." The line went mute, and then he returned. "Can I call you back? I just had another urgent call come in."

"Sure," Dar said, relatively certain he wouldn't. "Take your time and have that example when you do." She heard the line go dead and she put the phone down, chuckling softly under her breath. "Hasbro potty trainer, probably." She returned her attention to her screens.

There were two, large and vivid, attached to a docking station she currently had her laptop connected to. One held the framework design program, with its multiple windows and intricate circuit tracings and the other her programming software with its endless lines of code.

She spent some time rereading the last block of instructions, turning to glance at the window in her office when the branches outside hit the glass. They had left the shutters off this one as well, and Dar smiled a little, remembering that first, almost insignificant storm when she and Kerry had looked out of it together.

She turned back to the screen and reached out to her trackball, laying her fingertips on it and moving the cursor to select a section of code.

It was almost done. There was just some cleanup work to be done on the control surfaces, and she made the adjustments, tiny snippets of code that ran the training simulator and its mechanicals.

It wasn't as cool as the AI methodology she'd just submitted the patent for, but this was a bread-and-butter contract and a billable milestone. A big one, on a project that had wavered on the edge of being cancelled three times now, subject to government budget infighting.

The code itself was stored in their offices, in a secure server her machine was connecting to, encrypted and segregated from the rest of their systems, the programmers working on parts of it only allowed to check out specific sections.

With her being the only exception. Dar had the master encryption key for the repository, and access to all of it. She had the responsibility of being the check on the check, reviewing all the sections as they were worked on before she allowed them into the golden copy.

Her programmers were good people. They'd passed security checks. She liked them. Dar studied a line, then she went in and made a slight syntax change. But this would have her name on it and in so far as any software could be perfect, she wanted it to be.

A touch obsessive. Dar owned that and recognized there was a downside.

In a corner of her screen was the network communications app they used to quick chat and now it popped up. Seeing it was from Carlos, she clicked on it.

Good morning. So far just rain here.

She typed back.

Here too. Still have power?

Carlos had probably just woken, he and his buddies having set up cots on the second level, bringing supplies and a small gas stove into the break room there. For a brief moment, Dar almost regretted them not staying as well.

Yeah – hey the landlord stopped by! His plane was the last one to land at MIA he said, and he was kinda blubbering all over the place. I told him to expect a big bill for all the work and materials and all that stuff and asked him for a copy of his hurricane insurance on the building.

Dar pondered that. "We probably should have asked him for that before now," she said aloud.

He said he gave that to Kerry with the rest of the paperwork - might want to check?

"We might want to check." Dar touched the intercom on her desk. "Hey, Ker?"

"Yes, oh love of my life?"

Dar smiled. "We're sure they've got a windstorm rider on that damn building?"

There was a pause on the other end. "Don't they have to? I mean, it's required isn't it?"

"For a mortgage, yes," Dar replied. "But y'know, this is Miami."

"Let me check. I've got the paperwork scanned in. Let you know."

Dar put her hands on her keyboard.

Kerry's checking. Not that we can do anything about it now if they don't, and really, regardless, if the place takes a direct hit it's not going to matter.

There was a pause before Carlos answered.

I guess we just find someplace else?

They would, and now, Dar took a moment to think about what Kerry had asked her on the way across on the ferry. If the worst happened, and they did have to move the company, would she keep it here? So far trying to handle the expansion of the company in the area they'd picked had been tough.

Coconut Grove wasn't built for that, really. Dar sat back and considered. It wasn't, but it was funky and cute, and a nice place to come to work every day. There were shops and cafes to walk to, and it was right down the road from the water.

She liked it. She'd liked it when she'd lived here back in the day, and though sections had changed, the streets with their differentiated houses, overhanging trees, and just general air of old Florida appealed to her.

Yep, we'll find somewhere else. We'll figure it out.

Dar typed back to Carlos, because that, at least, was true. They'd figure it out. She didn't really want to go back into a business park, like ILS had been in, or move inland where it would be mostly strip shopping malls and traffic.

Kerry had meant, though, would they move the company outside Miami and no, Dar didn't think that was in the cards. For sentimental reasons, sure, but it meant relocating everyone who wanted to stay with them and that was a huge disruption that went past just her fondness for her hometown.

No. Dar went back to her screen, with a little nod. They would just learn from this experience, as she had in her past, and build ways to make it not matter that they were based in the middle of Crazytown.

A small alert flashed. She touched the intercom again. "Hurricane warning's up at the eight a.m., hon. We're centerline in the cone."

"Great," Kerry responded. "He's got a rider, for what that's worth, Dar. Hey, they're evacuating the beach. Do they evacuate here?"

"No," Dar said. "They know we're a bunch of rich assholes that won't listen anyway, or have bought here as investment property. And these things are bunkers."

"Okey doke." Kerry clicked off.

Dar returned her focus to her screen, making another small change, and committing it. She reviewed the last sections of code that had been checked in and went over the wiremap and flow one more time. She closed the repository and sealed it with the encryption key. "That's as good as it's gonna get for now."

She extracted a visible diagram and published it to an encrypted share for the team to review and felt a sense of relief that she could mark this closed before the uncertainty of the storm coming overhead.

She moved to her mail program and opened up a note to her project contact in Colorado, attaching the milestone validation and a link to the published schema and sent the note off.

By the time they'd reviewed it, she reasoned, it would be a week or so and at least they'd know the worst of what the situation would be here. She opened another mail, this time internal, and sent a brief, congratulatory note to her team for getting all the segments in by the deadline, then she stood up.

Mocha looked up at her from his spot on the couch, tail wagging gently.

Dar went over and sat next to him, scratching him behind his ears. "You ready for this, buddy?" She asked. "It's going to be loud and scary, and you're still just a baby boy."

"Gruff," Mocha responded, rolling over and wriggling on his back, rubbing his nose on her leg. "Arouf."

"Is it time for a cookie?" Dar laughed, as the dog tried to lift his ears upside down. "I think it is. Let's go get one." She got up and followed Mocha out of the office and into the living room, pausing to watch the television as the storm inched closer.

Like a slow-motion train wreck. Dar shook her head and moved on.

****

Kerry gazed over a mostly completed page, reviewing the answers she'd given to the request for proposal from a potential new client.

On the surface, it wasn't a complex request. They were looking to open up three satellite offices in the South Florida area, but needed to keep costs down and be highly flexible in the work environment. They weren't fond of the idea of having the staff work from home.

Home office was in Augusta, Georgia. The new locations were an attempt to make inroads in a new segment of their business, the nature of which was somewhat vague, but that apparently was sales related and required the employees to pitch face to face to new customers.

Kerry tapped her fingertips lightly on the keys of her keyboard, rereading the page. She'd given the standard answers to the standard questions, but as she read them, the whole thing felt a bit stale to her. There was nothing new or special about the proposal.

Sometimes, she reminded herself, a banana was just a banana. There were only so many ways to configure computing devices, connectivity, and desk space. But one of the things Dar had said she wanted to come out of their company was for their solutions to be, if not totally out of the box, at least have components that showed they thought that way.

So, was there something different here? Kerry exhaled, and her eyes narrowed a little bit. Reading between the lines she sort of got the impression that the company wasn't that confident in their ability to home run whatever it was they were going to peddle.

Hence, the request for flexibility and low cost. By definition, it made it lower risk.

Having the teams work from home would be both, but they'd written specifically into the request their strong desire to have the teams be collocated for supervision and management.

One team in each county meant they couldn't share a common space. that meant three rental offices, with three sets of connectivity, three build outs, and three installations of hardware. Aside from putting them in a tent on the lawn at Bayside that meant there were limits.

They wanted the offices to be client facing, so that meant more limits, because it meant Class A office space for 20 people per office.

Ugh.

Kerry leaned back in her chair, studying the screen and shaking her head. Then her mail dinged and she glanced over at the other screen briefly, seeing an advertisement come in trying to sell her a motor home. "Boy did that rental put me on a list."

She reached over to delete it, then paused. She opened the mail and studied the colorful pictures, remembering the cross-country convenience of having their little home away from home with them. "Hmm." Her mind, thrown unexpectedly on a completely different track, pondered.

What if?

She pulled a pad over and took a pencil, scribbling some notes. What if she proposed a single, industrial space as a home base, for back office, and three traveling, tricked out motor homes to sell their proposals to clients?

Weird and radical, and possibly just laugh inducing from the prospective client. Kerry discarded her almost finished proposal and started a new one.

But definitely out of the box.

****

More rain. More wind.

The shutters made the usually open and sun lit condo like a bunker. Dar peered out of the small window in the back door, watching the ruffled waters of the Atlantic churn past the seawall. Behind her, she heard the sounds of a press briefing on the television, by this time the storm having taken over all the local programming.

Not that she watched much on television in any case. Usually either it was Animal Planet, Discovery, or Cartoon Network.

That was an option now, but she was reluctant to turn away from the reporting, even though she knew it would be hours and hours before the storm's main event would take place. Literally, as she had thought earlier, like watching a slow-motion train wreck in process and just as impossible to look away from.

"They opened a pet shelter this time," Kerry said as she entered the kitchen behind her. "I can only imagine what that's like."

"Like the humane society on a bad day," Dar said. "But it's damn good they did with all the people who didn't evacuate last time because they couldn't take their pets." She watched a bird get blown backwards across the back area, landing in a flurry of ruffled and bewildered feathers.

"Very true." Kerry came over and looked out the window past Dar's shoulder. "Your folks still down at their boat?"

"They're socializing at the marina." Dar bit off a grin. "You know my mother. She's enjoying herself."

Kerry merely chuckled. She moved over to the fridge and looked inside, pondering her choices for lunch. "How do we feel about the generators?" She asked. "Should I use this chicken now, Dar? I can do some stir fry or fajitas in case we do end up losing power."

"Good idea," Dar said. "I know they tested the damn things, and with the Belcher tanks they've got fuel. Who knows?" She looked over at the television. "I think the storm surge is going to come right over us," she said. "I hope it doesn't trash the slips."

Kerry paused, a package of chicken breasts in her hand. "You think the Dixie's going to be okay?"

Dar made a face. "I secured the deck. Dad helped me," she said. "And if anyone knows how to do that it's him."

"True." Kerry drummed her fingers on the counter, then retrieved her wok from its hook. "I heard a couple of our neighbors in the market saying they wished they'd had their boats taken up state or into one of the covered Marinas in Lauderdale."

"They were full."

"That's what they said," Kerry agreed. "And it was too late to have them taken any farther."

"It is what it is." Dar turned. "I finished the drop and sent it over." She leaned against the refrigerator with one shoulder, folding her arms across her chest. "I'm debating on whether I should start setting up the delivery for Broward County or not."

"I'm pretty sure that's one you can hold off on for a few days, hon." Kerry got out her chef's knife, its long, silver surface reflecting the light. "I was just listening to the county manager up there on the TV and they're more worried about the fact they can't get the drainage canal gates open."

"Hmm."

"They're probably going to offer everyone west of I-75 a canoe."

Dar chuckled. "Well, let me do the setup for them and maybe I'll reach out and offer to redo their control software while I'm at it." She winked at Kerry, and then she wandered back out, idly pushing the sleeves of her long sleeve T-shirt up over her elbows.

"Don't offer to go out there today," Kerry called after her, glancing to her left as Dar's place was taken by two dogs, who seated themselves with hopeful eyes on her, tails sweeping across the stone floor. "Oh. You think I'm cooking for you, little pirates?"

"Gruff," Chino barked softly.

"Not with Szechuan peppercorns, my dear," Kerry informed them. She finished cutting up the chicken and deposited it in a bowl, sliding the cutting board over into the sink for washing along with her knife, trading it for a smaller one of both for the vegetables.

Bamboo shoots, miniature corn, and snow peas. She assembled the rest of the ingredients and turned the fire on under the wok, waiting for it to heat up.

On the television in the living room a man was standing, covered in a yellow rain jacket, on the edge of some dock somewhere with the obligatory palm tree behind him while rain blew sideways against his head.

The camera pulled back and then the picture was framed in a square panel in a newsroom, and you could see two other anchors seated half turned to watch it, with concerned expressions.

It was replaced with a radar view of the storm; the outer fringes now sweeping over land and soon would cover most of the area they lived in.

"Conditions will now start deteriorating." The anchor was intoning, in a serious voice. "Everyone should rush all their preparations to completion. Get off the roads and into secure shelter."

On the bottom of the screen, a ticker was running, listing off all the shelters that were open and had space to evacuate to, and what now was closed, like the airports and seaports, and government offices. Kerry walked over and glanced out of the window that faced due east, right into the oncoming storm.

Was it really smart for them all to stay here? She went back to the stove and poured some peanut oil into the wok, adding a spicy red pepper mix with it. Dar had weathered big storms here, and seemed confident, and Andrew had agreed, once he'd done his own inspection of the place.

True, they were not the only ones staying. Ceci had commented, in some amusement, that it was the most expensive hurricane shelter in the state and better attended than most, and she'd reported that the management of the commercial center had stocked up on damned near everything.

And well, they were here. Kerry mentally shrugged. No matter what happened it probably wouldn't end up either as uncomfortable or dangerous as their last vacation so what the heck.

What the heck.

****

Once she'd gotten back to her desk, Dar found she really didn't have an urge to sit down behind it, going over to the window and looking out over the front of the house instead.

This view was far less dramatic than the one from the kitchen, showing the common front area of the group of condos, one of which was theirs.

Her phone rang, and she reluctantly turned and went to pick it up, glancing at the caller ID and answering it. "Dar Roberts."

"Hey! Dar!" A man's excited voice came blurting out and made her hold the phone slightly away from her head. "I got that link... holy cow!"

Dar sat down behind the desk. "That didn't take long," she said. "I just sent it over, Scott. Figured I would before—"

"Yeah yeah!" He interrupted. "So, listen, I sent it to the team, and they loaded it up into the simulator and they're running it now."

Dar's eyebrows hiked. "Now?" She glanced at her watch. "You all are in full gear today."

"Anyway." Scott exhaled in audible satisfaction. "I was able to update the nabobs on the morning call, and they're pacified for now," he said. "Great way to start the week, you know? So, thanks for that, Dar."

Dar was a bit nonplussed. "I'm certainly glad we could make the checkpoint. I had some doubts since we have all this weather going on down here."

"Weather?"

Dar's dark brows contracted. "The Category five hurricane about to hit Florida?" She ventured, in a quizzical tone. "I'm sure the news up there gave it a brief mention?"

"Oh, news. I don't watch it," Scott said. "You know we're buried here in the mountain. Half the time when I leave, I have no idea what time it even is. Anyway, it's just rain, right? How bad could it be? I was a little surprised when you said it might be a problem for delivery."

"Well," she said. "The last Cat five that hit this area caused, I think… 28 billion in damages, took out a naval base and made part of the county unlivable for a year." She paused. "Had nearly a hundred and seventy mile per hour winds. Enough to peel the roofs off houses."

"Oh." Scott sounded truly surprised. "Does that happen often?" He sounded astonished. "I mean, we have snowstorms here but my goodness why do you live there?"

"Because we don't have snowstorms here and most of the time, we don't have hurricanes either," Dar said. "Anyway, let me know what the team thinks about the new algorithm. I made some adjustments based on their notes from our last meeting."

"For sure!" Scott said. "Thanks again, Dar. I'll probably be in touch later, after they run it for a few cycles. We should know if they have any big notes by then. Better plan on heading up here if it passes the smoke test. They've been holding off the bigwigs on this thing but the pressures getting crunchy again."

"Figured," Dar responded. "Let me know what the team thinks."

"Will do," Scott said. "Good luck with the storm thing," he added. "I should probably go look it up and see what that's all about I guess." He chuckled. "Later!"

Dar put her phone down and studied it in some bemusement. Then she shook her head and turned her attention to her screens, pondering a moment before she called up another project into her programming tool, leaning against the desk to inspect it.

Not the county one. This schema was completely different, a cryptic assembly of hardware instructions she now contentedly fiddled with, setting up a preview on her other screen, and glancing from one to the other to watch the effect her changes were having.

****

Kerry watched Dar watch the rain out the back window. "Hey, hon." She put down the magazine she'd been reading. "How about we put on some ponchos and take the cart out."

Dar turned. "Go out in the rain?"

"See what's going on," Kerry said. "Go see what your folks are getting into, see if the market's still open. It's not that windy out right now."

"Isn't that exactly what the news yonks are telling everyone not to do?" Dar, however, looked both entertained and interested.

"No one listens. You saw that guy who was wind surfing," Kerry countered. "Every time you see that reporter in the slicker on the pier there's someone strolling along behind them."

"That windsurfer got blown into the side of a building," Dar reminded her. "But yeah, sure. Let's go around the perimeter road." She went to the hall closet and opened the door. "I brought the foul weather gear in from the boat."

Kerry got up and joined her. "Ah ah ah." She turned and held her hand up to the two dogs, who came rushing over.

"Oh, let them come." Dar handed her a dark green rain jacket. "They're water dogs."

They donned the waterproof gear and pulled the hoods up. "Wear these." Dar handed Kerry a pair of water shoes. "They're grippy."

"And neoprene." Kerry followed her out of the front door, with the dogs frisking behind her. They walked down the steps and into the lower-level parking where their cars were, along with their cart.

Mocha and Chino jumped into the back of it, well used to the conveyance and Kerry put up the back gate behind them.

The cart was modified. It had four seats and a cargo bed, which had wooden braces with leather covered pads on them and a thick mat for the dogs. There was a metal water dish clamped to one of the supports and two leashes and collars were looped and fastened near it, though seldom used.

A squall had recently passed through, and they were in a lull between them, so there was only a spattering of rain and gusts of wind as Dar guided the cart out of the parking depot and up onto the road. She looked both ways, then turned left and started along the edge of the golf course.

"See?" Kerry pointed in the distance where other carts could be seen. "People are still out and about."

"Good time for a break anyway," Dar said. "Plenty of time to be locked inside."

****

The marina was a surprisingly busy place. Dar parked the cart on one side of the building that housed the facility among a scattering of other vehicles, and they went under the overhang that fronted the docks.

The dockmasters were all there, in their white shirts and blue shorts, with blue rain jackets on as they talked to the thirty or so boat owners who were gathered around.

A table was against the outer wall, with what appeared to be chilled dispensers full of lemonade and something pinkish in them, and servers were roaming around with trays offering cold canapes.

"So, this is how we cater a hurricane party here?" Kerry commented dryly. "There's your folks." She indicated the easily spotted Andrew Roberts near the edge of the patio. "I'll get us a drink."

A television was tucked inside a wooden framing, showing the National Weather Service broadcast, and next to it, inside the service window Dar saw two of the marine workers watching a large radar.

"It's gonna be nasty," Dockmaster Jack was saying as she came up next to a small group of other residents. "Oh, hey there, Ms. Roberts. Your slip's all secure."

"Yeah, my father said," Dar replied. "We just came down to see what was going on."

"Like everyone else," A man standing there, hands in the pockets of his Bermuda shorts said. "I'm already bored to death watching the Weather Channel."

Kerry came over with two cups full of the pinkish liquid. "Here." She offered Dar one. "Cranberry."

Besides the man in the Bermuda shorts, the rest of the gathering had fallen silent, most were watching Dar and Kerry with at best noncommittal expressions.

They had never really been that popular. Not, at least, once Kerry moved in with Dar and their lifestyle became known. It had become common to see them around the island together along with their sometimes, boisterous dogs.

Most had pretended they were sisters or cousins right up until the time Dar casually kissed her in the middle of the formal dining room, flipping off the shocked watchers as they just as casually strolled out.

But they were uniformly polite to everyone and so far, they'd avoided any unpleasant clashes. Their impending departure had become known and subtly celebrated until everyone encountered Andrew and Ceci and realized, belatedly, what the term out of the frying pan into the fire meant.

Certainly not everyone felt that way. Many were part-time residents and really didn't care one way or the other. Some, that certain percentage, were gay or gay friendly and made that known to them as well. But there was a core of conservativism that lately had become louder and some of the men there were part of that.

Dar took a sip of her cranberry fizzy drink and let her elbow rest on Kerry's shoulder, enjoying the faint twitch of some lips.

A squall swept through suddenly, and they all herded over near the wall of the building to avoid the sideways rain that spattered over everything. Mocha and Chino had trotted out onto the dock, and now they came back over, shaking themselves violently and adding that spray to the rest of it.

"Water's already coming over the seawall on the east side," Jack said. "They're bringing in a truck with sandbags just to throw them on the back side of that thing for safety's sake." He looked at Dar. "I know your back yard's right up against the edge there."

Kerry took a small fruit tart from the tray held out to her by one of the servers and handed it to Dar, then took one for herself, struck suddenly by the difference between the understated competence of the team around them and what they'd seen by their office.

There was a plan. A plan that was not only thoughtful, but executed by professionals with no sense of panic, or lack of preparedness here. Kerry had the sense that though the storm was dangerous, and everyone was worried, that they would weather it because the ground they were on had been thoroughly prepared.

Why wasn't everything like that? Kerry nibbled the fruit tart. Was it just a question of money? "Yeah, we saw the water coming over into the swale there, up to the inner gates by our place," she said. "What's the thought on the new generators?"

"Manufacturer's got a team here. They're going to stay through the storm with us," Jack said, with quiet confidence. "So, if it conks out, won't be for lack of attention. They ran feeder lines over from the Belcher docks, so we've got plenty of fuel available."

Jamlet, the server, paused to listen. "Yeah, we've got around a hundred of us on the hotel side who volunteered to stay on duty here," he told them. "Safer here than my place in Cutler Ridge." He offered the tray to the three other men who were standing around Jack. "We're all bunking out over at the mansion. They brought in cots and all that."

Jack nodded. "Marina staff has a full shift on base for the duration too," he said. "All of us were glad to be over here, not dealing with all the crap landside." He turned his head and looked out over the marina. "Everything's as locked down as we can make it."

"We'll be fine," One of the men standing by said. "I'm just worried about surge lifting up the docks. That eye's vicious looking." He indicated the television. "There's a lot of boats in the marina."

"True," Jack agreed, with a rueful smile. "I was a little surprised. I thought more would be heading out and over to the Med, but not so much this year."

"Staying away from going out there," the man said, shortly. "Too much chaos. I'll spend my money in the Keys this year or go out to Belize."

Andrew and Ceci came over to join the small group. "Hey, kiddos," Ceci greeted them. "Run out of problems to solve?"

Kerry smiled. "Taking a break from them. You never run out in our business."

"Ain't that true," Andy said. "'Lo, all you all," he added to the group. "Had me a chitchat with that there Coast Guard captain just came by and he said they closed up all the inlets."

Some of the men eyed him with a mixture of resentment and wariness, but others smiled appreciatively and nodded, accepting his authority in all things maritime related, having learned the hard way about all the things he really did know that most of them didn't.

"It was nice to see Larry again," Ceci remarked, with a smile. "We should do a barbeque for him and his crew after this is over."

"Could play us some baseball out on that green patch in the middle," Andy said solemnly.

Dar smiled and rocked up and down on the balls of her feet. The entire island social stratosphere was something her parents viewed as entertainment set up for their benefit, and they enjoyed poking and outraging everyone generally any chance they got.

The squall intensified, and as if by common accord all of them edged inside the marina building itself, which housed the business office and the dock shop where they offered boat supplies and fishing gear for sale. It was luridly fluorescent lit inside, the windows covered with mechanical shutters.

There was a large desk in the center, and past that, mostly darkened, was the command center with its weather radars and radio gear. The sound of marine frequencies drifted into the store from it, the harbor masters using headsets and boom mics as they responded to queries.

It smelled of plastic and fabric, and Jack pulled the doors closed after everyone had crowded inside. They watched in silence as the squall brought rain in such a heavy curtain that they no longer could see the boat slips or even the sidewalk past the edge of the patio.

"Whoof," Jack muttered.

The wind suddenly produced a deep howling sound and the doors rattled a little, and through the rain they saw palm fronds whipping by on the ground, rolling toward the water, and the contents of the table outside were pulled along to join them.

"Sorry," one of the marina staff stuck his head inside from the command center. "We saw that one coming, but it got here too fast to warn ya."

Andy eyed the door. "Once this here lets up we should get us back ovah to that there house," he said. "Ain't gonna get better from here until this thing's done."

Chino was sitting next to Dar's leg and now she let out a small bark of protest. "Gruff."

Jack stood against the wall between the store and the command center. "We just got a call from some commercial fishing boats that wanted to dock in here." He shook his head. "No way. I've seen the gear on those things get loose and take out a crane."

"Some of them are coming in and just dropping anchor in the bay," one of the residents said. "Hope they don't end up in anyone's backyard."

"Ton of hulls coming up from the Keys," Dar said. "I heard that on the news this morning, John." She looked at the resident, a man who'd always been friendly and once he'd found out Andrew's Naval background even more so having served himself. "Bet a lot of folks are just tying up in the mangroves."

He nodded. "Everyone realized over the weekend this was going to blow up." He pointed at the screen. "If I'd have known, I'd have taken a flight up to Long Island, but my wife has two cats and a poodle here she won't leave."

"We know what that's like." Kerry indicated the two wet Labradors. "Just as glad the whole family's here." She indicated Dar's parents.

The man next to him stepped around Kerry to lean on the counter, looking into the command center at the radars. "Well, I'm going to get out of here." He pulled the hood up on his jacket and fastened the flap at his throat. "Since I can't get my family all taken care of."

He pushed past Jack and went to the door, shoving it open and walking out into the squall, the wind yanking the glass door outward and letting in a blast of rain.

"Jamlet, can you—" Jack started away from the wall.

Jamlet put his tray down quickly and went over to grab the door, shielding his eyes from the rain with his other hand. He leaned back to pull it shut, but his shoes slipped out from under him on the wet concrete and he ended up flat on his back on the ground.

There was a moment of silence, then two of the dockmasters rushed for the door to help. They were beaten to the opening by Andy, who got his hand on Jamlets' belt as he tried to get up and hauled him to his feet, putting him gently behind him as he got a grip on the door and hauled it shut. "Easy there."

"Oh!" Jamlet grimaced. "Oh man that hurt." He reached for his back. "I hit the sill." He limped to one side of the store. "Thanks, Mr. Roberts."

"All right." Jack looked around with a touch of nervousness. "We should probably get everyone out of here and home and shut down. We need to get the shutters over the doors."

Kerry had dodged between the stirring residents and gone to Jamlets' side. "You, okay?" She asked. "You hit pretty hard."

He was gingerly moving his legs in a slight marching motion. "I think so. Teach me to volunteer, huh?" He gave Kerry a wry grin. "Glad the boss isn't here."

The rain, abruptly, slackened, and the wind died down outside. The view went from almost whiteout conditions to a soggy view once again of the marina. "Let's go," John said. "While we can." He started herding his friends out.

"Good idea." Ceci sidled up next to Andy. "The idiot meter's going up again," she added. "Wayne's pissed off because they wouldn't let his cousin bring in the boat he just bought at the boat show. Stupid thing is 72 feet long and they don't have space, but does he care?"

"Ah." Dar was waiting for the crowd at the door to ease. "What did he want them to do, kick someone else out? He's that kind of asshole?"

"Yes," Ceci said. "Us, actually. Not that the slip we're in could handle that size, but it didn't matter."

Dar swung around and stared at her mother.

Ceci patted her arm. "Don't worry, kiddo. Your father handled it." She smiled without much humor. "These Sir Buckalots talk a good game, but really they've got the backbone of a slinky."

The store emptied and Jack came over to them. "You guys are almost residents anyway," He said, speaking frankly. "So even if Mr. Roberts hadn't said he was going to kick the crap out of him, we wouldn't have moved you. Just so you know."

Andrew chuckled silently.

"Dingleberries," Ceci said. "I swear I'm going to paint a pentagram on the outside wall of that place once we move in here."

Chino barked softly then stood up and went to the door. She looked over her shoulder and Mocha got up and joined her, his tail wagging gently.

Kerry shook herself and went to the door. "Glad we missed that little scene." She eyed her father-in-law, who winked. "He's a jerk, but I bet he took you threatening him better than he would if Dar had done it."

"Probly," Andrew said and zipped up his rain jacket. "But I do swear people are just jackass sometimes."

"Most times," Jack remarked. "But I didn't say that out loud," he added. "Anyway, we'll keep an eye on your two boats, clan Roberts, and hope this thing passes over fast." He held the door for them as they went out, going around the corner of the building to where their cart awaited.

****

"Ugh. That's a job done." Kerry went into the laundry room and threw the two large and now muddy colored towels into the washing machine. "Amazing how much dirt can get on two dogs between the driveway and the door."

Dar leaned into the doorway. "They were chasing a squirrel. And given all the rain, the mud's not a shocker."

Kerry started the machine going. "Well, let me get these cleaned before something tragic happens and we have to live with the smell of wet muddy dog towel in the house." She wiped her hands off and joined Dar in the entrance to the room. "I have meatballs defrosting for dinner."

"Yum."

"You say that to everything."

"You don't make me salads," Dar countered, with a charming smile.

"And I have some eggplant parm for your mom." Kerry felt a sense of satisfaction at this inadvertent result in her casual planning. "So let me go see if anything blew up in my email while we were out." She bumped gently against Dar and went past.

Dar retreated back into her office, aware of the faint sounds of her parents upstairs in the second master suite. She went behind her desk and triggered the lift to raise it up to standing height, resting an elbow on it as she unlocked her desktop.

At the same time, her phone rang. With a sigh, she answered it without looking at the caller ID. "Dar Roberts."

"Hello, Ms. Roberts. It is Manuel."

Slightly surprised, Dar adjusted the phone against her ear. "Hey, Manuel. Didn't expect to hear from you today. I thought you were busy with your duplex in Hialeah."

"Si, yes," He said. "But I have just gotten a call from Ms. Hunter about the property we discussed yesterday. You did not give her your phone number?"

"No," Dar said. "Never occurred to me, and she didn't ask." She glanced up as Chino came trotting in and jumped up on the leather couch. "Why?"

"Because the young lady demanded of me that I give it to her," Manuel said. "And I did not, though it made her very upset with me."

"Well, good," Dar said. "Is that all you wanted to discuss?"

"No," he said, with a slight chuckle. "Not at all. It is this—she wishes to accept your offer."

"Yeah, she said she would probably do that," Dar said. "I sent the paperwork over to my lawyer. But we both know we can't close on anything without insurance, and I can't get that until the storm's over."

"The young lady does not seem to understand this law," Manuel said. "And...forgive me, Ms. Roberts, was it your intention to pay on cash basis for this?"

Dar was briefly silent. "Yes," she answered. "I did say that. I figured it would grease the skids for her to say yes. No bank process bullshit, as long as she has clear title."

"Si, that is what I thought. If you are not looking to secure a mortgage, you can purchase this property, yes? Without signed insurance coverage." He paused. "I do not recommend this, Ms. Roberts, is understood, yes? To purchase a property at this time, with this storm coming, and not insure it would be very stupid."

"O... K..." Dar knew she had a very confused look on her face. "We're on the same page there, Manny. That would be stupid."

"Si. But this young lady has said, if we do not complete the transaction today, she will sell it to some other person who is willing also to close very soon." He paused again. "So, I felt it would be good for me to speak to you about it."

What the what? Dar shifted and gave her trackball a spin, more to do something than anything else. "Why in the hell would a couple of days matter?" She wondered out loud. "Does she hate the place that much?"

Manuel cleared his throat. "I do not know, Ms. Roberts. But I can say this, it could be... "He hesitated. "If this person does in fact have clear title, it is possible there is no financing on it. She maybe owns this outright?"

"Could be," Dar said. "So?"

"Perhaps it is she who does not have insurance, and at this time, cannot obtain it," he said, in a practical tone. "And so, she is removing her risk."

Dar made a low noise in her throat.

"Not so stupid, in this view," Manuel said, in an almost apologetic way. "Because let us say, if the worst thing happens and the property is destroyed, it is of much, much less value."

"Would be," Dar agreed. "Okay, Manny, I need to talk to my lawyer, and I need to talk to Kerry. Let me call you back in around a half hour. That work?"

"Si, that works very well." He sounded relieved. "I hope you understand, Ms. Roberts. I am not looking to push you to do this. I feel it is unwise, and a very big risk. But I did think you would want to know about it."

"You're right on," Dar said. "I did want to know." She paused. "Even if I really didn't want to know. You know?"

"Si."

"Talk to you later." Dar hung up and put the phone down. "Ker!" She let out a yell. "Got a problem!"

****

"Dar, that's crazy," Richard Edgerton enunciated into the phone, with an audible sigh chasing the words. "Not only is it crazy because of the weather, it's just plain crazy. That woman is just looking to put a scam on you."

"Don't disagree," Dar said. "Can she do it? Does she have the standing?"

Richard sighed. "She has clear title," he admitted reluctantly. "The report came back about twenty minutes ago. But something else came back too, and that's even more dangerous."

Kerry, Ceci and Andrew sat on the couch in Dar's office, listening. They all had remarkably similar skeptical looks on their faces, given the vastly different faces involved.

"That is?" Dar leaned back in her chair, one knee braced against the edge of her desk. "Thing built on a super fund site or something? Or an old Indian burial ground?"

Richard chuckled. "No," but it is on the register of historic places, which means, you can't materially change that building."

"Ho boy," Ceci muttered and rolled her eyes.

Dar considered that. "What if it gets flattened in the storm?"

Richard was briefly silent. "I'd have to check on what the regulation would be on that, but it does mean there are limits to what you can do with any renovation. Maybe she knows that limits her choices in selling as well."

"Old man prob'ly got that done on purpose," Andrew said. He stretched his long legs out along the floor and crossed his ankles. "Grunty cuss. "

"Did you know him, Dad?" Dar asked. "I heard of him, but we never met."

Andrew nodded. "Met him a few times doing this and that," he said. "Didn't like nobody telling him what to do." He cleared his throat. "Had him an open hand. Gave food, and whatnot to them that needed it. See him sometimes downtown, just pulling along a cart with him and handing bags out to fellers."

Kerry, who had been watching Dar's face, smiled a bit, and leaned back into the soft leather of the couch. "You just engaged Dar's Robin Hood gene," she said. "For what it's worth—I think we should do it." She paused as everyone looked at her in some surprise. "Yes, I think she's trying like hell to dump this place, but I think we should risk it."

Dar regarded her with interest. "You do?"

"Yeah, I do." Kerry folded her arms. "I say we tell this chick we'll sign, but take fifteen percent off the offer since we're assuming the risk. Take it or leave it."

"Throw in we know about the historic designation," Richard suggested, sounding interested. "Let her know we know that limits its marketability."

"Does it though?" Dar asked, one dark brow lifting skeptically. "Yes, I know it's on the whatever, but this is Miami," she reminded them. "Throw enough money at it and some big suit could change that."

"Does she know that?" Richard asked. "You said she's from the west coast. Doesn't like it here."

Ceci chuckled.

"Old man'd like it," Andrew said.

"That place isn't bad looking," Ceci said. "From the pictures I saw it's a nice structure. Sort of reminds me of the frontage at Viscaya." She eyed Kerry. "What the hell you two are going to do with all that space though I've got no idea."

Kerry chuckled. "Yeah, it's way too huge for us. But I liked the idea of having all that space outside the house. We've been looking all over the area and we've seen some nice places, but they're all up crammed together. This isn't."

"I'm assuming you're going to move on this, Dar?" Richard said. "I agree with Kerry. Let's get her to discount for our assuming all this risk and getting her a fast sale. If she agrees, I'll set up the wire."

"Okay," Dar said. "I'll call Manny back. Let's see where it goes. Thanks, Richard. I'll let you know." She hung up the phone and regarded her family. "Crazy day."

****

"Where is it now?" Dar returned to the living room, after a brief view out the back window.

"Eye's reforming," Ceci said. "Just our luck it's going to be built back up right before it hits." She observed, as the radar pictured the huge, circular storm inching closer. The round eye, which had been razor sharp earlier, was now obscured with clouds.

"Going over the Gulf Stream," Dar said. "Look at those bands." She regarded the thick lines. "What was the last reading? 163?"

The faint smell of garlic and tomato sauce lingered in the air, and there was a pot of French pressed coffee on the table. The two dogs wandered around, sniffing here and there uneasily.

"They know," Dar said. "Air pressure's changing."

"I can feel it in my sinuses," Ceci said. "I think the last dropsonde reported what... 901? That's insane." She looked around. "As insane as we are to be sitting here right in its path, by the way."

"Mm." Dar had been perched on the back of one of the leather chairs. Now she let herself slide backwards and landed on her back on the seat of it, her head hanging down and her legs dangling off where she'd been sitting. She folded her hands over her stomach and regarded the ceiling. "Maybe we should have gone somewhere."

"Where?" Ceci asked. "You know how these things are. Go one place, think you're safe, the stupid thing turns, and you end up in its path again. We'd have had to go to Colorado, and the last time you went that direction turned out a little nutty, you know?"

"No, I know," Dar said. "Or you do all this dramatic stuff and the thing dies." She glanced to one side, as Chino came over and regarded her upside-down posture with a puzzled expression. "Hey, Chi."

The dog licked her face.

They could hear Andrew and Kerry talking in the kitchen, and the faint sounds of dishes clinking. A soft howling penetrated the walls, and far off, crashing waves thundered.

Dar pulled her phone out of her pocket and typed onto the screen, then paused to wait for an answer. "Power's still on at the office."

"Surprising," Ceci said. "I think they said a hundred thousand were out already?"

"Something like that," Dar agreed. "Carlos says so far so good. He says there's some street flooding, and branches down, but nothing else."

Kerry and Andrew returned at that moment and Kerry put a plate on the table next to the coffee that had some cookies on it. She regarded Dar's posture with some amusement. "Honey, are you that bored?"

Dar put her hands down, then pressed her body up into a handstand before she turned around and folded herself back into a seated position on the chair right side up. "It slowed down," she said mournfully. "Went from ten to six miles per hour. "

Kerry poured a cup of coffee and picked up a cookie and handed it to her, then got her own. She sat in the chair next to Dar's and exhaled. "Yeah, the beach is getting pounded. Even those reporters got the heck out of there."

It was dark outside. Kerry wasn't really sure if that was better or worse. When it was daylight you could look out the small windows at the windswept areas, the frothing seas, but now at night all you could do was listen to the sounds of wind thrumming against the walls.

"Do hurricanes always come at night?" She asked, suddenly. "Or is it just a fifty-fifty chance?"

"Just chance," Andrew said. "Though that one that done come through here last time came during the night."

"The one that's named for you?" Ceci snickered.

"That is not mah fault."

Dar checked her watch. "Guess Manny never heard back from our friend in California. Maybe she didn't like the deal." She shrugged slightly. "Which is fine," she added. "I was willing to leave that one to fate."

"Maybe she decided to hang onto it and continue to taunt everyone," Kerry suggested. "You know, put advertisements on billboards offering it for sale and then telling everyone no?"

"Maybe." Dar munched on her cookie and took a sip of coffee to wash it down. "I just don't get the attitude. Is that still a thing? Did I just miss out on that because I grew up here?" She glanced at Kerry, and then at her parents, who were exchanging looks themselves. "Or am I just oblivious?"

"Well." Ceci cleared her throat. "It's probably true that you're the only one in the room who didn't grow up surrounded by that attitude, Dar."

Andrew nodded. "Yeap. That is for sure the truth. Mah family did not care for anybody that did not look the same as we did." He looked at Dar. "Most folks feel that way."

Dar was silent, blinking a few times. "What?"

"It's true." Kerry reached over to put her hand on Dar's arm, rubbing the skin there lightly with the edge of her thumb. "You know my family," she said. "You knew my father. You remember Karl?" She paused, thoughtfully. "Until I went to school, and then moved down here, I lived in a bubble."

"There are still a lot of people, even here, some who live right on this island, who think immigration's a terrible idea, Dar," Ceci said. "They feel free to share that with me, because they assume I'm one of them." She paused. "And aside from a quirk in the brain, I would have been. My siblings are."

Dar set her cup down. "But everyone here – everyone, even your family were immigrants once." She said. "That's the whole point of the country isn't it? Everyone came from somewhere else?"

"It's true." Kerry said. "I took a class on this whole thing when I was in college. After I got over the whole shock of the whole evolution thing." She gave Dar a wry look, and her eyes twinkled. "I was interested, because I thought, well, maybe some of this weird stuff we do has to do with that, you know?"

"Tribalism?" Ceci nodded. "I watched a documentary on that the other week. No idea how they got funded to make it. Seemed radical, even for me."

"It all has to do with survival," Kerry said. "If you accept evolution, and that we evolved as primates, given what we see with groups of gorillas and chimpanzees then the groups we evolved into were small tribes who depended on each other to survive."

"What does that have to do with immigration?" Dar asked, cautiously.

"Let me get to it." Kerry held a hand up. "Maybe by the time I'm done that stupid storm will finally be here. Anyway." She said. "So, the idea is, your group is everything. Your mother and father, brothers and sisters, aunties and uncles, all that, they form an organization around you that's safe."

She paused. "Everything outside that, is an enemy." She said. "Everyone who isn't us, is them, and they are competitors for land, and resources, and food and if they have it, we don't."

Dar closed her eyes and gave her head a little shake, then opened them again. "We aren't hunter gatherers in Africa anymore." She pointed out. "We're smarter than that now. Aren't we?"

"Ain't been near long enough," Andrew commented briefly. "S'what war's all about, Dardar. You got what I want so I'm gonna take it." He put his hands behind his head. "We ain't much but critters yet. I seen it up close." His lips twitched a little bit. "From both sides."

Dar looked thoughtful.

"So, on top of that we have a natural, inborn instinct to trust people who look like we do, and act like we do," Kerry said. "And even though intellectually it doesn't make sense, we want that. We want everyone around us to think like we do, and believe like we do, and people who don't make us uncomfortable, and honestly, since it's below our thinking minds we don't really even know why most of the time. "

"Can't fight what's in the gut," Andy said. "Ain't up here." He tapped his head. "Ah think about folks I grew up with. Sweet folks, give you their shirts, last bite of food from their houses long as you're the right color, go to the right church."

"I really never thought of anything like that," Dar admitted. "It just seems so stupid to me. I've seen the contributions people make and read some history... I mean, we're all one species." She concluded. "Whatever differences we have are just cosmetic."

Ceci smiled. "As a radical anarchist parent, you make me very proud, Dar. Even though honestly we didn't subvert you on purpose."

Dar looked from her parents to Kerry and back. "Aren't they? People are all people?" She lifted one hand. "Biologically I mean. I realize we all have cultural differences. We speak different languages. We have different color skin and hair and all that, but at the cellular level. We're all homo sapiens."

Kerry nodded, with a faint smile. "Which is why bias, and prejudice is universal. We really are all the same, underneath. There's no one anywhere who doesn't feel, deep inside, that their way of thinking, their tribe, isn't the only best kind."

Dar frowned. "So, she's not the weirdo, I am?" She mused. "Or is she just honest."

There was an awkward silence. "I think," Kerry finally said, "It surprised me that she would actually say what she said, out loud. Because I know, in my family that's what all of them thought." She paused. "It was accepted, you know what I mean? But no one ever said it, not that way."

"Your pastor was pretty clear," Ceci remarked dryly.

"About our being gay you mean," Kerry said. "Yeah that's true. I felt when we were there the last time that everyone felt like they could say stuff like that whereas when I was a kid, it wasn't like that."

"No," Ceci said. "There were always code words. But I remember hearing conversations about someone Candy was going out with at one time and they grounded her because he was Puerto Rican." She paused thoughtfully. "I think that might have been when I decided to take off."

Dar grunted softly. "Never thought about it."

"No, because we," Ceci indicated herself and then Andrew. "Well, for one thing we were so different from each other where would you start? One week you'd go to a Southern Baptist Sunday school and the monster truck races the next. I'd take you to a coven after your oil painting lesson."

Kerry started laughing, covering her eyes with one hand.

"So, we decided to just see what you wanted to do and let you do it," Ceci concluded, with a grin. "It was a lot easier on everyone."

"Get ourselves out of the way," Andrew said. "Sure didn't want you to get any of what my family gave me," he added. "But don't you worry about that there gal, Dar. Life'll learn her one way or t'other." He got up. "Going to go close up that window back there. I hear it rattling."

Kerry half turned and looked at the television. "I vote we go to bed and maybe this thing'll be done when we wake up."

"Great idea." Ceci stood up. "Let's just hope for the best."

She and Andrew retreated up the stairs and Kerry turned back around. "Shall we?"

Dar sat with a thoughtful expression on her face. Then she gave herself a little shake and nodded. She put her hands on the chair arms and pushed herself upright. "Let's imagine tomorrow as a better day." She held out a hand and Kerry clasped it. "All the waiting is making me nuts."

Chapter Three

"Ker."

Kerry came abruptly out from a vague, beach involved dream to unusual sounds and Dar's hand shaking her shoulder. "Huh... uh?" She grunted and rolled over onto her back. "Wh..." She blinked, bringing Dar's face into focus. "What's going on?"

"Eye's coming ashore," Dar said. "All kinds of I don't know what are banging into the walls."

"Oh!" Kerry felt a jolt of adrenaline chase the sleep back. "Are we okay?"

"So far." Dar rolled out of the other side of the bed and pulled on a pair of worn jeans and a T-shirt.

"What tim..oh." Kerry sat up and braced her hands on the rail of the waterbed, as the clock swam into focus. "Power's still on," she said, after her brain acknowledged the four a.m. on the clock's LED. "That's good at least."

A loud bang jerked her right up to her feet and she looked quickly around to see Dar paused in the act of putting her shirt on, head cocked to listen. "Where the hell are the—" She sensed movement to her right and looked toward the wall. "There they are."

Mocha and Chino were sitting up in their beds, tongues lolling, ears pricked up.

In general, storms didn't bother them. Both had grown up from puppies in Florida, and half the year thunderstorms were a daily event, but the loud bangs were disturbing, and their brows were both furrowed.

Kerry pulled on her cargo pants and a T-shirt and patted her leg for the dogs to join her as she made her way out of their bedroom suite into the living room.

Dar turned on the television, and they were both aware of a howling sound that penetrated the walls and was growing louder. "Wish we could see outside."

Kerry went past her, rubbing her eyes with one hand. "I'll get some coffee on." She jerked as another loud bang sounded, this time an impact against the shutters covering the window. "Hope that's just coconuts." She went into the kitchen where a nightlight was glowing.

"Hope so." Dar flicked through the channels. "Cable's down," she said. "Guess it's over the air or nothing. Old school." She switched signal inputs and picked one of the local stations, somewhat jerkily as the signal pixelated in and out. "Oh wow."

Kerry popped back into the living room as she heard stirring upstairs. "What?"

"Looks like they're in a bunker." Dar indicated the screen.

The reporters were in polo shirts and pants, around a wooden table in a square room that looked completely unlike a television studio. "Looks like a conference room," Kerry said. "Hey, good morning," she greeted Andrew and Ceci. "Looks like the fun's starting."

"Been," Andrew said. "Ah been listening to the radio I got. Wind's ripped down them cranes in the port and blew out windows in some of them buildings already."

Dar watched the screen that showed a lurid radar of thick dense circular clouds around a distinct ring that was just about to their east. "Probably ILS's," she said, after a pause for thought. "Glad I didn't have to worry about that this time."

"Was that your problem?" Ceci asked, curiously

"Everything was her problem," Kerry answered for her. "Mostly because no one else had the common sense of a seagull in that place."

"Not until you got there." Dar folded her arms and smiled briefly.

The wind around them was a steady, ceaseless howling noise that vibrated through the walls and floor, and the two dogs trotted around the living room, for once without their tails wagging.

"Wow." Ceci curled up against one arm of the sofa. "That's a mess."

Andrew had an earplug in one ear, and a wire from it trailed down his tall body to one of his multitude of front pants pockets. "Power's out most places," He said. "Big old mess in the airport. Tore up one of them big hangars and put bits of airplanes all over."

"That airport's a mess anyway and always has been," Ceci said. "It's been under construction for fifty years. They probably won't notice."

The television team was just reporting the power outages, showing a map of the lower half of the state, where large blocks were shaded red.

"Roof just came off that there Coast Guard station cross the way," Andrew said, in a calm voice. "Damn good thing they sent them cutters off out of here."

The reporters looked scared. There were computers scattered on the table and screens leaning against the wall, and the lighting in the room was irregularly dimming and brightening.

Kerry inspected her phone. "Cell signal's out. I'm guessing our internet is out too." She shut the phone off and tossed it onto the table next to the couch.

"Probably," Dar said. "It's a separate circuit but with all that power out there's no way that POP is up."

"Hey, we still have air-conditioning." Ceci got up and went into the kitchen, where the coffee machine was just finishing up its task. "I think they just said that station's running on generator."

"They did."

Kerry went to go sit next to Dar, and both Chino and Mocha came over to press against them. "Does it seem surreal to anyone other than me to be sitting here watching this as that thing is about to hit us?"

The howling got louder and Kerry felt her ears pop. "Oh!" She swallowed in reflex.

Dar glanced at the shutters covering the sliding glass doors on the patio, then she walked over and looked more closely at them. "Holy crap!"

Andrew was at her side instantly, pulling a flashlight from one of his pockets and shining it where he saw Dar was looking. "What?"

"It's pulling the metal outward." Dar pointed. "The wind, I mean."

"Maybe you two should get the hell away from that glass then?" Ceci said, sharply. "I know you both can swim like fish but getting your asses sucked out into the Atlantic Ocean is not how I want this morning to go."

"They're bolted into the concrete," Dar said but she backed away from the windows and headed off into her office instead. "Hope that inside window's as protected as I thought it was."

Andrew crouched down and examined the outside floor, where the shutters had bolts extending into slots in the tile. The wind pressure was pulling the panels out, but the depth of the bolts so far seemed to be sufficient, and he stood up with a satisfied grunt.

"Andy."

"Ahm gonna get me some coffee." He ambled into the kitchen. "Figure that'll hold."

"I sure hope so." Kerry put her arms around Chino and Mocha. "We realized the other day we don't have any inside rooms," she said. "There are windows in all of them."

"There are," Ceci agreed. "Even the laundry room upstairs has one." She glanced over head. "When was the last time you had the roof inspected?"

The droning increased, and now the vibrations were palpable, and then they all heard, closer and more ominous, the sounds of the structure they were in creaking around them.

Kerry exhaled. "I don't know the answer to that question," she said as Dar reappeared. "Do you?"

Dar paused in the act of dusting her hands off on her jeans. "Do I what?" She asked, after a moment's silence. "The window's in a deep sill. Seems okay. But I'm going to close the panel anyway soon as the wind drops and the eyewall passes."

Ceci eyed Dar. "I asked when was the last time the roof was checked. I know you both have been pretty busy."

Dar came over and sat next to Kerry. "The association is supposed to take care of that," she said. "They do the whole complex at once since it's connected."

"Sure they do?" Ceci asked.

"They certify it and it's in their master insurance policy," Dar said, dryly. "So, they're motivated to."

"Ah." Ceci nodded, looking a bit relieved. "It's always better when someone's bank account is on the line." She looked up as Andy returned and sat down on the couch next to her. "The walls are creaking," she said.

"I wasn't sure concrete block could do that."

Dar got up and walked to the wall between the patio and the kitchen and put her hands against it, ignoring the roaring of the wind outside.

A flicker made her turn her head to one side, and she saw the picture go out on the television. Over the speakers, though, she heard a muted scream and a crash. "These walls are moving," Dar commented. "I guess theirs are too?"

"The walls are moving?" Kerry asked, sharply.

"Get away from them?" Ceci suggested. "In fact, maybe we should go into your office there, in the front? It's the furthest away from the ocean." She got up and grabbed a handful of Andrew's shirt sleeve to tug him along. "C'mon, people!"

Dar backed away from the wall, flexing her hands, and almost tripped over Chino, who had come up behind her. She hopped once or twice, then got her balance and joined Kerry as she circled the leather chair and they headed for the office.

They heard something rattle against the wall on the outside and then, a moment later, a cracking sound somewhere nearby.

"That's probably that tree," Dar said, after a moment.

"Maybe close that panel?" Ceci suggested, pointing at the window. "Not wait?"

"I don't think the mechanism is strong enough to pull against the wind," Dar responded, in a calm tone. "That's why I want to wait for the wall to come past, we'll be inside the eye."

Andrew went to Dar's desk and pulled the radio he had in his pocket out, setting it onto the surface and removing the plug from his ear, then the end from the device.

Radio crackling emerged from its front speaker, clipped and slightly garbled.

"Navy station," Andrew said, briefly. "Got them updates from NOAA too."

"They transmitting from that bunker down south of Card Sound?" Dar asked.

"Yeap."

The radio had a stream of non-stop content, the voices changing every few minutes as different sources checked in. Most of it made sense only to Andrew, who knew the jargon, but they heard when the storm's eye came ashore.

Heard on the radio, and then around them as the wind sound became so loud they all flinched and the walls around them shuddered in motion.

Andrew went over and closed the door, and the two dogs crawled up onto the couch, whining, ears pinned down to their heads. He came back over and sat next to Ceci and clasped his hands.

"Storm surge, twelve feet," the radio reported. "Structure collapse reported mid beach, twelfth street."

"Twelve feet. Holy bananas," Kerry muttered. "I hope like hell everyone is evacuated off Miami Beach."

The long, narrow stretch of land to their north was a barrier island that extended up the coastline and bordered the mainland on the other side of the intercoastal waterway. On the south end, though, it stood between the Atlantic Ocean and Biscayne Bay.

Fisher Island was the very southern tip of it, separated from South Beach by a man-made channel called Government Cut that had been built to allow cargo ships access to the mouth of the Miami River.

"Twelve feet is going to come up over the wall outside," Dar said.

"It's going to take out the parking garage too," Kerry said.

"They closed them doors on the outside," Andrew spoke up. "Heard em when we got back."

A loud crash sounded outside, and then they felt a deep thrumming through the floor. Bangs and cracks followed, and Kerry wrapped her arms around the shivering Mocha, his pale eyes wide and round and his nostrils flaring. "Easy, honey."

"Twenty-twenty hindsight," Ceci said, after a moment of silence when even the radio seemed to be pausing to catch its breath. "This was stupid."

Andrew snorted a faint chuckle. "Got too big."

Dar was next to Kerry on the other end of the couch, her arm curled around the apprehensive looking Chino. "Yeah. This was dumb," she admitted. "Let's not do this again."

"Shelter in place. Shelter in place." The radio burst out. "We have one hundred seventy knots at the buoy."

The roaring built and built and after a minute Dar lifted her hands to cover her ears, with a grimace, as the thumps and bangs got louder and louder and went on for what felt like forever. Kerry put her free arm around Dar's waist and hugged her close as they huddled there, just enduring it.

Felt like it was never going to stop. Felt like hours, and the noise was brutal and exhausting, the unexpected bangs making everyone jump.

And then like a knife cutting bread the howl abruptly faded.

Everyone opened their eyes and looked around in question. Then Dar got up off the couch and went to the window, triggering the controls that would close the mechanical shutter on the outside. There was a crack, then a whine, then the panel folded out and over the window, seating itself into the latch and bolts with a very audible crunch.

"Are we in the eye?" Kerry got up. "We must be, right?"

"Yeap," Andy said. "Got the back side of it coming."

"That means the edge is probably over the office," Kerry said. "Holy shit, Dar. That building's never going to hold up in this. It's going to be… "She paused. "I wish we hadn't had Carlos and his friends stay there."

Dar turned. "Too late now," she said. "Let's take a walk around and upstairs. See if we see any damage before the backside hits us." She paused and shook her head. "I'm damn glad all our support guys are up in Melbourne. Wish we'd sent the whole damn company on that bus."

"Me too. I'm worried about Mayte and Maria and Zoe and…" Kerry exhaled. "About everyone." She glanced at the radio on the desk. "I'm glad Mayte got those sat phones."

"Smart young lady," Andy said. "S'good idea to check out what we can." He indicated the door. "No sense fussing about stuff outside. Can't get there."

Kerry was closest to the door. She opened it and peered cautiously into the living room where the television screen was still on but the picture had returned. The reporters were all seated around the table, most with headsets on, two with microphones.

They looked completely freaked out. Kerry felt a certain sympathy as she went past the couch and leaned over to turn on the lights so they could see better.

Andrew and Dar went up the stairs. Ceci joined her as she went along the walls and then into the kitchen, a little surprised that despite all the chaos outside, everything inside seemed pretty much as it was before they went to bed. "Hmm."

"A little water here," Ceci said, inspecting the inside of the kitchen door that led down to the garden. "Got forced in under the sill, I guess." She went over to the roll of paper towels sitting on the counter and unrolled a few, returning to drop them on the tile floor.

Kerry checked the windows. "Dry here," she reported. "I'm going to check the patio." She went back out and turned on the dining room lights. The sliding glass doors were in one piece, and she could see past them, to the patio floor that was awash with water, the metal shutters folded across the front of the space visibly dented.

There was a gap in them, she realized, when she studied the small gray patch that puzzled her until she realized it was after six a.m. and the sun was coming up somewhere. "Those are bent."

Ceci came over to stand next to her, shading her eyes and peering out. "All sorts of who knows what blowing against them," she said. "Coconuts, chairs, small yachts, microwaves from people who didn't have the sense to lock their boats down..."

Kerry chuckled a little bit. "Must be a mess."

The wind was only gusting now, rattling the shutters, sending spatters of rain to hit the tile of the patio and the edge of the jacuzzi, covered and secured, outside.

"Gruff." Chino came over to stand next to them, looking out.

"Crazy that the power's still on," Ceci remarked. "Coffee?"

"Might as well."

****

Andrew stood on the set of drawers that he'd dragged along the carpet underneath the hatch that gave access into the crawlspace above the ceiling. "Hey, Dardar?"

"Hang on." Dar's voice sounded muffled. "I'm checking the laundry."

Andy grunted and shined the beam from his flashlight into the space, relieved at least not to see any slivers of outside light that might indicate a gap they had to worry about. The ceiling itself was unstained, and he didn't see any evidence of damage, but the sounds he'd heard of shattering tiles made him leery.

Dar appeared. "Seems okay," she said. "I checked the vent, there's water inside it. So probably from the hot air escape."

Andrew nodded. "This here looks all right. You want to take a peek?"

Dar hoisted herself up onto the chest of drawers next to him, feeling the furniture wobble a bit under their joined weight. "We should hurry up before that starts again." She put her hand on his shoulder and looked past his arm as he lifted the hatch up again and directed the light against the inside of the roof.

The crawlspace was full of insulation, and the roof was sprayed with it, covering the surface. But it was intact, and she saw no evidence of any water stain. "It's metal," she said. "Not sure I mentioned that. Metal frame and metal overlay, with felt and wood over that, and a rubber seal."

Andrew looked at her. "Do tell," he said, with some interest. "That's like they do in the military."

Dar nodded. "It's a bunker. I wasn't kidding. In order for them to get anyone to insure this place, since it sits on its ass at the edge of the damn Atlantic, they had to."

She jumped down to the ground and dusted her hands off. "I smell coffee."

Andy set the hatch back down and shut his flashlight off and slid it into one of the pockets in his military style work pants. He merely stepped down off the chest of drawers and then he turned. "Give a hand with this here."

Dar helped him move the chest back over to the wall. "That was pretty scary," she said. "I can only imagine what it's like everywhere else."

"Yeap." Andy clapped her on the back. "Let's go get us a biscuit and some joe before that all starts up again."

"I think we have doughnuts not biscuits."

"That's all right too."

****

Kerry lost track of what time it was. With the shutters down, and the howling seemingly never ending, it was just hour after hour of listening to Andy's radio, all of them huddled in Dar's office.

They had thirty minutes of respite, before the wind came back, in the opposite direction. Long enough to get cups of coffee, and some trail bars, along with the doughnuts they'd brought back from the market the night before.

Power was still on, and it seemed a little surreal for the inside of the condo to be warmly lit with the task lights on Dar's desk as though nothing were going on outside at all.

It felt real, and yet unreal at the same time. Kerry remembered being in this same office, but with no power. The stuffiness of the inside air uncomfortable, but without the incessant howling outside since the winds in that older storm had been only half at most what they were now.

The intermittent bangs and crunching sounds made it impossible to do anything needing concentration. Even Dar abandoned her desk and sat on the floor between Chino and Mocha, leaning against the couch.

Her forearms rested on her knees, twiddling her thumbs idly. "Wish I had a deck of cards."

"Knew we forgot something," Ceci said. "We have one on the boat."

"Last time I saw a deck of cards was playing Solitaire on my desktop," Kerry admitted. "Cards were not an item in my past."

Ceci eyed her. "Your father didn't play poker with the boys?" She asked in a mildly disbelieving tone. "Really?"

"Oh no. Gambling wasn't done in his house," Kerry said. "He thought that was an absolute sin against God. Not to mention there was just no way he was going to have that surface in some article, with all the campaign claptrap he used about purity and clean living and whatever."

"Huh," Andy grunted. "Don't that figure."

"Peculiar religious hypocrisy," Ceci said. "One of the reasons I ran from Christianity." She idly played with one of Mocha's dark, silky ears. "It's just an excuse to self-righteously frame your bias in a way that makes you feel virtuous."

"Asshole justification," Dar said.

"That's what I said," Her mother smirked. "Admittedly, religion was mostly window dressing in the hallowed halls of my growing up, but nothing quite gave me a thrill more than announcing my paganism in company in the living room."

"Christianity ain't got nothing to do with Jesus Christ nowadays," Andy said. "All them folks better hope he ain't really coming back here cause they're gonna get their butts whipped."

Kerry chuckled then flinched as a bang came from the shutter covered large window behind them. "I like belonging to a family of anarchists," she said. "I remember a time when I thought I was the only one in the world." She tilted her head and regarded Dar. "Then I met you."

Dar grinned, then propped her head up against one fist. "Is this thing ever going to end?" She asked plaintively, glancing over at her father. "Feels like it's been over us for eight hours."

"Almost, Dardar." Andy patted her shoulder. "Offshore drop's down sixty."

And then, in time, the wind died down. At least enough so that it no longer thrummed the shutters, and the howling had muted. They still heard rain hitting the aluminum, but it was more in spurts and it seemed, at last, that the worst was over.

Dar looked at her watch. Then she got up and went to the door of the office, opening it and looking out into the living room. "Okay."

"Eye just went over the airport," Andy said. He stood up as well and collected his radio, stuffing it into his thigh pocket. "Turned some north. Going all up the Palmetto, seems like."

"Went right across the center of the city," Kerry said.

They all went into the living room, where the television was still on. The reporters were still in their conference room and a screen hung on the wall behind them showing the radar view.

"Everything Andrew didn't do," Dar said. "Let me see if I can look out the back door." She went into the kitchen, almost getting thumped into the door itself as the two dogs eagerly clustered behind her. "Hang on, mutts," she warned. "I've got no idea what the hell's out there."

Kerry and Andrew grabbed the two animals and moved them back, as Dar triggered the window shutter. It whined and groaned but stayed in place. "Hmm."

"Bent," Andy said.

"Probably." Dar unlocked the door and cautiously pushed against it, feeling resistance as the seal around the edge of the door gave way with a faint sucking sound and she took in a breath of waterlogged air as she leaned her weight against the panel.

Warm wet and salt-tinged wind blew into her face as she pushed harder. She finally got the door open enough to stick her head out and look around.

The door was blocked by palm fronds and debris. One was across the back of it, and Dar hesitated when she saw the thick spines. "Ker, give me that pair of gloves in the drawer willya?"

"Hang on." Kerry fished the leather work gloves out of the miscellaneous drawer and handed them over. "Here you go. What's out there?"

"A lot of junk." Dar got the gloves on and gingerly eased the frond back, shoving it aside sufficiently to push the door open enough for her to get her body sideways through the opening and out onto the small porch at the top of the stairs.

She looked around for a long moment. "Holy crap!"

"That doesn't sound good." Kerry poked her head out and peered past her elbow. "Whoa, Is that the Atlantic Ocean there right below us?"

The little walled garden at the bottom of the steps appeared as though a junkyard had been emptied into it. Debris covered the ground and plants were uprooted and most washed away. At least half of the space was covered in water.

Dar took a step farther and allowed the rest of them to ease out behind her, as she took a few steps down. The gates that had been in the wall were gone. Waves were lapping past the opening and the seawall that had been past it was no longer there.

Chino came out and stood behind Kerry, emitting sounds of doggy astonishment.

Dar turned around and looked up at the wall of the condo that looked like it had been painted over with Army camouflage paint. "What the hell?"

Ceci walked down the steps and turned to see what Dar was looking at. "That's actually sort of attractive," she commented. "Must have been from all the branches and trees hitting the wall. Look, there's a pile of branches on the ground there."

Chino and Mocha descended warily, staring around at what was usually their neatly kept playground. The winds were still gusting, but they were between squalls. And between the shredded gray clouds whipping overhead there was even a very brief splotch of sky.

"Careful, kids." Kerry went down to join Ceci, and they picked their way through the debris to look at the water surging through the gates, bringing a white foam and both flotsam and jetsam as waves rolled up to where they were standing. "Holy crap the whole beach is gone."

"Some mess," Andy said. "All that there wall's down." He made his way over to where the gates had been, the surf soaking his boots and pants as he got to the edge and looked around it. "Mah, lord!"

Everyone hurried over to join him. "What?" Ceci said, grimacing a little as the water washed up against her knees. "What is it, And..." She stopped talking, as she got to where she could see past him. "Whoa."

"Oh wow," Kerry whispered. "Is that water up over the streets there?"

The rock ingress that lined Government Cut was completely gone, and past it, what had been the southern end of Miami Beach showed buildings with floors caved in, glass blown out. The marina was a wreckage of collapsed and capsized boats.

In the middle of the cut was a large fishing vessel, turned sideways and half sunk. Only the bow protruded up from the waves that lashed across the opening, no longer restrained by the seawalls that had once protected the channel.

Water lapped up to the wall they were standing behind. Fully eight to ten feet of land was missing. What was once a beach and path could no longer be seen.

"Is that ... "Kerry started to ask.

Andrew went past where the gates had been and sloshed into the surf, the wind blowing against him and plastering his T-shirt and cargo pants against his body. He looked to his right, then he paused and extended his hand into the surf surging around him. "Wall's still here."

Dar edged out after him around the curve of the wall, looking past it. All along the beachfront she could see waves breaking, some rolling up past where the pools were and swamping them.

"Mah, God." Andy came up next to her and put his hands on his hips. "Some damn mess."

"Yeah." Dar exhaled. "Well, we should probably make sure the rest of this place is in one piece, then break out the sat phones. It's maybe clear enough to use them."

"Probly not." Andy glanced up, as another squall came over, and they were suddenly drenched in rain. "Got nother name here they're gonna retire I figure."

"Oh yeah."

****

Dar entered the kitchen, ruffling her hair dry with a fluffy light blue towel. Behind her in the living room the television was on, the local station now evacuated out of their conference room and back in the more familiar confines of their studio.

Chino followed her inside, then sat down next to her bowl and barked.

Dar paused and regarded her, then she looked over at the clock in the microwave. "Oh," she said. "Sorry, Cheebs. I guess there was so much going on we forgot about that." She draped the towel around her shoulders and then went over to pick up the two steel dog food dishes near the wall.

It all seemed so weirdly normal, surrounded by surreal lack of anything being that at all. She filled the dishes, the sound of the food hitting the metal attracting Mocha from where he'd been sleeping on the couch.

He trotted in and sat next to Chino, tag wagging happily. Chino turned her head and licked his ear.

Dar watched them and chuckled. Their fur was damp, and she smelled the wetness of it, but they had towels spread out on the tiles to sop up most of the rain and sea water they'd brought back in as the squalls returned.

"Looks like everything's pretty much intact, at least from the inside." Kerry entered from the living room, running her fingers through her hair, a dry terry cloth short sleeve hoodie having replaced the T-shirt she'd been wearing. She was barefoot and had traded her wet jeans for a dry pair of cargo shorts.

"Yeah, we should leave the shutters in place though." Dar put the food bowls down and stepped back out of the way as they were engulfed. "Dad checked the crawlspace again. Still dry."

Kerry came over to stand next to her. "You sure were right about this being a bunker," she said. "I saw what those winds did to South Pointe."

"Lower profile," Dar said. "The way they built these, with all those angles there's not much surface for the wind to grab." She nodded in satisfaction. "They just said the winds are down to a hundred twenty."

"Still bad."

"Still bad," Dar agreed. She took a glass from the cabinet and opened the refrigerator, dispensing milk into it. "No one really knows though. They can't get out to do any visuals yet." She set the glass down and then retrieved a jar of peanut butter and opened it.

"Should we consume our cans of beanie weenies?" Kerry mused. "Can't think of any other opportunity for it."

"No." Dar spread peanut butter on a slice of bread. "What they usually do is collect any of the canned goods no one uses after the season and donate them to Camillus House or one of those things." She folded the bread in half and took a bite. "I'm fine with this."

Kerry settled for a bottle of iced tea and a container of yogurt. She followed Dar into the living room and sat down on the couch next to her, as they watched the news reports.

"Front's going to pick that up and take it back out over the Atlantic," Dar predicted. "They just put up hurricane warnings up the coast."

A ticker was scrolling across the bottom of the screen, providing them with snippets of information in a repetitive loop. "Numbers to call," Kerry said, thoughtfully. "Could we call any of them right now, Dar?" She asked. "Since they took out all the old copper, I mean?"

"No." Dar chewed her sandwich. "One of the reasons I was so against that." She frowned. "No internet, no VoIP, no digital, no phones."

"Good thing Mayte got those damn sat phones for sure," Kerry said. "Maybe we should have one all the time?"

"Maybe I'm going to order an Inmarsat dish as a backhaul."

Kerry diverted her attention back to the ticker. "Twelve foot storm surge. Does that mean a twelve foot high wall of water, Dar?"

"Something like that."

Kerry was silent for a moment. "Twelve feet high? That's what washed across our back area there?" Her voice was hollow with disbelief. "Twelve feet?"

Dar nodded. "That's where all that debris is from. Probably when it sucked back out it took the gates with it. Good thing this place held up. We would have had our asses pulled out into the ocean. Probably be halfway to Nassau by now."

Kerry stared at her in silence, eyes wide.

Dar glanced at her. "Didn't happen, right?" She took a sip of her milk. "No point in freaking out about it." She watched Kerry's face, and it almost made her smile, so vivid and evident were the emotions crossing it. "Wasn't half as scary as going down that river was."

"But we chose to do that," Kerry said, after a long pause.

Dar half shrugged. "We chose to do this. All relative risk."

Kerry gave her body a shake, and then she went back to peeling the cover off her yogurt. "Mother Nature doesn't mess around."

"Mother Nature does not," Dar confirmed. "What is that, is that from the television station?" She indicated the screen. "Yeah, it must be," she said. "They're in Kendall."

"Where I used to live," Kerry said. "Holy crap."

The wind was still whipping, and trees were in motion as the camera panned around. It was being handheld, spots of water collecting on the lens.

Then it tilted down and showed a lake, water lapping against the feet of the camera holder, standing on some platform.

"He's standing on the top of the station mobile van," Dar said, after a moment.

It was the parking lot of an office plaza, but all that could be seen was water, washing out any landmarks save the tops of some trucks parked nearby. Then the camera turned around to show the building the station was broadcasting from. A three-story building with a parking garage. On the roof was a square, bunker like structure they could just see the top of a satellite dish sticking out of.

Long cables ran from the camera, up a flight of concrete stairs to a second level door, propped open. Stunned faces could be seen just looking around. The sound cut in now, and they heard the loud rumble of a generator nearby, and far off the sound of a siren.

Kerry paused in mid spoonful. "My entire apartment would have been flooded," She said, after a moment. "Our parking lot used to flood in a bad rain. I can't even imagine."

"If that's what it's like in Kendall," Dar said, "and they were in the fringes."

Kerry put her yogurt down. "What are we going to be left with at the office, Dar? What are we going to do?"

Dar folded her arms, regarding the screen with somber concern. "Well," she said, after a pause. "Let's see what contacts we can make as soon as the weather clears. Find out what's going on."

****

Kerry eased the front door to the condo open and peered outside. "Looks like a Christmas tree blood bath happened out here." She pushed the door open, gently kicking the branches covering the steps out of her way.

She pulled the hood on her jacket up as she felt rain splatter against her face and started down toward the ground level driveway that angled one way toward the road, and the other under the building where they had their cars parked. "Don't try opening the gate, Dar," she called out. "It's flooded."

"Figured." Dar emerged with both dogs on their seldom used leashes. "Got your camera?"

"Got it." Kerry removed one hand with her digital camera in it, then waited as Dar got herself untangled and picked her way carefully down to join her.

It was overcast. Rain was still intermittent. Winds were still gusting. But the gaps in all that had been slowly increasing. Now they were going to see what there was to be seen on this, the more protected side of the facility.

Kerry turned the camera on and took some pictures. The front of the condo was covered in broken branches, coconuts, metal debris, wood debris, pieces of net from the tennis courts, and paper. The walls were scuffed with green, but not as wildly as the back was, and the gates that protected the walk up to their front door were intact.

Dar pushed the gate opened and they emerged onto the path, looking both directions warily.

There was water everywhere. Across the path, where the golf course was, a lake now stood, the wind making rough waves in it as it spread through the trees as far as they could see.

And the trees were mostly either leaning over, or on the ground, as though a giant hand had flattened them. Branches stuck up out of the water, many laying across the road.

"Which way you want to walk?" Kerry asked. "Toward the cut, or toward the marina?"

"Toward the cut," Dar said. "Maybe the sat phone'll connect." She handed one of the leashes to Kerry and pulled a phone out of her pocket and checked the display. "It sees the bird," She said. "Let me try Mark. He lives down south. Might be clear enough there now."

They turned and walked slowly along the road, as Dar fiddled with the handheld device. She tried dialing Mark, but though the phone seemed to be reaching out, there was no answer. "He might still be inside."

"Yeah, he's a smart guy," Kerry said. "Try Carlos."

Dar dialed, but again, got no answer. "I guess it's too early," she said. "I just wish I knew what was going on." She juggled the phone, then put it back in her pocket.

They heard the rumble of generators in the distance. But otherwise, aside from the wind, there was almost no sound. Dar looked over at the golf lake. "Birds are gone," she said. "I remember that from the last big one. They know and they all disappear."

"I noticed the ducks weren't around," Kerry said. "I wonder where the peacocks are? Where would they all go?"

"I think Clemente puts them in a compound." Dar paused as they reached a bend in the road and could see past it, to where the ferry ramp was. "Oh wow. Is that a ... I think that's a pilot boat." She studied the wreckage piled up against the ramp, the boat turned on its side. "Must have broken loose."

They walked closer to the edge of the island, as the wind gusted fitfully against them, fluttering their jackets against their bodies.

"Gruff," Chino barked softly.

"Hope no one was on it," Kerry said. She shaded her eyes as she peered across the cut at the end of South Beach. "Jesus. The whole damn beach is gone. Is that sand up on the sun deck there?"

Kerry saw two figures inching along on what was the second floor of the nearest building. They looked down at the ocean, surveying the damage much as she and Dar were. Kerry was sure there were more people starting to get out and look around, despite the news saying not to.

Very human, to be curious. Kerry was surprised they hadn't met any of their neighbors yet in fact. "Think everyone else went the other way?" She asked Dar.

"Probably."

Dar kept walking until they were on the concrete pad that led to the ramp for the ferry. The security shelter was closed up tight and empty and the ground around it was littered with shards from the barrel tiles that had come off its roof.

She got to where she could see up the shipping channel, past the berths that had once held some decrepit old cruise ships toward the turning basin and the line of buildings that edged the waterfront of the city.

"Trees down all along the causeway," Kerry said. "There's a truck in the water over there, near the Star Island turnoff." She took out her camera and started taking pictures. She used the digital zoom to get a better look. "Oh, hell, the whole road into Star Island's gone."

"South Pointe Marina's a mess," Dar said. "Glad mom and dad at least weren't there." She shook her head, the hazy light and mist obscuring the scene, but the toppled sails and capsized hulls were evident even from where she stood.

They heard the sound of tires crunching on gravel and turned to see one of the island golf carts coming toward them, with two men in rain gear in it.

"They're going to yell at us, Dar," Kerry said and took a picture of the cart as it approached.

"They're going to try." Dar smiled briefly and without much humor. "If they whip out a bullhorn, I'm going to shove it up their asses."

Kerry stuffed the camera into her pocket and took the leashes of the two dogs from Dar as her partner turned to face the two men.

Dar had a particular way of standing when she was facing confrontation and now she fell into that posture. Her weight over her center of balance and her hands resting half open at her sides, she positioned herself between the cart and Kerry.

Kerry really didn't think the men were any threat. They were both sweating under their rubber rain gear and they looked more flustered than angry. She recognized them as security, but one of the many that spent time in roving patrols rather than at the ferry dock.

"Ms. Roberts!" The driver called out. "Oh, Ms. Roberts!"

"Yeeeessss," Dar rumbled a response, eyes narrowing.

"Great. Glad we found you," The man said. "Mr. Lou said if we could find you, to ask you to come over to the command center." He jumped out of the cart and came over to them. "Everything okay at your house?"

Kerry watched Dar's freight train of attitude get abruptly derailed, and she relaxed. "Everything's fine," she assured him. "What's going on? Is there a problem?"

She drew his attention to give Dar a chance to take her hackles down and muffled a smile as her partner eased over to her side, hands now in her pockets.

The man nodded vigorously. "They got some stuff not working and Mr. Lou, he knows Ms. Roberts knows all about that stuff. So will you come with us?" He looked from Kerry to Dar. "We were headed your way when we saw you out walking. George recognized the pups."

"Um. Sure." Dar glanced around. "Give us a ride back to our place, and we'll drop off the dogs," she said. "How's the other side of the island?"

"What a mess!" The other guard said. "Surge threw a manatee up onto the Beach Club porch! Some of the guys were trying to get it back into the water when we left there."

"Oh, my goodness." Kerry got into the back seat of the cart with the dogs, while Dar stood on the back gate. "Dar, hang on!"

****

Ten minutes later, after dropping off the dogs and giving Dar a chance to grab a backpack they were in the back seat of the cart heading up the road toward the marina. As they went past the other condos, a few residents were visible, most taking pictures of their homes, and the damage all around them.

Two men had crossed the road and were standing on a slight rise, looking at the lake that now filled the center of the island.

"Those are the golfers," George said, half turning in his seat to face Dar and Kerry. He was a man in his mid-forties, with thinning brown hair and a stocky build. "Ruined their fun for a while huh, Sam?"

"They're gonna have to pump that out." Sam shook his head. "Just glad this rain's mostly done."

No sooner than he'd said it, a squall came over and swept across the road, drenching the cart, and George cursed as he scrambled to get his hood up and hauled the plastic rain guard down. "Ya had to say that didn'tcha?" He yelped.

Dar blinked the rain out of her eyes, glad they were alone on the road as the cart careened from one side of it to the other, nearly going through a deep puddle. "Yew."

"You didn't pack our scuba gear in there did you?" Kerry said, under her breath. "We might need it."

"On the boat," Dar muttered back. "I was going to bring it back to the house, but figured hell, if anything happened, we were due for new gear anyway."

"Mm."

"Sorry about that, ma'am," Sam said. "Here we go, hang on."

Dar had her hand clamped around the roof support post and her other arm wrapped around Kerry, and it still almost wasn't enough to keep them from sliding off the seat as the cart turned sharply and went up a narrower path toward what looked like a huge thicket of downed trees.

"What th..." Kerry paused. "Oh wow," she said. "That whole ring is down."

The command post for security was a thick, squat building artfully hidden in foliage that was now toppled everywhere, exposing the concrete block structure and blocking the path save a small gap that Sam was aiming for. Inside the ring of destruction was a small parking lot, and the two cars that were parked in it were buried under fallen branches.

The building windows were covered in shutters, and the shed to one side of it had been blown open, tools and supplies scattered across the area randomly. The tall radio tower that had been on the roof was over in one corner, wrapped around a tree trunk whose top half had fallen over.

One corner of the overhang roof near the door was hanging down, but the building seemed intact aside from that.

Sam and George got out and they joined them, hurrying over to the door as another squall came through. The front surface of the door was dented, and the light fixture outside was bent aside and destroyed, glass from it littering the ground.

Going from the windy, damp, warm outside into the ice box chill inside was a shock. Kerry almost flinched, and now she was glad they had their raincoats on as she blinked her eyes against the cold, dry air.

Inside the building there was a lot going on. There was a desk near the door that under normal conditions some administrative person would have been seated, attending to visitors.

Now, it's surface had been cleared, its contents behind it wrapped in black garbage bags, and the top of the desk was covered in various types of food along with jugs of things to drink. Stacked on the side of the furniture were boxes of paper cups, plates and plastic silverware.

Behind that there was one big room, with consoles along every wall of it, desks and monitors. Most of the stations were empty and the monitors were either dark or full of fuzzy nothing.

To the right was an office, and that's where most of the noise was coming from. Sam and George turned and headed into it, pushing open a partly closed door that released a din of voices outward toward them along with the strong smell of coffee.

"Wasn't figuring this to go this way." Dar said, as they stood there somewhat awkwardly. She had her backpack on her back. "Let me go see if this phone's any good yet." She pulled the sat phone from her pocket and went outside.

Short attention span; gets bored easily. Kerry went over to the expresso maker near the wall and picked up a small paper cup. Then she pressed the buttons required to obtain a shot. "Lou!" She called out, as the machine grumbled and sputtered, steam wisping from it.

A moment later, a tall man with a crew cut and surprisingly large ears stuck his head out into the room. "What was that? Oh!" He came all the way out into the room. "Oh, hey! Uh..."

"Kerry," she supplied amiably. "Dar's outside trying to make a phone call. What is it you need her to look at? We've got a lot of stuff going on."

"No, yes, Kerry, I know... sorry." Lou Rogers came over to her. "Sorry about that. I didn't realize George and Sam brought you back with them. They just said they found you. Our big system, you know, the one that runs all the cameras and all that stuff? It won't turn on."

"Okay." Kerry nodded. "I'm going to assume it has power."

"What?" Lou said. "Oh! Yes, of course it does. We checked the outlet, it can run the teapot, so we know there's juice there, but it keeps stopping at some screen. Could you... or could she look at it? They didn't keep any of our IT people island side. They sent them all off."

He looked at her with an anxious expression. "I know there's so much to take care of, but it's hard for us not to be able to see all our cameras, you know? We have to send patrols out and the place is a mess."

"Where is it?" Kerry asked then took a sip of her expresso. "Sure, we'll take a look, but next time, take my advice and keep a nerd around," she said. "You always need them."

"It's over in there." Lou pointed at a closed door in the back. "That's where all our IT stuff is. Door's unlocked." He glanced behind him. "We're going to rig up an antenna for the radio...so..."

"Go on. I'll take Dar in there when she comes back."

A moment later, the door opened and Dar reappeared, a frown on her face.

"No luck?" Kerry read the body language effortlessly. "C'mere, let's see if you can fix their system. Then we'll steal a cart and go check out our boat. Sound like a plan?"

"Mm. Coffee." Dar observed her cup. "That what they're paying us? Sure. Where is whatever it is? No answer yet on these damn phones."

Kerry led the way over to the closed door and pushed it open with one shoulder, the very familiar sound of technology escaping at once and washing over her like sea foam.

No matter the size or content, they all looked and sounded alike. The smell of cabling, forced air, metal and components being cooled, and the sound of fans pushing hot air out of densely packed gear with a particular, peculiar scent of ions.

The pitch of the noise was known to both of them.

This room had two rows of racks on either side of an open aisle, and the doors were open on several of them, with keyboards and monitors pulled out keeping them propped open.

Dar, predictably, went one by one and pushed the keyboards back into place, then closed and latched the rack doors as they went down the aisle. The workbench at the back had a single console and a thick, padded chair.

Kerry waited for Dar to shrug off her backpack and sit down. "Let me get you a cup of this, hon."

Dar paused, and turned. "Kerrison."

"Yes?" Kerry's brows quirked a little, as she took in Dar's surprisingly stern look.

"You are as much a computer professional as I am," Dar said. "Why the hell would you be running around getting me coffee?"

"Aw." Kerry went over and ruffled her hair. "Because there's only one chair, my love. And I know how to quantify and qualify my tools and make sure they're applied in the best use case." She leaned over and gave Dar a kiss on the forehead. "Go fix."

She bumped Dar toward the table, then turned, chuckling, and went out of the IT room and back to the coffee maker.

Dar did surprise her sometimes with things like that. Though they were both aware of their relative subject matter expertise, and level of nerdiness her partner sometimes seemed to think—or at least often vocally expressed—the notion that they were total equals.

Socially, yes. Kerry busied herself with the expresso maker. They were partners. But Dar's aptitude for technology was at a genius level. Hers was not. Though she had a significant knowledge base of her own, and she had far stronger pure business skills than Dar did, there was one true master nerd in the family, and she wasn't it.

Her technical skills were acquired. She'd gone through school and gained knowledge the old fashioned way, and built on that as she'd built her career. Dar's were far more innate. She had a synergy with how things worked and how to make them work that was absolutely instinctual.

She'd watched Dar problem solve sometimes. Dar had done something, or drawn a solution to something, or typed something and Kerry asked her how she'd known to do whatever it was. The answer was almost always just a look at her with knit brows.

Dar didn't know how she knew. She didn't know. And that was why, Kerry realized, that they'd left ILS in such a pickle when they had because though Dar had documented what she did as thoroughly as any human being could have, with full integrity it hadn't helped.

Hadn't helped because she could not document, could not mentor, could not teach anyone how to do what she did because she didn't know herself how to frame that information and it was so natural to her that she didn't understand why everyone else didn't think the same way.

Kerry picked up both Dar's cup and her second, and made her way back to the room, bumping the door open with her hip. She let the door close behind her and went over to the worktable, setting down the coffee at Dar's elbow.

There was a screen there, and Dar was reviewing it, her hands draped in a relaxed pose over the keyboard. "Take a power hit or something?" Kerry asked. "Or maybe a bad hard drive?"

"No...well, I don't know," Dar said. "I don't think so. It's more like... some change or something got done and then it restarted and barfed." She indicated the screen. "It's all compiling and missing link errors."

"Can you undo whatever it was?" Kerry said as Dar picked up her cup and took a sip.

"Well." Dar regarded the screen. "It would be easier if I knew what it was," she said. "But yeah, let me script a routine to go find all the changed files in the last twenty-four hours and see if there were backup copies made." She shook her head and started typing. "Nice of them to leave this logged in as root for me."

Kerry covered her eyes with one hand and snorted in soft laughter. "Maybe I should pitch them a deal to take over their IT."

Dar stopped typing, and looked at her, both eyebrows lifting nearly up to her hairline.

"Too soon?"

****

Dar took off her raincoat and draped it over the padded office chair. It was chilly in the room, but the damp squeak of the jacket got on her nerves and she'd decided the trade off was worth it.

The problem she was working on wasn't that complicated. The system itself was a Linux variant. One she was tolerably familiar with, and the file structure wasn't overly obscure.

Whoever had tried to do whatever they tried to do had made a mess of it. Dar had to wonder why anyone would want to change anything right before a humongous hurricane came over. But, since there weren't any IT people around, there was no one she could ask that question of.

Part of her questioned why the hell she was even doing this. Dar reviewed the results of her script, comparing it to a scratch file she'd built. The island management weren't friends of hers, and she was trying to move off it anyway.

Some jackass would probably walk in any minute and demand to know what she was doing here. Dar could almost hear the blustering horn honking in her head as she wrote another script to rewrite the backup files back to original and copy the new ones to a different directory.

Probably some dipshit old buddy of Jim's, who would then throw her, and Kerry, out of the security building where at least then they could be on their way toward doing something more personally meaningful. "Jackass." She spoke aloud, giving the screen a little slit-eyed glare.

On the other hand, she would probably get a little bit of warning because he would have to get past Kerry, who had gone back out to try and find out the status of the rest of the island and try her own sat phone.

She finished typing, reviewed her results, and then shrugged. She restarted the system and leaned back in the chair, folding her arms and watching it as it booted back up.

Idly she looked around, approving the orderly cable trays and neatly tied bundles of cable, some of which came into the room from large, round penetrations on both ends of the room. She got up and went over to one of the racks in the back, peering inside at the equipment.

Lots of blinking lights. She studied the machines, opening up one rack to stick her head inside.

Someone had done a good job. She approved the neatness. She closed the door and wandered back to the console, leaning on the back of the chair and peering at the screen.

The lines of code crept along as the machine went through its startup sequence, then it began to assemble itself for some kind of use. "Well. That's farther than it got the last time," Dar said, encouragingly. "C'mon, buddy. Get your act together so I can go do something else."

She watched the green text scroll across the black screen, the monitor's edges covered in bits of old tape, and dark with the fingerprints of a thousand nerds whose hands had recently left a pizza.

It was always pizza. Dar could even imagine she could smell the distinctive scent of old, cold pizza congealing on cardboard and only just kept herself from looking around to find it.

In their new office there was occasionally pizza, but more often burritos from the taqueria that had opened up on the next block. You could eat both with one hand, she mused, but at least with burritos you didn't end up with large greasy pieces of cardboard hanging around.

"Ah." Dar regarded the computer screen. "The crap you think of while waiting for Linux to boot." She leaned closer. "Finish damn you!"

The system obligingly finished its work and presented a login screen to her, and since Dar had no login, she considered her job done. She peeled her jacket off the back of the chair and shrugged into it, then she turned and made her way to the door.

****

Kerry crossed her legs at the ankle as she leaned against the wall, ostensibly watching the television mounted to one side of her.

What she was actually doing was listening to the argument inside the office that didn't seem particularly confidential, and was certainly loud. These tidbits of information could end up valuable at the most, or mildly amusing to relate to Dar at the least.

She had her cup of coffee in one hand, and her other hand tucked into her cargo pants pocket, Her right ear twitched as she heard someone slam their hand on a table.

"God damn it, we don't have enough people here to run those kinds of patrols!" A loud, exasperated male voice echoed into the outer room.

"Larry, look," Another male voice interrupted. "It's not anyone's fault the surveillance system isn't working. We're bloody lucky that's the only thing down right now."

"No one's fault! My ass!" The first voice said. "Someone screwed around with it. Those things don't just break themselves."

Kerry suppressed a smile. Sometimes they did. Sometimes what seemed like cosmic rays from space would send a system sideways.

In this case, though, given what Dar had found, she had to admit, in the private silence of her own mind, that Loud Mouth was probably right. She cleared her throat, and glanced up as the front door opened and a tall, slim man entered and shoved a rubber rain hood back off his head. "Hey, Miguel."

The man looked surprised to see her. "Well, hello there, Kerry." He undid the catches on his rain gear. "Something wrong? I mean..."he glanced around. "Aside from the obvious? Everything okay at your place?"

"Fine," Kerry said. "We lost a lot of beach and it's a mess on the ocean side, but everything else's intact as long as the garage didn't flood."

Miguel took off his raincoat and put it on a peg near the door, then went over to the table full of snacks. "Cold pizza for breakfast. Nice." He sighed. "Marina's a mess." He looked over at her. "Some of the floating docks came up out of the water and slammed into the boathouse."

"Wow," Kerry said, after a brief pause.

"I think your boat's okay." He picked up a piece of stone-cold pepperoni and walked over. He looked to his left as he did and came to a halt. "Oh. Hah," he said. "Stupid thing started working again! Hey, Lou!" He yelled. "Your pictures are back!"

"What?" Lou came hauling out of the office, almost plowing into Kerry as she hastily moved out of the way. "Where... what happened?" He went into the command alcove. "Oh, shit look!"

Sam came over to stand next to Kerry. "Where's Ms. Roberts?" He asked, in a low tone. "She do that?"

"I'm sure she did," Kerry replied. She watched as the men all clustered into the area, tuning screens as two of them pulled out chairs and sat down to work. "I mean, that is what you asked us over here for, right?"

The door to the IT room opened and Dar ambled out and glanced at the now active monitors. "Nice," She said. "If it was always that easy, everyone'd do it."

"Good job, honey," Kerry said. "Sam, want to give us a ride around to the marina before they ask us to fix something else? I'm going to have to start charging by the hour for her."

"Sure," Sam said. "But you know, he shoulda at least say thank you." He gave his boss's back a sour look. "I mean, that's not nice, you know?"

"Don't care." Dar poked Kerry toward. the door. "C'mon."

They moved away from the alcove, but their motion caught the eye of Lou, who turned hastily and waved at them. "Oh! Hey!" He said. "Did you... I mean, was that something you did?" He pointed vaguely at the screens. "They didn't just start working, did they?"

"It was something I did," Dar said in a mild tone. "Kerry said that's what you wanted?" She eyed him with raised eyebrows.

"Absolutely!" He looked around. "How did you... um... Hey can you come into my office for a second?" He sidled back out of the way. "I just want to ask you... um... "

Dar looked at Kerry, who sighed and shook her head. "I'll go wait in the cart. C'mon, Sam. Make it short explanation please, Maestro." She pointed to the door. "Scoot."

Dar followed Lou into his office and he closed the door behind her.

The office, a large space with a worktable in the front, a bulletin board on one wall, a white board on the other, and in the back, a big, plain desk covered in papers.

Stuff was everywhere. Blueprints, and plans, and on the wall, a mounted television playing the same local channel they'd had on at the condo. "Cable's down," Dar said. "That, internet, and phones."

"It's a mess," Lou agreed. "But hey listen... what was wrong with that thing? It went down halfway through the storm and we were going nuts. I couldn't see anything that was going on and couldn't send any of my guys. All we had was the radios, and they tanked when the tower came down."

"Someone tried to upgrade it," Dar said, in a straightforward way. "Not really sure why anyone would try that in the middle of a Category five hurricane, but they did. I rolled it back."

Lou sat down on his desk and looked at her. He was a big man, who'd spent two years as a professional football player with the Dolphins. He wore a bush shirt with large pockets and work cargos in dark blue. "Huh?"

Dar sorted through the words, searching for a simpler way to answer. "You got anyone on your staff here who likes to play around with computers?" She asked. "Someone was on the system playing around. Probably trying to make it do more things. Probably didn't mean to tank it. Maybe thought they were going to be a hero, give you guys some extra features or something?"

Lou frowned, then shook his head emphatically. "I got two guys who take care of the cameras and all that stuff. I sent both of them off the island yesterday on the last staff ferry. None of the rest of us knows a damn thing about it."

Dar put her hands on the back of one of the worktable chairs and glanced down idly at the blueprints. "All I can tell you is what I found. The program stopped working because somebody made changes to it and made it stop working. Didn't get that way by itself."

"You know, I said that myself. I mean, I don't know anything about this computer stuff. I'm a physical security guy. But that thing's been running for years. I don't let nobody mess with it. They keep asking me to upgrade to some new thing but I ... huh."

"Huh," Dar echoed. "Maybe talk to whoever it was who wanted you to upgrade the loudest."

Lou looked at her for a long moment. "Someone'd just do that?" He asked, cautiously. "I mean, could they?"

Dar's pale eyes twinkled gently. "I could," she said, with a smile. "And I know my own kind. We like new and shiny."

He made a face, wrinkling up his nose. "I'll talk to those guys," he said. "Wasn't the time for anything like that, y'know? This stuff lets us do more with less people. Budgets are always so tight around here."

Dar cocked her head to one side a little. "Really?" That surprised her, since she'd never had the impression the operational staff ever lacked for funding, given the yearly fees they all paid and the price of the real estate.

"Talking out of turn." Lou stood up and waved his hand at her. "Anyway. Thanks very much for coming over here, ma'am. It really helped us out." He looked at Dar, then looked away. "I know you and the big cheese don't see eye to eye and all that, but my guys all say you and your friend are good people."

"Glad to help." Dar wasn't sure if she should be amused, or disgusted, or just throw up her mental hands in a whatever shrug. "Don't be too hard on whoever it was. I'm sure they didn't expect it to end up with a call to me."

"Sure they didn't," Lou said, with a wry smile. "Thanks. Maybe we could talk about this whole thing after all this is over." He got up and offered a hand. "And for sure, I'm gonna let Jim know you saved our behinds."

Dar escaped from the office, going past the group of security guards now contentedly doing whatever it was they did with their camera systems, oblivious of her passage. She slipped out the door, finding that it had once again stopped raining. At least for the moment.

Miguel was outside, with a bit of pizza still clutched in one hand. He was talking to Sam and Kerry who were seated in the cart. Kerry had one booted foot propped up against the dashboard, and both hands wrapped around her knee, head tilted slightly in a listening posture.

As Dar angled toward them, though, Kerry turned her head and their eyes met, a wiggle of an eyebrow and the slightest hint of an eyeroll telling her all she needed to know about the subject matter.

She increased her pace and the two guards broke off the conversation. "That's that." She got into the back seat of the cart and folded her long legs into a somewhat comfortable position.

"See you later, Miguel." Kerry gave the other guard a slight wave. "Hope things work out."

"Thanks, Kerry." Miguel stepped back and away from the cart as they turned around and started back out along the road.

Kerry half turned in her seat and placed her elbow on the seat back. "Miguel thinks our boat's fine. But there's a lot of damage. But looking at the other condos on the way here seems like they held up pretty well."

"Yes," Sam agreed. "All the places I saw, except the beach and the marina, and... well, we can't get around to where the maintenance docks are. A bunch of trees are down across the road there. But anyway, the houses all look okay."

They came around the curve in the road that arched along the side of the island where the protected marina was built in. Along the way they saw a lot of trees down, and near the road the flash of a white hull of a boat that had been thrown up onto land.

Like on their side of the island, much of the edge of the land of the island was gone, sucked into the ocean along with bushes and trees that had been planted there. Flotsam and jetsam was everywhere, and a huge pile of sea wrack was stuck in the small square cutout usually frequented by manatees.

Sam steered the cart around a fallen tree, both Dar and Kerry hastily grabbing hold of the seat supports as they bumped and trundled over the branches and debris before they could get back onto the road. As they emerged from behind a thicket of flattened bushes they could now see the marina.

"Holy crap," Dar uttered.

Kerry just let out a soft whistle. At least a dozen large, expensive yachts were in pieces, half sunk in the water, or lying on their side. Two rows of docks they had been tied up to were exploded into thousands of shards, a dumpster worth, lying on the roof of the marina building itself, which was half collapsed.

Along the marina past that there was debris and wrack, the docks themselves awash with ocean waters and their lines pulling the boats askew.

"Yeah. A mess," Sam said. "Glad all those guys ended up bunking at the mansion. They were going to stay down here, y'know? But they heard they were doing a cookout up there since that's where the chefs were bunked so they went up there to get in on that."

Dar peered past Sam's head as they got closer and caught sight of both the Dixie and her parent's boat, tucked into slips along the most protected side of the marina, apparently intact. Unlike most of the boats, theirs had been moored nose to tail with their backs to the wind.

Most of the slips sat sideways to the onshore winds and the craft had taken the brunt of their force. Dar saw some debris on the back deck of the Dixie, and it seemed like the radio antenna was bent, but her lines were in place and the dock structure alongside the seawall was in one piece.

Her father's expert preparation, no doubt. "Looks like they both made it, Ker." Dar pointed at the boats. "And they're in slips we can get out of." She added, shading her eyes as she looked at the entrance to the marina. "Barely."

"Yeah the rest of these, it's gonna be a while," Sam agreed. "You want me to let you off or take you back to your place now that you seen this?" He pulled the cart to a halt and leaned his elbows on the steering wheel. "Cause I don't' want to be round here when some of them other fellows start showing up to see their stuff."

"Back to our place I think," Kerry said. "We've got things to get sorted out, too."

Sam nodded and turned the cart around just as a couple of men in rain gear appeared near the edge of the marina building. "Just in time."

He sped off, as a shout sounded out behind them.

****

More people were out on the road, some wandering over to the lake that was the golf course and looking at it, when they came back around the curve of the island to where Dar and Kerry's condo was.

"A lot of people stayed out here." Kerry commented.

"Sure." Sam nodded. "Anyone who didn't fly out did. Why stay in some janked out shelter if you could stay here? In your own place with your own stuff?" He slowed down as they approached the turn in and the slight rise that would then slope down to the parking garage and the path up to their doorstep. "Hang on!"

Both Dar and Kerry grabbed hold of the roof support bars and Dar braced her feet out as the cart turned and went up over the slight bump and between the gates of the concrete half wall that bordered the complex.

A moment later a huge blob of water headed their way, coming at them from near the path to the door. It hit the oncoming cart, and since the plastic sides were rolled up in deference to the mugginess, it drenched all of them.

"Hey!" Sam yelped, as the cart nearly went out of control.

"Oh crap!" Kerry got her hands up in time to intercept the water before it hit her face. She swayed as the cart veered to one side but was grabbed by the shoulders from behind and steadied.

Dar let out a bellow. "Dad! Hey!"

Sam got the cart to a halt, blinked the muddy water out of his eyes, and shook his drenched hair. "What in the world was that all about?"

From the slope to the understructure parking, Andrew Roberts appeared, dressed in cargo shorts and a tank top, damp from the rain and wearing knee high fishing boots. In one hand he was holding the handle of a very large bucket. "Sorry bout that. Ah did not spect you all to come round that corner right then."

Kerry got out and shook herself off. "What are you doing, Dad?"

"Bailin," Andrew said and walked over to them. "Wanted to get that door opened, see what the underneath looks like."

Sam wiped his face. "Yeah, there's supposed to be drainage, but Lou figured it's all full right now."

Dar walked over and saw that the slope to the garage that had been flooded to the level of the road when they'd left was now half emptied. She glanced at her father, who'd come over to stand next to her. "Both our boats look good."

Andrew nodded. "Figured it might be like that."

"About a dozen of the ones tied into the floating dock got trashed," Dar said. "Two of them ended up upside down on the beach."

Andrew clucked his tongue. "I done told them people. Didn't figure to listen to someone who knew something about boats."

Dar chuckled, a touch maliciously.

Kerry trotted up into the house and returned with a towel, which she handed to Sam who showed no inclination to get back in his cart and leave. "I'm going to try my phone again." She went over, and out into the roadway.

Sam walked over to join Dar and Andrew. "You made a dent in that, Mr. Roberts," he said. "Had someone stop me on the way over here and ask me to find a pump for them. I didn't think about suggesting they try a bucket."

Dar stifled a laugh, and Andrew didn't bother to. "Lemme get back to it," Andrew said. "Ain't nothing to do anyhow but watch them weather people." He picked up the bucket and went back down the slope into the water.

Sam backed away toward the cart. "Let me get out of the way and back to work. Anyway, thanks for coming to help out, Ms. Roberts. I know Lou really appreciated having all those screens back on. It sure helps us."

"My pleasure," Dar lied amiably, giving him a little wave as he backed the cart up and turned it around. She stepped up onto the stairs as another wave of water came up from the garage. She leaned against the railing and put her hands into her pockets.

It was still overcast, and the air was so thick with water it might well have been raining. She felt the sweat gathering under her shirt, and the wind only brought a sheen of moisture to her face.

After a moment of random thought, she took her hands out of her pockets and removed her shirt. That didn't make the air any less muggy but exposing her skin to the breeze helped make it a little more comfortable.

She still heard the sound of trees being whipped by the wind, and it howled as it came through the buildings. But the clouds overhead were not as dark and there was a sense that the storm was passing. Dar wondered where the eye was, and if it had dissipated any.

She wondered if Melbourne, where they'd sent their team, was safe. The last angle she'd seen on the path of the storm was moving it south of the town, but you never knew.

You never knew. Their whole office could be gone. Everything she and Kerry had built up in the last half year could be gone. That they had been so lightly touched so far was mostly a matter of luck. Dar twisted the fabric in her hands and watched the droplets land on the tile steps.

Luck. When she'd decided to move into May's old place, she'd never considered hurricane security. It was just a cool place to live away from people that had a great view. What it would be like to sit in it while a monster storm came over head never crossed her mind.

Now she knew. Dar draped the damp shirt over her shoulder and went down the steps.

"Paladar, what the hell are you doing?"

Dar paused as her father came up the slope with another bucket of water. "Going to see if Kerry's having any luck with the phone," she said. "Why?"

"With half your damn clothes on?"

Dar spread her arms in a gesture of inquiry. "No worse than a bathing suit," she said. "It's too sticky."

"Here then." Andrew tossed the bucket's contents at her unexpectedly. "Cool yer self."

"Yah!" Dar tried to dodge but there wasn't space to, and a moment later she was wet through again. She pulled her shirt off her shoulder and stretched it out, spinning it between her hands and then heading her father's way. "C'mere!"

Andrew bounded backward as she approached, snapping the shirt with audible cracks in the air. "Don't you get saucy there, young lady!" He ducked the makeshift whip as Dar jumped into the puddle with both feet, sending a splash of water over him. "Gimme that!"

Dar got in a hit on his leg, ducking as he scooped up a bucketful of water and slung it in her direction and plunging sideways through the puddle. She sent another splash heading his way by hopping up and down and a moment later they were in a full-out water fight.

Kerry heard the commotion and folded up her mostly useless phone, trotting across the street and into the driveway. She arrived just in time to get smacked in the face with a torrent of warm muddy water. "Blah!" She let out a squawk, as the chaos now turned into laughter.

She wiped the water out of her eyes and put her hands on her hips as Andrew and Dar sloshed out of the puddle, both completely soaked. Andy still carried the bucket, Dar had her shirt in her hand, wrapped around her fist in a ball.

They had almost identical grins on their faces.

"What in the hell's going on here?" Kerry asked, spitting a bit of debris from her mouth from the water.

"We were just messin round," Andy said. He glanced behind him. "Ahm gonna open up that there door, Dar. Ain't enough water left to drown much on the back side."

"Yeah, I think I soaked up a good bit of it." Kerry regarded her now wet through body. "I guess it doesn't really matter now if it starts raining again?"

"Not much, no." Dar started idly twisting the shirt in her hands, watching the water drain from it again.

The door to the condo opened and Ceci peered cautiously out. "Ah." She emerged and closed the door quickly to keep the dogs from escaping. She looked from her husband to her daughter and chuckled dryly. "I see some things never change."

"The boats are okay, Mom," Kerry told her. "There's a lot of damage around, but I didn't see anything catastrophic."

"Not to us," Dar added. "Not sure some other boat owners would agree."

"They're starting to get pictures in from the rest of Miami," Ceci said. "I think we were lucky. I just saw one where all the windows in the Intercontinental hotel were blown out and one of the interchange overpasses collapsed." She considered. "Not really sure if that'll make the traffic better or worse."

"Which one?" Andy asked.

"836 and the Turnpike."

"Lord." Andrew grimaced. "That all's where that flooding is at."

"No luck?" Dar asked Kerry.

"Can't even get a signal now," Kerry replied. "Said whatever the sat equivalent is of all circuits are busy."

"Crap."

Andy retrieved a manual crank from a box near the garage door and inserted it. He cautiously started rotating it, applying pressure when it resisted. He braced his booted feet apart and pulled harder, the muscles standing out under the skin of his bare arms.

Dar half turned and watched. "Hang on," she said, handing her shirt to Kerry. "Hold that for a minute, wouldja?"

"Sure." Kerry took the wet item, silently laughing. "But there's only room for one of you to haul on that crank, hon."

Dar looked over her shoulder at her dryly. "It's the seals."

"It's A Seal," Kerry amiably agreed, pointing at Andy. She glanced up to where Ceci was now sitting on the small bench outside the front door, holding her sides laughing. "C'mon, it wasn't that funny."

"Nooo," Dar whined. "The seals on the door." She went over to the box where the crank had been. "I need a crowbar," she said. "Which are all of course inside the damned garage."

Andrew stopped trying to turn the crank and looked at the door speculatively. "Ah do believe you are correct there, Dardar." He let the crank drop onto the ground at the top of the slope and started off down the driveway. "Lemme see what I can find round here."

"I'll go too." Ceci trotted down the steps. "Goddess I'm tired of that damn weatherman." She caught up to Andy and tucked her hand inside the crook of his elbow.

Kerry watched them disappear around the corner, then returned her attention to Dar, who was smiling, eyes slightly unfocused. "You and your dad are so funny."

Dar looked up, the blue of her eyes looking surprisingly vivid in the overcast, gray light. "Kinda stupid." She half shrugged and looked a touch embarrassed. "We used to have hose fights in the yard when we lived down south. Drove the neighbors nuts."

"Kind of beautiful actually," Kerry said. "You realize I never even got

invited to play golf with my father? He wouldn't so much as play catch
football with Mike for the press." She shook out Dar's wet shirt and hung it
over the stairway railing. "I don't think I ever even saw him in a T-shirt."

"Muppet," Dar said. "Why have kids if you're not going to have some
fun with them, given what a pain in the ass they are?"

Kerry laughed, leaning against the railing and folding her arms across
her chest. "Having a water fight definitely would not have been his idea of
fun," she said. She glanced up at the entrance. "I guess we should go back
inside and see what the television is showing. Maybe we'll see something
of Coconut Grove."

Dar looked around. "Yeah, there's not much else we can do out here.
Saw what we needed to see for now, I guess. When we get this door open,
we can take the carts out." She fished the sat phone out of her pocket and
turned it over, watching some water run out of it's folds. "Hope these are
waterproof."

Kerry chuckled.

"If we stay outside, more chance for the team to get hold of us," Dar
said. "Worse comes to worse, we can take the boat out and go over to the
shoreline there. See if we can dock close enough to get to the office." She
looked up at the sky. "We'll either beat the Coast Guard out or get our
asses chased down by them."

Kerry exhaled. "I'm thinking about how much email I'm eventually
going to have to look at.

How many pissed off clients to deal with."

"It's a storm, Ker."

"They don't care, Dar."

Dar sighed and folded her arms over her mostly bare torso. Her skin
was spackled with storm debris sticking to her and moving as she breathed,
visible muscles shifting under her tanned skin. "Yeah, I know."

There was a leaf plastered along her ribcage and tucked into the waistband of her cargo pants a twig was poking out.

Kerry went over and removed it, twirling the twig in her fingertips.
"I'm worried about our people," she said, after a long pause. "I'm worried
if they're safe, and I'm worried that if something's going to happen to our
company it'll affect all of them."

Dar regarded her somberly. "What about us?"

"Not worried about us," Kerry said. "At least... I mean, Dar, there's
any of a hundred companies who'd hire either of us in a heartbeat. And, we
have a lot of personal resources."

"True," Dar agreed. "And worse comes to worse..." She winked at
Kerry. "We can live on my little island, and I'll fish for our dinner." She
smiled. "Cause that's all I need in life," she added casually. "You."

Caught off guard, Kerry blinked a few times as her mental train ran off
the tracks and ended up floating in a lake somewhere.

"Let's worry about things when they happen," Dar said. "And before
we do that, let's go take a damn shower because I think I have a pollywog

in my underwear."

****

The condo had partially at least returned somewhat to its usual internal view. Kerry had gotten the shutters on the kitchen window and the door open, and cleared the debris off the backyard steps, and Dar was outside on the patio working on the bent panels protecting the outside.

Chino and Mocha were seated inside the sliding glass doors, watching her intently. Behind them, the television was showing loop after loop of storm wreckage and destruction, and if Kerry concentrated, she could hear helicopters outside, now that the winds had mostly died down.

"Power is out throughout most of South Florida," A reporter was saying. "Pumping stations are down, and there's a boil water order in effect."

Kerry stood in the doorway to the kitchen, a pot of chili on the stove behind her softly bubbling away as she watched the scenes flash on the screen. An airborne view of the Port of Miami, just west of them, showed multiple cargo loading cranes toppled into the channel.

The docks that would normally have cargo and cruise ships, were, of course, empty. Port Miami had closed before the storm and every ship had run from it, going south and west into the Gulf of Mexico.

"The storm surge, measured at over a dozen feet high, picked up containers and they're now in the water on either side of the terminal," the reporter said. "Palm and Star Islands are completely cut off. The surge washed over and destroyed the causeways onto those man-made islands."

Kerry shook her head. "What a mess."

"Parts of MacArthur and Venetian Causeways are underwater, and the police are advising everyone to please stay off the roads. I am going to repeat that. Please stay off the roads, and do not try to travel away from your homes unless you are in need of emergency medical assistance."

It wouldn't stop people. Kerry knew it, the reporter knew it, and the police surely knew it. There were people out right now, she was sure, who were driving around looking at what there was to be looked at. After all, wasn't that what she and Dar had done?

People want to see what's going on. With no power, and no internet, no cell service, no way of surfing around to see what was being said, the only real way to know was to go look. So, they would. She was almost sure that aside from random drivers, there were people out taking drone movies, and soon, there would be boats on the waterways.

She felt bad for the police. They were people. They had families, and those families had also been in danger, and were possibly in homes that were damaged or somewhere unsafe, and yet they reported for work when perhaps their own homes were destroyed.

The reporters at the television station, there in their flooded out building, were showing up. At the staging yard on the edge of the Everglades in Sunrise, Florida Power and Light's linemen were gathering.

"The eye of Hurricane Bob has moved off the coast and is now going northeast as it gets caught up in the flow of the frontal boundary," the reporter said. "The edge of the eyewall has just missed the south of Port Canaveral, and hurricane watches and warnings are now going up along the southeastern seaboard."

A flood of new light made Kerry turn her head to see the metal shutters peeling jerkily and reluctantly back from the edge of the patio, with some strenuous encouragement by Dar. She went to the sliding glass and slid one panel open, allowing the dogs to scoot past her. "Nice job, hon."

Dar dusted her hands off as she finished shoving the shutters back into their side pockets. "We're going to have to have those replaced. Bent as hell." She turned and put her hands, encased in leather gloves, on the railing of the patio wall, looking out over the still roughly churning ocean.

At that moment, however, the clouds parted just a bit, and a wan, pallid bit of sun came through, splashing the dark green and white ruffled surface with an emerald sparkle and as if in signal of it, a muffled burble sounded from the thigh pocket of Dar's cargo pants.

'Here we go." Dar fished it out. "Ready or not."

Chapter Four

"Ain't nobody else answering." The voice echoed a bit, the sound of wind behind it. "So, I figured since you people were the most east, maybe it was clear."

"About right, Scott," Dar said. "Glad everyone's safe there."

"Yeah, on generator, noisy as hell," Scott replied. "Had to hump my ass up the stairs to the roof here to use this thing since they can't power the elevators on it. Cheap jackasses."

Dar was momentarily silent, her mind busy imagining Scott in his wheelchair effectively hopping up the emergency steps. "Ah."

"Wasn't real bad, just wind, rain and crap. Came over us, went up the coast." Scott said. "Everybody on the damned planet is calling this number to find out what's going on down by the office. You know anything?"

"Not yet," Dar said. "As you figured out, no one else is answering their phones yet. We can see a lot of damage everywhere from here but no pictures yet on the television from Coconut Grove."

"Figures."

"So, you can tell anyone who's calling that we're still evaluating the storm damage," Dar said, briefly. "I'm probably going to have to go over there by boat and check it out."

"Figures," Scott said. "Anyway, that cloud phone thing worked out at least. No problems there. Stupid things ringing off the hook downstairs. I better get back there." He paused. "Only thing we can't call from that thing is these stupid sat phones."

Dar frowned. "You should have been able to... "She paused. "Oh, crap. We probably didn't turn on the codes for them to allow the dial out." She sighed. "Damn it."

Scott laughed. "Better for you," he said. "Otherwise someone'd have some bright idea to forward calls to you from this thing and it'd never stop."

Dar chuckled a little herself. "That's true. Anyway, thanks for taking the time and hassle to get a line out, Scott. Glad everyone's okay. Just keep things going best you can there. I'll see what I can do on this end to figure out what's going on."

"Roger that." Scott sounded relatively content. "Bye."

He hung up the line and Dar did the same. She put the phone back into her pocket and regarded Kerry, who stood next to her listening. "Well, at least they're okay up there."

"I can only imagine the calls they're getting." Kerry grimaced slightly. "Twenty-twenty hindsight. I should have sent an admin with them to field all that cruft."

"Twenty-twenty," Dar agreed. "Anyway, let's see if Dad's had any success in finding a crowbar to open up that door." She went past Kerry and slid the doors open, crossing from the fitfully windswept moist heat of the patio into the chill interior of the condo.

Kerry followed, sliding the door shut as Mocha and Chino came over to investigate, a little puzzled and doggily concerned about all the uproar in their normally sedate home.

They all went to the front door and Dar opened it, just as they heard a loud bang very nearby.

Kerry grabbed Dar's arm. "What the hell was that?" She asked. "Was that a gunshot?"

"Hope not." Dar paused, blocking the door with her knee. "Chino, Mocha, stay!"

Kerry went and opened the nearby hall closet, ducking her head inside and flipping on the light. She reached over and grabbed the shotgun from its rack on the wall and swung back around the door frame, pausing to check its load.

Then she cradled it in the crook of her arm as Dar cautiously eased her body around the front door and peered outside. "Dad?"

Andrew came up the slope and craned his neck to look up. "Yeap?"

"Was that you?" Dar asked. "That noise?"

"Yeap."

Dar paused. "Did you shoot the door?" She asked, in a puzzled tone.

Andrew came a few steps farther and planted his hands on his hips. "Did I what?" He asked. "Why in the hell would I do that?"

Dar came out onto the landing. "Heard what sounded like a gunshot. Thought maybe you shot the door in frustration."

"Say what?" Her father said, his voice lifting.

"I would have," Dar said. "That's why Kerry's the gun owner." She moved aside as Kerry appeared, having put the shotgun back in its rack. "Any luck?"

Ceci entered the gate, a small digital camera in one hand. "I got some great shots," she said, in a satisfied tone. "I think I'll start a new set of paintings. Start with all the mourners over there at the golf lake." She grinned. "Call the first one Disaster Strikes the Senseless Rich. What do you think?"

"I think it's going to be a hit." Kerry went down the steps to join her, coming around to see the screen of the camera as Ceci displayed her shots. "Ceci Roberts, the Irony Series."

Ceci chortled. "I like that. Nice ring to it." She flipped through the pictures. "I really shouldn't laugh, because it's a goddess awful mess. But no one here's hurting."

Dar went down the slope to where there was a handle poking out of the remaining puddle. "What is that?"

"Sledgehammer." Andrew went over and picked it back up, bringing the head of it out of the water, and moving farther down the line of the door. "Ah figure I can give it a few good bangs here."

"Yeah, I want to get the carts out," Dar said. "Get over to the marina and get the boat over to see what's going on shoreside."

Andrew looked over his shoulder at her. "No word from them all?"

"Just from Scott, up north," Dar said. "Nothing yet from anyone else." She watched as her father selected another spot and swing the sledgehammer, producing another sharp report as the head of it hit the frame of the protective roller door.

She went over to the manual crank and inserted it, applying pressure first in one direction and then the other as Andy kept up his pounding, making the door shift jerkily up and down in its tracks.

Ceci regarded them as she stood next to Kerry. "Single minded," she commented.

"'Always." Kerry watched Dar with an affectionate smile. "Door has no idea what it's up against."

A helicopter rattled overhead, and they both looked up to see a large Coast Guard chopper heading due west, its large rotors shimmering in the gray light. Kerry pulled out her phone again and opened it. "Might as well give this a try again."

"I'm going to see what's on the news," Ceci said and walked up the steps to the condo. "They were showing the airport before we left. I think I saw at least one of the jet things across the runway."

"Ugh."

****

"Got it." Dar poked her head inside the kitchen, where Kerry was setting down a double bowl of kibble for the seated and waiting Labradors. "Finally."

"Good job, honey." Kerry straightened and looked over at her, then started to laugh a little. "You need another shower."

"Muggy as hell out there." Dar glanced down at her sweat drenched shirt and debris-stained skin. "But we got the door open. Sort of."

"Sort of?" Kerry got out a glass and went to the refrigerator, opening it to dispense milk into it. She handed it to Dar.

"Ended up taking it out of the track completely and bending it flat against the wall," Dar said. "Really at the end it was just me and dad shoving." She took a swallow of the milk and winked at Kerry. "Good to do something not involving a keyboard for a change."

"No damage inside?"

"Just some debris, and the puddle that we let in," Dar said. "Cars are fine. Dad took one of the carts out to go see if his truck survived."

"Well. Not much we can do with the cars anyway right now, with that ramp the way it is." Kerry said. "I think your idea with the boat is probably our best bet right now. "She looked out the window at the still gray skies, though the trees outside that still stood were only fitfully waving.

"I'm going to get dry." Dar took her milk with her and disappeared back into their bedroom.

Chino stood at the back door, and now she turned her head and barked gruffly.

"Are you done?" Kerry went over and opened the door, checking her watch and then following the dogs down the steps into the wreck of their back garden. She moved away from the walls a little and went down nearer to the outer gate, where ocean still surged, washing sea foam and debris up into the yard.

She opened the sat phone, and to her surprise it rang. She quickly answered it. "Kerry."

"Poquito, boss!"

Kerry felt a sense of relief. "Mark! It's great to hear your voice."

"I can hear the ocean in the background there," Mark said. "What a bleeping fricken mess." He went on without waiting for her to answer. "I just got this stupid phone to work. Nothing else is. We don't have power, cable, phones, nothing."

Kerry glanced at her surroundings. "We have generators," she said. "But no cable, or net or anything. "Cellulars all down everywhere I hear." She paused. "Our place here made it through okay. The back wall got taken over by ocean, but everything else is fine."

"My house made it, but I lost part of the roof," Mark said. "It was the part over the bedrooms. We're camped in the kitchen but we're lucky. Did you see those pictures of Doral?"

"I did," Kerry said. "That whole area's flooded. Did you see the airport?"

"Hell yes!" Mark said. "Someone said it's going to be closed for who knows how long, and that whole interchange collapsed over by Sweetwater."

Kerry looked out the gate over the ruffled surface of the ocean. "The channel's full of who knows what," she said. "We could see it from here. The cargo cranes are all toppled over." She walked down to the water edge. "South Beach is a mess."

"I got a pair of solar panels here. We saw a little bit of the coverage," Mark said. "This ain't gonna be a quick fix, boss."

"No," Kerry murmured.

Mark was silent for a moment. "It was scary as crap," he finally said. "Barb's really freaked out. When the roof went, I was wishing I'd taken her and stayed with the guys at the office." He paused. "I haven't heard from anyone else yet. There are trees down everywhere here. I'm going to take my bike out and see how far I get."

"Mark, be careful," Kerry said. "We're just running around here with golf carts and it's dangerous."

"No, I know," Mark said. "But I'm worried about the guys. Carlos and his buds."

They were both briefly silent.

"Yeah, me too, and the rest of the staff." Kerry sighed. "I think we're going to take the boat out and see if we can get over to the shore there, by the end of the waterfront."

"They're telling people to stay home," Mark said. "Not that anyone's gonna do it."

Kerry chuckled briefly. "Dar figures even if the docks are gone down there, she can get us close enough to swim in."

Mark made a small sound of protest. "And you're telling me to be careful? Jesus, Kerry. There's like whole National Guard things being sent here."

"And?" Kerry said, watching a seagull appear, skimming over the new shoreline. "On a list of what they're going to care about, where would a small IT services company end up, Mark? They're going to be focused on hospitals and facility."

"Ouch."

"Just the truth. Besides, you know Dar. The eye barely cleared us, and she was out fixing the island camera systems and annoying the neighbors. She's not going to hang around waiting for the National Guard."

Chino came over and sat down next to her, observing the wake coming into the yard and depositing luridly purple seaweed at the dog's feet. She bent her head and sniffed at it, then she stood up and gingerly walked into the water.

"Chino, stop," Kerry said. "Anyway, Mark, I'm going to keep trying to get hold of Maria and Mayte. They're over near the airport."

"I'll let you know what I find." Mark promised. "We're pretty far south but I might be able to get up around there using 27." He paused thoughtfully. "Might want to pack an inflatable kayak past that though."

"Be careful!"

****

"It's kinda late," Kerry said, as they drove carefully around the edge of the marina, heading toward the protected side. Near the front, where the most damage was, a number of men were out, some with cameras and others just standing by.

"Yeah," Dar agreed. "But we can probably get over there and back before it gets all the way dark." She aimed the cart around the back of the marina building, detouring around two fallen trees and one of the island pickup trucks that was serving as a workspace for the five or six marina staff standing around it.

Dockmaster Jack was one of them. He spotted them and took a step back from the truck and waved. They slowed down as he walked over.

"Hey there."

"Hi, Jack," Dar said. "What a mess, huh?"

"What a mess," Jack agreed. "I told the chiefs those floating docks were going to be a humongous bad idea, but they didn't want to pay to sink pilings like we did on the perimeter." He looked at the marina building. "Total loss. They're going to have to rebuild the whole thing."

The entire roof caved in, a further collapse since they'd been there before. The storage shed behind the building had been deconstructed, and two of the four walls were lying on the ground, the contents of the shed scattered all along the back part of the path.

Jack shook his head. "Weather station's gone, radio sets... Jesus." He looked around at them. "And everyone coming over here to chew us. I think you and your folks did all right."

"We did. We came over to check it out earlier, and dad was here before," Dar said. "Matter of fact, we were going to take a ride out over across Biscayne Bay."

Jack blinked. "Now?"

"We've got some people over there we're concerned about, who stayed in our office." Kerry explained. "We can't get hold of anyone."

"Oh, I don't know." Jack seemed taken aback. "It's   dangerous out there. Currents are crazy, and there's so much debris... I'd hate to have you all get through the storm fine then crack your hull," he said, as the winds rose again. He indicated the sky. "Honest, I would wait."

It was good advice. Kerry knew that. She also knew they weren't going to take it. "Thanks Jack, we'll be careful." She felt Dar's body shifting, the twitch of the muscles in her hands as she gripped the wheel of the cart and the faint jumping of the muscle just over her kneecap indicating her impatience. "We've got some pretty solid gear onboard and Dar's a great driver."

"Oh, I know. I've seen you come in." Jack said. "Well, like I said, take care." He stepped back from the cart and gave them a little wave as he rejoined the rest of the staff standing by the truck.

"Are we being... um..."

"Stupid?" Dar hit the pedal and started the cart along the path, having to take the time to dodge debris every few feet. "No more than we usually are." She grimaced as they bumped over a bit of aluminum decking. "I can't cope with more sitting in our living room watching endless loops of helicopter footage."

Kerry chuckled briefly. "Fair point."

"Besides, we're taking my father," Dar said, as she edged the cart along the far side of the marina, where the seawall had protected the two slips that were aligned alongside it, the furthest from the marina. "We'll be fine."

Two slips on the very end of the inlet, tricky to maneuver into, tucked into the curve of the protective stone wall with lines only on their port side.

Dar found a place to park the cart and removed the fob from it, in case anyone got the idea they'd like to borrow the vehicle. She lifted a backpack from the back of it and joined Kerry as they carefully made their way along the plaswood surface toward the boats.

Andrew was visible on the bow of theirs, which was tied up in front of his own. He was coiling a line expertly in both hands, watching idly as they approached. "Lo there," he greeted amiably.

"Hi, Dad." Dar stepped from the edge of the battered dock onto the gunwale of the boat and then onto the deck with easy grace. "Amazing nothing's broken." She inspected the space.

"Just that there whippy." Andrew indicated the antenna. "Back here got washed out. Got me a coconut out of that there corner of it but the sump took care of the water." He looked around the back of the boat. "Nothing cracked, and it's dry down there in the engine well."

Dar nodded. "Let's get this party started," she said. "I don't really want to be dodging bits of someone's backyard barbeque in the dark." She slid the backpack onto her shoulder and started up the ladder to the flying bridge.

****

Kerry heard the dual inboard engines start up, and she left off checking the interior of the cabin to return to the back deck. She looked over the aft well wall where the engine wash was bubbling up debris, and then to the starboard side where bits of wood and chunks of foam were floating.

Andrew stepped up onto the gunwale and walked along the side of the boat to the bow, kneeling to untie the ropes that held them to the dock.

Kerry did the same for the aft cleat and felt the boat shift and start to drift away from the pilings. She looked up at the flying bridge and saw Dar standing at the controls, legs braced as her hands worked the throttles.

Out of habit she went to the radio console, opening up the teak hatch and taking out the handheld transmitter before she paused in thought. Normally, she would call the dockmaster, and clear them out.

Did the dockmaster even have a handheld radio to hear it?

Would the dockmaster even for one moment give a damn?

Kerry put the transmitter back into its clip and closed the hatch.

"What'cha doin there, kumquat?" Andy came back from his task and joined her. "Everything shipshape in there?"

"Yeah, it's all okay I think." Kerry said. "I was going to call in our leaving, but I don't think it matters."

Andrew shook his head. "Naw." Then he went over to the side of the boat and watched as they drifted toward the wreckage of the floating dock and the first of the overturned yachts lying on its side. It was mostly underwater and the fully fitted out cooking pit it had on its deck was hanging half bent across its port railing.

The Dixie's direction gently changed, moving backward in the water at almost idle as Dar nudged the big boat past the damaged craft, sliding it also past her parents on their port side.

Andrew stood there with his hands in his pockets and watched calmly as they came within a foot of his boat's fiberglass hull.

"She's pretty damn good at this," Kerry commented from her place next to him. "She brings this thing into those little marinas down south and everyone's usually going—how in the hell?"

He chuckled. "One thing mah kid did not get from me," he readily admitted. He drew in a satisfied breath of the warm, damp air as they cleared the second slip and Dar started to swing the boat around almost within its own length.

"I'm going to go grab my camera," Kerry said, as they completed the maneuver and headed cautiously for the entrance to the marina basin. "I'm totally sure I'm going to need it."

"Ain't no doubt." Andy glanced up at the flying bridge. "Good job there, Dardar."

Dar smiled, but didn't turn, her attention focused on avoiding the sunken structures and nudging the floating debris out of their way. She did glance to her left as they approached the edge of the protective sea wall and saw the dockmaster on the far side of the destroyed marina building watch them go out.

She took one hand off the throttles and waved, and Jack waved back. Then she moved past the last overturned boat and reached the opening, feeling the chop of the water start to jostle the hull.

The channel water was rough and churning as she edged out into it, and the wind hit them, pushing against the boat and making the guy wires stabilizing the flying bridge sing. Dar reached over to turn on the marine radio out of long habit, settling into the captain's chair as her eyes flicked over to the digital sonar screen and the depth gauge.

The marina let out onto the southern side of the island, into Norris Cut, and she turned west from there, moving very cautiously along the coast. The wind was sharp enough to make her blink, and she wished she'd remembered to bring her sunglasses with her as it felt like particles of salt were being driven into her eyeballs.

Along the edge of the channel she saw trees by the hundreds down. The entire south side of the island had been laid bare and much of the landscaping was in the water forcing her out a little to avoid it. Ahead of her was the causeway, and beyond that the heart of the city and the mouth of the Miami River.

The storm surge had gone pretty much right up the river's path. This far away Dar couldn't see what damage there was yet, but one thing was obvious and that was there was no power anywhere. The only lights showing were the channel markers winking red and green on either side of her.

It felt lonely. The Dixie was the only vessel moving in her sight, and the sound of the diesel engines rumbled softly underfoot as the boat rocked in the chop while she went at a dead slow speed, keeping one eye on the waters ahead of her and the other on the sonar.

Would suck to run into something. Dar had no intention of being a sound bite on WPLG, some stupid nitwit out for a joyride that had to be towed in by the Coast Guard after running aground or into sunken debris.

She only hoped Kerry would forgive her for the motion that caused, a side by side swaying that tended to trigger nausea in most.

****

Kerry looped the strap of her camera over her head and made her way back out onto the deck, glad of the bit of ginger candy she was sucking on. She swallowed some of the ginger flavor, the hard candies something she kept stock of onboard to fend off the discomfort she hadn't quite outgrown.

She'd gotten more used to the motion of the boat over the years. Especially when they went out for some diving, and they had to anchor in place. The back and forth, up and down rocking had become familiar, and she'd developed reasonably steady sea legs in moving around on deck.

Andy sat in one of the comfortable back chairs and watched the passing scenery with interest. Kerry sat beside him and took off her lens cap to test her focus.

There was a pile of debris along the southern coast of the island they were passing, and she zoomed in on it and took a picture, then paused, trying to determine what it was. A small boat, probably.

They passed another and she lifted her head from the eyepiece and pointed. "That's a car."

"Yeap," Andy said. "Probly came up off the front there." He pointed at the approaching coastline. "Road's all washed out." He extended his long legs along the deck, crossing his worn military boots at the ankle.

Was there someone in it? Kerry hesitated, then refocused, but it was impossible to tell. Should they stop? She looked at the angle and then slowly lowered the camera. The water covered the entire cab, lapping over the top of the vehicle. "Hope it was empty."

"Probly," Andy said. "Though," he added, thoughtfully. "Some fellas do live inside their cars in that city there." He sniffed and folded his hands over his stomach. "But them probly went into them shelters with all that yelling on the radio."

Unexpectedly, Kerry's phone rang. "Ah." She rapidly put the cap back on and dug the phone out of her pocket, opening it up. "This is Kerry."

"Kerry!"

"Hey, Col." Kerry felt a sense of relief hearing the familiar voice. "Great to hear from you. How'd it go?"

"Oh, my goodness gracious. I'm digging a cellar to get into for the next time." Colleen said, in an exasperated tone. "We're swamped up to the second floor here, girl. That your generator rumbling?"

"Um. No." Kerry said. "We're on the boat, heading to see what's up at the office."

For a moment there was dead silence.

"Col?"

"Of course you're on the boat heading for the office." Colleen was half laughing and half groaning. "Have you seen the news? Are you out of your ever loving? Kerry, for the love of God!"

Kerry glanced at Andrew. "What?" She asked. "I saw the stuff on the TV, sure. What does that have to do with anything? We left Carlos and some of his guys at the office. We want to make sure they're okay," she said. "We did all right out on the island."

Why was Colleen so surprised? Kerry wondered. When Dar suggested this idea, it sounded eminently logical, and both Andrew and Ceci had nodded in agreement as well. Was it so surprising they'd want to do this?

"Figured you would. That place is a bunker," Colleen said. "Well, you just be careful. I heard there's all kinds of flooding down near the water there, and buildings damaged."

Kerry glanced to her right and shifted. "Yeah, we're passing it right now. No kidding." She stared at one building on the coastline, one whole side twisted and tumbled into the water. "Wow." She added. "No, Dar's being careful. We have sonar onboard, and her dad's with us."

"Ah," Colleen said. "Well, with no power, no phones, no internet, no nothing – soon as the water goes down here, I think we should shift ourselves up to the north, with the support folks. You think?"

"Yeah. Not sure we're going to have any other choice," Kerry said. "I talked to Scott. They did fine up there."

"Righty ho. Let me know how it all works out, now that it's clear enough for these lovely phones to work," Colleen said. "Thank the lord Mayte thought of it." She paused. "You hear from her yet?"

"No," Kerry said. "We're worried about that too. Not her, or Maria. I heard from Mark."

"Well. This one just started now, after the clouds cleared up a bit. Give it some time," Colleen advised. "Let me go get the candles out. Going to be a hot steamy night."

Kerry hung up the phone and sighed. "This is such a mess."

Andrew got up and mounted the gunwale and started up along the port side toward the front deck of the boat.

After a moment, Kerry got up and followed him, holding onto the railing as they hit some chop. She jerked as the boat's horn sounded lightly, and she looked up to find Dar standing at the controls, peering at them.

"Careful, people." Dar's voice sounded on the intercom, echoing softly over the engines.

Andy half turned and gave her a thumbs up as he took up a position on the front of the boat. He stood with his legs braced and his arms folded, surveying the waters they were crossing through.

Kerry stayed where the cabin arched up to the bridge on the port side, where there were grab bars fastened into the fiberglass and she could lean against it. She took out her camera and took some shots, then, as the boat wallowed a little in the cross current, she decided more ginger was required.

She returned to the cabin, which was blessedly free of wind and comfortably cool. She put the camera down on the galley table and went past it into the compact bedroom with its queen size bed and maximized storage space.

On the countertop was a soft fabric bag and she grabbed it, fishing inside for another of the candies.

The intercom crackled. "Hey, Ker?"

Kerry went to the wall and pressed the response button. "Aye Aye, Captain."

Dar's deep, warm chuckle came through the speaker. "You think we have a pair of sunglasses down there?"

Kerry blinked. "Is the weather gotten that much better in the two minutes I've been down here?" She asked in a puzzled tone. "Really?"

"No," Dar said. "Spray's getting in my eyes."

"Oh!" Kerry said. "Yeah, let me look around for some and I'll bring them up. Want some coffee?"

"Absolutely."

Kerry went back up the steps into the main part of the cabin and detoured into the galley, flipping on the coffee machine as she hunted in the various drawers for glasses. She found a pair of wrap around Oakley's and stuffed them in her thigh pocket, then got some coffee going.

It occurred to her, then, that they had satellite access onboard and she turned and removed the seldom used controls from the drawer and turned on the bulkhead mounted television.

"Poor signal." Kerry sighed and just turned the mute on and went back to getting the coffee sorted. The satellite was subject to rain fade and never that reliable in any case. They usually only used it for some random CNN watching and the weather.

She poured the coffee into a thermos, added cream and sugar from the small fridge, after checking the date on the cream, and capped it. Then she put the strap of the thermos around her neck and went back outside.

Behind the boat the twin prop wash from their engines was frothing the water and the air was full of the smell of rain, of sea water, and a touch of diesel. Kerry climbed up the steps to the flying bridge, and joined Dar, standing behind the console.

The bridge was mostly white fiberglass, in deference to its exposure to the weather. There was the console that Dar used to drive the boat, which had a circular wheel with hydraulic steering controls down to the large inboard engines, and the twin throttles that fed them fuel.

That was at the front of the bridge, with plastic flaps Dar had rolled up to allow her a good view of the front of the boat and the water around it.

Behind the bridge were fiberglass seats and teak tables on either side, where the boat's guests could sit and socialize while keeping the driver company.

Kerry had never used them. When she was on the bridge and keeping Dar company, she would sit in the second pilot's seat next to her, and slowly over time had learned all the controls and gauges that covered the space.

She had never driven the boat anywhere. She certainly had started up the engines and a good working knowledge of the dials and switches, but she knew that the casual ease with which Dar handled the large vessel was deceptive.

"I love you," Dar said and accepted the offered cup. She ducked her head briefly for Kerry to put the sunglasses around her ears. "Damn spray." She put the cup in its gimballed holder and adjusted the throttles, increasing the speed of the boat a trifle. "We're in deeper water here."

They were moving past the channel that went under the bridge, and directly in front of them was the mouth of the Miami River and the city buildings on either side of it. A little farther west and Dar would turn south and go along the coastline toward the Grove.

Ahead of them, the triangle of manufactured land that was Brickell Key showed stunning damage. Two of the condo apartment towers were missing parts of most floors, and the hotel on the south end had collapsed onto itself.

Now that they could see the buildings a little better, they could see the damage. Windows were blown out everywhere. Drapes and tattered blinds were lashing in the wind. The storm surge had come up over the seawall and debris had been pulled back out into the water as far as the eye could see.

They turned to go south and passed by what had once been their daily commute endpoint. The tall glass building that was ILS's Southeast headquarters had taken a lot of visible damage. Kerry's eyes went wide. "Jesus, Dar, I hope no one was in there."

"I'm sure no one was there." Dar took a sip of coffee. "The only idiot who would have stayed in that place keeping things running doesn't work for them anymore."

Kerry gave her a sideways look. "Idiot, and idiot staff," she corrected her. "Because, my love, if you'd have stayed, all of us would have."

There were no people yet visible, that close to the water. As they went by the buildings, they could see between them streets full of water, debris, trees, concrete, piles of roof tiles, flooded cars... Kerry went back down and got her camera, then returned and started taking some random pictures.

That area had been evacuated, mostly. Kerry knew that in the midst of that, there were people who refused to go, ignored the mandatory evacuation, hid from the police, from the county officials patrolling the streets before the storm, struck getting people out.

The radio crackled, making them both jump. "Coast Guard, Coast

Guard." A voice said. "Anyone out there?"

Dar looked at Kerry, who picked up the radio mic, and held it. "We're not the Coast Guard," Dar said, after a pause. "Let's see if they answer."

"I was waiting," Kerry replied. "But I can't... I mean, they must be somewhere out of this area, Dar. We haven't seen another boat on the water."

"Just us," Dar agreed, as they started through the South channel, and approached Rickenbacker Causeway. "That seems to have made it." She indicated the concrete and steel pylons of the bridge, which were visibly intact. "Tore up the toll plaza though."

Kerry went to the side of the bridge and peered across the water at the roadway. "There's a truck parked across it too," she said. "Boy this is going to be creepy after dark."

The bridge itself was empty. They passed under it.

"Coast Guard, Coast Guard, do you copy?" The voice on the radio repeated, as Andy climbed up onto the bridge and settled in one of the tables behind the bridge. "Hello? Is anyone out there?"

Kerry sighed, and lifted the mic, then held off when she heard the channel open again.

"Calling station, this is Coast Guard Ops."

With a satisfied grunt, Kerry put the mic back down.

"Thanks, Coast Guard. This is Crandon Beach. I just want to report... well, there's a tanker here on the beach," the voice said. "It's leaking oil all over the place and we can smell diesel everywhere. It's huge."

"Roger that, Crandon." The coast guard answered. "We'll put it on the list."

"Someone going to come look at it?"

"Not right now, Crandon. We have to bring all the craft back into the area."

"Explains why we didn't see any of them," Kerry said. "Coast Guard, I mean. Or hear them on the radio."

"Went up to Virginia," Andrew said. "Captain that stopped by said they were all going out." He paused thoughtfully. "Might have ended up better going to Orleans, turns out."

Dar adjusted the throttles a little, as they cleared the bridge, and moved along the flooded coastline. "Oh, crap that's right. Damn storm is heading right that way." She paused. "Where'd they send Navy, Dad?"

"South."

"Gitmo?"

"Yeap."

Dar shook her head a little. "Bet that was popular." She increased the speed of the boat again, now that they were clear of the bridges, and solidly in what seemed to be unobstructed waters. "See if I can make up some time."

"Ain't nobody round to stop ya," Andrew said. "Let's go."

****

Dar started to doubt her decision to start off so late in the day as they rounded the bulk of Dinner Key and through the shallow channel that fronted the part of the coastline near where their office was.

The sky was still very cloudy, and the light was dimming to a dusky hue. They'd passed cluster after cluster of shattered docks in the large marina at Dinner Key, but few boats since most had apparently been evacuated.

Now, as they came closer to the much smaller set of docks at the Coconut Grove sailing club, they found the wooden structures perilously destructed, most of the planks cracked or missing and the pylons at almost right angles to the waves.

No boats were in the dock. All of them, smaller craft, had been lifted out and were stored in the nearby concrete shelters, which seemed to be relatively intact.

Dar backed the engines down to dead slow, and the roar settled into a low rumble as she held the boat against the current while Andy and Kerry went onto the bow to look around.

She saw trees down. The sailing club had a parking lot, and a road behind it, and past that was the back entrance to their office. There were so many trees around the place though, she couldn't see past them.

Kerry turned around on the bow and looked up at her, the faint shrug working through her body visible.

Dar regarded the scene, then she triggered the anchor, hearing the harsh rumble as the chain unrolled in the hull and released the heavy iron hook into the water.

Watching the sonar, she saw the anchor hit bottom, and gently backed the engines a bit as she angled the boat across one of the pylons, catching the anchor on the debris to hold the Dixie in place. Once she was sure it was snagged, she put the engines into idle and waited as the current realigned the boat.

It stayed in place. With a grunt, Dar shut down the engines and then the air was filled with the rush of wind through the debris and the creak of building parts moving when they shouldn't have been. She paused to see if anything was going to happen, then she shrugged and went down the ladder to the back deck.

"What a mess." Kerry came around the corner of the gunwale and joined her, stuffing her camera back into her pocket. "Can't see anything. Can you see the place from up top?"

"Nope." Dar went to the side of the boat and regarded the water. "Guess we'll have to..." She paused in mid word, as Andrew put his hands on the railing and hoisted himself over it, going boots first into the water. "Dad."

"He just did it before you could," Kerry said wryly. "But I think you were right not getting any closer. I saw a bunch of stuff in the water just ahead of us there." She went to Dar's side as they watched Andrew pop to the surface, shaking the water out of his eyes. "Careful, Dad!"

Andrew turned like an otter in the water and regarded her with a grin, then he turned again and started swimming toward the wreckage of the dock, using a sweeping underwater stroke.

Dar went up the side of the boat to the bow to keep him in sight, walking across the deck of the gently rocking craft as she looked up and down the coastline, wrack filled and silent.

She spotted something. "Dad!"

Andrew paused in mid stroke and turned, eyes scanning.

"Snake!" Dar pointed to his right.

"Got it." Andrew drew one hand up, the bulk of a large knife tucked into his fingers as he tread water watching the snake skim toward him, it's rounded head about six inches off the surface.

But the snake veered off and went past him, intent on some target that wasn't a large human being blocking his way. Andrew turned to watch it go, then he restored the knife to its sheath and continued to swim toward the shore.

"Hmm," Dar said.

"Hmm," Kerry echoed.

Dar went to the back deck and picked up the backpack she'd put on the boat. She opened up one of the storage lockers and removed a large dry bag from it and put the backpack inside the drybag and closing the top of it.

Kerry had grabbed one of the smaller bags and dropped her camera and her sat phone into it.

Dar went and opened the hatch in the back deck that would allow them to walk onto the fantail, where there was a ladder that could be extended into the water.

"Did you bring the keys?" Kerry asked. "I don't really want to come back here to find out someone stole our boat, hon."

Dar paused and regarded her. "Maybe you should stay here?" She said. "The gun's in the cabin, right?" She added. "Because that's a damn good point. Even if I take the startup key, if someone lets the anchor loose this thing is heading for Havana with that current."

"We don't want that to happen," Kerry said, somberly. "But I don't really want to not go with you either." She pondered. "Why not stay here and let Dad explore?"

Dar considered that, leaning both hands against the back wall of the deck. "I could," she admitted.

"But you don't want to," Kerry said.

"I think I should go," Dar said. "I know dad's got mad skills, but it is our people."

They looked at each other for a long, silent moment. Then Kerry nodded. "Okay. I'll keep trying the phones." She put the small dry bag down and watched Dar as she slid the straps of the dry bag over her shoulders and then entered the water. "Want some fins?"

Dar grabbed the edge of the fantail, judging the current. "Yep."

Kerry went and retrieved a set of them from the storage and came over to hand one and then the other to her as Dar fit them over her boots and tightened the straps. "Be careful, hon."

"I will," Dar promised. Then she released the boat and started toward the shore, the ripple from her fins stirring the surface behind her.

The water was cold after being in the heat for the ride over, and Dar briefly regretted not putting on a wetsuit for the swim into the dock. The passing of the storm had sucked heat energy with it, and left a chilly upwelling that was less than comfortable to swim in.

She approached the broken spars cautiously, just spotting Andrew pulling himself up onto the edge of the pier.

It was easy enough to make headway against even the brisk current with her fins, and she edged around the first broken pylon, moving aside the wood planks hanging crazily off of it as she got between the two destroyed piers.

At least there were no upended boats to get over. Most of the debris there was furniture from the deck of the sailing club, for some reason left out, and now jumbled just below the surface as she approached the shore.

Something moved and she went vertical in the water, her hands coming up defensively until she realized the small object that had emerged from the water was the head of a turtle. "Jesus, buddy."

The turtle swam past, seeming a bit confused as it sought something to haul itself up onto. It was a small animal, about the size of a salad plate and after a brief pause Dar swam after it and grabbed hold of its shell.

Its small legs churned in the water, trying to get away from her, but she went shoreward again to the seawall that Andrew had climbed up onto, dragging the turtle with her until she reached the concrete wall. "Hang on." She put one hand on the wall and hoisted the turtle up with the other, placing him on the surface of the dock and out of the ocean wash.

The turtle scrambled away from her, as Dar gave her fins a kick and pulled herself up. She turned around and sat down on the concrete facing the boat. She gazed across at the Dixie, spotting Kerry on the flying bridge, watching her.

She lifted her hand and waved, and Kerry waved back. With a contented grunt, Dar removed the fins from her boots and set them down on the ground, then she stood up, dripping seawater everywhere and feeling quite soggy in her cotton twill pants and shirt.

With the humidity, she'd never dry but at least it was warmer in the air. Dar sighed and skirted the fins, leaving them on the edge of the wall as she tramped across the sailing club deck, stepping over a fallen palm tree and a pile of twisted aluminum that had once been part of a patio awning.

She walked along the side of the club, whose windows were covered in plywood and whose back door had, incongruously, two large refrigerators placed across it.

It was quiet. A loose piece of plywood swung in the wind, slamming fitfully against the wall. She walked along the sidewalk to the front of the club, toward the road it sat on. It was once lined with tall, graceful palm trees but now they were all collapsed, two of them on top of cars that had been left in the lot, and a third having taken down the electrical and phone cables hanging from a pole that had snapped in half.

In the near distance, a car alarm was going off. She could also hear, on the wind, the sound of sirens.

She climbed over one of the palm trees and ducked under a second, squeezing between two cars in the road and across the sidewalk on the other side. Beyond that was a gravel yard, with a boat lift, and past that a coral wall, old and discolored, that ran along the back of the property their office sat on.

Her father was nowhere is sight. The office sat in a commercial area, and there were no houses nearby. The block had been deserted when they'd left the previous day. Dar walked past the coral wall and could see the back of the office.

She saw the angle of the roof, and the loading dock, and she went between the heavy Ficus trees across the back, emerging across the delivery tarmac to get a good view of the building.

There was no building debris on the ground, which she considered a good sign. She walked up the steps onto the loading dock and then circled the wall and headed along it toward the front on the footpath that circled the office between the line of trees and the structure.

The window boards were all still in place. She thought for a moment how much they likely owed her father for that. Along the left-hand side, trees were down everywhere and as she reached the corner, one of the huge Ficus there was uprooted entirely and blocked the whole road.

She heard Andrew's voice, and as she came around the corner she saw him, and Carlos on the porch talking. The big muscular guard seemed none the worse for wear, though he was in a tank top and shorts. He spotted her and waved.

"Hey, boss!"

Dar climbed up onto the porch, noting that above her head, even the company sign was still firmly bolted into place. "Hey."

"We've been trying to call you all." Carlos held up the sat phone. "It just won't get a line out. Keeps saying it's busy, busy, busy." He half turned. "The place did all right! I was listening on the radio, and other places got trashed. My apartment's roof's gone."

"Wow," Dar said. "Glad you were here then?"

"Glad I was here, and my buds too," Carlos said. "No power though. It's kind of a mess inside, some of the skylights blew out and we got rained on, and when the storm hit... holy damn... waves came right up and came right through up to the windows on the first floor. See?"

They looked at the wall, which had water stains and debris along it.

"We set up a grill in the middle there," Carlos said. "That did pretty good, and Scott's bus lived." He turned and pushed the door open behind him. "Wanna scout it out? I figured you would show up here... Pete heard boat engines off in the distance."

"That was us. Kerry's guarding the Dixie," Dar said. "Let me see how bad it is in here, and then try to give her a call."

****

"We're by the edge of the water, near the office," Kerry said into the phone. "Dar and her dad went ashore to check things out. I'm guarding the boat."

"Guarding the boat?" Ceci asked, in a somewhat surprised tone.

"Well." Kerry glanced to one side. "It's pretty creepy out here and it's getting dark. I've got the shotgun out and loaded. Dar didn't want to take a chance of anything happening to the Dixie and stranding us."

"I see." Her mother-in-law pondered that for a minute. "Are you tied up at the dock there?"

"We're at anchor. Nothing left of the dock here," Kerry said. "Or not much, anyway. Just a lot of broken pylons. The whole Dinner Key marina is trashed."

"Saw that on the news," Ceci said. "Some of the flooding is going down, but they got nothing on the power yet. National Guard is starting to do some searching."

"I heard the helicopters before," Kerry said. "Not right now though."

"They had to ground them. Wind's too heavy," Ceci reported. "So far they say about a hundred people dead, and a couple thousand in the hospital, but no idea what percentage of reality that is."

Kerry sighed. She was sitting on the bridge of the Dixie, in the chair Dar usually used, and she had the floodlight lit pointing at the edge of the land where Dar and Andy had climbed out. "Yeah," She said. "And I haven't heard from any of our other folks. I tried calling Mayte and Maria, no answer."

"It's probably still the weather," Ceci said, in a consoling tone. "Hopefully you all make it back here soon before it's too graveyard dark."

Kerry grimaced a little at the term. "It's creepy out here. I'll sure give you that. Postapocalyptic, actually." She thought she saw some motion, and shifted, one hand dropping casually down to rest on the stock of the shotgun on the seat next to her.

"People are starting to gather in the streets here," Ceci said. "Well, golf cart paths anyway. Catering'll probably show up any minute."

Kerry chuckled a little bit. "Okay, let me turn on some more lights here. I thought I saw someone heading this way," She said. "Talk to you in a bit." She hung up the satellite phone, then, tried dialing Mayte's line again.

Just a busy signal. With a sigh, she canceled the call, and then she got up and went to the searchlight, turning it slightly. She was rewarded with the sight of two tall figures coming from between the boathouse and the downed trees.

Dar was slightly in the lead, and she saw that Dar was sans the dry bag she'd taken with her. Kerry watched her body language carefully and calculated that the news at least was not entirely horrible.

She wished she could take the boat closer or that Dixie carried a small punt as some of the other large pleasure craft did, but she did what she could, She started up the engines and noted Dar pause to retrieve the fins she'd left on the dock.

She went down the ladder and to the back deck, going through the hatch and tipping the dive ladder into the water as the two swimmers approached and came around the stern to where she waited. She had the back deck lit, and a couple of towels ready, and she backed up a step out of the way as Andrew pulled himself up. "Hey, Dad."

"'Lo, Kumquat." Andy cleared out of the way for Dar to climb up after him. "Them kids in there are all okay."

Kerry felt a sense of relief. "Glad to hear that."

"Office is a mess," Dar said, as she took the towel being handed to her. "Roof's in one piece, but the pressure sucked out two of the skylights and there's water damage everywhere."

"Ah."

Dar sat down on the edge of the platform wall, wiping her face. "Whole first level got flooded halfway up to the ceiling," he said. "I think we're going to have to replace all the walls and the flooring." She looked at Kerry. "No idea when we can get back in there and work."

Andrew had gone up onto the back deck and taken off the heavy cotton shirt he'd been wearing and draped it over one of the equipment prongs then wrapped the towel around his neck. "Some mess," He said. "Carpet's going to come on out of there and the plaster off them walls."

Kerry considered, folding her arms. "Once they have power back on, we can see where to start," she said. "I'm just glad Carlos and his friends are safe. That's what matters." She exhaled. "I only wish I could get hold of Maria or Mayte."

"Carlos says he couldn't get his phone to work either. I left him mine," Dar said. "And some of the supplies I brought with me. They were putting up a pot of chili outside when we left." She stood up. "Let me just change and I'll pull the anchor. We were starting to see some folks roaming around down there when we came through to the pier."

****

It was quiet, and absolutely deserted as Dar carefully maneuvered the

Dixie back into her slip in the marina. The floodlights were on, outlining the overturned boats and destroyed docks, but they brought the only sound with them, the low rumble of the twin inboard engines.

Andy stood on the bow, hands braced on the rail. Kerry was on the back deck, one foot up on the gunwale waiting to hop off to tie them up.

The water level had dropped, Dar noticed, tide was out and had taken some of the flooding with it. She could see the edge of the island, once more in dry air, where there had been high water levels before they'd left.

She put the engines in neutral and let the boat drift a little, coming past her parent's craft as the current nudged her toward the dock. The marina building was dark and deserted and she figured everyone was finally getting a little rest.

She was glad they might now as well. She was tired, and the salt-tinged wind had her eyes burning a little and her lips chapped. She felt more than a little depressed about what they'd seen.

Onshore, she saw motion and looked up into the shadows to see their cart coming down off the ridge toward them, with her mother driving it.

It made her smile. She felt the edge of the boat gently impact the rubber bumpers, and she cut the engines as Kerry jumped to the dock and wrapped the aft rope around the nearby cleat. "We're back," Dar commented to nobody, making a note of the diesel levels and the charge of the batteries.

Once the engines were off, she could then hear the distant rumble of the island generators and the creak of the pylons as Kerry tightened the forward line and the boat went still. She turned off the controls and made her way down the ladder as Andrew came around from the bow.

"Glad them boys ended up okay," he said, as they joined Kerry on the dock. "Figure we should go on back there tomorrow and get stuff on out of there."

"Because of the water damage?" Kerry asked, as they started up the dock toward the oncoming cart.

"Looters," Andrew said. "Won't take long."

Dar nodded. "Yeah," she said. "I mean, those are all big guys. But it gets pretty dangerous pretty fast."

Kerry pondered that as she trailed along in Dar's footsteps. "Wow," she finally said as they reached the golf cart. "Here I was picturing people helping each other."

"There's some of that too," Dar said. "They'll send the National Guard in, and all that but everyone's pretty fast to take advantage at a time like this. Especially downtown where all the evacuations were."

"That sucks," Kerry said.

"It does." Dar slid into the back seat and exhaled. "What's up here, Mom?"

"Not a damn thing," Ceci said amiably. "They announced a buffet up at the mansion for everyone. I thought it would be fun to go over there and see what that was all about. Those uniformed manbots came around with what looked like a mimeographed paper for all the things they were doing."

"Sure, why not," Dar said. "Faster than cooking up our beanie wee-nies."

"Sounds good to me, too," Kerry said. "It's a mess by the office," she added. "But everyone's all right."

"Suspected it would be," Ceci said. "There's a lot of trees around there. A lot of damage?"

"Water," Andrew supplied. "Them vents got sucked up out the roof."

"Ew."

"We're going to have to put in new carpets and drywall," Dar said. "I gotta figure out where we're going to work from. Where's the storm now?"

"Haven't looked in an hour or so," Ceci said. "I've been driving around annoying the neighbors."

"Why d'you want to do that for?" Andrew asked, eyeing her. "Ain't crazy enough today?"

"Why not?" Ceci navigated a large puddle in the road as they headed toward the looming bulk of the Vanderbilt Mansion. "After all, you got to enrage the entire boating populace of this island of misfit toys and swim ashore in downtown Miami."

Kerry muffled a smile, and felt Dar move a little as she silently laughed. "They should all be glad they're here," Kerry said. "Mainland's a real mess."

"Exactly." Ceci steered around a downed tree and they pulled up through the entrance to the mansion, where a cluster of haphazardly parked carts blocked any further progress. "They need to shut the duck up and realize how lucky they are."

They found a spot for the cart and got out and made their way through the crowd of vehicles to the front steps. There were still covers over the windows, but the lights were on inside and as they approached the doors a puff of chilled air hit them.

Chilled air and the scent of wood soap and sterno. The terrazzo floors were covered with rubber mats, far different than the woolen rugs that were usually there and unlike its usual pristine and sedate décor there were boxes and carts against the walls and the stairwells had cases of water on their landings.

Inside the lower lobby there were island staff in jeans and T-shirts, with trays of plastic cups filled with what seemed to be wine and one of the staff spotted them and came over to offer them some. "Roberts family! Welcome."

"Hey, Juan." Dar picked up a cup of white wine and handed it over to Kerry and then took one for herself. "Everything survive here okay?"

"This place?" Juan looked around. "Heck yeah. Old man Vanderbilt knew what he was doing," he said. "Water came up over the pool and was up the back stairs out there." He pointed over his shoulder. "But they had all that covered, and it went back down again. But whoa, it left a shark in the pool."

"The swimming pool?" Kerry asked. "A shark? What are they going to do with it?"

Juan nodded and shrugged. "Grounds too soggy to bring over the boat lift to get it out. No idea what they're gonna do." He pointed to the dining room, past a pair of tall wooden doors. "There's some food set up in there. It's kinda pick your own today. They just put out what they had, you know?"

"Maybe they got some Ritz crackers then," Andrew said. "C'mon you all."

They went into the large dining room, which usually had tables set up in an elegant pattern, with crisp white linen and china. Now the tables were bare, exposing their plywood reality and one side of the room had been cleared to allow a long row of banquet style supports filled with chafing dishes.

Scattered at various tables were groups of their neighbors and there was a buzz of conversation in the air. The overhead speakers, which usually had refined classical music playing were silent, but there was a large television on a cart near the back wall, with a cable running from it through the door, one of the local stations on the air.

The plates were Chinet heavy paperware, and the silverware was plastic. Kerry picked up some of both and moved down the line. There were various manufactured salads, potato and carrot, and some plain lettuce shredded into chunks with plastic jugs of dressing nearby.

Completely unlike what was usually served in the room. Kerry smiled to herself, having eaten there occasionally with Dar. Neither of them were particularly fond of the place and its staid pretentions, preferring either the beach club or the trattoria near the docks.

She regarded the lettuce, then she kept moving and chose some Salisbury steaks and mac and cheese.

"Mmm." Dar sounded pleased with the choices. "This is not too bad."

"I think they have chocolate pudding on the other side, hon," Kerry said, as she half turned and scanned the room. She selected a table near some of their more amiable neighbors. "I'll be over at that second one there." She pointed.

"Be there in a minute."

Kerry walked over to the table and set down her plate and cup, giving the woman nearest to her a brief nod. "Hey, Jalinta."

The dark haired and deeply tanned woman nodded back. "Everything is okay at your house?" She asked, in south American tinged speech. "My husband is stuck in El Salvador. He is very upset he missed this." She had a bowl of rice and beans, and a piece of chicken on her plate.

"Everything's fine." Kerry sat down. "I wouldn't have minded missing this. That was pretty scary last night."

"Si." Jalinta nodded. "It was. How are your doggies?" She squeezed a bit of lime over her rice.

"Oh, they're fine." Kerry smiled. "They've got no idea what happened in our backyard though. What a mess." She glanced up as Dar came over to sit down next to her.

Andrew and Ceci arrived and took seats at their table. "Lo," Andrew greeted Jalinta, before he tucked into the cheeseburger on his plate. "Them fellers want me to give them a hand tomorrow," he told Dar and Kerry. "Told them has to be sunup cause we got things to get done."

"At least they asked nicely." Ceci regarded her plate full of miscellaneous non animal food items with relative content. "Best thing I've had here yet," she announced. "They should cater natural disasters more often."

Clemente, the manager of resident services came across the room and took a seat at their table. "Hello there," he said. "We are arranging for deliveries of supplies. What can we get for you?"

All four of them regarded Clemente in silence for a moment. "I think we're okay," Dar finally said, pausing in her decimation of a hot dog. "We've got supplies in the house. Water still okay?"

Clemente nodded. "We have a treatment plant on the west side of the island," he said. "So, we are fine. You have everything you need? If you do not, we will have our staff come by in the morning and please tell them." He patted the table. "Please enjoy your dinners."

He got up and went to the next table, one of his minions scurrying over to join him with a pad and pen.

"So, the kids are all okay?" Ceci asked, as they were left in relative peace. "Glad to hear that. I was a little doubtful about leaving them there, so close to the bay."

"Carlos and his gang came through fine, yeah," Kerry said. "And we've heard from Colleen, Mark and Scott up in Melbourne. Nothing from Mayte or Maria though, and I'm really getting concerned about them." She forked up some of her mac and cheese. "We go back tomorrow."

Dar nodded. "I have to figure out where we're going to put the code repository and where we can get people back to work on in." She picked up a potato chip, dunked it in some ketchup and ate it. "No way to know when they can even get power back there, much less the rest of it."

Kerry nodded. "You think Melbourne?" She asked. "We can probably get space up there where the call center guys are."

"Maybe," Dar said. "Problem is, all our folks are here and we've got no idea what's going on with them." She pondered the last bit of her hot dog. "This is a mess."

"Why not bring your stuff back here," Ceci suggested. "We have power and AC." She said. "You could rent one or two of those cottages around the corner. String some cable between them." She picked up a pickle and bit into it. "Bring all the nerds here and really drive them crazy."

"That's not a bad idea," Kerry said, after a brief pause. She put her fork down and got up. "Let me go put a bug in Clemente's ear and grab them." She pushed her chair in and went after the services manager, who was now a few tables away.

"I'm pretty sure those cottages don't have enough power to run our gear," Dar said. "But we can arrange for temporary runs." She glanced at her mother. "But you're right it's going to drive these people nuts, and if power stays off on the mainland, all the big shots are going to want to stay here."

"Screw em. We get there first." Ceci smiled. Andy just chuckled and shook his grizzled dark head, leaning back to pick up a cup off one of the trays being passed nearby.

****

It felt amazingly good to lay down in bed in the cool comfort of their home with the knowledge that no storm was going to interrupt their night's rest. Kerry stifled a yawn and stretched, feeling the water bed's surface shift under her.

Outside in the living room she heard the drone of the television, but she had no desire to go and look at it, see the scenes of destruction played over and over again.

It reminded her, a little, of what it had been like after the terrorist attack on 9/11. Those same images in a never-ending loop, until you just got exhausted from it.

Now that it was dark, there was no new news, really. Just a recap of the day, the starting of—not recovery, but a sense that a reckoning was still being taken, that a corner had not yet been turned.

There were two hundred and fifty known dead people, but everyone knew there were more, buried under rubble or washed out to sea. Some of the hospitals were in trouble—their generators weren't functioning and shelters were overrun with people escaping from the ruins of their homes.

The pictures drove home to her, in a very sobering way, just how lucky she and Dar were, and what exactly their means had provided for them.

But tomorrow they would be out early, in the heat and the mess. She knew she had a long day of sweating and labor ahead of her.

Dar came into the room, closing the sat phone in her hand up and plugging it into the charging cable on the table next to the bed. Then she sat down on the bed and lay back, stretching her arms out across the shifting surface. "That was Mark."

"How's things with him?"

"They're okay. He's going to take his bike and meet us at the office tomorrow," Dar said. "He thinks the idea of using this place here is pretty good, except we don't have comms."

"No, but nothing really does around here."

"True," Dar agreed. "If we can get the core programmers here and working locally, it gives us time to get something set up farther upstate though."

"That's just the repository, Dar," Kerry said. "My problem is the rest of our systems have to talk to the world. I can't get anything else going. We can't order or pay bills or any of that." She turned her head and looked at Dar. "So, we need to get that part somewhere we can reach it."

Dar nodded. "Agreed," she said. "We have payroll on Friday."

Kerry put her hands behind her head and regarded the ceiling. "One thing I'm not worried about paying is the rent on that building, because I'll be damned, you know? Not after what we had to do to board it up."

"Could be the least of our problems." Dar rolled onto her side and propped her head up on one fist. "What are the chances that landlord's going to have the resources to start repairs on that place before his insurance pays?"

Kerry grimaced.

"Ah well." Dar rolled over and got up. "Let me go shut off that damn TV. I'm tired of listening to it."

Kerry rolled off the other side of the bed and followed her. She wanted a hot cup of tea to end the night with. She diverted into the kitchen while Dar went to find the remote. She started some hot water going as she casually glanced out the window in the kitchen.

It was very dark. She went over and opened the door to the back yard and walked out onto the top of the steps as the moon emerged from the clouds and spread a silver blanket over the ocean very nearby.

The water level had dropped. It was once more beyond the wall outside their yard, and she could see the edge of the seawall above the waves again. There were still some rollers coming in, but the surface of the water had calmed, and only had normal ruffles of white offshore.

She could smell strongly the salt, and the tang of seaweed lining the shoreline and the pungent scent of bruised vegetation.

Chino came out on the steps behind her, tail waving idly. Then Mocha bustled past and ran down the steps, eliciting a bark of objection from the older Lab.

"No crabs!" Kerry called out. She heard the kettle chime behind her, and she returned to the kitchen, leaving the door open for the dogs to return. She found Dar getting herself a glass of milk, and they stood together in silence for a few minutes.

Dar rinsed her glass and put it in the rack to dry and then turned and folded her arms. "Remind me to load our gear onto the boat tomorrow."

Kerry's brows creased.

"Our dive gear," Dar clarified. "I just realized while I was standing here that trying to swim to the boat with our server rig isn't a great idea."

Kerry's brows creased even further. "So… you're going to take it underwater?"

Dar looked at her. "I'm going to see what we need to do to bring Dixie into a dock there, hon," she said. "C'mon."

Kerry chuckled a little in embarrassment. "Sorry. It's late and I'm exhausted." She went to the door and whistled. "Let's go, kids!" She called out. 'We've got a long day ahead of us tomorrow."

Dar came up behind her and encircled her with both arms, as they watched the dogs make their way back to the steps, noses pinned to the ground. "We'll figure it out," she concluded. "We always do."

"We always do."

****

The next morning brought clearer skies, a stiff onshore wind to ruffle the waters, and more activity around the marina as everyone adjusted to the new disaster shaped reality and started to get on with recovering things.

Kerry walked in and out of the early morning sun with a coffee cup in either hand, moving along the dock that bordered the marina and toward the Dixie. She had on hiking boots and cargo pants, and a tank top with a light cotton shirt over it in deference to the sun.

Dar was on the back deck stowing their diving gear and she looked up as she heard Kerry's footsteps, walking to the edge of the boat.

Dar reached over to take one of the two cups as Kerry stepped onto the gunwale and then down onto the deck. "Busy?"

"Busy," Kerry confirmed. "And your dad's the most popular man on this side of the island it seems. He's over near the tent they set up next to the marina building giving advice to everyone."

Dar chuckled as she took a sip of the coffee. "People are idiots. He offered to tell them how to secure these damn boats before the storm got here. You think anyone listened?"

"You did."

"He's my father," Dar said. "Of course, I did. And anyway he did most of it himself." Dar moved over and sat in one of the deck chairs. "I think that's everything." She indicated the boxes on the deck. "Carlos said they managed to get a generator going."

"From where?"

"Didn't ask," Dar said. "He said two or three of our staff just showed up."

Kerry sat down in the other deck chair. "For work?" She hazarded. "Or breakfast?"

"Yes."

"Okay we should probably get going then," Kerry said. "Let me finish this and go get Dad."

Dar extended her long legs out and crossed them at the ankles. She was wearing neoprene booties and light cotton pants over her bathing suit, her shoulders bared to the sun. She sipped her coffee while watching the breeze ruffle the water, appreciating the moments of peace before what she reckoned would be a very busy day.

There was no power at all on the mainland all the way up to Palm Beach. Some emergency locations, hospitals and the emergency management stations had it from generators, but large areas were blocked off by flooding and downed trees.

The National Guard was starting to slowly move in. She could hear helicopters in the distance.

The storm was inching its way up the east coast, now a Category four. It was skirting the edge of the Carolinas and there was flooding there, as the hurricane had slowed down, pumping rain inland as the weather team raced to cover it.

Leaving the devastation in South Florida behind, as they often did. The only silver lining to that in Dar's view was that she was relatively sure it was distracting her major government customers for the moment and that might give her a chance to get things sorted out.

With all the destruction it seemed crazy to be worried about that, but she was. The weight of the commitments she'd made to deliver that contract felt heavy on her shoulders, and so, in a funny way she was thankful Hurricane Bob was on his way right up the coast toward them. A big, dangerous storm people in those parts were not used to dealing with.

Dar sighed. She watched a seagull come drifting in, coasting into the marina as though surveying the upended boats, pausing in midair, and then diving down to pick up a bit of debris in the water.

She watched it float for a moment, then she got up and climbed the ladder to the flying bridge and went to the controls, setting her cup down into one of the gimballed holders.

Across the marina she saw Kerry talking to Andrew near the tent, and then she spotted the marina manager heading down the dock toward the Dixie.

She delayed starting the engines and went back down the ladder instead, coming to the side of the boat as he reached it. "Morning, Jack."

"Hey, Ms. Roberts," he said. "You off to the Grove again?"

"We are," Dar said. "Bringing some supplies to our staff there and seeing what we're going to have to do to get things done."

Jack nodded. "Can I ask you for a favor?" He said. "I got about ten guys who could really help us out here, but John said even the work barges won't be moving for a couple days. Could they catch a ride back with you?"

"Won't be till late," Dar said. "But if they can get down to the sailing club marina down there, sure."

"Great," Jack said. "They can't come out until later anyway. Most of them have stuff to do at their own places, you know? But I offered them a hot shower and AC." He winked.

Dar chuckled in reflex. "Yup. That'd do it. I could probably rent the head in this boat by the minute once we're parked down there. Sun'll be out all day and it's going to be steamy." She looked past Jack to see Kerry and Andrew coming toward them, and behind them there were three men following. "Hey."

Jack turned and then put one hand out onto the pylon. "Morning."

"Hey, Dardar," Andrew said. "You go on out, and I'm gonna follow you along there." He pointed at the boat behind Dar's. "Give these here fellers a ride ovah to the Coast Guard station."

"Sounds good," Dar said. "I'm going to park by the same spot we did yesterday and do a quick look under there to see if we can get closer."

Her father nodded. "Keep your ears on." He motioned the three men past the boat, and they followed him, giving Dar and Kerry, and then Jack, polite nods.

"Do we know those guys?" Kerry asked, in a low tone.

"They work for one of the residents," Jack said, after the men had all boarded the boat behind them. "They seem a little... "He made a face.

"Spooky?" Dar asked, with a faint smile. "As in, maybe they have a government ID somewhere?"

"Yeah," Jack said. "They're definitely military or something. The guy they work for is a retired something or other from the government. They're nice. I like them, but they always have that look, you know?"

"They remind me of Secret Service." Kerry said. "So, I get why they get along with Dad." She circled Dar and went into the cabin of the Dixie. "I'm going to rearrange the boxes in here, Dar. In case you hit some waves."

Jack looked at Dar with a puzzled expression.

"Kerry's family's involved in the government," Dar explained. "Her mom's a senator."

"Really?" Jack sounded surprised. "Oh wait, now I remember someone saying that sometime... from Michigan, right?"

"Right."

"Anyway, you all be careful and thanks for the favor, Ms. Roberts. I'll tell those guys to be down by the sailing club before it gets dark." Jack lifted his hand. "Want me to let you loose?"

"Let me get the engines on first," Dar said. She went up to the bridge and settled into the captain's seat and started up the inboards as she heard Andrew do the same behind her. "Call us on the radio if you need anything, Jack," She called over the side of the boat.

Jack waved, and went over to the forward ropes, untying them and tossing them onto the deck. "They just got the marina radio going," he yelled back. "Heard there were some idiots near Star on jet skis. Watch out for em!"

Dar lifted her hand in response, as he walked past toward the larger boat behind them. She nudged the engines into gear as they drifted away from the dock.

Chapter Five

Dar tightened the strap on her gear and eased into the water, using the ladder to lower herself into the green blue depths that surrounded the boat. She was wearing a tropical wetsuit, in deference to the potential wreckage under water and the chill and she pulled on a pair of gloves and fastened the wrist holds to keep them in place.

Kerry was on the deck, on the sat phone, watching her. "I hear ya Col. I just got off the phone with the team upstate and they got hold of some office footprint next to them."

"Be right back," Dar told her, before she submerged her head and let herself sink under the surface, the cool water penetrating her suit as she adjusted her gear. She tightened the tank a bit and rerouted her regulator as she looked around.

What was left of the club marina was a mess.

Literally a mess. The structure of the dock was collapsed in on itself and as she swam slowly under the water, exhaling bubbles, fish darted in all directions away from her, then drifted back as they explored this new world they now inhabited.

The visibility underwater was limited. The storm had churned up the bottom and it was hard to see much. Dar went ahead cautiously, unsure of what she was going to encounter, unable to clearly see details until she was almost within reach of things.

The pylons that had supported the aluminum walkways were skewed and, in some cases, split in half. The walkways themselves were twisted into a maze of wreckage that, though interesting if diving for pleasure, were nothing but obstructions right now.

The Dixie was anchored about fifty feet offshore. Dar felt the current pulling against her as she made her way toward the rock lined shore, searching for a path that would allow the boat closer to land. Her bubbles sounded loud in her ears as she paused, then reached out to tug on a bit of debris.

It moved a bit and she tugged harder, pulling a stretch of aluminum decking toward her and away from a set of still intact pylons.

She measured the space with her eyes, then she finned to the surface, emerging with her head out of the water as she moved in a circle.

The Dixie was drifting about thirty feet away and as she tipped her head up, she spotted Kerry on the bridge with a set of binoculars, keeping her in view. She waved, then went back under the water.

Well, it would get them a bit closer. Turning with her back to the boat, she regarded the narrow wedge of relatively clear space. If she brought the Dixie in here, they could tie up to the pylon at the top end, which was partially extruding into the open air.

She swam over to it, and shoved against it, then grabbed hold of it and tugged, to judge its general permanence. It didn't budge in either direction, so she grunted in satisfaction, then turned and nearly levitated out of the water as she found herself face to face with a massive grouper.

A burst of bubbles came out of her regulator along with an audible squawk and she instinctively tucked her hands under her arms, moving back away from the large fish as it watched her with one of its large, round eyes, opening its wide jaw as it swam easily against the current.

She got her back against a piece of aluminum debris and put her hand on the hilt of the dive knife strapped across her chest as the big fish, easily three hundred pounds, sauntered past, inspecting the wreckage as smaller fish darted around.

Grouper generally weren't dangerous. However, they had big jaws and sharp teeth and Dar didn't want to take any chances. She waited for it to disappear into the murky distance before she went over to the pylon and removed a safety sausage from a clip on her gear, inflating it and tying it off.

The sausage was a bright orange tube, meant to bob to the surface and mark a position. After it was tied firmly in place, she heard the hoot of the Dixie's horn as Kerry spotted it.

Then she went to the other edge of the open space and deployed a second sausage, which would give her a target when she was steering the Dixie in.

She checked the tangled wreckage one more time, pulling some out of the way of the passage and looking for anything that might get caught up into the boat's engines before she made her way back to the Dixie's anchor line, barely visible in the murky gloom.

She swam under the boat, seeing the edge of the dive ladder moving in the current ahead of her. She grabbed it and swung around under it, then paused with her head still submerged to remove her fins and fit their straps around her wrists.

The boat was moving with the waves, and she waited a moment for the ladder to come a bit deeper before she got her booties onto the bottom step and lifted herself up out of the water as the chop lifted the aft of the boat upward.

Kerry was standing in the dive well, already reaching out to grab her tank yoke. "I saw the markers come up."

"Yeah. I heard the horn." Dar climbed up and moved into the well alongside her, shoving her mask down around her neck and leaning forward to toss her fins into the back deck. "Not much space, but it's a little better."

"Our team thinks so," Kerry told her. "They're dragging debris out to try and make a plank for us pirates to walk." She moved aside as Dar slid her tank into the clamps and released the straps off her rig attached to it. "Carlos said they spotted the Dixie coming in."

"Yeah?" Dar stood up and walked over to the edge of the well, peering around the side of the boat to where she could now also see the sausage bobbing at the surface. Past it were a half dozen figures on shore, two of them carrying over what looked like a door. "Huh."

"Colleen's picked up two of her people, and one of the receptionists and she's on her way upstate. Took her almost three hours to get gas and that was only by bribing the station owner," Kerry said, as she shut off the air in Dar's tank and secured it. "I told her of course to expense it."

"The gas or the bribe?" Dar found the whole thing a little surreally funny. She stood still as Kerry came over with the freshwater hose and rinsed her off, blinking at the faintly chlorine scent. "Thanks."

"No problem, hon." Kerry finished with the hose and then handed Dar a fluffy towel. "Not that you really need this. With the breeze and that sun you'll be dry in a minute."

Dar dried her head with the towel, and then unzipped her wetsuit and pulled it down to her waist. "Okay let me move the boat in. We can tie off to that structure where the marker is. It's pretty secure." She headed for the ladder. "Keep an eye out, I'm gonna pull up the anchor."

"Yup." Kerry got up onto the side of the boat and walked up to the bow, as she felt the rumble and heard the anchor chain retracting and the Dixie started drifting in the current.

The engines caught a moment later and she felt the motion as they moved toward the shore, the breeze fluttering her shirt against her body.

There was a small crowd onshore. Carlos was there and two of their programmers, and as she watched, one of Carlos' gym buddies crawled out along the split edge of the dock, dragging along a piece of wood and wedging it in place.

It occurred to her, just for a moment, that doing this on their own was probably a little strange. There were probably people somewhere on shore, watching this bunch of nerds with flotsam and jetsam and a pleasure yacht thinking what in the actual hell were they doing?

Probably most everyone else were watching the battery powered televisions or walking out to find gas for their generators or waiting for help to show up, based on what she'd seen on the screen before they'd left. The sound of a helicopter in the distance made her wonder how long it would be before someone told someone about them and they'd end up on the news.

With a smile, she shrugged, and then waved at the gang ashore, holding up the coiled forward rope and preparing to throw it over.

****

"Get that barrel," Carlos said, pointing toward what had been the bar area of the sailing club. "If we put that in the water there, we can prop this board on it."

"Got it," his buddy replied, dusting his hands off and climbing up the beach to the ruined pool deck. He skirted the debris filled pool and went behind the collapsed bar to where barrels of soda syrup were lying on their side. He pushed one, and heard it slosh inside. "Hey, gimme a hand this one's full."

His lifting partner climbed up the deck to join him and they wrestled the barrel loose of the debris, hoisting it up and over the bar then walking with it back down toward the water.

The big Bertram yacht was tied off to the part of the dock that was still in one piece, and they had managed to get wood planks and pieces of table in place to get almost all the way out to it.

One of Carlos' bosses was standing on the shore, clothes dripping wet from the swim in, and the other stood on the side of the boat holding one of the planks in place while the computer kid nailed it. "You know what, Mickey?"

"What?" Mickey went into the water up to his knees and got the barrel wedged in place.

"Glad we came down here instead of staying by that apartment. I bet those guys are still stuck on the second floor sweating their asses off."

"Yeah. This is okay," Mickey agreed. "Nice breeze and a little work-out." He straightened up and nodded. "That'll hold up." He turned and watched the other computer guy get out on the planks, as the woman on the boat started to bring boxes out. "Let's go see what that is."

They walked over to the edge of the twisted end of the dock and joined Carlos and the blonde woman he was talking to. "Think that'll be okay," Jerry commented. "Should hold up, at least for a while."

"Thanks, guys," Carlos said. "Yeah, so Kerry, we got a lot of stuff cleared out and onto the delivery dock at the office. Mick and Jerry were awesome," He said. "And some other people just showed up there too... they said they knew you."

"Knew me?" Kerry asked. "Boy, that could be either good or bad," she said. "Were they customers or..."

Carlos shook his head. "Didn't stop to talk to them since we saw the boat coming in. We cleared a path up to the office from here. We were trying to find a flatbed cart, but we figured we could get some stuff up by carrying it anyway."

Kerry ran her fingers through her drying hair. "Well, we've got a bunch of supplies. Dar's dad'll be by in a little while. He had to run some people over to the Coast Guard station," she said. "Let's go see if we can scrounge up something to move this stuff with since we're going to need that to move gear back down here."

"Sounds good. Lets go." Carlos motioned the other weightlifters ahead of him.

Kerry half turned. "Dar!" She let out a yell. "I'm going up to the office!"

Dar waved.

Kerry started climbing up off the wrecked dock, and they followed, leaving the others to stack boxes on the edge of the shore.

****

The heat was oppressive once they got a block inland and Dar felt the sweat gathering as they crossed the parking lot of the club and entered the back of their building.

Piled on the loading dock were stacks of soaked paneling and boxes, the large garbage container already full of stripped up carpet. "Wow," Dar said, as she walked alongside Arthur and Elvis, the two programmers. "Lot of stuff got done."

"Nothing else to do," Arthur said. "My dad was here and helped us. He was tired of watching the news."

"Know how he felt," Dar said, as they walked up the concrete stairs to the propped open back door.

Inside it was dark and quiet. The building was surrounded by trees, and though they had been thinned by the wind it made the inside gloomy. Dar felt the lack of the usual sound of air-conditioning, and the ever-present humming of electronic equipment that had been a part of her normality for as long as she could remember.

It smelled musty. The floorboards creaked as they walked down the hall, the doors on either side flung wide open and the windows facing outward open as well. What breeze there was came through it, bringing the smell of mud and garbage steaming in the sun.

The door to the server space was open, but it was dark and silent inside and Dar walked past it. Ahead of her she heard Kerry's voice and as she passed the downstairs kitchen, she smelled coffee brewing.

She paused.

"Camp stove." Carlos read her mind. "Want some java?"

"Not yet." Dar continued on, looking from side to side and frankly wondering where to start.

Not where to start cleaning up, because they had gotten a start on that. Ripping up the carpet to keep it from molding and throwing away all the things that the flooding had ruined. Dar stopped and reversed her steps, going into the server room and pulling her flashlight from her pocket.

It smelled like wet concrete in the room. She'd only spent a moment inspecting it the previous day, and now she took a little more time to look around, checking the floor with her hand. "Dry."

Carlos came in behind her. "Yeah, water didn't come in here," he said. "Cause of this raised thing. I think it might have gone under it?"

Dar stood and handed him the flashlight, then she took the tile puller from the wall and knelt again, getting the suction cups in place and yanking a tile free. She set it aside and held her hand out for the light. "Let's see what this looks like."

Carlos handed her the light and then knelt next to her as she lowered her head to look under the floor and shone the light around.

She came up in a swift motion that made Carlos hop backwards. "What?" He said. "Is it bad?"

"Eyes."

Carlos stood up and looked around, finding a bit of conduit and taking hold of it. "What kind of eyes?" He asked. "Like... alligator?"

Dar picked up the tile puller and moved over a few feet.

"Are you going to pull that floor up?" Carlos said. "Should I get... I dunno, a knife? Or a hammer or something?"

"Wasn't that big." Dar set the cups and yanked the second tile up, moving quickly aside as a moving thing sped past her, claws scrambling on the tiles as it skirted Carlos' powerful leg and bolted out the door. "Hmph."

"What in the hell was that?" Carlos went to the door and looked out. "Watch out everyone! Some kinda animal's out here!"

Dar shone the light down under the floor where the eyes had been, then knelt, inspecting the multicolor cabling that ran in a number of directions. It was covered in mud and gunk, and there were leaves and debris coating it, but the strands themselves seemed to be intact.

She grunted in satisfaction and put the second tile back down then went over to the first, laying down on the floor and looking beneath it.

****

Kerry looked around quickly hearing Carlo's warning, glad they'd left the dogs behind today. "What kind of animal?" She asked, coming out of the conference room where everyone had gathered. Outside the door was the reception desk, which was covered in paper cups and gallon jugs of Publix water.

Carlos' two friends came out after her, and their two visitors followed.

Two ILS employees in fact, security guards Celeste and Jerry, dressed in jeans and polos. They lived nearby in the Grove. "Maybe it's a cat," Celeste suggested. "I thought I saw one outside, and there's dogs running loose everywhere."

But there was no sign of anything moving. "Could have gone anywhere," Kerry said. "Okay, so, Celeste you were saying?"

The young guard was peering around in the nearby offices. "Jerry and I live on the same block here," she said. "We have Ficus down everywhere. You can't get a car through, but anyway, they closed the building up and sent everyone home before the storm hit."

"Makes sense," Kerry said. "Dar was saying no one stupid enough to stay there in that kind of storm still worked for ILS."

Both of them looked at her, a little uncertainly.

"Meaning us." Kerry motioned to her chest, and vaguely over her shoulder.

"Oh! Right." Celeste laughed. "No that's true. It's not the same since you all left. We miss you," she said. "We were all saying that before they sent us all home."

Jerry nodded.

"You guys worked at the old place?" Carlos asked.

"We did," Celeste said. "We're security guards."

Carlos grinned. "Me too."

"Well, the building's a mess. Dar and I went past it on the waterside yesterday on the way down here. Windows blown out all over the place." Kerry paused, as she heard a helicopter rattle overhead, and as that faded, she could hear in the distance the sound of a motorcycle.

"We saw on the news," Jerry said, with a grimace. "No way we're going back to work in there any time soon." He put his hands in his pockets. "So, we said, hey, since we're in the neighborhood, why not come down here and say hello."

"That's cool," Carlos said. "Want to help us around here?" He asked, after exchanging the briefest of looks with Kerry. "You can share our pizza."

"Sure!" As though they were just waiting to be asked, which they obviously were, they joined Carlos and his friends as they went back to sorting through the debris.

Kerry watched them and put her hands in her pockets, smiling a little to herself. Then she turned and trotted up the steps to the second level.

Here, the damage was a lot less evident. The skylights were covered with garbage bags and tape, the walls were stained with rainwater, but the water that had come in had run down the stairs and through the floor. While the offices on either side of the hall were damp with humidity, they were mostly intact.

She walked into the end of the hall and paused to look into Maria's office. It stirred a pang of worry and she felt that tightening in her chest as she went through their outer office and through into her own.

Here the windows were all flung wide open and a steady breeze was coming through. She went to the window and looked out it at the sodden destruction all around.

On the ground beneath the window were the boards that had covered them. She heard the sound of a power drill nearby as Arthur's father moved along the outside, removing more.

Depressing. Kerry acknowledged the knot of anxiety she felt as she looked out over what had been their quaint and laid-back neighborhood, where now trees were down everywhere, and the streets were debris covered and deserted. She took a breath and could smell the salt tang of the sea, and the scent of bruised foliage on the walls next to where she was standing.

She heard the motorcycle getting closer now and crossed back over to Maria's office and went to her window to look out and down the street. The machine itself came into view and she recognized it and its rider. "Mark!" She let out a yell and a wave as he came coasting into the parking lot in front.

He parked, took his helmet off and gave her a wave in response. As he headed for the front door two bicycles came into view, the sound of their spokes audible to her from where she stood.

They spotted her and called out. "Ms. Kerry! Hello!"

Angela their receptionist, and one of Colleen's data entry clerks. Both women pulled their bikes up next to where Mark was parked, and she returned their wave as they headed toward the door.

Why? Kerry wondered, as she backed away from the window. She headed downstairs to greet them. Why, with no power, and no communications, why come here? She thought about that as she paused to look into their outer office, where Zoe would usually be seated.

Zoe, with her soft, lisping speech, who would at this time of day have been very busy with phone calls and opening the mail. Her desk was empty, her phone packed into the cases. Kerry wondered how Zoe had fared, and remembered she lived out where Maria and Mayte did.

Whole area still flooded; she'd heard.

The sound of the newcomers now seemed loud as they all gathered near the conference room. Mark's deep voice mixed with Carlos, and Angela's lighter tones, and then Dar's distinctive speech, clear and crisp with that touch of music in it.

That hint of an accent that shaped a voice that was practical and pragmatic and utterly confident even when Dar herself wasn't feeling any of those things.

Kerry started down the steps and then gasped suddenly, as something moved at her. "Yow!" She let out a yelp, jerking to a halt as she found herself facing off a large striped cat who stopped short and hissed at her.

Predictably, Dar came bounding up onto the landing and nearly ran into the cat, who turned hastily and lifted a fully claw extended paw and hissed again.

"Hey!" Dar barked at it indignantly, coming up onto the balls of her feet and lifting both hands up in a defensive posture. "What the hell!" She glared at the cat. "Who are you hissing at you little..."

The cat put its ears flat back onto its head and closed one eye as it squinted up at her, one paw still lifted up, but the claws now retracted.

The rest of the assembled crowd came pouring around the corner hearing the commotion and Angela let out a squeak. "Oh, it's Rudy!" She came forward, kneeled down and extending a hand toward the animal. "C'mere, Rudy. You must be starving."

Dar turned in place and looked at her, both hands coming down to rest on her hips. "Rudy?"

The cat skirted Dar as widely as it could and scuttled over to where

Angela was kneeling, accepting a head scratch. "He lives outside," Angela said. "I feed him ham croquetas in the morning. I was worried about him, you know? I mean, he's an outside cat, but still."

Kerry continued down the steps until she reached Dar's side, one step up. She rested her elbow on Dar's shoulder and regarded the cat with a bemused expression. "Is that what was under the server room floor?"

"I think so," Dar said. "It got out of there too fast for us to see it. But it was about that size." She sniffed reflectively. "Glad we didn't bring the dogs with us today. That would have been a circus."

"Mm," Kerry agreed. "Hey, Mark."

"Hey, Ker." Mark had shrugged out of his riding jacket in deference to the muggy heat. "This place looks better than our house does," he said. "Riding in, didn't look too bad."

"Considering how close we are to the water? No," Dar agreed. "Storm surge drained out. It's all coral edge around here, like out on the beach islands."

"No place for the water to stay," Arthur said. "That's what it looks like anyhow. Gets worse the farther west you go here."

"Two of the server guys are headed in here," Mark said. "We can unrack the gear and use those pelicans up on the second level if we unpack the stuff in them now."

The rest of the group looked at him with interest. "So, there's a plan?" Elvis asked. "Where are we taking the servers? I'm guessing we're going where they go." He indicated Arthur and himself.

"There's a plan," Dar confirmed. "Repository's going over onto the island we live on. We got space there."

There was a moment of contemplative silence. "Oh, sweet," Arthur said. "That's where they've got all the generators right? I heard about it."

"Sweet," Elvis agreed. "Lan party at Dar's, Rockstar."

Arthur hit himself in the head. "So that's why we had to build a bridge to the boat."

"We're going to get to go on the boat?" Elvis seemed absolutely delighted. "This is turning out to be a lot better than I figured it would."

Dar and Kerry exchanged looks. "So now that the plans in work," Kerry said. "Mark, how do you feel about you and I taking a ride west to see if we can find out how Mayte and Maria are doing."

"Right on with that," Mark said. "Let me just get the server guys going when they get here, and we can take off. I don't know if my motor's gonna survive all that water, but we'll get farther than a car would."

"Okay, gang," Carlos said. "Let's go get those cases unpacked. It's nice and breezy up there now they got the wood off the windows."

"See?" Angela had Rudy the cat in her arms and followed them. "I told you to stick around here, Rudy. This place always has it together. No matter what's going on."

****

Dar draped her shirt over the seat in the conference room, leaving her in a teal blue tank top with tropical fish on it and her cargo shorts.

Upstairs she could hear the thumps and scrapes as the team got things unpacked. Down the hall, she heard the server techs talking, laughing, the sounds of cables being thrown out to their length down the hall and then recoiled.

Everyone was, she thought, just glad to have something to focus on that wasn't the Weather Channel.

She walked over to the jalousie cranks and worked them, "Thanks, Jerry!" She called out, as the last piece of wood was removed off the windows, and they were able to open to allow in the breeze.

Jerry leaned against the windows on the other side, peering in at her. "My son said he figured if any place had things moving it would be here."

Dar grinned. "He's a damn good coder," she told him. "We were lucky that day you had him stop by with his skateboard."

Jerry nodded. "Yeah, you know we talked about it, his mom and I. Didn't figure all that gaming stuff would go anywhere and then he showed me his first pay stub from here." He laughed. "I felt like an idiot, waiting so long to push him."

"Tech's like that," Dar said. "it's this generations industrial revolution."

Jerry nodded again. "Different world," he said. "Still a place for people like me." He indicated his tool belt. "Definitely now a place for people like him." He said. "But not everyone's got a place, just like they didn't back in the day, those that drove horse buggies and the like."

"No," Dar said, after a thoughtful pause. "Techs like that too. It takes us places some people can't follow." She ran her finger along the edge of the louvered glass. "But you can't stop inventing stuff. That's not what we are, as a species."

"Hang on." Jerry seated the drill in one of the pockets of his work belt and walked around and into the entrance, then entered the conference room. "Mind if I grab a drink?"

Dar waved a hand at the table, which was covered in bags of chips, bags of granola bars, gallon jugs of warm iced tea, and other items.

"Mind if I ask you a question?" he said.

"No." Dar sat down and drew on a large pad of graph paper, with their company name and logo on it. "Have at it."

Jerry sat in one of the chairs and stretched his feet out, his work boots covered in grass and mud and speckled with paint and glue. "You hired that boy in the chair."

Dar glanced up at him. "Scott?"

He nodded. "Why? What you pay, you can hire anyone. Why that kid off the street?"

Dar considered the question as she sketched out a design diagram for how she wanted the servers set up once they got them over to the island. "Because he's a good tech," she finally said. "What I've learned out of screwing around with this stuff the amount of time I have is that you gotta have a specific set of skills to do it."

Jerry just waited for her to continue.

"Logical common sense is probably the rarest of them," Dar said. "He has it. I didn't care what his other issues were. I wanted that skill." She looked up at him. "Was it also a decent human thing to do? Sure. But if he'd been a lousy tech, I wouldn't have done it."

Jerry nodded. "Arthur said that and I wondered."

She twirled the pen she'd been using between her fingers. "It's a quirk in the brain. This... whole tech thing. I realized that, at some point," She shrugged casually. "So, I recognize it when I see it. You want that in what we do."

Jerry smiled and lifted his cup of warm iced tea in her direction.

****

"Hear me?"

Kerry adjusted the ear bud. "Yep." She settled her boots on the foot pegs of the motorcycle. "Let's go," she said, tightening the strap a little bit on the helmet she was wearing.

Mark nodded, and throttled forward, sweeping up the ramp and onto the interchange. "I'm gonna see if we can get off at 25th and go west. I heard 36th's a mess."

His voice was slightly crackly, fed through the Bluetooth radios between their two helmets, removing the communication challenges the motorcycle's engine caused.

There was little traffic, unusual in the daylight. Mark gunned the bike's engine as they crossed over the Interstate, and headed west. Light poles were down, and debris scattered everywhere. Boxes and palm fronds were littered over the surface of the highway, making navigation delicate.

A few National Guard trucks moved along in the commuter lane, and two Florida Power and Light trucks in tandem were going the opposite direction they were, headed for the city center.

It was still windy. The trees that weren't down, or missing fronds, were swaying hard, some streaming sideways as the high-pressure gradient that follows a storm like Bob took hold.

Kerry felt the wind shove against her, exposed as they were on the back of the bike and she was very content that the far more experienced rider was in control instead of her, especially as he evaded the debris on the road crossing between lanes.

"You guys leave your bikes down south?" Mark asked, as though reading her mind. "Any idea what went on down there?"

"We did," Kerry said. "They're locked up in the shed behind the cabin so if that ended up okay so did they." She watched as they crossed over stretches of glinting water and half submerged houses. "Something to worry about later."

She looked to her right as they passed the huge complex that was Jackson Memorial Hospital. There were lights on, and a row of large generator trucks lined up outside. "Looks like they're okay."

"Only trauma center we got. They better be," he said.

"Wow, check those boats out," Mark commented, as they crossed over the Miami River. "Some of them ended up in the court parking lot."

The storm surge must have been crazy, coming up the waterway. Kerry saw the glint of sun on flood waters extending on either side of the river, and collapsed buildings in the river itself, the bridges in an up position on either side.

It had funneled the surge up from the bay and the boats that had lined the edge of the river were thrown inland. The restaurants and shops both upscale and down ripped and in some cases collapsed into the water. A boatyard was in pieces, the aluminum panels littering the shore.

Once they were past the government and civic centers she saw houses destroyed under the freeway, wood, a stretch of street blocked by a huge tree down, the flashing lights of a police SUV.

"Glad 836 goes all the way out west," Mark said. "No way could you get through there on the ground."

"No," Kerry agreed, as she spotted a group of people standing up to their knees in the water. "My old apartment complex used to flood in a regular rain. I can't even imagine what it's like today."

"That place in Kendall?" Mark asked. "Oh yeah, you said you were on the first floor." He crossed into the next lane to avoid a downed light pole, collapsed into the right-hand passage with a piece of metal debris wrapped around it. "It must be a freak show here at night."

"Must be. It was for us coming back in with the boat last night through the channel," Kerry said. "Pitch black until we got near home. Dar had the lights blasting just in case someone was out there paddling around."

Mark laughed. "When Dar told me she was going to take the boat out and like, make a landing out on the edge of the bay to offload our ops to that place I cracked up."

Kerry chuckled a little. "I pissed off you don't want to know how many people by reserving the big cottage out there to move that stuff and our coders to. Dar's mother laughed her ass off."

"They gonna like live there?" Mark sounded skeptical. "Her parents I mean?"

"Oh yeah," Kerry said. "To know they're going to just make everyone crazy every minute between the pagan stuff and Dad's working on machinery in the front yard. Dad can't wait to invite his buddies over for a cookout." She felt Mark laughing through her grip around him and had to laugh a little herself.

There were some there, she reckoned, that were going to look back with nostalgia on the days when the most disruptive thing coming from the Roberts family was she and Dar throwing balls for dogs on the golf course and kissing in the dining room.

The road they were on was elevated, and ran from Interstate 95 to State Road 826. Aside from themselves, several power trucks, several police cars, and a file of National Guard trucks, it was empty. Kerry leaned a little to the right as they came up to the airport that the road skirted on the south side.

The field was awash and empty. Most of the facilities were on the north side of the field, so all they could really see were several planes upside down off in the distance, and a glimpse of a damaged roof in the nearest concourse.

There were trucks out on the field, driving back and forth. "Inspecting," Kerry said. "They want to open. I heard that on the news this morning."

"Sure," Mark said. "Fastest way to get supplies in." He risked a quick glance. "Wow the tower's a mess."

Kerry looked, and her body jerked a little upright when she saw the tall structure, missing half its roof, all of its windows, with cables and lines hanging down on the outside just barely visible. A blue tarp was flapping out of one window.

"Wonder how they're gonna work that out," Mark said. "ILS still does the tech for them."

"Glad I'm not going to get that call," Kerry said. "I can just hear the governor screaming."

They were both silent for a moment. Then Kerry shook her head. "Just keep going. Don't think about it."

Mark got in the right-hand lane as they passed the end of the airport, going over the bridge and heading north. All the airport parks on the right-hand side were flooded, and the office buildings were missing roofs, some crushed under fallen trees and lamp posts.

"We got kinda lucky," Mark said, after a long pause. "Y'know?"

"We did," Kerry agreed.

"Lot of these places ain't gonna make it back."

"Yeah." Kerry shook her helmet covered head a little, as they started down the exit to ground level. "Are we going to even be able to get through there?"

"Good question." Mark slowed as they reached the bottom of the ramp. The lights were out, and to the right, they could see a few cars trying to make their way around the fallen trees and collapsed electrical poles. "Let's see how far we can get. They live off 90th and something I think."

He cautiously turned left and kept his feet off the foot pegs, ready to stop and brace the big bike as they moved through the intersection and under the highway. Ahead, there were power lines down across the road, and in the distance, they could see a tractor trailer overturned and blocking the road.

Here, at ground level, they could really understand the level of damage. Storefronts were boarded up, but roof damage was visible. Pieces of tar shingled surface flopping off down the sides of the buildings and overhangs ripped off and collapsed.

The street signs were blown down. The light poles and traffic signals were all on the ground, and Mark was gingerly crossing over the downed lines with little bumps that made them both flinch. In the distance they could hear helicopters and the rumble of generators.

The buzz of a chain saw.

To the right, the echo of a crying child, and angry shouts in more than one language.

All around they smelled wet vegetation, stagnant water, a waft of garbage, and somewhere off in the distance, someone was cooking bacon.

"Weird." Mark concluded, after a long pause of them just moving down the street, slowly. "Kinda Mad Maxy."

"Kinda," Kerry said. "Dar said after that last big hurricane it got pretty elemental pretty fast."

"It did," he said. "My dad ended up sitting on a futon chair in front of what was left of our house with a gun in his lap and a tiki torch."

"Oh boy." Kerry muttered. "Let's hope this gets sorted out fast."

****

Dar was seated in the conference room with her pad at her elbow, listening to one of the two server techs who had been working on securing the gear. "Thanks, Mike," she said. "So, we're ready to pull them from the rack and put them in the case?"

"Bout as much as we can be," Mike said. "Everything looks like it's all secured. Far as I can tell nothing got super wet, and nothing smells like it got burned out."

Dar nodded. "All we can do here," she said. "We'll have to wait until we can power them up to really know."

"Right."

"Jose, we have all the network gear to bring this stuff up?" Dar asked one of their handful of network techs who had recently arrived, surprisingly, on the back of a horse. She could smell the animal on him, not entirely unpleasant.

The horse was tied in the central open space, contentedly cropping grass on the far side, a bucket of water nearby resting in the shade.

"We got cables, no problem," he said. "But I'm gonna need the appliance for dot1x and its not gonna like not seeing the cloud."

Dar regarded him in silence for a bit. "Take it," she said. "We'll spin it up and see what we get. If we have to, I'll crack into the switches and remove the config."

Jose nodded, seeming unsurprised. "Okay. Let me go get started." He got up and went through the door, with Mike right behind him.

Carlos appeared in the doorway. "We're done unpacking. I had my guys bring those cases down to the server room." He came inside and took a cup, pouring it full of warm iced tea. He sat down and exhaled, his skin glistening with sweat. "We all going to go over to the island?"

Dar fiddled with her pen, turning it in her long fingers. "The high value is the repository in those servers," she said, reflectively. "But we have all kinds of hardware here, and I think if we all abandon this place it'll get looted in a heartbeat."

Carlos nodded as Dar spoke. "Zactly what I was thinking," he said. "My buddies said they're all up to stay here, and Micky said he's going to go get some hardware just in case. You know?"

Dar regarded him. "Hardware like the shotgun Kerry has back on the boat," she asked.

"Yeah," Carlos said. "So, we figure we'll lock everything up tight down on the bottom level, and park ourselves up on the second floor outside your office in that open space. It didn't get any water, and we got a good view." He paused. "Those two people from your old place want to stick around too."

Dar smiled briefly. "They're good people. I was sorry to leave them behind."

Carlos smiled gently back at her. "Not as sorry as they were from what they said. But hey, we can use them right now so all's cool, right?"

"Absolutely," Dar said. "Wouldn't surprise me if more folks show up here from there. Anyone does, they're welcome to share whatever we've got here. If they want to help out, let em. I'll pay everyone our rate for it."

Carlos smiled again, but remained silent.

Dar got up. "Let's go walk the upstairs." she said. "I'm making a list of what we need to get done." She picked up her pad and they walked out of the conference room and up the steps to the second level.

Now, with the boards off all the windows, light flooded in and Dar entered one of the inside offices to go to the windows and look down at the central area in the middle of the square structure.

There were branches and debris everywhere and in the middle of it all was Scott's trailer home looking basically untouched. It had a pile of leaves on the top of it, but the outside was undented and right now the folding back grid was providing a surface for a charcoal grill.

"Protected." Carlos commented briefly. "But you figured it would be."

"I did. Wasn't sure about the storm surge though." Dar turned and made her way out of the office and into the hallway. She crossed over and stood in the area outside her and Kerry's offices. This was an angular corner, the largest space that had Zoe's outer area on one side, and Maria and

Mayte's offices on the other.

There was a skylight overhead, and it was covered now with a blue tarp, tacked into place. The floor under it was stained from the rain, but now dry. With all the windows in all the rooms open, a cross breeze was moving through and though it was warm, it wasn't horrible.

Dar went through Zoe's area and paused. "See if we can close off the back stairs and make the main set there the only way up," she said. "Hang out here."

Carlos leaned against the wall, with his brawny arms folded. "Yeah, the doors are pretty solid. It was more secure when we had all the boards on the windows though. But it's a lot easier to breathe in here with em off."

"True." Dar went into her office, which had been restored to its apparent functional use. She walked over and put her pad down on her adjustable workspace. The surface was set to allow work while standing, and she decided she'd stay here and use it that way.

The windows were wide open and she smelled the sea on the onshore wind as it gusted in and ruffled the tank top she wore, bringing with it the sound of generators somewhere in the distance and a siren.

Her desktop machine had been set back up on her desk, it's monitor neatly centered for her, all the cables carefully arranged and managed.

Useless, certainly. But the precision made Dar smile just from the respect it showed because those techs who had arranged the machine knew her attention to detail and didn't want to fail to show her they knew she'd note it.

And of course, she had noted it. Dar went to the desk and sat in the chair behind it. She regarded Carlos who had taken up a pose against the door sill. "Wish we could get a truck size generator and just run things here," she said. 'What a pain in the ass."

Carlos came over and sat on the couch against the wall, since Dar had no visitor chairs in her office. "Could we have?"

"They were all rented anywhere in the area by the time I looked," Dar said. "Lesson learned for next time. Either we get a generator truck, or we have a big one installed, like they did out on the island." She folded her arms as the sun came in the window and splashed across her shoulders, catching the inky darkness of her tattoo.

The squeak of rubber against the wooden floors sounded outside and then Arthur was in the doorway. "Another boat just got here," he reported. "And some cops. They yelled at us," he added. "They're probably going to come up here, they saw where we ran off to."

With a sigh, Dar stood up. "The boat's probably my dad. Let's go see what's going on now." She motioned the two to join her. "Cops probably think we're pirates."

"Yo ho yo ho!" Carlos rumbled. "Maybe we are!"

****

"What do you think?" Kerry stood on the sidewalk, her helmet in her hand, as they studied the scene ahead of them. The road had three lanes, and all three were blocked by a cascade of fallen trees, as well as stretches of murky looking water.

"Let's try going behind that mall," Mark suggested. He pointed to their right. "Gets us in the right direction, anyway."

Kerry regarded the path. "We're going to have to walk for a little bit. Too much stuff in the way." She started forward and stepped over a fallen stop sign as Mark came along behind her pushing the bike.

"Yeah." Mark eased the tires over the sign and then up and over the median. They sloshed through ankle high water and then off the road and through a half flooded parking lot. "Keep to the edge over there," he said. "Not sure what's in all that."

Kerry agreeably shifted her path to the left, threading between a car turned on its side and a garbage dumpster. The west edge they made their way along was relatively dry and for several minutes they walked along in silence.

Then a loud sound made them both stop in mid motion. Mark pushed the bike up next to where Kerry stood and they saw two men coming out of the back of one of the stores, carrying boxes. They jumped into the water and waded toward a pile of material on the northern side of the mall.

Mark got back on the bike and started the engine, the sound of it echoing sharply. The two men dropped the boxes waded faster.

"Maybe we should stay on this thing," Mark said, after a brief pause. "Kinda like when you're walking around in the glades, y'know? Make noise. Scares the snakes."

"Well, maybe they... "Kerry regarded the door the men had come out of. "No, they're probably not getting things to survive with at the Verizon store." She resumed her seat on the bike and they started forward slowly.

Mark shook his head and they wound their way through the loading area and squeezed between two turned over dumpsters, thankfully empty, into an alleyway that ran behind the mall.

There was around a foot of water in it. They took it slowly to keep the wake from swamping the bike's engine until they emerged into one of the smaller streets behind.

Here the larger roads split from commercial buildings to residential. As they rumbled carefully through the flooded ground they saw people on either side of them out and about, and the sound of chain saws was audible.

"What street is that?" Mark asked.

"Can't tell." Kerry could see where the street signs had been, but they were either blown off somewhere or under the deep water just to the north of them. "Look at those houses."

They were blown apart, as though a tornado had touched down and possibly it had. To the right, a man dragged a mattress out of a home that was missing a roof. He hauled it over and laid it on top of a half-submerged car.

"Is it like this where you live, Mark?"

"Not this bad," Mark said. "It's a lot more flooded here. We mostly had wind and stuff by us." He gunned the engine a little as they moved onto a less wet part of the road. "All the area we're in was rebuilt after Andrew. New codes."

They made it another three blocks before they found a street sign. "Let's try and go south from here." Mark navigated carefully around a stop light sitting in the middle of the road amidst a pile of cables and they found themselves on a two-lane street, full of downed trees.

Mark turned and they went south along the road, slowing where there were puddles that extended across the road, some splashing up over their boots. "Okay there, I think that's 96th." He said, after a few minutes silence. "Should be just west from there."

They slowly approached the intersection, which had a bus overturned in it, seemingly deserted. Mark steered around the bus and they had a view along the road, which had a median that was the only dry part. "Okay, I'm gonna have to go up on that," he said. "This thing ain't gonna make it through that water there."

"You want to stay here and I'll walk down?" Kerry asked.

Mark stopped, braced his boots, and then took off his helmet to turn and look at her.

Kerry also removed her helmet hastily; afraid she was missing something. "What?"

"What?" he said. "What what? As in what the what? You want me to hang out here and let you go into who the hell knows what?"

Kerry regarded him. "What do you think's going to happen? I'm not that short. I'm not going to drown in that water. It's only up to my knees."

They both then paused and chuckled. "C'mon, let's see how far we can get." Mark put his helmet back on and started up the bike's engine and then cautiously gunned it up onto the median that split the road in two.

Ahead, they could see a pair of fallen trees and past that, there was some activity going on. "You see those trucks?" Mark said. "I think they're army or something."

"Something," Kerry agreed. "National Guard maybe... and I see some flashing lights." She held on as they bumped over the swamped, grassy median, weaving around the posts and slim, planted trees, most of which were lying on their side.

They got to the fallen trees and then had to stop. Mark parked the bike and they got off. He set his helmet down on the seat and then started to break off branches to make space for them to pass.

Kerry took hold of a larger branch and tugged on it. She was standing in water up to her ankles, and the tree moved a little. It slid sideways and allowed her to see past it. "Ah." She paused and regarded the scene.

In the next large intersection there were, in fact, several National

Guard trucks and a tarp shelter. From the back of one of the trucks, water was being handed out to a line of people. Blockades were set up to prevent farther progress along the road.

The flooding past it seemed extensive. Where the trucks were it was up over the tires. Past it, along the roads, it was easily double.

"Holy crap." Mark had cleared enough room to come stand next to her. "Well, we're gonna have to stop here anyway."

"We are." Kerry admitted. "Let's go see what's going on."

They walked together, Mark guiding the bike through the water until they were across from the little encampment. They took off their helmets and shrugged out of their jackets, glad to be rid of them as even the hot breeze now felt cool. "Downside to bikes," Mark said.

"No kidding." Kerry riffled her sweat soaked hair, thankful for the feel of air against her scalp. She followed Mark as they walked off the end of the median into the flooded roadway. She grimaced as the hot, dank water soaked into the leather of her hiking boots and the cargo pants she wore.

There was a crowd gathered around the trucks and a buzz of conversation. The National Guard had set up a platform of boxes under the tent, so they were able to be dry-shod and the tarps kept the sun off a long table with radio equipment and papers on it.

The guardsmen and women who worked under it looked hot, and sweaty and most had wet uniforms up to their thighs.

One of the guardsmen stood a little way off, up to his knees in water, a satellite phone to his ear. "Look!" He said suddenly, audibly to them. "These people want to go into that area, and they're pissed!" He had a clear Southern accent.

Mark and Kerry eased through the crowd and paused. Kerry looked at the scenario, trying to decide where she might find some indication of who to ask questions of.

"Look, you can't go past here." The young man at the front of the platform said. "Ma'am, it's dangerous, and there's all kinds of chemicals and all in the water, you can't go."

The woman speaking to him was repeating what she said in Spanish. It was relatively obvious the young man had no idea what she was saying. Kerry herself could only catch a word or two. "Any idea what she's saying?" she asked Mark.

"Her house is back there," Mark pointed. "She was in Orlando when the storm hit, and she just got back here."

"See if you can translate for them." Kerry nudged him. "Yelling's not going to help anyone."

"Got it." Mark eased between the crowd and the edge of the platform. "Hola," he said. "Dime. Dime." He patted his chest. "Les dire."

Kerry went closer to the guardsman, as people started to raise their voices, anxiety and some anger audible. "Hi, my name's Kerry. What's the situation?" she asked him, quietly.

His shoulders relaxed in some relief, responding to both the clarity of her voice, and the calmness she projected. "Ma'am, are you a resident around here? These folks are trying to get back into the area, and it's just dangerous, you know?"

"I'm not actually but I have some staff who live here that I'm trying to find," Kerry said, "Where are you from?"

"Alabama," the young man said. "We just got here. Been driving most the night." He removed his cap and wiped the sweat off his forehead. "I don't speak that language those people are talking I guess."

Kerry nodded in sympathy. "I don't much either. My father-in-law's from Alabama." She smiled at him. "I thought I recognized the accent."

The guard got up and offered her a hand. "Ma'am, c'mon up here out of that water." he said. "Where is it your friends live at?"

Kerry accepted the help and stepped up onto the boxes and followed him over under the tarp to the table that held a street map. The group of guardsmen glanced at her as she came up, then went back to their work, accepting her presence without comment.

She studied the map, with her guard friend at her elbow. "Here, this is where they live." She indicated a set of streets. "I haven't heard from them and I'm really worried about them."

An older guardsman who had been talking to someone at the rear of the tarp came over. "That area's busted up pretty bad, ma'am," he said. "Most of the houses there are under water to the first floor." He glanced at the truck handing out water. "We can't go farther neither."

One of the men came over from the front of the platform. "Sir, these people just won't be reasoned with. Even with that fella's help. Is he a friend of yours, ma'am? I thought you came up together."

"He's a friend, yes," Kerry said. "So, what's being done for the people back there? I'm sure they need help, right?"

"Ma'am, there's nothing we can do right now," The older guard told her, with some exasperation, but not without sympathy. "We can't drive our trucks back in there, and we're not medics or nothing like that. They just sent us here with these tents, and some water."

Kerry paused thoughtfully, folding her arms over her chest. "Are they going to send in helicopters? I know you can't do anything, but is someone doing something?"

The man shrugged. "Our radios just talk to other folks like us." He indicated the set. "What's Miami-Dade doing? We got no idea," he said. "I heard they were setting up a command center downtown. Something like that. They just loaded us up with tarps, and some rope, and a whole bunch of water and told us to get out here as far as we could. So, we did."

"Absolutely you did," Kerry said. "Well, let me go see what I can do." She walked over to the edge of the tent and went back into the sun, pulling out her sat phone and patiently pecking at the small keyboard. She glanced up as Mark came over to her. "Cluster."

"Cluster," he agreed. "I get why everyone's upset but like, what are these guys supposed to do? They can't drain shit."

"They can't." Kerry said. "Hang on." She listened to the odd buzz that was the sat phone's ring and then it was picked up. "Dar?"

"Hi," Dar said. "What's up? Make it kinda fast cause Dad's explaining to the cops we're not burglars."

"Ah."

"I'm gonna have to go over and get my captain's license before they haul us off to jail," Dar said. "Get anywhere out there?"

"We got near their neighborhood but it's a nightmare here," Kerry said succinctly. "There's some guard trucks but it's all flooded and no one has any way farther. No plan to that they know of."

"Not good."

"No, and..." Kerry paused as she heard her name called. "Wait, hang on."

"Kerry! Kerry!" A slightly slurred, Latin inflected voice cut through the clamor and Kerry and Mark turned to see Zoe splashing her way through the water toward them, arms extended.

"Just found Zoe," Kerry said into the phone. "Let me call you back." She shut the phone in time to hop off the platform and accept the hug as Zoe reached them. "Zoe! Wow I'm glad to see you!"

Zoe looked exhausted, terrified, and overwhelmed. "Oh, Kerry, I am so glad you are here." She paused and then looked at Mark. "And you too!"

Mark just chuckled.

"It is terrible," Zoe said. "The road where Maria's and Mayte's house is, is so flood and no one can get to it. I think people are hurt there. My family's house is destroyed."

"Is your family okay?" Kerry asked. "Where are they?"

"They went out to the shelter, and we are all okay," Zoe said. "But Mayte and Maria and Tomas were not there." She drew a breath. "Have you call them?"

"We've tried. They haven't answered. That's why we came out here to see if we could find you all," Kerry said. "Now we have to figure out how we're going to go do that, because I didn't bring any scuba gear with me."

"I am just glad you are here," Zoe said. "My mama said you would do something. I tell her everything about all what you do, and she says you are better than the government."

Kerry looked around the woebegone scene, somewhat at a loss to know what to do in order to live up to that expectation. "Kind of a low bar right now."

"Too bad we don't have a couple jet skis," Mark said. "That'd do it. Better than my bike, anyway."

Kerry thought about that. "Too small really," she said. "But you know..." She glanced behind her at the National Guard troops. "I wonder." She turned around and got back up onto the platform, looking for and finding her young friend. "Hey..."

"Oh, hello, ma'am. Saw you found one of your friends," the boy said. "Sorry there's not much else we can do for you here."

"Well..." She eyed him. "You gig?"

Surprised, he blinked. "Uh... I mean, sure." He glanced around. "But I tell you, ma'am, I wouldn't be eating anything out of these here waters. No telling what's in there."

"Oh gosh no," Kerry said. "But I wonder if there are any guys around here that we could call on the radio that maybe have airboats. I bet they could get in there to help people, and we're out here kinda close to the glades, huh?"

He thought about it a moment. Then he nodded. "Done got a good idea there. Let me hook in the captain." He turned and trotted over to where the older man was talking to an agitated gray-haired woman.

"Okay," Kerry said, rejoining them. "Let's see where that gets us." She turned to Zoe. "Any other shelters around here they could have gone to? We can check those in the meantime." Her glance went around the street scene. "I don't think there's much else we can do here."

"Not much they can do either," Mark said. "That water's going fast."

****

"Sorry, folks." The police officer accepted the cup of coffee offered to him by Angela. "You have to admit it's not what we expect to see in all this kind of mess." He added. "Thank you, ma'am."

Angela smiled at him. "No problem, we've got plenty," she said. "The bosses make sure we're taken care of, y'know."

"I can see that." He smiled back at her. "That why you came to work?"

"Honestly?" Angela said, glancing around. "I knew they'd have their act together here. I just didn't want to stay at home and listen to everyone complain. There's no power, but things are getting done, you know?"

"That sure is true," the officer agreed. He looked around the conference room. There were boxes of supplies, most of which had been transferred off the boats that morning, and two long chests full of ice. "Too bad you don't have a generator here."

"We got one, we're just saving it for nighttime," Carlos said. "Everyone's going nuts trying to get gas for theirs. I heard that, and no power anywhere so not much gas around." He paused. "We got a few tanks in the back but it ain't gonna last forever. And Port Everglades closed."

The officer nodded. "Yeah, there's that. We got calls all morning seeing folks trying to break into service stations. No sense. How'd they think they were going to get gas out of those pumps with no power, I'm sure I don't know."

There were two other officers with him, and now they were all seated at the table in the conference room taking advantage of a moment to rest and consume coffee and some cookies.

"We just got a call from someone saying there were people looting along the shore here," the second officer said. "And you know, that's kinda what it looked like," he added. "With that ramp and all you made." He paused. "But you know we saw those boats and they're not really the pirate type, if you know what I mean."

"It's true," Carlos said. "But I told the boss that some old busybody'd call ya." He straddled a folding chair, his muscular arms folded over its back. "People ain't got enough to worry about they're calling the cops."

"Well," the first officer, whose breast bore a patch with the name Cruz on it, said. "Been a lot of reports of looting and all that already today. People getting out, breaking into stores and grabbing TV's and stuff." He dunked a cookie into his coffee and popped it in his mouth. "People take advantage, you know. We see that all the time."

Dar entered with a folder and took a seat at the head of the table. "Here's all the paperwork." She offered it to them. "For some reason, someone here thought someday someone would want to see physical copies of something we always keep in digital that we can't access right now."

She handed over the registration documentation for both boats, and a copy of their office lease. "Almost like someone was psychic."

"Probably Maria," Carlos said. "She keeps everything on paper. She says ya never know."

"Ya never do," Dar said, and rested her elbows on the table, then she reached out and took one of the chocolate Oreos and regarded it with a skeptical blue eye. She twisted the cookie apart and consumed the bare half.

The first officer took the folder and opened it. "Thank you, Ms. Roberts," he said. "I really appreciate the cooperation." He scanned through the papers, while the other two sat there quietly having their coffee and cookies. "Okay, this looks pretty straightforward."

Angela returned and set down a steaming mug in front of Dar. "We're fixing up some tuna fish sandwiches and Fritos in the break room."

"Yum." Dar removed the top off another cookie and ate it, then put the two non-eaten halves with their double crème together. "Kerry said they got out to the edge of Doral," she told Carlos. "Flooded to hell after that. But she found Zoe." She dunked the joined cookie into the milk and held it there for a few seconds before she removed it and put the whole thing into her mouth.

"Heard on the radio," Carlos said. "Least we can run that off that UPS. Ain't much good for nothing else right now." He rocked back and forth on the chair. "Glad Zoe's all right anyway."

Andy entered and pulled off a pair of hide gloves. His hair was wet and there was a faintly briny scent about him. "Lo there." He removed a plastic covered packet from his back pocket and put it down next to Cruz's elbow. "Got that off mah boat."

Cruz glanced at the packet, then he closed the folder and pushed it back toward Dar. "Here you go, ma'am. That's all right, sir." He picked up the damp plastic and offered it back. "I've seen enough for my report." He took a sip of his coffee. "Now I need to tell you, this is not going to be a really safe area after dark."

Carlos smiled. "Yeah, it was a little creeptastic last night," he said. "But we got a plan to bunker in. And the boss here's going to take some of the gang with her over to where they live."

"Where's that, ma'am?" Cruz asked.

"Fisher Island," Dar responded. "We have power out there."

"Oh yeah we heard." The police officer laughed a little. "That explains the boats, I guess."

"Got some fellers coming ovah here to keep an eye on," Andy said. "It'll be all right." He sat down next to Dar and folded his hands across his stomach. "That there case's ready to go, Dardar."

"Your crew is always welcome here to share what we got," Dar said to the officer. "We've got some sat phones."

"Ah got me a spare shortwave ahm gonna hook up to that big old battery fore we go," Andy added. "They can call the boat on it. These phones ain't hardly worth nothing."

Cruz laughed again. "Glad to see some people being self-sufficient," he told them. "Everyone else I saw this morning, walking through the streets was either running from me with a box or asking me for a handout."

He leaned back in the chair, apparently loathe to surrender it. "That's what I hate about these storms. Everyone comes out after looking to take advantage, taking whatever they can get. You're supposed to have three days of food and water in your house you know?"

"Some folks don't have the cash," Carlos said, bluntly.

"They can go to a shelter." Cruz shook his head. "And I don't buy people can't afford it. Cops don't make that much and I went to Costco and got two cases of canned stuff for my house, and it was twenty bucks. Hey, it's junk like SpaghettiOs, but it'll feed my kids." His jaw jutted forward a little. "My wife made the biggest pot she had of rice and beans. That probably cost two bucks."

"Wall," Andy said. "Folks are like that. Wanting to blame folks for e'vrything."

Cruz got up and motioned to his two companions. "That's the truth, but not here. I'll mark you all as friendlies and let the patrols know about your two boats out there." He grinned a little. "And they can stop by for cookies if they're around."

He winked at Angela, who had come in with some plates and set them on the table. She offered him one, but he declined, and they left with casual waves and words.

"Well, that turned out better than I expected," Dar admitted after they'd passed beyond hearing. "I wasn't much looking forward to dealing with you and I frog marched down to Miami Dade jail."

Andy laughed. "You evah been?"

"To the jail?" Dar asked. "Yes." She paused. "Busting someone else out of it," she conceded, as everyone swung around and gave her an interested look. "And they're actually a customer now. Got a new computer system going in," she added. "Anyway."

"Yeap," her father agreed. "Got them an attitude ah seen a time or two, them boys." He picked up the hide gloves, and flexed one big, scarred hand. "Glad they moved on."

"They weren't gonna mess with us," Carlos said, confidently. "They know better. Not after the boss said where you all live. Those guys know." His lips twisted wryly. "You'll be getting a call from the PBA after we get phones back I betcha."

Andy grunted. "Anyhow, let's get a move on that there box of yours." He got up and headed for the conference room door.

Dar stood up and pulled her sat phone out. "Let me go see what Ker's up to." She walked around the table. "Be right back." She ducked outside the front door and into the sunlight, walking away from the structure and into an open area before she tried to turn on the phone.

This was a pain in the ass. She recalled the phone number that Kerry had been carrying and dialed it. "When the hell are they going to get the damn cell towers back up?"

****

"How about you stay here?" Mark asked. "Me and Zoe'll see if we can go south a little and get to the Palmetto shelter. Maybe you can help these guys?"

Kerry pondered, regarding the shelter. In the short time they'd been standing there twenty or thirty more people had shown up, including a man with a child holding a broken arm.

The guardsmen were trying to help. One man knelt next to the child with a first aid kit, another was going around the crowd handing out plastic bottles of water.

Everyone was standing in knee high water, and Kerry could smell the muddy tang of it. She had retreated back to the median near where they'd left the bike and was for the moment dry shod. "Yeah, I guess."

Zoe would be more use to Mark when searching in the shelters as she was a native Spanish speaker. Kerry herself only understand and spoke a handful of words in the language but in truth she had no real desire to stay here, in the sun, with the muggy heat and the rising mosquitos around her.

But it was also true if they had to divide and conquer it was likely her who could encourage anything positive out of this particular situation. "Okay, you guys get going," She said. "Let me..." She paused as the phone in her pocket buzzed. "Ah."

She recognized the number that had originally been Dar's and had been handed off to Carlos. "Hello?"

"Hey."

There was something that Dar's voice did to her. Kerry half turned and focused on a clump of dead brush poking up out of the water. "Hey," she responded. "You're not calling me from the joint, are you?"

Dar chuckled, a low deep sound of amusement that was both wry and relaxed. "How's it going there?" she said. "I was trying to remember if we had any way of contacting any of Dad's friends who could help, but god damn it there's no signal anywhere."

"That's why I told them to try the radio," Kerry said. "No, nothing much here. Mark and Zoe are going to go check out Palmetto shelter, see if they were seen or heard of there." She watched the men on the platform huddle in a small group around the older man with the sat phone. "Dar, I hate to think of Mayte and Maria out there in some trashed house, in trouble. You know?"

"Is there something you can do?"

Kerry thought about that for a long moment, both of them silent and comfortable with it. "Crap I should be able to, shouldn't I?"

"Ker," Dar said, in a wry tone. "I know it's kinda normal for us to pull rabbits out of our asses, but there are limits to what even we can do."

"That sounds so damn reasonable, except I think about what we did in New York, and you saving that raft, and I'm sitting out here in this gross swamp wondering why I don't have a drone and a paddleboard with me."

Dar laughed softly. "You gonna drive the drone while you're on the paddleboard?" She asked. "Tricky. Let me see if I can get the... oh crap. That's right. All I have to drive is a yacht."

"I know. I'm being a dork." Kerry chuckled along with her. "Let me see if they're making any progress with the radio. I don't know what else to do, Dar. We can't go any farther west with the bike." She ran her fingers through her hair and pushed it back off her forehead. "Maybe I'll have Mark check that one shelter, then bring Zoe back to where her family is."

The faint sound of buffeting wind came through the phone as Dar turned and faced into the breeze in front of the office. "Let me think a minute."

Kerry was content to wait and watched a lizard appear on one of the nearby fallen trees, jerking it's head up and down. She glanced to the side as Mark came up next to her and raised one brow at him.

"They called the Red Cross for that kid," Mark said. "They're gonna maybe bring a chopper for him." He paused. "You talking to Dar?"

Kerry nodded. "Go on to Palmetto," she said. "I'm waiting to see if Dar has something else for me to try."

Mark nodded back. "Okay, we'll call if we find anything." He motioned Zoe to come over to the bike, and then handed her the helmet Kerry had been wearing. "Buzz me if you need me."

Kerry raised a hand in response as he started the bike's engine and Zoe timidly got herself arranged on the rear seat. She took a few steps away as Mark turned the machine around and started carefully back along the ridge they'd come in on.

They brought the young child, a dark-haired boy, up onto the platform and he sat on a box. His arm was now in a roughly made splint held on with white gauze that was stained rust with blood. His face was twisted in pain and an older woman crouched next to him.

"What about."

Dar's voice almost startled her. Kerry returned her wandering attention to the phone. "What about what, hon?"

"I know it's out of the way, but why not try to get out to US 27 and come into Sweetwater from the other side?" Dar suggested. "Get up on the Turnpike and off at Okeechobee road."

Kerry's brow creased a little. "Won't that be even more flooded?"

"Canals all drain out that way across the Everglades," Dar said. "Sweetwater's in a dip between the city and the swamp and you might find some folks with boats out there that'll be useful," she added, almost as an afterthought. "Airboats."

"Places out off 41. Yeah," Kerry said. "The tourist places, where you can take rides out. Dar, that's a good idea. I told them to try and find some airboats but these guys are kind of clueless here. They're from out of state."

"Well, it's something," Dar said. "Don't spend too much time out in the sticks there. It's lunchtime."

"I'm going to call Mark," Kerry said. "If they haven't gotten down to the shelter by now, I'll have him drop Zoe off and we'll go out that way." She felt a sense of mild relief. "Thanks, hon."

"No problem," Dar said. "I gotta go. They're starting to haul the servers out." She paused. "Be careful, okay?"

"Will do," Kerry said. "Any word from Colleen?"

"They're almost up there," Dar said. "She checked in about ten minutes ago."

Kerry hung up the phone and then dialed Mark's number. The sat phone buzzed, but there was no answer. She assumed they were underway and couldn't pick up. She closed the phone and put it in her pocket, and then she turned around and started for the platform.

****

"Okay stop it there a minute." Dar stepped back to consider their progress. They had gotten the rolling cart through the office yard and across the street and were now trying to maneuver it across the destroyed pool deck of the sailing club.

Carlos wiped his forearm across his forehead. "Crap it's hot."

"It is." Dar felt the sweat rolling down her back and was glad of the tank top. She straightened up and shook her hands out, tired from the effort of carrying the case down a set of four broken, coral stairs. "This is the hard part." She studied the rough terrain they had ahead of them.

Arthur took his shirt off and hung it from the back of his belt. "Yeah, at least over there we could roll it. We sure that ramp is going to hold up for this? I'd hate to have it sink after all that work." He sat down on an upturned bench and took a drink of water from the bottle in his shorts pocket.

Dar walked past him to the beachfront where the Dixie was tied up, and where Andrew's boat was anchored behind it, both boats shining white in the sun.

It was going to be a real bitch to maneuver the whole rig onto the boat. Dar folded her arms and took in a breath of salt-tinged air. Ahead of her, past the boats, she saw a dozen watercraft in the distance, three of which had flashing blue lights on them.

She was relieved to see that the chop had come down in the bay. It was light and ruffled, and the Dixie was only rocking a little bit against her lines. Still, her hull thumped against the inflated pontoons they'd draped over her side.

"Need a beach lander," Andy said as he joined her. "Some bitch," he said.

"Like the ferry, with a ramp," Dar agreed. "Well, we don't have one so let's just do this." She walked along the makeshift platform, testing its sturdiness. It was relatively stable under her weight, but Dar knew the case they were shepherding was an order of magnitude heavier.

She walked up next to the Dixie and stood there a minute, looking at the deck. "Tricky." She turned and motioned Carlos over, and watched both him and Andy come along the ramp. She kept an eye on the stability of the path. "Meh."

"What's the plan, boss?" Carlos asked. He'd also taken off his shirt. "You think we can make it down this?"

Dar glanced at her father. "You've got a hell of a lot more experience loading things on boats than I do."

Andy looked at the Dixie, then at the makeshift ramp, then at the case full of high-tech servers. He snorted a short laugh and shook his head. "Some bitch," he concluded. "Ain't got no idea if that there box'll make it all the way long this here thing and us not end up swimmin."

"Well. Is what it is." Dar extended her hands in a light shrug.

"True." Andy kicked the pylon with one booted foot. "Ain't gonna find out standing heah." He hopped up and down on the planking. "Be some easier if that back deck was other way round." He eyed Dar meaningfully. "Shorter."

"Got it." Dar agreeably untied the aft line and stepped onboard. "Get ready, and I'll turn her around."

Andy untied the forward line and tossed it onboard, then he motioned Carlos back toward the shore where the rest of the staff were seated. Sweating and waiting. "C'mon, boy," he said. "Let's get this heah done fore ever'body melts."

"Right on, sir," Carlos said, and followed after him. "Worst comes to worst we can all jump in and hope that case floats."

****

It was stifling under the tent but it was at least out of the sun. Kerry ignored the pungent smell of heated canvas as she climbed up out of the water and onto the wooden platform.

The young guard she'd befriended turned and saw her approach. The rest of the group he was with looked up as well but went back to leaning over a map on the makeshift plywood desk after a moment.

"Oh, there you are, ma'am," he said. "I thought you'd done gone off."

"My friends did," Kerry said. "They're going to look for our other friends at the Palmetto shelter." She put her hands into the pockets of her cargo pants. "What's your name?"

"Billy," he answered promptly. "Harris."

"I'm Kerry. So did they... I mean, are you all going to stay out here or...?"

Billy sighed. He took off his camo hat and wiped the sweat off his brow. "We don't know," he admitted. "I hear they're bringing in more supplies, but my cap'n there said the more they bring stuff in here the more people'll show up."

"Probably true," Kerry said. "And they'd have to bring in some kind of shelter. You can't stay here. The mosquitos will eat you all alive at night."

Billy nodded his head. "I done told him that. They need to get us one of those big bus things at least. With a big old battery like a RV, you know?"

"I do know. I've driven one." Kerry smiled; her ears pricked to listen into the conversation around the table. It wasn't particularly low pitched. "I went on vacation in the Grand Canyon. We drove there from here in one of them. It was cool."

"Let's just pack up and get out of here," Kerry heard the older man say, "We can't do anything useful. These people are just going to keep showing up wanting more than we got."

"He's right, sir." One of the women dressed in camo gear said. "We should be doing search and rescue, that's what we're trained for. Go over back into the city."

Billy also heard the conversation. "Just when we done setting up." He sighed.

Kerry studied the crowd. "But these people need help too," she said, quietly. "Someone has to."

"Can't go no farther," Billy said. "You see that water there."

They heard the sound of the chopper approaching, and two of the other guard called out to Billy as they moved away from the tent and started to clear a space. "Gotta go," he said. "You can stay up here until we're ready to pack. I know the cap'n don't mind."

Kerry did, in fact, remain where she was as she watched the guards, now grown to a group of six, push the crowd back gently as they made an open circle around the injured boy. She sensed motion to her right and turned her head to see the captain standing next to her. "Is there enough space?"

"Drop a basket," the man said. "Listen, Ms...." His brows lifted.

"Roberts," Kerry supplied.

"Ms. Roberts, there's not much you can do here. We're not having any luck contacting anyone around the area who can help, and we don't got the gear to go no farther in the wet there."

"Yes, I can see that," Kerry said. "We need some punts, or something. I'm hoping my friends got to a shelter. Everything back there looks like it's sunk." She glanced at the name patch on his chest, which said Dodge, J. "Captain Dodge? Thanks for letting me hang out on your deck."

The captain nodded his head as she spoke. "That's right," he said, then hesitated. "Billy done said you had family back where we come from." He looked briefly around with studied casualness. "I know some Roberts where I come from."

Kerry wasn't entirely sure where this was going. "My father-in-law's family still lives back there," she said. "His siblings... well, his brothers. His sister moved to one of the cities not that long ago."

"He wouldn't be one of old Duke's boys, now would he?" The captain's gray, steady eyes watched her face, with a slight, noncommittal smile on his face.

"Yes, he is," Kerry said. "He hasn't lived there in a long while though. He..."

"Went for the navy." The man now smiled more easily. "I do know the family. We go back a ways." He stopped speaking as the helicopter came to hover over the open space around the boy. "Let me go make sure this goes right."

He went to the edge of the platform, clapping one hand to his head to hold his hat in place as the downdraft from the rotors flattened everything underneath it.

The young woman had come to stand next to her. "That poor kiddie," she said. "We're going to find a lot more, for sure." She was roughly Kerry's height, and had curly auburn hair. "Command said they already knew they'd need to send the dogs in."

"Dogs?" Kerry asked.

"Cadaver dogs," the woman said, placidly. "Best thing to search with. I mean..." she hastily corrected herself. "Not at first, they'll send in the rescue dogs first. I mean... I know you're looking for some friends and all that."

Kerry felt at that moment, both nauseous and lightheaded as she considered the potential result of her search. The muscles in her jaw tightened.

"That was a crappy thing to say. Sorry," the woman said. "I've just done this before. You never really get used to it but you do know the drill."

"No, I know," Kerry said. "It's all right."

The captain came back over, and the sound of the helicopter began to fade away, the boy being hoisted up in the rescue basket with his tiny, terrified mother with him. "That's done," he said. "Betty, let's see about getting us packed up here. Ms. Roberts can come with us. She's family."

"Yes, sir," Betty produced a brief grin, then went back to the makeshift table and hauled a crate out from under it. She put it on top and started to pile things from the tabletop into it.

"I'd probably better stay here and wait for my friends to come back," Kerry said. "But thank you very much for the offer."

The captain smiled at her. "Ma'am, we can't leave you out here in this mess," he said. "We're not gonna go that far, just up into Doral and meet up with our main unit at the base there. Them friends of yours can get there easier than back here."

Kerry hesitated, regarding her surroundings. She really had no desire to stay out here with a gathering crowd that was a bit more agitated since all the water had been disbursed and there seemed to be nothing else forthcoming from the trucks.

She didn't feel really in danger of anything, but she also didn't think she could get anything useful done by standing around in water up to her knees either and the water level didn't seem to be going down any.

A loud and angry yell distracted them, and the captain turned, his hand dropped to the holstered firearm on his belt.

Two of the men in the crowd were grappling with one of the guard, who was trying to pick up empty boxes and put them back on the truck. Two of the other guardsmen started toward them and then a bunch more of the crowd surged forward. They reached out and grabbed for the boxes.

"They're empty!" The captain called out. "Stop! Stop it! There's nothing left!"

The voices were rough and mostly Hispanic, with a few interjections of the sounds Kerry knew was Creole. She felt at a loss and helpless. Without anything else to offer she went to the table and helped Betty pack up.

"That's gonna end in a bad way," Betty said. "Let's get going." She picked up one end of the box and Kerry grabbed the other end. They moved the crate off the table as one of the guards picked up the piece of plywood and lifted it over his head, throwing it into the back of the truck.

"Fall back!" The captain yelled. "Get in the truck. We're moving out. Jack, leave them the damn boxes. They're empty and these idiots don't speak enough English to understand me."

Kerry hastened along the edge of the platform with her burden and then stepped down off it into several inches of stinking mud between the platform and the truck. She helped Betty lift it up and slide it into place, then before she could react, she was grabbed around the waist and lifted up into the truck herself.

Three soldiers vaulted into the back of the truck after her, and the captain let out a whistle. "Jack, get rolling. Go east! C'mon!"

Kerry caught her balance as the truck jerked into motion and Billy landed next to her on the bench that served as a seat on either side of the middle cargo area. "Where are we going?" She asked, more than a little rattled.

"Southcom," Billy said. "Least they got cold water and hot coffee there, we done heard."

Southcom. Southcom. "Oh, okay. I know where that is." Kerry felt a sense of relief. "I'll just call my friends when we get there. It's probably a better path for them to pick me up anyway." She braced her mud-covered boots against the floor of the truck and held on.

Captain Dodge had a seat on the other side of her, and he reached out and patted her knee. "You just stick with us, ma'am. No sense you staying out here in the muck."

Kerry smiled, and folded her hands.

Chapter Six

Dar stood at the controls, her head turned to look over her shoulder as she popped the engines in and out of idle to keep the Dixie in place as the team literally manhandled the large pelican case down off the dock and onto the wooden ramps they'd built.

There were seven people there working on the case. Carlos and his two buddies provided the real horsepower, their bodybuilder physiques glistening with sweat in the sun.

Arthur and Elvis, the two programmers were there, but they were both slight and slim and mostly of use in climbing around the case to keep it straight on track. Celeste their old security guard from ILS was helping them, and Andrew was in the water, directing the action.

Dar felt a little unsettled, torn between a desire to be down there with her team at this difficult task, and knowing she was without a doubt the person who needed to drive the Dixie here in the tight quarters of the half-destroyed dock.

Andy hung by one hand off the makeshift dock. He pointed with his other hand where to bring the edge of the case. "All right. Bring that there end ovah here. Watch out ovah there don't step on that there edge."

"Got it." Arthur caught his balance as he almost fell off the other side of the repurposed aluminum door. He inched around the edge of the case and tugged it forward. He pivoted the front end around to where Andy had indicated.

"Push," Carlos told the nearer of his two buddies. "Yeah, get it … yeah." They shoved the case along the planking toward the end of the ramp, where the Dixie idled just out of reach.

Andy turned his head toward the boat and raised the volume over the engines "Dar!".

"Yeah?" Dar answered. She craned her neck so she could see her father's dark head at the waterline. "What?"

"Back on in here," Andy said. "Squitch by squitch now!"

"Easy for you to say." Dar shifted into reverse, one hand toggling the two throttles that controlled the big inboard engines as the Dixie eased toward the shore. The current pulled against the bow and it was hard to keep the big boat straight as she slowly approached the dock.

The rumble of the engines covered the sound of wood cracking, but Andy heard it and he turned quickly in the water. "Hey!" He let out a call of warning. "Y'all look out there!" He shifted his grip as the wood planking moved. The pylon cracked and collapsed under the weight of the case. "Oh lord!"

"Whoa!" Carlos let out a yell of alarm, as the case started to tip. It leaned over on one side toward where Andy hung on. "Grab it! Hey! Look out! Watch out!"

Dar heard the commotion and leaned to one side to look along the port side of the boat. "Oh crap." She saw the case shift and start to slide toward the water as the planks tilted and twisted as the team tried to grab hold of it.

"Dad! Move!" Dar hollered, her hands freezing on the controls until she saw her father's tall form disappear under the surface of the water and then she gunned the engines, swinging the back end of the boat around and under the edge of the dock as the case turned and tumbled with everyone scrabbling for it. "Let it go!"

"But..." Arthur protested.

"Let it Go!" Dar bellowed, only barely keeping the back end of the boat from collapsing the makeshift ramp.

Carlos released the handle but lost his balance and went into the water. The rest of the helpers scrambled for hand and footholds as they let go, reeling to keep their balance. Celeste sat down abruptly and grabbed the edge of the door.

The big case hesitated, and then fell off the ramp in a rush and onto the back deck of the Dixie. It tipped sideways and then back as it hit the diving well and tilted toward the surface of the ocean. "Oh crap," Dar muttered. "Wasn't what I wanted that damn thing to do."

Her mind was already going through the steps of dropping the anchor and whether she'd refilled her dive tanks, but a second later, Andy emerged from the water and launched himself up and over the gunwale. He grabbed hold of the edge of the case and hauled it backward to keep it in place.

A ragged cheer came from the team watching on shore.

Andy braced his boots against the lip on the back deck and leaned forward a little, booting the dive ladder into the water. "C'mon here, boy!" He yelled to Carlos.

Carlos swam through the water, keeping clear of the engine wash. "Okay?" He eyed the churn of the diesels warily.

"C'mon," Dar called out. "Just grab the ladder!"

Carlos swam forward and did, hanging on as Dar shifted out of idle and the Dixie surged forward. It brought her stern away from the rocks on the shore that had been washed with her engine outflow. They'd been so close. The edge of the hull brushed the dock and made it sway crazily, nearly throwing the team on it into the water.

"Crap." Dar adjusted the throttles. She got the bow out and ahead of the dock. They were clear, so she put the engines back into idle. "Carlos! Get on!" She yelled, as the boat drifted out a little from the shore and into the bay.

"Oh boy!" Carlos climbed up the ladder and into the well, getting his weight against the case as he helped Andy tip it onto its end. "Holy crap, pops!" He said. "That was nutzo!"

"Yeap." Andy glanced around. "Need me some rope," he muttered. "Put you a dent in this here fiberglass, Dardar!" He called out, as Dar maneuvered the Dixie back around to bring her bow to the shore again.

"I'm going to drop anchor and give you a hand," Dar said. She felt the rumble as the heavy device dropped from its housing and plunged into the lightly chopped water, and then pulled taut as it hit the bottom and the Dixie swung against the current and held.

Dar waited until she was sure the boat wasn't going anywhere, and then went to the ladder. She put her hands on the railing and let her body weight take her downward in a rush that ended with her boots on the deck.

"Get me a rope," Andy said, as he and Carlos kept their grip on the case and kept it tilted toward the cabin. "Tie that to this here thing here."

Dar reached into the deck box and removed a coil of rope. "Let's get everyone onboard and see if we can get it out of the well and onto the deck." She tossed the rope out to uncoil it and then fed the end of it through the handle on the case and tied it into a neat knot. "It's waterproof but I don't want to test having it ride back with my prop wash a foot up over it."

She ran the rope over the edge of the well to a deck cleat and secured it.

"Stay there," Andy told Carlos as he released his hold and went to the box. He removed another rope and repeated the tie down on the other side. "All right."

Carlos cautiously let go of the case and then straightened up. "Whoof."

Dar came over to inspect the case. It was tilted on one edge, the ropes holding it against the low wall that separated the diving well from the back deck. She could see the dent her father mentioned where the edge of the case must have impacted when it fell.

"Nice catch, boss," Carlos said.

"I was lucky I didn't take out the dock with you all on it," Dar responded, with a brief wry grin. "Okay, let me get her back in there and give Kerry a call to see if she's on her way back here so we can get this thing back to the island before something else happens."

****

"You're where?" Dar's voice came through the phone with a full compliment of disbelief attached. "At the what?"

"Long story," Kerry said. "I couldn't get hold of Mark and the guard was pulling out. They offered me a ride and it was that or stay in the middle of that flooded area with a lot of pissed off people." She glanced around. "That was a no win situation, hon."

"Holy crap," Dar said. "Let me see what we can do to come get you."

"I'm fine. This whole place is crawling with National Guard," Kerry said. "They've got power here at least, and I got a hot cup of coffee. I tried to call Mark again but he's not picking up."

"These sat phones suck."

"Well, hon." Kerry took a sip of her coffee. She stood in the shade of a large block concrete building that sprawled along a flooded street. "A lot of things suck right now."

The front grassy area was covered in water, but it was not enough to stop the military trucks who were driving in and out. There were men and women moving in all directions, most carrying boxes and crates and sloshed through the shallow flooding.

The building had a large wall on the outside, and a guarded gate and the front door she was standing near was six feet above the water, up a set of cracked and weathered concrete steps. "Anyway, just wanted to let you know where I was. I'm going to see if I can talk anyone into giving me a ride back down there and keep trying to get hold of Mark."

Dar sighed unhappily. "I've got a rack full of servers tied to the back of the Dixie probably melting in that case."

"Go on and get those servers over to the island," Kerry said. "I'm pretty sure I can get someone here to ride me back over to the office. They have to be patrolling there too, right? Might as well have one of us doing something useful since I utterly tanked at finding out about our people."

"You found Zoe."

Kerry cleared her throat. "She found me, hon.'"

"You were in the right place."

Kerry gave the sat phone an affectionate look.

There was a deep rumble of generators behind her, and she heard the air handlers cycling on, cooling down the building. There were more guard trucks arriving every few minutes and in the distance on the other side of the building she could hear a helicopter firing up. "They're using this as a staging area. Sorry about the noise."

"Figures," Dar said. "Are you sure it's okay, Ker? I hate thinking of you stuck out there alone."

Kerry smiled. "Hon, I'm in the middle of like a thousand soldiers. I'm fine. I'll meet you back at the office. Give you a call when I get there, and you can come pick me up."

"Hmph."

Dar didn't like the idea. Kerry knew from the tone of the grunt. "Okay? I know you want to get our satellite office going." She paused. "Even without an actual satellite."

"Yeah, okay." Dar finally said, with an audible sigh. "Anyway, we managed to get the case onto the back deck, but it took a fall in the process. No idea if the damn things'll work when we get them powered up," she said. "If they don't, I'm going to just head back over there with the gang, and we'll meet you."

"Deal," Kerry said. "Drive safe, hon. Let me get off. I see a call coming in. Maybe it's Mark."

"Okay. Call me if he's got any issues."

"Will do." Kerry hung up the line and took the incoming one. "Hello?"

"Colleen here," her friend and their finance director said. "We just got up here to the space and glad I am to have air-conditioning and power back. I will tell you that."

"Hey, Col." Kerry smiled. "Glad you got there. Everyone okay?"

"Fine as rain," Colleen said. "We're going to get things set up, and then turn our admin phones on. You want anything forwarded or should we just take your messages, you and Dar?"

"Messages." Kerry answered at once. "Otherwise it's just going to be a mess, because these sat phones only randomly work."

"Got it and will do," Colleen said. "How's it going at the office?"

Kerry glanced around at her surroundings. "They got the servers on the Dixie. Jesus only knows if they're going to work," she said. "Dar's on her way back to the house with them now."

"Good luck then, lassie," Colleen said. "Give all me regards and I'll have my fingers crossed they at least get the cellular towers back up there."

Kerry hung up and pondered the controls of the phone, then she dialed Mark's number again. It rang several times, but again, there wasn't an answer.

She cursed under her breath and then shut the phone down and put it into her pocket.

****

Dar regarded the back deck of the Dixie for a long moment and rubbed the edge of her thumb over the keypad on her phone. She stood on the dock and felt a touch indecisive about what to do next.

Carlos and his buddies had gone back up to the office, using the hose near the loading dock to rinse the salt water off their skin.

The programmers sat on the boat in the deck chairs, sucking down bottles of iced tea from the Dixie's compact kitchen. Angela had just come over the rise with a basket along, with Celeste.

Andy had just swum over to his own boat and hoisted himself up onto the back deck of it. He was making the vessel ready to go, and Dar lifted her hand to give him a wave as he appeared at the side facing her.

"Okay." She turned as the approaching women got to the ramp. "All aboard," she said. "Let's see if we can get the gear up and running and the office set up before Kerry gets back."

"Right you are, boss." Angela looked pleased. "Glad I can be a help, you know? I hoped I'd get to go with you." She eyed Dar hopefully.

Dar waved her forward. "G'wan get on. You too, Celeste. We need all the help we can get."

"Right you are, Ms. Roberts." Celeste grinned. "I'd be glad to. There's nothing at all we can do over at the ILS office. Jerry went over there, and it's blocked off due to all that damage. No one's allowed inside. He came back and told us and he's going to help out Carlos."

Dar nodded, and followed them over to the hastily braced end of the dock and then onto the deck of the Dixie, pausing only to untie the ropes holding the boat to the shore.

As Dar stepped onto the deck, she felt the boat move and start drifting. She quickly dodged around her passengers and got to the ladder up to the bridge. She climbed up and went to the controls, perching on the edge of the captain's seat as she pressed the starters for the engines.

The inboards caught and started up and she reversed the boat back from the shore until she had enough clearance to swing the bow around and face the east. Ahead of them, Andy was already underway, moving cautiously through the debris field and into the channel.

"Can we come up there?"

Dar looked at the ladder. "Sure," she called down. "Better do it now before I have to maneuver."

Arthur and Elvis came up immediately and went over to the console. They looked at the controls with avid curiosity.

"This is a nice boat," Arthur said.

"Thanks." Dar checked the depth sounder and looked at the bottom outline. She turned the Dixie out from the shore and into the marked channel ahead of them. There were dozens of boats out on the water now, mostly police and military, but a few pleasure craft out to see the damage.

The breeze picked up as she gave the engines a little nudge, and then they crossed the bay in Andy's wake, heading back across the water toward the shipping channel.

"What's all the stuff down there?" Elvis asked, pointing at the lower deck. "The tanks and all that?"

"Scuba," Arthur answered for her. "It's cool you have your own stuff. Me and my dad are certified, but we rent ours all the time."

"We go out on the weekends sometimes," Dar said. "Or when we go down to our place in the Keys. Faster if you have everything. There's a compressor at the marina, and down by our cabin."

"That's cool," Elvis said. "My dad has a Skidoo. We take it out sometimes. "

"What's he doing with it right now?" Dar asked, thoughtfully.

"Riding around looking at all the storm stuff. He brought some animals out of the flooding already," Elvis said. "I bet he's the most popular guy in the neighborhood right now." He paused, considering. "Bet he's raking it in too. Buck a ride or something."

"Wish I had a couple of them," Dar said. "Kerry's out west trying to get over to where Maria and Mayte live. It's all flooded. She can't get past the turnpike and twelfth and apparently the National Guard showed up with tents and trucks."

"Need some airboats," Arthur said. "That's what my dad said before. He saw on the news all those people were floating around on wood debris and stuff. Cars all flooded, houses all flooded. What a huge ass mess."

"They live out there in Sweetwater," Arthur said. "Mayte showed me pictures of her house. It's nice. All full of flowers and things in the front and a garden."

"We've been out there. It's a nice neighborhood," Dar said, adjusting the throttles a little as they went past the bridge. "We can't get hold of them."

"That's what Mark said. Hope they find a way out there," Arthur said. "That whole area got trashed. Did they stay in their house or go to a shelter?"

"We don't know." Dar admitted. "I think they said they were going to stay in their house, but crazy as it got... not sure I would have."

Arthur blinked at her. "But you did."

Well, that was true enough. Dar adjusted one of the throttles and peered at the depth finder. "We figured it would be as safe as anywhere. You'll see when you get there."

They turned into the shipping channel, on the cargo side that would take them up along Terminal Island, and then across the short channel that separated it from the island. Dar picked up the speed a little and kept a sharp eye on the depth gauge.

The engines roar made more conversation difficult, and so the two programmers went over to the table behind the console and sat down, content to watch the passing scenery as the drone of the engine rose around them.

Dar's radio crackled. "Dixie, Dixie. C'mon back," Andy's low, growly voice emerged.

She lifted the transmitter. "Dixie. Go ahead."

"Got me an idea. Pull up into the service bay at the front there when we get by," Andy said. "Got them a boat lift," He added. "Haul that big old box up out to the dock."

"Roger that," Dar agreed at once. "Great idea. Not sure if the cart can handle the weight. I probably need to bring the truck around."

"Yeap," Andy said. "Ce'pt some of them roads on there are still blocked up."

The radio crackled. "I heard that," Ceci's voice interrupted. "Where are your keys? I'll drive that thing over the backs of these wingnuts here still arguing about that flooded golf course."

Dar chuckled in reflex, glad they had set up the marine radios that were proving far more reliable than any other technology so far. "In the stone dish on the kitchen counter," she said. "We're still about twenty, thirty minutes out from docking."

"That'll give me enough time to stop by the club and grab some box lunches they claim they have ready." Ceci sounded satisfied. "Be there in a jiff and oh by the way, they got amateur hour TV rolling from the security building. Funniest thing you ever saw, got a camera pointed at the radar and everything on an in-house channel."

"Nice."

"Lord."

****

Kerry walked down the hallway, its surface covered in nondescript gray weave carpet that matched the mostly nondescript gray walls.

Like all the government buildings she'd ever been in, this one smelled of linoleum polish and bureaucracy. Like places she could remember since childhood she heard the sound of an old-fashioned telephone ringing somewhere along with the clatter of a typewriter.

Randomly, she wondered if someone wasn't just playing that into the PA system somewhere, an MP3 track like one of Halloween noises. "Government background soundtrack." She said, under her breath, as she turned a corner and went into the large open conference room where the National Guard leadership was camped.

Here there were televisions on rolling carts, and several on the wall, a bank of wired telephones, a lot of men and women in fatigues. Against the wall, boxes of water.

People walked in and out in Army and Navy uniforms as well, and Kerry saw her new friends from the edge of Doral. They were over near one corner where there were folding tables set up in a large square, and laptops where information was, she supposed, being collected.

Billy saw her and trotted over. "There you are. So, where did you say your friends lived?"

Kerry promptly provided Maria's address, and followed him over to where the woman who had been at the table in the tent typed into a keyboard.

The woman looked up and gave her a brief smile of welcome. "Nice to be back in the AC."

"It is." Kerry didn't deny it. She sat down on a folding chair next to the table as Billy took a seat behind one of the laptops and typed into it himself.

"Stupid system is slow as hell," He commented.

Kerry wisely kept her mouth shut and didn't offer an opinion. The last thing in the world she wanted to get entangled with at this moment was a government computer system that possibly needed some kind of technical adjustment.

And then the nerd kicked in. "I guess you guys are using satellites," She said casually. "They are slow."

Billy glanced at her, and then other woman did too. "You know something about it?" He asked.

"More than I want to right now," Kerry admitted. "But at least you have satellite backhaul. Everyone else is kinda stuck." She leaned back in her folding chair and took a drink of her coffee. "Wish we'd thought to have a dish put on the roof."

Billy went back to his screen. "Okay. That area's totally underwater." He wiggled aside in his seat and turned the screen so she could see it. "See here? It's about five to six feet of water."

"Holy crap," Kerry said. "That's like a swimming pool."

"It is," the woman agreed. "That's why we had to get out of there. Ain't nothing we could do."

Kerry regarded the screen, then she looked at the two young soldiers. "So, what are they going to do?" She asked. "I mean... there are people there trapped, aren't there? I saw video of people sitting on top of their roofs."

Billy shrugged. "Wait for the water t'go down," he said. "I heard the Cajun Navy's coming over, but it'll take time for that. Some places, I guess they can bring choppers in like we did for that boy, but not with all them trees."

The woman nodded. "They're getting some pole skiffs from Orlando," she said. "Maybe down here by tomorrow."

Kerry sighed. "I'm just worried about my friends," she said. "Let me go try and... "She paused. "Figure out what to do." She got up. "Thanks, I really appreciate the info."

She walked through the room and headed for the door, aware in her peripheral vision of the captain trotting after her.

****

Andy already had his boat tied up to the maintenance dock by the time Dar maneuvered into the narrow channel.

Two of the ferries were tied up there, relatively unscathed, but the docking area where the third of the three of them would usually have been was empty. Andy had tied up at the front of that space, leaving the rear part of it, with its hoist, for Dar.

As Dar eased in, she saw the dockmaster, Jack, and two of the marina staff come out of the hut near the end of the dock area, wiping their hands with some paper towels. The dockmaster lifted his hand and waved casually at her, indicating the cleats on the pier nearby.

Jack walked over to the side of Andy's boat as he stepped off, and they started to speak with each other. The other staff waited on the pier for Dar to come alongside.

"Can we help with anything?" Arthur asked. He came over to stand next to the controls.

"There's rope on the front deck there." Dar indicated with a tilt of her jaw. "If you want, go grab it and toss it to the guy on shore."

Arthur retreated down the ladder, with Elvis right behind him. Then he climbed up onto the side walkway and made his way along the cabin to the front of the boat.

Dar positioned the Dixie up against the pier and waited for the lines to be secured, and then she shut the engines down. She then climbed down the ladder and arrived at the deck as the door to the cabin opened and the rest of her passengers appeared. "Okay. Let's see what we can do with this thing."

"We're here?" Angela asked.

"More or less," Dar replied, and stepped up onto the gunwale. "We stopped here to get the servers hoisted off." She crossed to the dock as Jack and Andy came over to her. "Think we can do it?" she asked, as Arthur and Elvis climbed up after her.

"Hi, Ms. Roberts," Jack said. "Whatcha got there?" He regarded the large, long case on the back deck. "Looks like a coffin."

"Big box of IT gear," Dar said. "We have to get it over to the cottages. We rented the big one near the club."

"Oh yeah," Jack said. "I heard all about that. Got in ahead of some other folks and they were roaring." He glanced past her. "Get the lift down to get that box up, willya, Sam?" He said. "They should be done clearing the roadway so's Mrs. R can get you all's truck over," he added as an aside to Dar and Andy. "Heard you on the radio. S'how I knew you were heading in here."

"Sure." Sam unhitched the cradling gear and stepped onto the dock. "You ladies want to get inside there, or up on the pier? I don't want you to get hit with nothing." He was a tall, well-built man with a silver-gray crew cut, and tattoos up the length of one arm.

"Probably need all of us to move it. It's heavy," Arthur said. "Took all of us to get it down to the boat and then it almost fell in the water."

Sam nudged the case, then bent over and gave it a shove. "Oh boy," He straightened up. "Thanks for warning me. Jose, go grab the rest of the gang inside there wouldja, if they're done with the tree?"

"Sure." Jose hopped ashore and jogged over toward the shack.

"Had a tree come down across the driveway," Jack explained to Dar and Andy. "We were in the middle of chain sawing it into chunks and moving it out of the way."

"They have a lot of customers for the rest of those villas?" Dar asked. "I didn't figure they would, since we didn't have much damage that I could see." She frowned a little. "Thought they'd be glad of some income for the thing."

Jack snorted a little. "Not folks here, folks on the mainland who want to sleep on those fancy sheets," he said. "Friends of friends, you know what I mean?" He eyed her. "You know what I mean. The mayor's a buddy of someone out here, and he wanted some place for the feds to stay."

"Jackassery," Andy said.

"Pretty much," Jack said. "Like all the rest of it. I've had about up to my eyebrows with it this past week." He put his hands on his hips and exhaled, visibly frustrated. "One guy was giving me a hard time for coming over to get lunch."

"One of them folks with their boats sunk?"

"You got it." Jack nodded at Andy. "I told him one more hour of it soaking ain't gonna matter."

Dar grinned wryly. "Then we show up." She indicated the Dixie.

"You have never been a problem," Jack said, bluntly. "You and your family are nothing but good people, and there's no one on staff here'll say otherwise." He indicated the group of men who trooped around the corner of the shack heading toward the dock. "Glad to help you out here."

A moment later, Dar's truck pulled around on the service road and crunched to a halt near the lift, the driver side window down and Ceci's silver blonde head poking into view. Andy went over to the car and leaned against it, catching his wife up on the details.

Dar glanced around her, at the service docks that seemed mostly intact. "Doesn't look too bad back here."

"No," Jack agreed. "No one wants to live on this side. Got views of the cargo ships going in and out mostly. They all want to live on the east end, and the south. South got the worst of it."

"I saw."

"Hey." Jack looked at her. "True you fixed the cams? I heard that in the mess there." He indicated the shack. "Sam said you went in there and sorted them out."

"That shouldn't surprise anyone," Angela spoke up. "Everyone knows Ms. Roberts is a computer genius."

Dar frowned. "Someone tried to mess around with it." She half shrugged. "I just rolled it back. Wasn't that complicated."

"Whatever it was, it made em happy." Jack grinned at her. "They're just glad they don't have to foot patrol in the heat and I don't blame em. Some of those guys were working all night and they just let them come over for some chow about an hour ago."

Dar put her hands in her pockets, cocking her head slightly to one side. "Why not just feed everyone up at the mansion? It's not like its fancy food. It was something like hamburgers and mac and cheese."

"No mingling," Jack said. "You know how it is."

"Give me a damn break," Dar said. "We're in the middle of a natural disaster. They should grow the hell up." She turned and stepped back onto the deck of the Dixie and climbed down onto the back deck and walked over to help Pete lift the edge of the box to slide one of the canvas lift straps under it.

Jack watched for a moment, a faint, wry smile on his face. Then he hitched his belt up and stepped onto the deck of the Dixie, pulling a pair of worn leather gloves out of his back pocket and fitting them onto his hands. "Move over guys."

"Hold on there." Andy ambled over to join them. "Cec, back that there truck up around ovah theah." He got down into the deck and wiped his hands on his cargo shorts. "Least ah didn't hear no parts moving round."

"Let the cradle down!" Pete called up to the dock. "Need more slack."

"Want me to drive that back around, Mrs. R?" Arthur asked Ceci. "My dad has a truck like this one," he added. "It's a pig to turn around."

"Sure, kid, have at it." Ceci willingly opened the door to the vehicle and hopped out. "Angela, let's go see if we can find a drink in there. These guys are gonna need it." She led the way over to the nearby shack. "How'd you do?"

"It's a mess," Angela said. "Glad I'm here. Specially over here, though they had a nice little setup at the office. And with Carlos around I wasn't worried about being where we were."

"I just bet." Ceci chuckled. "And who's this?" She asked, as Celeste joined them.

"Hello, Mrs. Roberts," Celeste said. "You don't remember me. I work security at the ILS building. I remember when they brought that cake in you did for Kerry. I'm Celeste Cruz," she said. "I live in Coconut Grove. A few of us thought we'd stop by and see how you all were doing."

Ceci regarded her. "Welcome back then! C'mon." She led the way forward. "The more the merrier."

****

Kerry was already at the door before the captain caught up with her. She slowed reluctantly as he called out her name. "Oh, hey." She took a step back from pushing the outer door open and turned. "Something wrong?" She asked. "I didn't leave anything back there I don't think."

"Oh no! Nothing's wrong. Just wanted to see if there was anything we could do for you," Captain Dodge said. "My name's Jerry, by the way." He held out a hand. "Don't think we proper met back there."

Kerry returned the grip. "I'm just going out there to use the phone." She held up the device. "Get hold of my friends and have them come pick me up."

"Where's home? Where you trying to get to?" He pushed the door open and they went outside into the hazy sun and nearly breathtaking humidity. "Whoa." He took off his glasses and rubbed them with his shirt. "Fogged that right up."

"Yeah, it's crazy hot." Kerry picked up the faint sound of angry voices some distance off. "Anyway, our office is over in Coconut Grove," she said. "That's where we're all gathered. I live out on Fisher Island, though. Near the Coast Guard station."

The name meant nothing to him, and he just nodded. "So, you all went to that big shelter, right? The basketball stadium? Why don't you let me get you a ride back down there? Meet your friends," he said. "East, we got plenty of patrols."

"If someone's going that way, I'd love a ride," Kerry said. "Figure out what to do next to find our people out there in Sweetwater." She stuck her hands in her pockets. "Go find someone with a jet ski maybe."

"I got ya." He smiled at her. "You hang on here a minute and make your phone call. I'll see what we can cook up," he said. "Did they do a lookup for ya inside?"

Kerry nodded. "No record of them, but their house is definitely in the flood zone. I hope they just went to a shelter."

"Sit tight." The captain went back inside the building, releasing a puff of cold, dry air into the heat that almost drew her back after him.

She sighed, though, and went over to stand under the overhang, one edge of it ripped and damaged but providing a bit of shade as she got out the sat phone and tried Mark again.

No answer. She folded the phone and crossed her arms as she breathed in the moist, warm air. She felt the sweat gather under her shirt, and was aware of being a little hungry, and more than a little frustrated.

She suspected the captain would get her a ride. Which was great, but it didn't help her find Mark or Zoe. She wondered if they were back where she'd last seen them, hunting for her. Should she ask the nice Jerry if he'd arrange to have her taken back there?

No. Kerry reluctantly sighed. The guard was here to help people, not escort her around South Florida searching for a guy on a motorcycle. "We should have stuck together," she said aloud. "We're so damn used to cell-phones working."

The loud voices grew louder, and she saw figures behind two parked trucks. Since nothing was coming to mind, she walked in the direction of the sound and came up next to one of the trucks. Three men behind it faced off against one other man with his hands spread out to either side of him.

Definitely a situation to avoid and so naturally Kerry stayed right where she was and listened, ready to stick her nose in when the opportunity presented.

The three were soldiers, in muddy fatigues with sweat stains across their backs and down each side. The single man facing them was in jeans and a T-shirt, with a thatch of thick black hair and a lean rangy body.

"Look, I just want to talk to someone," the black-haired man said. "Don't be such douchebags."

Kerry leaned casually against the truck, wincing a little as the heat of the metal hood penetrated the light material of her shirt. She remained there though, crossing her ankles as she punched in another number into the phone and held it up to her ear.

"We told you, get the hell out of here, buddy," one of the soldiers said. "We don't want your kind mooching around."

"My kind?" The man repeated. "What the fuck is that supposed to mean? Who the hell do you think you are, you plastic ass GI Joe?"

The phone rang through to the message service. "Mark, give me a call," Kerry said quietly into the phone. "I'm not where you left me."

"Shut the fuck up."

"Get your hands up, jackass. Let's see who's plastic. I'll put this plastic right up your ass."

Kerry folded up the phone and pushed off the side of the truck. She turned and walked around the other end and stopped short as she came upon the group of them. "Oh!" She called out loudly. "What on earth's going on here!"

One of the soldiers had his fist wrapped in the dark-haired man's shirt, his other fist drawn back. A second soldier had his sidearm drawn, and the third had just been moving to grab the black-haired man's arm.

They all froze at her exclamation and the man closest to her spun around and threw his hands up in surprise as the rest just turned their heads.

"Sorry." Kerry gave them all a smile. "Didn't mean to interrupt anything..." She put the sat phone in her back pocket. "You all okay?"

The soldiers were young. The dark-haired man was too, maybe early twenties. One of the soldiers still had peach fuzz. Kerry felt slightly ancient as she strolled toward them. She put her hands into her front pockets in a casual move.

"Oh. Uh." The closest soldier to her let his hands drop. "Sorry, ma'am. Are you...? "He looked around, clearly surprised to find her there. "Um..."

The other soldier somewhat furtively put his gun away, and the third released the dark-haired man and shoved him backward. "We're just taking care of a trespasser, ma'am. We're fine here, thanks," the soldier said, gruffly. "No problem."

"Get out of here," the second soldier told the dark-haired man. "Clear out and stay off the base." He took a step toward the man again.

"Hold on," Kerry said. "He's not doing anything. Why not go back inside and get some of the fresh coffee they just finished making in there? It's hot," she added, with a gentle grin. "I was just in there. They've got sandwiches too."

They were all taller than she was. They were full of bravado and young aggression and at least, in the case of the soldiers, were hot and irritated and probably in no mood to deal with some strange chick who obviously wasn't part of the guard.

Kerry drew in a breath and studied all of them with a direct stare. Her eyebrow lifted, a veneer of confident command exuding from her she'd learned mostly from watching Dar.

Who hadn't had to learn it from anyone. It came as naturally to her as breathing and Kerry knew well there'd have been a lot less hesitation if it had been Dar here with her supremely macha attitude and the truly surprising level of raw aggression she could produce.

For a minute it was a true tossup. She saw the twitch, almost smell the testosterone flare. "Go on," she told them with quiet confidence. "We've got enough to deal with, don't we?"

"Can't do anything out here anyway," the man nearest her said, with a faint shrug. "Let's get a drink and get out of this damn sun."

They left, not without giving the dark-haired man, and Kerry, stares before they trooped off and around the truck, one of them hitching up his fatigue pants with a jerk.

Kerry watched them go, then turned back toward the dark-haired man. "Hi."

He stared frankly at her. "What the hell are you? Some Sergeant Major or something?" He was a little scruffy. He had a few small scars on his hands, a deeply tanned skin and an angular face with a pointed chin. His eyes were a surprising hazel.

"Random nerd," Kerry said. "Did you need something from these guys or were you just messing with them?"

He was only an inch or two taller than she was, but he had a wiry toughness evident under the soft cotton of his shirt. "I came here to see if these jerks wanted to rent my ride," he said. "Didn't even get far enough to talk about it."

Kerry looked past him. "What kind of ride? You got a swamp buggy or something?"

"You don't think I brought it close enough for them to just grab, do you?" The man snorted. "Got it around the corner." He paused. "It's an airboat. Not that I expect you to know what that is."

"Ah, you never know." Kerry smiled at him. "Matter of fact, it's music to my ears. They might not be interested but I certainly am."

"You are?" He eyed her doubtfully. "What the hell does a Sergeant Major want with something like that? I just came here because I saw some of those dodos walking through the water half a mile over cause no one thought to bring any boats with them."

"Friends of mine are missing south of here. I want to go find them," Kerry said. "I was going to see if I could get out to Tamiami and find someone who had an airboat and what do you know? Here you are."

He tilted his head a little to the left. "Why not have the GI Joes find em?"

"They don't have boats." Kerry smiled briefly. She felt the sun beating down and it gave her a headache. "Yes or no? You for hire?" She asked. "What's your price?"

He looked around and then back at her. "Thousand bucks." He sent the words at her like a slingshot, with an arrogant little jerk of his chin.

"Done."

"I don't take credit cards."

Kerry smiled again, as charmingly as she was capable of. "I've got cash," she said. "Let's go." She pointed back toward the gates. "Before some captain comes back and makes me go in a Humvee." She added, "what's your name?"

"Joe. What's yours?" He countered, caught between outrage and grumpy delight. "Are you serious?"

"Kerry." She herded him toward the gate. "Yup. C'mon, time's a wasting."

"Sergeant Major Kerry." He turned and headed down the street with her at his heels. "Weird ass day just got a little weirder but hey, at least you're not pointing a gun at my ass."

****

Dar studied the long, somewhat now battered case seated in the back of her truck. One side had a dent in it, from where the box had fallen into the back of the Dixie. She pondered if she should open up the case and inspect it, before they spent more energy on getting it to the other side of the island.

Then she shrugged. "We're this far." She turned and leaned her back against the sun warmed truck side. The heat penetrated the sweat soaked shirt she had on.

The team was seated at a picnic bench nearby, having some actual iced tea. They were chatting with the dockmaster team, and now that the sun was angling to the west, an onshore breeze had come up and it felt good against her skin.

Andy came over to her. "What'cha think?" He jerked his head in the direction of the box.

"I think they're probably dead as a doornail," Dar said. "That stuff isn't meant to be dropped off the side of a building and do anything useful afterward."

"Wall." Andy's expression was philosophical.

"Is what it is," Dar said. "What a pain in the ass."

Her father chuckled a little. "Yeap," he said. "This whole thing is."

It was. Dar paused, then glanced sideways at him. "You think we should move out somewhere else?" She asked. "Midwest or something?"

Andy shrugged. "Got tornados there," he said. "Fires out by the west. Floods in some places. Always something. Least you see these here things coming."

"True," Dar said. "Next time we'll have a better plan. We didn't think about any of this after we started up."

He patted her on the back. "S'all right, Dardar. All happened so quick," he said. "That there ten-watt bulb you got for a landlord didn't think of nothing and he's had the building for years." He paused reflectively. "Y'never do think these things'll come right at you."

No, it was true. They all came into the area, and you expected them to turn north, or turn south. Or get ripped apart by having to come up over Cuba, whose mountainous terrain served as an effective though somewhat unintentional barrier.

Even when they came closer, even when the cones started including your area, because they were so fickle, and so erratic, no one ever really though they'd be ground zero.

And yet, here they were. Dar sighed, and straightened up. "Well, might as well know the worst." She waved at the seated team. "Let's get this over to the cottage."

Jack had just finished a sandwich and he wiped his hands off and stood up. "We'll give everyone who won't fit in that truck a ride over on the cart," he said. "That metal must be burning hot by now. No one wants to sit back in the back there."

"Thanks." Dar opened the driver's side door then paused, cocking one eyebrow at Ceci.

"Don't give me a look, kiddo," her mother said. "You certainly did not get those long legs from me." She shook a finger at Dar. "Not my fault."

Dar adjusted the seat all the way back and got in. "Uh huh."

Andy got in next to her, and Ceci climbed into the back seat, along with Angela. The rest of the group got into the golf cart and a moment later, the odd little parade was bumping across the debris strewn pathway toward the newly re-opened tarmac road.

Dar focused her attention on the road, which curved around the end of the island heading back along the route that would take them past their house. They were just coming past the ferry dock when her sat phone rang.

Without looking, she fished the phone out and answered it. "Dar."

"Hey, it's Mark."

Dar nodded in reaction "Hey, what's up."

"What's up is we got no idea where Kerry is. She's not where we left her," Mark said. "The guard was here, and trucks and everything with a tent and now they're all gone!"

'I know," Dar said. "She tried to call you. She went with them to the big Southcom facility in Doral, off 41st." She steered around two golf carts that were moving in the opposite direction, shiny models with addresses on them that marked them as residents, not workers. "She said she was going to try and keep calling you."

"Oh! Great," Mark said. "Thanks. I know where that is." He sounded relieved. "I'll go find her."

"Any luck with Maria's family?"

"Nothing," Mark said. "They haven't seen them. Zoe and I checked three shelters, then I left her back at the one her family's at. She's going to try and get a ride over to the office to be with everyone else. Those shelters are a mess. Just loud and screaming kids and ugh."

Dar pulled into the turnoff that would take them over to the area where there were cottages and villas to rent. "Better than a house with no roof."

"True that," Mark agreed. "I'll call ya when we hook up. I don't know why these phones are being so damn flaky."

They arrived in front of the cottages and as they did, they saw in the putting green to one side of the rentals a helicopter landing. It was sleek, and dark green and anonymous, and two men in guayaberas got out, ducking under the rotating blades and shielding their face from the downdraft.

Dar regarded the helicopter. "That would be handy. Faster than the Dixie."

Andy studied the craft. "I could maybe fly that," he said. "I done a course on it. While back though."

"Can't have changed much," Dar said.

"No," Ceci told them. "Stop it. Both of you."

They got out of the truck as the golf cart pulled up alongside. A moment later, as they walked across the emptied central patio, the islands hospitality manager spotted them and hurried over. "Ah! Ms. Roberts. Good you are here."

They all halted in the middle of the patio. There were cottages and villas on all sides of the central area, two of them larger with steps leading up to them and patios, and some smaller units that were original to the place, then side paths to another area behind them that held a circle of newer villas that had more recently been built.

"Hi, Clemente," Dar greeted. "We've got the—"

"Yes, yes I know," Clemente said. "Of course we know, and we have moved the furniture in the living room aside for you to bring in your things to work." He indicated the steps up to the biggest of the cottages. "May I show you?"

They trooped up the patio steps and the manager pushed open the wood front door, which stuck a little. "It has swollen up," Clemente said. "From the water."

"Sure."

Inside was a large, square room, with an elegant wooden table in the center. A couch had been moved against the wall, and two lamp tables had as well, leaving as much as the stone coral floor open as was practical. "It is okay?"

Dar nodded. "Good as it's going to get," she said. "We can put the rack in the corner there." She pointed to the far side of the room where there was an empty space. "It's fine, Clemente. We'll get set up best we can." She turned. "I've got four folks who'll be staying here too."

"Si." Clemente nodded. "Come, I will show you the bedrooms." He indicated a back hallway. "And now that you are here, I will tell the electricians." He hustled over toward the back of the cottage. The two programmers and Angela and Celeste followed him.

Dar walked over and looked into the small kitchen. "This'll do."

It was refreshingly cold inside. They had taken out all the carpets, though Dar wasn't sure if it was because of their presence, or to remove water from them. The cottage had two bathrooms and the kitchen, and three bedrooms along with the large living space.

Angela came back out. "We can have two more people here. Are you taking another trip back there, Ms. Dar?" Maybe more folks are there now."

Dar nodded. "Gotta go pick up Kerry," She said. "I'll see who else is around, but let's get that box in here first. This going to be okay for you all?"

Arthur just laughed.

"Dude," Elvis said solemnly. "C'mon."

Celeste spoke up. "This is pretty nice. And oh my gosh that air-conditioning feels so good." She sighed happily. "If we can borrow one of those carts, we can bring in those supplies from the boat."

"You can take my truck," Dar said. "Let's get things going." She went outside with the rest of them and they gathered around the back of the truck. The case was lying on its side, it's weight more than enough to keep it in place.

Elvis took a mover's dolly the marine group had loaned them and put it on the ground. "This is gonna be tough," he said. "If we miss that thing it's gonna hurt."

"How are we going to get it up those steps?" Angela asked. "Maybe we should get some help? Wish we'd brought old Carlos with us!"

"Let me go get some fellers," Andy said. "Stay put." He walked off toward the path between the cottages, and the rest of them looked over at Dar in question.

"Let's see if we can find some boards," Dar said. "We'll make a ramp." She pointed toward the road where the landscapers were still dragging debris around. "See what we can find. "

****

Kerry sloshed along as they walked west from the military base of operations, toward the Everglades. Joe splashed on ahead of her. He reached out to grab and break the idle twig as they went deeper into the flooded area here at the industrial end of the street.

Kerry caught up to him and asked, "How did you make out in the storm? Your house, I mean."

"Don't live in a house," he said. "I live outside." He glanced at her, a crooked smile appearing. "I know where there's some limestone caves, you know? Little ones. I just ducked into one of em."

Kerry was impressed. "Wow," she said. "That's gutsy."

He shrugged. "S'what's the problem with everyone in these parts. It's all of it swamp. All of it floodplain, you know? You build against it, she comes." He indicated the sky vaguely. "Stupid." He led her around a stretch of trees. "Here we go."

Tucked into a gap between a thick patch of sawgrass was an ungainly creation, two rickety seats on top of a flat bottomed, broad beamed platform. Behind the seats was an eight-foot-high screen of rusted metal poles that formed a protective grid.

Behind the grid there was a large vertical propeller. Attached to that was a gas engine. Under the seats was a weathered wood box and the floor of the platform had a hand hammered look as though the metal of it had been repurposed.

It was stupendously weird looking. Kerry, however, thought it looked great. "Nice."

"Built it myself," Joe told her, with a proud expression. "I hunt with it. Bring back skins and game." He walked up onto the boat and went to the back of it. He yanked a pole with a long spike on the end of it out of the ground. "C'mon up."

Kerry climbed up onto the boat, glad to have her boots out of the murky, pungent mud. The boat shifted under her and she put her hand on the back of one of the chairs to hold herself steady as Joe knelt beside the engine and started it up.

It rumbled to life. Joe listened to it for a minute, then reached over and engaged a clutch and the propeller started to turn. He quickly got up and sat in the left-hand seat, taking hold of the rudders as the boat started to move. "Siddown."

Kerry did, without complaint. The breeze picked up as they headed west, the propeller driving the boat through the flooded grass and out over where the water covered the road. The sound of the engine prevented easy conversation, so she spent some time looking around as they turned along a deeply flooded road and went south.

"Twenty-seven," Joe said, raising his voice. "Underwater all the way to Tamiami."

There weren't any people out here. The depth of the floodwaters was, Kerry reasoned about five feet or so, but as she looked between the trees, she saw houses buried up to their first floors and cars completely covered. Overhead, she spotted birds circling.

Joe noted her glance. "Buzzards. Lotta dead stuff around," he said. "Cows. Some horses." He paused. "People."

"Yeah," Kerry said, briefly. On the wind they were heading into she could smell a hint of decay, the distinctive scent of death mixed with the smell of water and foliage. It made her tense up inside. As it did, the thought occurred to her that being out here with a very random and unknown man was probably not the smartest thing she'd ever done.

She felt she had a good instinct for people. She knew, in fact, that she had a finer talent for judging intent than Dar did, and Dar told her that on more than one occasion. She was the one who made the business deals, evaluating customers and deciding if they were the kind of customer who would end up being a good investment and long-term partner.

So was it smart to be riding on a rickety airboat along the edge of the Everglades with someone she didn't know? Kerry's lips twitched. It was a good cause. She wanted to find Maria and Mayte, and make sure they were safe. The mission was one she knew her partner would have accepted.

It probably wasn't smart, but then again, it didn't really matter now did it? Because after all, here she was.

Here she was, driven by that innate risk-taking part of her that raised its head sometimes utterly unexpectedly, surprising her colleagues, their customers, and occasionally herself.

She settled back into the rusty seat and kicked a bit of the mud off the bottom of her boots. The sun glinted off her wedding band and she rubbed her thumb against the bottom of it, finding obscure comfort in the warmth and the solid feel of the metal.

To the right was a line of trees. Behind that she could see swamped grass for as far as she could focus. Every so often they would go past a flooded house, and on the left, a continuous flash of them as they came even with blocks interspersed with wooded areas.

It seemed desolate. Joe fished under his seat into the box and pulled out a headset that he crammed onto his head then pulled out a second for her and handed it over. "Put that on."

Kerry took it, glanced at it, then pulled it on over her ears. The headset, earmuffs actually, blocked out the sound of the engine, though they were a little loose and not that comfortable. "Thanks," she said after a moment. "That was making my ears itch inside."

"Loud," Joe said. "Gonna turn up there, see what we can find out for ya." He pointed ahead of them to where a huge stand of trees had collapsed, and were lying across the roadbed they were traveling over. "S'close to where you said."

Kerry straightened up in her chair and braced her boots on the floor of the airboat, taking in a breath and then releasing it.

If they found them, if they were okay, it would make for good end to the day.

****

Dar wiped the sweat out of her eyes and paused to catch her breath. They had the case on its end, on the dolly and part of the way to the cottage entrance.

Jack had his guys bring over two pieces of three by twelve long enough to get up the steps and they were propped against them now, waiting for them to push the case up them and into the cottage.

"Holy crap," Elvis said. "This is crazy hard."

"Almost there," Dar said. "But something just occurred to me." She left her spot and went up the makeshift ramp to the door, standing against it and measuring its height against hers.

"Oh crap," Arthur muttered. "Don't tell me it's too big."

Dar came back over to the case and stood next to it. "I think it'll just fit," she said. "Otherwise we'll have to take it around the back and around the Jacuzzi through the patio."

"Everything's a bitch," Elvis said, mournfully.

"Sometimes." Dar put her shoulder against the case. "C'mon." She and the two programmers started pushing the case toward the steps.

It was difficult. The ground was covered in gravel. But it was at least even and they made good progress until they had the dolly lined up against the planks. Dar then took a step back and studied the case.

"That's gonna fall on top of us if we try pushing it up there," Arthur said. "I bet you."

Dar exhaled. "We'll put a rope on the top of it, and someone'll pull while the rest of us push," she said. "I've got some rope back in the boat. One of you take the cart back and go grab it. It's in the box in the back."

"No problem." Elvis trotted off.

Dar went over to one of the stone benches in the center of the square and sat on it, the white stone warm but not unpleasantly so. She let her boot slide forward as Arthur came over and sat next to her.

The square was quiet, at least for now.

Arthur looked around. "This is pretty ritzy. I mean, you can see it's money here, you know?"

"It is," Dar admitted.

Arthur was silent for a moment. "I didn't figure this was your style," he said. "I mean I knew you lived here but I didn't think..." He paused. "You're not really the Gucci type I didn't figure."

Dar smiled briefly. "I'm not. I inherited the place here from an aunt. It's not really my style. That's why Ker and I are looking for another place near the office."

Dar glanced past the case to where the two men from the helicopter had reappeared and covertly watched them. "They don't much like me here." Her lips twitched. "Though I'm not really sure what they hate more, my redneck background, the fact that I'm gay, or my dogs."

Arthur regarded her with a bemused expression in silence for a long moment. "Fuck them!" He finally said. "Like why the hell should they care? I remember when I started working for you. When Kerry told me about you guys, I was kinda weirded, but after a week it was like—a nothingburger."

Dar chuckled. "A lot of the people we started the company with already knew." She put her hands behind her head and crossed her ankles. "Some of the other owners here are just jerks. Just like anywhere else."

"Like everywhere. I have people call me a geek all the time," Arthur said. "Cause I like computers and comic books and gaming. They don't know me." He studied one of his sneakers. "Making fun of me because I don't' like to play football."

"I don't like to play football either," Dar said, in a reasonable tone.

"You're a girl, you don't have to," Arthur said. "If you're a boy, and you don't like to play football, everyone thinks you're gay."

Dar folded her arms thoughtfully. "Well, if you're a girl and you do like to play football, they think you're gay. I'm not really sure what that says about football," she concluded. "But anyway, I never liked it. I'm not really a team player."

Arthur laughed unexpectedly. "I never liked it because I'd rather be in the air-conditioning with a keyboard," he said. "I only liked to do skateboarding outside." He kicked his heels against the gravel. "But it's cool.

I've got a bunch of friends who like the stuff I do now."

Dar glanced at him. "You found your tribe," she said. "I get it." She indicated the surroundings with one hand in an idle circle. "I don't care about this place or the morons who live here. I'm giving my place to my folks, so if they had an issue with me just wait."

Arthur laughed again.

"Juuuust wait," Dar repeated, with a wry grin. "My mother already has plans to invite her coven over to have some midnight thing in the middle of the golf course and my dad's already told half the men here they're useless jacktards."

Arthur held his hands over his stomach and laughed without restraint.

"Only thing good about the place is it's built like a brick shithouse," Dar said. "We didn't even lose a shingle." She lifted her hand and exchanged a wave with one of the young maids who worked for Clemente. "Hey, Juanita"

"Hola, Ms. Roberts." the young woman said. "Who is your friend?" She gave the shirtless, and now somewhat sunburned, Arthur a smile. "Buenos Dias, senor."

"Hi." Arthur returned the greeting with a somewhat embarrassed grin. "I'm Arthur."

"He's going to be staying in the big cottage. He works for me," Dar said. "Trying to get some work done, since our office on the mainland has no power."

"Si, of course," Juanita said. "We will take very good care of them, Ms. Roberts. What can I put in the kitchen?" She asked. "Coffee, yes?"

"Coke, Doritos, and Snickers bars to start," Dar said. "Try to stock it with some Pop Tarts too."

"Pop Tarts!" Arthur sat up. "Now I want one!"

The golf cart from Dar's unit came bouncing back into the courtyard, fully loaded. Elvis got out, along with Andy, Jack, two of his men, and Chino. Andy had a coiled hank of rope on his shoulder. Chino trotted over to Dar and jumped up into her lap, tail wagging enthusiastically.

"Oof. Chino." Dar got her arms around the large animal and gave her a hug. "I missed you too. Now get down." The dog obediently hopped off. "Did you leave Mocha behind?" She asked, as Chino wriggled between her knees and cocked her ears in response.

"He's busy guarding the back yard," Andy said. "Them folks are doing some cleanup back there."

"Hi, Chino," Arthur said. "Did you get scared in the storm?"

Dar gave the dog's tail a tug. "Not really. They didn't like all the noise, but they did all right."

"Okay here we go," Dar said.

Jack and the two other dock workers surrounded the case. Dar joined them, as Arthur took the rope from Andy and climbed up the steps to reach out and tie it onto the top handle. "Almost there, guys, almost there."

****

They slowed as they reached a thick pile of trees and Joe maneuvered the airboat around the end of them. Going through a thick patch of half-submerged logs, the bottom of the vessel scraped over debris. The throttled down engine muted to a low rumble in response, as they went forward cautiously.

Kerry missed the breeze of the travel, the heat of the sun and the humid air gathered around her like she'd walked into a spa. She put that aside and stood, keeping hold of the back of the seat as she watched the horizon.

They moved from a patch of trees and onto a street, where houses were half buried in water.

It was quiet. The sound of their engine the only noise. She couldn't hear anyone nearby, no shouts or yells, or babies crying. No sound of generators.

They passed by a car that was almost fully submerged, and as they did, both she and Joe spotted at the same time that someone was inside it.

Kerry drew in a breath. "Oh... did you see..."

"I saw it." Joe steered the airboat in closer, and slowed, then he turned and focused forward again. "Nothing to help there," he said. "Got a lot of that I figure."

The figure inside the car was upside down. There were fingers sticking out of the gapped window, and they were dark purple, and stiff. Kerry felt a chill ripple across her body and she slowly let her breath trickle out. There were flies buzzing around the hand.

"Don't know what they were thinking, sitting there."

"Storm surge came in too fast, maybe." Kerry watched over her shoulder as they moved past. "Should we tell someone?"

Joe looked at her. "Who?" He asked, with a faint shrug. "Family's either not there or gone." He focused his attention on the path ahead. "Cops can't do nothing. Plenty of time later for cleaning all that up."

"I guess you have a point there." Kerry took out her cell phone though, and opened her note program, taking down the address of where they'd seen the car with its gruesome contents. "Anyway."

She slid the phone back into her pocket, firmly directing her thoughts away from the possibility that she might find the same when they got to Mayte and Maria's house. "This is horrible," she said.

"It's bad," Joe agreed. "They knew it would be. My brother said that's why they didn't say to leave until last minute. They knew all these people would stay in their houses."

Was that true? "I thought it was because they weren't sure where the storm was going."

Joe gave her what could only be described as a look of pity. "Come on, lady."

"Or they were betting it was going to turn," Kerry said, but with a doubtful tone in her voice.

"You don't know much about the government," Joe said, and shaded his eyes with one hand as he peered ahead. "They don't give a shit about people unless they've got money."

Kerry took a breath, then smiled grimly. "Sometimes," she agreed, moving up closer to him and peered ahead. "What do you see?"

"Hear it?" He abruptly cut off the engine and let them drift, the sound of water lapping everywhere and crickets surrounding them. Then she heard it too, the far-off rumbling of an engine of some kind, and the sharp retort of a hammer striking. "No idea what's that about," he said.

"Well, whoever's making all that noise isn't dead at least," Kerry replied. "Let's go find out."

He started up the engine again and then they lurched forward as the fan spun into gear. It pushed them forward into the humid air as the sun slanted in from behind them, casting their shadows forward across the flooded road.

As they moved closer to the sound there were houses now that showed signs of life, and several had people sitting on top of the roof. One man had spread out a tarp over the roof and was tapping nails into it to hold it down. There was a woman next to him, hugging herself.

There was a cat swimming across a yard. It didn't look happy. It swam past a car that had a man standing on top of it. "Hey!" He called out and waved at them.

"Later!" Joe held a hand up.

Kerry felt sorry for the man, who stood looking after them with his hands planted onto his hips. But she wanted to find out how her friends were doing, so she remained silent as they came to a T in the road and Joe paused. "Which way?"

Kerry looked right and then left. The street signs were nowhere to be seen. She'd only been to Maria's twice, and both times Dar drove. And, on both occasions, they'd come from the east, not from the west like they were now.

"To the right there," she said, after a long pause. "Right, and then left," she added, following some instinct tugging her in that way.

Joe nodded, and steered the boat in that direction, glancing behind him and then back forward as he navigated the turn and cleared it. They saw a large group of people standing in the floodwaters half a block away around an RV turned on its side.

Two men push a door, floating on the surface of the water. On the door there was a huddled figure, writhing in what seemed to be pain.

"Whoa." Joe slowed their forward motion.

The people in the group closest to where they were turned, and gestured to them, beckoning them closer with definite urgency.

"That don't look good," Joe said.

Kerry scanned the crowd intently. "My friend's house is just past there," she said. "Two houses down on the left. Let's see what's going on here."

"No choice. They're gonna stop us." Joe turned off the big fan engine and let them drift forward. "Hey!" he called out. "Watch out, stand back. Yo!"

The man nearest him yelled back in Spanish.

"You speak that?" Joe asked Kerry. "Your friends live here, figure you do."

"I don't," Kerry admitted. "And I..." She straightened up. "Okay, over there." She pointed, spotting Mayte's slim form climbing up onto the roof of a car parked in a nearby flooded front yard. "Mayte!" She lifted her voice in a clear bellow. "Mayte!"

Mayte saw her and a moment later recognized her and let out a scream of acknowledgement. She scrambled off the roof of the car and plunged into the water and started wading toward them.

Now five or six people were heading in their direction, all raising their voices, all urgent, all in Spanish. The men pushing the door guiding it toward them, another woman pointed at the figure on it emphatically.

Kerry glanced sideways at Joe. "How many people can you take on this thing?"

"Three more, maybe," he said. "Six, including you and me, tops."

"Can you get to her?" Kerry indicated Mayte.

Joe looked at her, at first in a little surprise, then with a faint, crooked grin. "Sure." He started the engine with an expression of relief and started forward moving into the crowd of people who reeled to get out of his way. "Move out!" He yelled. "Move it!"

No one took him seriously at first, one of them reaching out to grab the edge of the airboat but Joe gunned the engine and shoved the man backward and he fell into the water,   turning and scrambling away from them with a shout of incoherent outrage.

The woman pointed at the figure on the door and yelled.

Kerry went to the front of the boat and braced her boots on the edge around the roughly square deck. She reached out with one hand as Mayte got to them and offered her a hand up. "Hurry," she said. "C'mon!"

Mayte grabbed her hand and was yanked upward out of the water with a powerful surge. "Oh, Kerry!" she gasped. "Oh, it is so good to see you here..." She sucked in a shuddering gasp. "They are up in the house, and my papa is so sick. Please we need help."

"Steady. Hold on" Kerry pulled her back away from the edge and gave her a hug. "Keep going toward that second house," Kerry directed Joe. "Don't let those people take hold of this thing."

Joe gave her a one handed, somewhat mock salute. "Right you are, Sergeant Major." He increased the speed. "And here I had ya pegged as a bleeding-heart liberal," he added in an approving tone. "Freakin good surprise. Hang on." He moved away from the crowd and headed east.

Kerry grabbed a one-handed hold of the seat and kept her other around Mayte's upper arm. "Now what's going on?" She asked. "What happened?"

"Dios mio where do I start," Mayte said, and then she looked past Kerry. "Thank you so much for coming here!" She told Joe. "They told us no one could come help us, they had a helicopter come over here this morning." She took a breath. "And I could not use those phones!"

"I know," Kerry said. "What's wrong with your dad?" She asked, as they came around a fallen Ficus tree and into the front yard of the house she knew Mayte and Maria lived in. "Maria!" Kerry spotted a familiar face at the second-floor window. "We're here!"

Joe glanced behind them, and then up at the window. "This is gonna be a mess," he said. "Knew I shoulda just gone hunting."

Chapter Seven

"OMG." Arthur sprawled across the couch pushed against the wall. "I'm dead." His shorts were sweat stained, and there were red marks and bruises along his bare torso. "That was crazy." He spread out his arms along the surface of the stiff fabric. "I thought for sure that thing was going to tip over."

"Like right on top of Dar," Angela said. "Would not have been good!"

"Good thing pops was here," Arthur said, his eyes closed. "Cause none of us were gonna stop that thing falling over."

Dar stood next to the upright case, the top edge just clearing the ceiling, the bottom still resting on the dolly that she had one booted foot propped up on. "Well, it's in here." She removed her sunglasses and stuck them through one of her beltloops and then raked the disheveled dark hair back out of her eyes. "Good work, people."

"Yeap," Andy said as he worked the latches on the far side of the case. "Let's see what we got here." His dark green T-shirt was almost black with sweat, as were the fatigue pants he wore tucked into worn military boots that matched Dar's. "See if it was all worth something."

"Right." Dar twisted the fastenings on the other side, and unlatched them, then leaned over to do the ones at the bottom of the case. "I didn't hear anything rattling around when we were moving it. That's a good sign."

The door to the cottage opened and the housekeeping staff came in, two of them carrying boxes that alternately clinked and tinged as they walked.

Ceci followed behind them and pushed the door closed after them. "We're back!" She announced. "And as I was coming around I saw them using some crowbars on the ferry lift."

"That'd be nice," Dar said. "I'd rather take the truck back to get Kerry than the Dixie and then have to steal a car if I have to go chasing after her."

"Did that boy not find her with that motorcycle?" Andy demanded. "What in the world were they thinking?" He planted his hands on his hips in one of his daughter's favorite poses. "Gov'mint's got all kinds of trucks and what not out there helping people."

'Didn't stop us now did it?" Dar shook her head. "Kerry's got a mind of her own. Hopefully by now Mark hooked up with her at Southcom and they're on their way back."

"Okay, take it off." Dar straightened up and grabbed one of the front handles, as Andy grabbed the other and they wrestled the cover off the case, stepping backward with it so they could remove it and see inside.

"Let'r go, Dardar." Andy took the case front and leaned it up against the nearby wall as Dar inspected the rack full of hardware inside.

Elvis and Arthur sat up to watch. "That one plates broken," Arthur commented, pointing at the facing of one of the servers, which was hanging down sideways. "Is that just the LED panel?"

The case had been built with a framework designed to allow machines to be fastened securely inside, and the framework had done its job keeping the systems relatively in one piece. The front of the one had cracked, and there was a dent in the railing on the right-hand side.

"Yeah, just the LED's." Dar inspected the panel, and then she tapped it back into place with a rap of her knuckles. "Everything else looks okay."

"Might have knocked some DIMMS loose," Elvis said, pulling his legs up under him crossed. He pushed his glasses up onto the bridge of his nose and leaned forward. "Hope they locked the hard drives down before they powered off."

"Mark's got an encrypted blob backed up for all of them," Arthur said.

"Don't help, since we ain't got no internet here," Elvis said. "Do we?" He asked Dar. "I mean, they got power and everything here I guess."

"No cell, no internet," Dar said. "There's a fiber that goes landside from here, but the pop's dead."

"Pofth." Elvis stuck out his tongue.

"Well," Dar said. "Lets power them up and find out the worst." She glanced around. "Where the hell is the thirty-amp service I asked for?"

"They're bringing in cabling from the pool back there," Ceci supplied helpfully. "They're trying to figure out how to bring it inside without having to leave a door open." She stuck her hands into the pockets of her painters' pants. "I told them to knock a windowpane out, but it wasn't' a popular idea."

"Can't they…" Dar looked up at the ceiling, and then at the doors to the pool area. "I guess drilling a hole in the wall isn't' gonna be popular either."

Andy chuckled softly. "Got me a big old bit on mah drill'd get through that there wall," he said.

Dar went to the window and peered out of it. "I'm sure that'll make me even more popular with the management," she said. "If possible."

Ceci rocked up and down on her heels. "Kiddo, I think you managed to piss off more people with this little rental than I woulda believed possible. Talk about panties in a wad."

"Why?" Dar glanced over her shoulder at her mother, with a puzzled expression. "What the hell is the problem with everyone? We rented this place. I didn't' steal it." She turned and put her hands on her hips. "What's their beef?"

"Ah. This is the only comfortable place to live in three counties," Ceci promptly supplied. "I mean, literally. They have all the bigshots helicoptering in here to sightsee and the best the mayor of Miami can offer them is a spare mat in the back room of the command center."

"Mother," Dar said. "People are dead, and houses are blown up all up and down the coast. Who the fuck cares what politicians are sleeping on?"

"They do," Ceci said. "And if we want them to give us lots of money to recover and help people, I get that it matters to the folks in charge here."

"I don't," Dar said. "Because half the condos on this high-priced Alcatraz are investment property and empty. They should farm those out if they want to house their buddies from DC." She walked across the living room of the cottage and entered the small kitchen.

Ceci tapped her chin with one fingertip. "Now that's a fine idea," she mused. "Where the hell is that hotel man."

Inside Juanita and her colleagues were stocking the refrigerator and setting up a coffee service. "Do not pay attention to them, Ms. Dar," Juanita said. "Mr. Clemente said he would take you and your friends over the other people any day."

Dar smiled briefly. "He's a good guy," she said. "He's been one of the best things about living here since I moved in. We're going to mess this place up, tell ya that in advance."

"No problem," Juanita said. "Do the young men and ladies have luggage? Manuel can go get it for them," she offered. "They seem very nice."

Dar paused in the act of opening a can of orange Crush. "Oh crap. Thanks for mentioning it. I totally lost track of the fact none of them has anything with them." She took the can and went into the living room. "All right folks, listen up."

"Can I listen from here?" Elvis asked.

"Sure," Dar said. "We've got a little time until they get those cables in here. So, let's go over to our local market and get you all some supplies. They don't have a huge choice but it's something."

Arthur opened one eye and looked at her. "Oh," he said. "You mean like clothes and stuff?"

Dar nodded. "They've got laundry service, but you'll need something to wear while what you have is being washed. I've caused enough problems without everyone running around naked."

The team chuckled with some tinge of embarrassment.

"All golf shirts and khakis, huh?" Angela asked, in a mournful tone. "I shoulda packed a bag, but who knew we'd end up here?"

Andy came in from the back patio. "Figured it out," he said. "But they got some fellers out there want to talk to you, Dardar. Said they got some deal or something or somesuch."

Dar sighed. "Great. More bullshit."

Andy shook his head. "Don't think so," he said. "Ah hear you all want to go riding out to the shop. C'mon, Cec. Ah could do me with a snack. Been all right with what they done got over theah."

"They have greasy cheeseburgers and ketchup," Ceci translated. She waved at the rest of them. "Everyone in the cart! Let's go invade." She snickered in evident enjoyment.

"Try not to have too much fun," Dar said, dryly.

The gang gathered and they trooped out the front door, while Dar took her time, drinking down her Crush before she crumpled the can and dropped it into the tiny, mostly useless trash can in the corner of the room.

She paused in front of the mirror and regarded her reflection, then just chuckled wryly before she went to the back door. If she'd already pissed off the world, facing it in a ratty tank top and cargo shorts probably wouldn't make it any worse.

She pushed the door open and went out into the stifling heat and walked out onto the pool deck of the cottage. It was bare of any adornment. All of the chairs and tables and niceties having been stored away for the duration of the storm.

On the far side of the deck were two electricians wrestling with a spool of heavy black cabling. Nearby watching them were two strangers in actual Polo polo shirts and pressed khakis. They were in the shade provided by the thick privacy hedges, which hadn't suffered much from the storm.

Figures. Dar exhaled, then skirted the pool and approached them. "Can I help you gentlemen with something?" She asked, in a brisk tone. "My father said you wanted to speak to me."

The nearer one, slightly older, thick black hair short and cut neatly around his head, nodded. "Ms. Roberts? My name is Alex Redondo." He held out a hand to her. "This is John Delacruz, my associate."

Dar took his hand and returned a firm grip. Then she lifted an eyebrow and waited.

"We heard you're in the computer business," Redondo said. "One of the security directors told us. He said you fixed something for him, said you were a real whiz."

Dar's brow remained raised, as her mental train went off the track and headed off on an unexpected highway. "Well." She paused briefly. "Whether or not I'm a whiz depends on who you talk to, but yes, in fact, I run a computer consulting company."

He nodded. "We need some help. The security guy said to ask you."

Dar felt a certain sense of the absurd surfacing. "I'm kind of up to my neck in my own crap right now."

Redondo nodded again. "I get it. Everyone is," he said. "But I think we can maybe help each other out. Here's the deal..." He paused and looked around.

Dar needed no assistance in interpreting the look. "Want to go inside?" She offered. "It's air-conditioned," she added wryly.

Both men smiled in response. They followed her around the pool and into the cottage. The second man, Delacruz, glanced at the rack as he walked in. "That's a box of gear," he said. "That what you all were bringing off that boat?"

"Yep," Dar said. "So, what's your pitch?" She waited for Redondo to close the door to the patio and join them in the center of the bare room. "As you can see, we're pretty busy trying to get something done here."

"Us too," Alex said. "Here's what it is."

****

The water was halfway up to the window. Kerry stood on the deck of the airboat, shading her eyes as she looked up at Maria. "We've got to get you guys out of here," she said, aware of the noise of the crowd behind them.

Mayte was behind her. "The whole house is flooded," she said. "It is terrible," she said to Joe. "Thank you for coming with this machine."

"Don't thank me," Joe said. "Thank her. She's paying for it." He looked behind them. The crowd started to drift over. "But if you all don't hurry up all that cash ain't gonna do anyone no good."

"Kerrisita he cannot come," Maria said. "His leg is I think broken."

"Oh, crap," Kerry muttered.

"When the water came, he went to run downstairs to get some things," Mayte said. "Mama tried to stop him, but the water came in too fast and too hard."

"Si," Maria said. "We put some things around it, to keep it still but he is in so much pain. And there is blood too."

Kerry looked over her shoulder, then she turned and went to the edge of the deck, stepping off it and plunging into the water to wade toward the open front door to the house. "C'mon Mayte. Let's see if we can get him down the stairs," she said. "Joe, just be ready to move it."

"You got it, Sarge." Joe kicked open the gear box under the seats and leaned over to pull out a worn shotgun. He settled it into the cradle of his right arm against his chest. "Don't be slow."

Inside there were things floating and it was hot. The stench of standing water making Kerry's nose wrinkle. The flood was up to her chest and she was glad to get to the steps and get out of it. She hauled herself upward by grabbing the banister.

Mayte was at her heels. "I was so scared," Mayte said. "We thought... we are so far from the water, yes? We thought it would be okay to stay. Mama didn't want to leave our house behind."

"We'll get you guys out of here," Kerry said, projecting as much quiet confidence as she could. "I get it, Mayte. We didn't want to leave our place either and there were some scary times during the storm."

"Is it okay by your house?"

They got to the top of the stairs. "Yeah, we're fine," Kerry said, after a brief pause to take in the blown-out windows and gap in the roof. "We found Zoe, too, and we heard from the guys we sent north. Colleen, and some of the staff showed up earlier at the office."

They went down the hall and met Maria as she came out of what was the master bedroom. Inside Mayte's father, Tomas, was lying on the bed, his face very pale and covered in a sheen of sweat.

"I'm really glad we found you," Kerry said, after a slight pause. "I can't wait to tell Dar. But right now, let's see how we can get Tomas out of here."

****

It looked like it was a compound fracture.

Kerry knew very little about the subject, but just looking at the blue, swollen, bloodstained skin on Tomas' leg nearly made her sick to her stomach. She could hardly imagine how Tomas himself and his family felt about it. "Oh boy," she muttered, under her breath.

Mayte knelt next to her. "Kerry, if we leave here they will come inside and take our things. We saw that already."

"She is right," Tomas said, wanly.

Kerry glanced around the bedroom. There was a beautiful wood cabinet against the wall, and on the dresser was scattered a collection of mementos.

"We came here with so little," Maria murmured, as though reading her mind.

"Things are just things," Kerry said. "What's important right now is that we get Tomas to the hospital." She was at a loss, though, as to just how they were going to do that. "Can you stand up?" She asked. "If we help you? If you can get to the stairs…"

"I know." Mayte stood up. "I have a blow-up thing in my room, let me get it. You can sit on that." She trotted out, and Maria took her place.

"It sounds so silly," Maria said. "But you know, Kerrisita, we have worked hard for the things we have, and we do care about them."

"It's not silly, and I get it," Kerry said. "But you can't stay here, Maria." She braced her knee against the edge of the bed and extended her arm. "Let me help you try to sit up."

'Si, of course not," Maria murmured. "Let me help also."

Tomas said something to her in Spanish. Then he took Kerry's hand and she leaned back, and pulled him up toward her. He managed to sit up and braced his other hand against the bed as he slid his good leg off it and onto the floor.

He paused, his face white, as he muttered a soft curse under his breath. "Un momento," He said. "My head is going around."

"No worry. Take your time." Kerry patted him on the shoulder. "We'll get through this."

"It is amazing you found us," Maria said. "With this machine outside," she added. "What is that?"

"It's called an airboat." Kerry stood up and went to the window and peered outside. Joe had tied off the airboat on the lamppost that stood outside the door and he stood on the far side of the boat. "Okay?" Kerry asked him, holding one thumb up in question.

Joe turned and looked at her, and she saw the shotgun cradled in his arm. He lifted his free hand. "For now," he said. "They seen this." He lifted the gun up and lowered it. "But don't take too long," he warned. "I ain't sticking around if they all start coming at us. Ain't got enough shells for that."

"Got it." Kerry pulled her head back inside and went back over to the bed. Behind her, outside the door, she heard Mayte working on something. "Okay?" She studied Tomas. "How about we get you up and you can lean on me."

Tomas shook his head. "It will be too much. I am too big."

"We'll get it done," Kerry said. "I'm stronger than I look, honest." She stood in front of him and extended both hands to him. "Maria, help him on that side," she directed. "Let's get you moving and before you know it, you'll be out on the boat and we'll be on the way to help."

Tomas seemed doubtful, but he took her hands. She leaned back and hoped they weren't going to end up crashing right back down onto the bed as he struggled to get upright on one leg.

Maria anxiously grabbed his arm on the side with his bad leg and urged him upward.

"Mayte!" Kerry called out. "Give us a hand here!"

"I am coming!" Mayte's voice accompanied an odd, rustling, squeaking sound and then she appeared in the doorway, rushing over to take hold of her father's arm just at the moment when Kerry was sure they were going to lose control.

Her assistance literally tipped the balance and then Tomas was upright, if shaking. Kerry released one and got one of his arms over her shoulders. "Get on that side, Mayte," she said. "Maria, move that chair out of the way."

"Si." Maria went to move the small, low stool that had been tucked against the bed and dragged it out of the way.

Mayte got up against her father on the other side, and they all paused a moment to take a breath.

Kerry studied the path to the door, as she considered their next move. It occurred to her that it was a good thing both women were used to taking her direction without much question because she really was making it up as she went along.

Briefly, she wished Dar was with her. Everyone carried their own internal troubleshooting toolbox, and in truth Dar was like having the world's most capable multi tool in the box with you and it came with a self-guided high-quality intelligence to boot.

Super useful. Utterly dependable. You needed a computer thing solved? No problem. You needed a mechanical thing solved? No problem. You needed something lifted off a high shelf? Really no problem.

Kerry sighed and dismissed the internal conversation since it was pointless. Dar wasn't there, and so she had to carry on. "Okay," she said. "Let's get over to the door, then let me go in front and we get through sideways. Just take it slow, Tomas."

"Kerry, this is so amazing," Mayte said. "All of the things outside, no one knows anything, no one knows where to go or what to do, and you are here."

"Yes," Tomas added, before Kerry could demur. "God bless you."

Kerry smiled briefly in response. "I am, for sure, blessed," she said, after a pause. "But I will be even more so if we can get out of here and make you feel better." She could see the pallor in the older man's face and sweat rolled down all of their faces. "So, let's go."

They started inching toward the door. Kerry, being on the side of Tomas that his bad leg was, felt the strain as she took his weight on her shoulders, trying to be very careful not to jostle the injury as she moved.

As they turned to get through the door Kerry saw a large, brightly colored object on the ground. "Wha...oh," she said. "That what you were blowing up, Mayte?"

"Yes," Mayte answered from behind her. "I got it at a surviving show."

It was a... kayak? Kerry nudged it a bit out of her way. An inflatable kayak in distress orange. "For this you mean?"

"Si," Mayte said. "Scott said I should. He knows about that like Dar's papa."

"Good advice." Kerry got around the kayak. "Here, Tomas, rest against the banister." Outside the open door, she heard Joe yelling. "Let me see what's going on out there, then we'll get you into the kayak and float you on out."

She made sure his grip was sturdy on the railing before she ducked under his arm, grabbed the kayak and hauled it up and over the landing, letting it slide down the banister and into the water that covered the lower level.

She squeezed past it, entered the water, and moved down the stairs. "Be right back."

****

"So, we have this new technology," Alex said, now seated on the couch, a mildly cool Coke in his hand. "It's a high-speed ground-based satellite and it fits in the space of a minivan." He held his hands out the full width of his arms. "Totally portable."

"Be freaking useful right now," Dar said.

"It would," John agreed. "We know it, freaking priceless because between the damage and the power, it's gonna be who knows how long before they get full cell or anything back."

"Lot of towers down," Dar said. "There's a repeater on the island here, but it doesn't do crap without the rest of it." She tilted her head with some interest. "What kind of technology is it?"

Alex took a sip of his Coke. "It's what the military uses, you know? But it's different targets, LEO, and it doesn't use the same channels they do so right now they're kinda open," he said. "It's a classified frequency but they classed it as experimental."

"If it's classified, how is it you can use it?"

"I'm attached to the naval research lab," John said, in an offhand way. "I have a license for it."

Dar's eyebrows lifted.

"It's legal," Alex said, quickly. "We've got a grant to try and develop a commercial use for it. You know? So, when this all happened, I said to John, hey, I bet we can figure a way to get this up and get commercial with it." He paused. "So here we are."

Dar folded her arms. "What do you need me for? You could get whatever price you asked for right now. You've got a whole damned island full of deep pockets jonseing for Internet."

"We do." Delgado smiled at her. "Problem is, we have the gear, and I know how to operate it, and John here knows how to bring up the service, but all that gets us is an internet connected minivan. Which is great, but limited. We want to sell this to everyone."

"Ah," Dar said. "You need a way to parcel it out."

"Exactly."

Trivial for her, in reality. "I might have the gear for that," She allowed, in a thoughtful tone. "Or where to find it, anyway."

"Sam said, if anyone on this island did, it would be you, or you'd be able to get it," Alex said. "But we got a limited timeframe, because we need to sell this package and get our money before they get everything else running again," he said. "I'm not pretending to any altruism here. I want seed money to prove this out as a new gig and these people here will pay anything for their convenience."

Dar found this comfortingly clear. "Got it," she said. "I want it to bring up my business. I'll hook you up and manage it as my cut," she said, in a decisive tone. "How's that?"

Alex smiled at her. "Man, I was hoping you were going to say that," he said. "My question is, can you really do it?" He asked her. "No offense. I have no idea who the hell you are and you're not my idea of some geeky cable brain."

He regarded the tall, mud stained, windblown, half clad woman leaning against the ornate French desk in the corner. "I've known a few of those in my time."

"I mean, you're obviously IT related." John pointed to the rack. "But I've never heard of your company." He sounded a bit apologetic. "Sorry."

Dar pondered the response, mostly feeling amused and not really offended. "I have no idea who you are either," She reminded them. "We try to stay low key," she added. "You'll just have to take my word for it when I tell you I can do what you're asking, and..." She casually shrugged. "And it'll be pretty apparent whether or not I can when I do it."

"Good point," John said. "Same with us."

"True," Alex said. "When can we start?"

"Where's your minivan?" Dar asked. "And how did you get it here?"

"Over by the club," John said. "In the parking lot behind that big building. I didn't get it here, it was here. Some guy had contracted us to look at it to bring in some soccer game or something for a party."

"What?"

"Yeah, I don't know. I was just hoping he'd have lots of rich friends we could talk to about it to be honest. I guess he couldn't get some game. He's from Spain," John said. "We got over here and found out he took off to get away from the storm."

Dar straightened up. "Let's go take a look," She said, briefly closing her eyes and picturing the layout of the island. "See what you got."

They got up from the couch. "You need anything to review it?"

"No. Just the eyeballs." Dar put her sunglasses on as they went out the door and back into the muggy heat. "Let's hope someone's got a spool of cat six somewhere."

****

Kerry waded outside and shoved a floating palm frond out of the way to allow her to see what was going on. Joe had his shotgun cocked. Its butt rested on his hip as he yelled at a small crowd of people on the other side.

"There are people trapped!" One of the crowd said. "C'mon, man!"

Kerry got to the edge of the boat. "Just me, Joe," she called out and boosted herself up and onto the deck, it's surface rocking under her weight. She got to her feet and came over to him. "What' going on?"

"What do you think?" Joe asked. "They want this boat and ain't none of them got near the bucks you do." He said. "Get back from there, buddy!" He added, angling the gun. "Don't come no closer."

"Listen, our friend is stuck in his house and we have to get him out." The nearest man said. He was standing in the chest high water, his T-shirt soaked in mud and a kerchief tied around his head. "Stop screwing around here, man."

"There's someone trapped here too," Kerry said. She gestured behind her at the house. "We need to get him to the hospital."

The man stared at her. "In there?" He pointed at the house. "We didn't hear anyone in there," he said. "We went to all the houses around here. No one answered."

Hard to tell really if he was accusing them of lying or excusing the group of ignoring someone in need. Kerry acknowledged it really didn't matter. "There's someone there, he's hurt, and we're going to get him help."

"There's people in there. I seen em," Joe added. "Maybe they didn't like the looks of ya. Thought you were gonna take their stuff."

"We're neighbors!" The man shot back, angrily. "They know us!"

Joe shrugged insolently. "I wouldn't let some of my neighbors in my place. Don't blame em."

Kerry glanced behind her. "Well, we're wasting time here," she said. "I'm sorry about your friend, but we're going to take care of the injured man in there first," she said. "So please get out of the way since I don't want anyone else to get hurt."

Joe nodded in agreement. "The guard'll get here eventually," he said, as the little knot of people reluctantly retreated. "Or it'll dry out. They should have stuff to eat in there if they stayed," he muttered. "Not be scrounging so fast."

"Maybe they stored it all on the first floor," Kerry said. "I don't think anyone expected this." She indicated the flooding. "They thought about the wind and all that stuff, not so much about the place being four feet under water."

"Could be true," Joe agreed. "I heard them talking it all up. We knew, though. Everyone by me found a place to hole up, off the ground. But we're used to the wet."

"Well. They didn't and we were lucky." She went back to the other edge of the boat. "Anyway, let me get Tomas out here before they come back."

"You figure they will?" Joe watched them. "They don't look like tough guys."

"Yeah, I do, since there's more of them than us, and it's hot and they're pissed off." Kerry jumped off the boat and back into the water. "And because people suck sometimes, you know?"

Joe chuckled briefly. "Heard that, Sergeant Major," he said. "Okay, get your buddies and let's get the hell out of here."

Kerry was totally on board with that idea. The heat and the never-ending seeping, dank smelling wet were getting to her. She plowed ahead through the floodwaters, stumbling a little as her foot struck some obstructions in the yard.

"Okay guys let... oh." She came around the edge of the downed tree and in view of the front door to find Tomas already sitting in the kayak with his leg awkwardly propped on the side of it, the front part of it framed in the open doorway. "Wow. Great job guys!"

Tomas looked like he was all in, though. His face was white as a sheet and Maria had hold of one of his hands, her face frightened. There was fresh blood on his leg and the bandage that was wrapped around it was now soaked. He was visibly biting the inside of his lip.

Mayte was behind them. "It was not so good, Kerry. Papa fell down the stairs," she said. "It was just a lucky thing the raft was there, and he went down on top of it."

"Oh, Kerrisita." Maria looked overwhelmed, as Kerry waded into the house. "This is a horrible thing." She looked around the lower level of the house and then firmly turned her head and looked outside instead.

Kerry got hold of the edge of the kayak and towed it back out toward the boat. "Yeah, it's a mess, Maria. But at least we're getting out of here now. Let's get you to the hospital fast as we can. Hang in there, Tomas," she said. "Easy... it's... there's a lot of stuff on the ground here."

"Oh." Mayte gripped the back end if the raft. "It is the rocks from the front, I think." She said. "Mama's little garden." She said. "The drinking fountain for the birds."

Now Kerry remembered, a vague picture in her head of the neat front yard, and its mango tree shaded rock garden with its stone bench and the table for dominos. She gently steered the kayak around the tree into view from the airboat. "Easy around that corner."

Joe put his gun down on the tackle box and come over to the near side. "That's a mess." He indicated the injury. 'You weren't kidding there, Sarge." He looked at the bloody fabric. "Broken?"

"Yes." Kerry pulled the raft over and came to a halt next to him. "What's the best way... I don't think he can get up on there." She looked at the edge of the boat, about a foot higher than the edge of the kayak. "Can we... "She paused. "What if we..."

She fell silent for a moment, then watched the edge of the deck dip down as Joe knelt on it and touched the front of the kayak.

"Pull the whole thing up on the deck," Joe said. "We can try it anyhow. Lemme get a rope on the front of that. Hang on." He went over to pick up a coil of rope near the chairs and then he paused and looked out past the other side of the boat. "Oh, crap."

Kerry turned her head and looked through the metal cage that wrapped around the engine fan. "Ah," she said. "Figured they'd be back." She spotted the group of men, now augmented by several more, heading back in their direction, with at least two guys wearing camo T-shirts.

They had sticks in their hands. It could have been to help them walk in the flood, but Kerry wasn't going to take the risk and she figured Joe wasn't in the mood to either. "Well, hell." She sighed. "That's not good."

"What is going on?" Mayte had worked her way around to Kerry's side. "Oh, those are the men who live down on the side of the block," she said. "They make noise with their cars all the time."

"Are they friends of your folks?" Kerry asked her. "Maybe we've got it wrong, and they'll help us get him onboard."

The younger woman looked past the edge of the boat, and then shook her head. "My papa does not like them, no," Mayte said. "We are friends with some of the families on this side of the block, but they went to the shelter."

"So, they're probly shitheads like we thought. Got it," Joe said. "Lemme get the engine going." He quickly returned to the edge and handed Kerry the rope. "Tie that on, yeah? Maybe we can pull the thing behind us if we haveta." He took his seat and pressed the starter on the engine, the sound of the huge fan spinning up filling the air.

"Mayte get up there." Kerry boosted herself onto the edge of the boat, getting the bow of the kayak between her knees as she laced the rope through an eyehole on the point of it and tied a knot in it. "Get your mom up there too."

Mayte climbed up onto the boat and walked over to where Kerry was sitting. "Can we... oh if we stand here..." She knelt. "Mama, come here and see if you can sit so we can bring the front on the top of this."

Joe came over. "Better hurry," he said. "I'm not stopping to argue with these shitheads." He took hold of the rope. "Help her up here and let's get this onboard."

Kerry scrambled over to the edge of the airboat and braced her boots, extending her hands to Maria. "C'mon," she said. "Let's get out of here, Maria, before we get into something I can't get us out of."

"Dios Mio." Maria was in tears. "Oh no, this is so terrible."

"It is." Kerry gripped her hands and hauled up with all her strength. "But we'll get through it."

"Get on!" Joe yelled. "C'mon c'mon!" He pushed Mayte ahead of him. "Get this and pull!" He put the end of the rope into her hands. "I gotta steer!"

Kerry managed to pull Maria onto the deck, both of them tumbling to the ground as Mayte wrapped the rope around her hands and tried to keep it taut. "I don't think I can hold this. "She yelped in alarm, her feet skidding on the deck as she was pulled toward the water. "Oh!"

Kerry got to her feet and got her hands around the rope. "Maria, stay there!" She yelled. "Stay on the side there and lean toward the water!" She glanced over her shoulder at the approaching group, who were yelling words being blown right back over their shoulders by the draft from the engine.

"I gotta back out of here!" Joe yelled. "I'm not letting them get their hands on this so hold the hell on to that rope!" He shifted the engine into gear and the airboat fan sent a wash of water backward as it started into motion.

"No, wait..." Kerry yelled. "Let me..." She jumped over and took hold of the front of the kayak as the airboat lumbered into a turn. "Hold on Tomas! Hold on to the side!"

Maria let out a yell of alarm. She reached out and grabbed hold of Tomas' good leg, leaning over the edge of the boat and making it dip down as Kerry bent her knees and tried to will the edge of the airboat to further dip so she could pull the front of the kayak up onto the edge of the deck.

"Mama!" Mayte lunged forward and grabbed hold of her mother's belt, and the weight of the three women was enough to send the edge of the boat low enough for the front of the kayak to slide up onto it.

"Mayte, grab this and pull!" Kerry scrabbled backward and grabbed onto the chair with one hand as she hauled the kayak with the other. "Pull!"

Mayte and Maria grabbed the kayak as it swayed and they all pulled, as the airboat swiveled in place and backed away from the house.

Kerry went to her knees and reached out to grab the other side of the kayak, trying hard to avoid slamming against Tomas' injured leg as the edge of the boat lifted up and lifted him with it, out of the water

"Oh!" A moan escaped him, as the inflated raft flexed under his body and he almost slid backward into the water. "Oh! Oh!"

"Crap!" Kerry leaped off the boat and into the water and got her shoulder under him. "Pull!" She yelled. "Hurry!" She saw the crowd approaching and heard Joe yelling something at her, but the sound of the engine overwhelmed the sense of what he was saying.

Kerry felt the boat moving and she grabbed hold of the edge of it, grimacing as she felt herself pulled over some underwater obstacle, something that felt like branches slamming against her legs. She tightened her grip and pulled herself forward, setting her shoulders against the side of the kayak.

She heard Mayte yell, and then a moment later the kayak moved onto the airboat and she pulled herself up onto the edge of it and out of the water just in time to avoid being scraped off and impaled by a broken off light post.

It caught the edge of her shirt though and a moment later she was being throttled by it, her breathing cut off abruptly. She heard Mayte cry out but there was no time to find out why as she was being dragged along the edge of the deck.

Gagging, she twisted to one side and ducked her head as the felt the shirt fabric rip. She grabbed the edge of the engine casing and turned, as the shirt was pulled off her body and left behind, the boat now moving faster and past the group of men.

The branches whipped against her bare skin as the boat moved past, leaving a stinging burn across her shoulders. The noise of the engines were deafening as she pressed against the cage around the blades for balance.

Ow. She ducked as they moved through another set of downed tree branches and turned, warding off a thick patch of leaves. She looked anxiously over at where Mayte and Maria were huddled over the kayak and Tomas, Mayte staring at her with one hand outstretched in protest, her eyes wide in shock.

At least he was onboard. Kerry reached up to rub her throat, and coughed, taking a moment to catch her breath. "That wasn't fun."

"Oh, Kerry! Are you okay?" Mayte gasped. "Your shirt is gone!"

"Better the shirt than my neck." She hauled herself to her feet. "Get the hell out of here." She got up next to Joe, who maneuvered through the debris, going through what had been Maria and Tomas' front yard and was now mostly just destroyed trash.

Behind them, she saw the group still yelling, one of them waving a piece of cloth in their direction. She saw the anger and frustration in their faces, but in that moment, found she didn't have it in her to care.

Joe glanced at her. "They were yelling something about the cops, no way I wanted to stick around for that." He paused. "That was kinda badass. You weren't keeping those bucks in that shirt pocket were ya?" He asked. "Cause I ain't going back for that unless you were."

Kerry's lips twitched slightly. "No." She ignored the knowledge she was dressed from the waist up in just a bra and pretended she had Dar's complete lack of body consciousness instead. "But they're wet. Hope you don't mind that."

"No problem," He said. "Where you want to take this guy? I can't get to Jackson in this thing."

Kerry thought about that. "Any place you know nearby? No, probably not, huh?"

"Probably not," Joe said. "Not with that. You got a dog bite or something, maybe." He steered the boat back out and onto the main roadway again, heading north. "He's gonna lose that leg or worse you don't find a fix for it."

Kerry glanced past him, hoping Maria and Mayte hadn't heard him. "Go back to the base," she said. "Back where you found me. I can get some help there."

"From the Guard?" He looked dubious. "Not from those dudes you told off," He said. "Though I dunno, they may like you better with your shirt off."

Kerry folded her arms over her chest, a brief, wry smile appeared on her face. "They might," she agreed mildly. "But at least there, I knew my sat phone worked and there might even be a guy on a motorcycle looking for me," she said. "I can give you your fee, and maybe someone else wants to hire you."

Joe looked sideways at her. "Kinda too bad, Sergeant Major," he said. "Don't think I'll find anybody like you there again."

"No, probably not."

****

Dar examined the gear stuffed in the back of the van thoughtfully. It was an expensive rig, and it smelled like machine oil and new electronics, planted into the back of a Mercedes cargo van that had been stripped of any interior except for the carpet.

"So, we figured we could hook up to maybe a wireless access point or something and do a trial," Alex said. "I picked up a few of those Linksys ones at the Best Buy before we came out here."

Dar pulled herself around the back of the rig and examined the connections to it. "Made for a cable plant."

"Mostly," John agreed. "Military, you know? All of it shielded and stuff." He was in the passenger seat, and Alex was in the driver's seat, both of them hanging over the back of their chairs watching Dar.

Dar studied the console. She reached over and flipped on the power and watched the lights and dials illuminate and the small integrated sine wave meter spin up. Over her head, she heard the dish power up, the roof of the van reinforced with a steel frame.

Alex got up and came into the back and sat on a small wooden stool next to the gear. He opened a hatch and folded it down to reveal a keyboard. "Let me get a signal. John, can you get the dish aligned?" He typed in a few commands.

John came over and with an apologetic look, edged past Dar to the back of the rig. He crouched down, his knees popping and cracking. "Ugh" He adjusted the settings. "Getting too old for this stuff."

Dar watched the readout's change, and the graph go from random patterns to a squared regularity. "That was fast."

Alex glanced at her. "You know that stuff?"

Dar smiled. "I know a little of everything," she said. "Enough to know what a pain in the ass aiming a satellite is. That was a fast connection."

"It's got a digital preset," John said. "And they're LEO, so they're a lot closer... there," he said. "Go ahead, Alex."

"See here I..." Alex sputtered as he found himself gently moved away from the keyboard when Dar took it over, examining the screen. "It's—"

"Unix," Dar finished for him. "SCO, I think." She pecked out a few commands. "Yeah," she said. "Let's see what this thing can do."

Alex and John exchanged looks. "Were you ...er... in the military?" John asked. "Or something?"

"Or something." Dar finished inspecting the machine's configuration. "This is relatively simple," she stated. "But it's meant to hook up to something else. Not just be an internet terminal." She looked at them. "I don't care, but did you walk out of a base with this?"

"No."

"Yes."

Alex glared at his partner. "What in the hell are you saying? You want to get us both in trouble? No, we didn't walk out of no place with this thing!"

"Yes we did," John repeated. "Drop the BS, Alex. Don't bother. It's not worth it and she said she doesn't care."

"And you believe that?" Alex seemed disgusted. "You're the one who said not to get my hopes up. What the hell changed your mind so fast?"

"What changed my mind was I just realized who the hell this is. Remember I said the name seemed a little familiar to me?" John asked. "You worked for ILS, right?"

"I did." Dar was busy with the keyboard. "Now I own my own consulting company. Worked out a lot better for me all around," she said. "But yeah, I don't care. One less thing for them to ask me to mess around with." She called up a configuration and reviewed it. "You might as well make some cash on this now. Once everyone realizes the market for this type of thing they won't' be able to make enough of them."

"Exactly," John said. "Cats out of the bag, you know. Key is this has access to that satellite net."

"It does." Dar ran some tests. "That's always been the bottleneck. This is pretty damn good speed and capacity." She glanced at them. "Hell, I'd buy one if you had them in production."

John smiled easily, and after a moment, Alex joined him in rather a bit more forced way.

She finished her work. "This'll work. I'll have to write drivers to let me hook up a router to it. Drive this thing over as close as you can get it to the security shack."

"The security shack?"

Dar nodded. "It's the only place they got any decent cabling out to the rest of the island. That's where all the cameras feed into." She leaned one arm on her knee. "They'll be serving lunch in that building over there. You want to sell your stuff? Sit down at one of the tables and just start talking."

"For real?" Alex said.

"For real. Tell them it'll take about six or seven hours to get things set up and sell them per device access, so they don't start putting their damn kid's gaming toys on it. I've got to get a router and get some cabling in place, but that'll give me plenty of time to get it done."

"Just like that." Alex half shook his head.

"Just like that." Dar squirmed out of the back of the van and stood up moving away from it as she felt her phone start to buzz in her pocket. "Scuse me." She pulled out the sat phone and opened it. "Yeah?"

"It's Mark," Mark said, sounding more than a little frustrated. "I'm out here at Southcom."

"You find Kerry?"

"No. She ran off with some guy on an airboat."

Dar stopped in mid motion and stared right ahead of her. "What?"

"You heard me," Mark said. "I talked to some guy here. She was here, no question. Some of these guys were around looking for her in fact," he said, pausing for a rush of noise to go by. "Some guy came around with an airboat and she took off with him. About an hour and a half ago."

"Well. Shit," Dar said, after a brief pause.

"She borrowed your one-track mind I think, boss," Mark said, in an almost apologetic tone. "She was really worried about Maria and her family."

"Yeah, now I'm really worried about all of them," Dar said. "Okay, stay there for now. Let me try to ... figure something out."

"Roger that," Mark said. "I'm gonna offer to help them fix something since at least they got power and AC here. Maybe they'll give me some ice water. I'll keep popping out to get signal."

"Okay," Dar said, closing the phone. "Soon as I find out something I'll call ya." She tapped the phone against her leg, then opened it up again and dialed. She listened to it ring, then she disconnected, and dialed again.

****

Kerry crouched down next to Tomas. "It's a really good thing we got you on this raft," she said. She rested her elbow on the edge of the kayak. "I know you're really hurting, but it would be a lot worse sitting on the deck."

He managed a faint, brief smile, his hands clenched on the edge of the raft.

Maria patted his arm. "We will get you help soon. It is fine, Tomas. It is better, we can get a doctor. Jesu knows how long it would take them to get to us for help."

"They don't have this kind of gear," Kerry told them. "Not even one of these." She indicated the inflatable. "They brought a lot of trucks and tents. Things to help people if they had holes in their roofs, that kind of thing."

"I did not think this is how we would use it," Mayte said. She sat next to the kayak, her back against the supports of the second chair. "Kerry, I feel so bad about your shirt."

"Don't," Kerry said. "Given how much time I spent in that water I was probably going to throw it out when I got home anyway. Or used it as a dog toy." She exhaled, aware of the sun blanketing her mostly bare body, glad she had a reasonable tan.

The breeze felt good against her skin, and riffling through her hair, drying the sweat damp discomfort. "I'm glad it ripped, and I didn't." She glanced at her watch. "And I'm super glad we found you guys."

"I was so mad at the phones," Mayte said. "We could get nothing. I was trying to see what I could do to get to help or get to call to you." She glanced up at Joe, who was focused on the flooded roadway they were coursing over. "This is amazing."

Kerry did cop to feeling a certain bit of internal satisfaction. It would have been easier for her to stay at the office and help Dar out, or hell, even cooking hamburgers and relying on the government to do their job. Much easier.

However, she, of all people, knew just how far to trust the government.

"If there is anyone who could find us, it would be Kerrisita," Maria said, blinking a little in the sunlight. "You and Dar will not be stopped."

"Si." Tomas nodded a tiny bit.

Well, that was sort of true. Kerry stood up and stretched out her knees. She stuck her hands into her pockets and fluffed out the fabric of her cargo pants to try and get them to dry, sighing a little inwardly at the squishiness of her boots.

She was glad, at least, she was wearing one of her solid-colored bras, which was almost like a bathing suit top and wasn't really too different than the gear she typically worked out in and she only wished they would stop going through clouds of insects as they intermittently bounced off her abs.

"I told them to go find the guys who run these out in the glades." Kerry said to Joe, after a long period of silence. "I told them to get on the short-wave radio and see if they could get hold of anyone."

"Who, those military guys?" He asked.

"Not the ones you talked to. The ones I was talking to before you got to Southcom," she responded. "It's the first thing I thought of you know? These airboats."

"What'd they say?"

"They thought it was a good idea. Those guys I talked to. They're from Alabama," she explained. "One of them catches frogs and things, so he got it."

Joe nodded. "Gigger."

"Yes."

He glanced at her. "What do you know about gigging, Sergeant Major? You're not a backwoods chick." He steered the airboat a little to the west, going around one of the highway islands the top of which was barely visible in the floodwaters.

"Definitely not," Kerry readily agreed. "I'm a WASP from Michigan and if I want frog's legs, I'll go to the nearest fancy French restaurant and order them." She paused thoughtfully. "But I do know what it is."

"Gigging?" Mayte looked up at her. "What is it?"

"Frog catching, Mayte." Kerry briefly smiled. "You take a pole with a sharp fork on the end of it and go out at night and catch frogs in the swamp."

Mayte stared at her. "You have done this?"

Joe started laughing.

"Absolutely not."

****

"So, what are we doing?" Arthur looked around the inside of the cottage. "Did they... oh yeah, they got the power in." He went over to the tall case and around the back of it, where a thick coil of black cable was now resting. "Let's see what we got."

"Great." Celeste came over to help him.

They uncoiled the cable and stretched it around the corner of the case, as Elvis reached up and unlatched the side lower hatch of the case, pulling it open.

Inside attached to the inner frame that the machines were racked in was an industrial power switch with a heavy twist lock plug in it and they connected the power to the plug and then stepped back.

"Wait." Elvis said. "How do we know it's the right power?" He said, as Arthur was about to engage the switch at the end of the strip. "What if it's wrong?"

Arthur studied the cable. "How in the hell can you tell?" He said, then he shrugged. "It's got a fuse in it." He hit the switch and jerked his hand back as it lit up.

They all waited and watched the light. It stayed on. "I don't smell burnt toast." Elvis observed. "Guess it's okay." He examined the stack of servers. "Let me pick one that's not like super urgent though to turn on."

"Crap." Arthur said. "You know what we don't have?"

Elvis paused. "Keyboard and monitor." He sighed. "I'm sure the boss has one."

"Has one what?" Ceci came over from the kitchen, where she'd been storing some supplies.

"We need a computer monitor and a keyboard." Arthur explained. "So we can see what's going on with these things. We got power."

'They didn't bring a KVM?" Elvis frowned. "I thought I saw one in there. Didn't I?"

Ceci studied the case. "Not my circus." She said. "Let me go get one of my monkeys." She turned and headed for the door, almost colliding with Andrew as he entered. "Turn around, sailor boy. We need our kid."

Andrew hauled up. "Ya'll got... "He saw the cable. "Yeap, they done got that done." He took a step back and held the door open. "Ah do not know where Dar went off to, but I expect we can find her."

"Stay here kids. We'll be back." Ceci sailed through the door and it closed after them.

The four of them sort of looked at each other. "We can let them boot." Arthur decided, pressing the start button on the machines one after the other. "See if we hear post beeps."

"And see blinkies." Elvis agreed, crouching down to look at the switch at the bottom of the rack the servers were plugged into. "That'll tell us something."

"Something." Arthur agreed, as he finished hitting the power buttons and then sat back to observe the results. "That'll take a while." He decided. "I'm gonna finish putting that stuff up." He went from the living room back into one of the bedrooms.

Inside there were two full size beds, with fluffy, luxurious bedding over thick mattresses. They were at right angles to each other, and between them were wood cabinets whose surfaces glowed with polish.

On the other side of the room was a door into a bathroom. Arthur fished inside the bag from the store and took out the supplies inside, bringing them into the bathroom and putting them down on one of the two sets of brass shelves.

He glanced around at the fixtures, which were all gleaming metal, and the surfaces, which were all glowing marble with the exception of the sink stand, which was teak. It smelled of polish and pine scent, and there wasn't even a bit of a stain in the perfectly even grout between the tiles.

The bathroom had an old-fashioned claw foot tub in it, but the tub had been fitted with brass piping and an arching showerhead that he figured had to spray the hell out of the tiles every time someone used it.

A sound made him turn, and he took a step back as one of the staff entered, with some bottles in her hand. "Oh, sorry, senor." The maid stopped. "I have some things here."

"No problem!" Arthur backed into the sink to let her pass. "This place is rich, huh?"

The housekeeper smiled and arranged the bottles onto a crystal glass shelf next to the tub. "Si, it is. Very much so." She said. "We take very good care of it here."

"Oh yeah." Arthur nodded. "There's not a speck of dust around." He said. "It's really nice."

The girl finished and turned. "It is nice for you to see that. Most guests who stay here pay no attention."

"They're used to it." Arthur guessed.

"Si, because they are here mostly to look at the houses, to buy one." The girl explained. "It is nothing special to them, you understand?"

"I get it." Arthur said, looking up and past her as Elvis entered. "It's swank. But it's cool, and it's sweet our boss brought us over here."

"For sure, we lucked out." Elvis joined him at the door to the bathroom. "Super slick idea to come out to the office, dude." He said. "But I can't see the chiefs hanging out here. It's like if Dar started driving a Ferrari."

They backed out to let the housekeeper get out of the bathroom. "I got the scoop on that." Arthur said, as he went back over to the bed and started taking the polo shirts out. "She inherited that place she got over here"

"Yeah?"

"Yeah. I seen pictures of their place down in the keys. Way more like I pictured their style." Arthur examined the shirts, and removed the neatly pinned tags from them, tiny little brass safety pins he set aside on the dresser. "All stone and beach and stuff." He said. "And a place to dock the boat."

"That boat's nice." Elvis said. "Wish I had one like that."

"You see the way she drives it? That was nuts, with the case." Arthur said. "I thought we were all gonna be jumping in to grab that case and it wouldn't have done no good. Woulda been dead, and we'd still be over there sweating."

"But we ain't." Elvis piled his clothes up and took out a bag of the chocolate covered pretzels, opening them and offering the bag to Arthur. "Let's see what those boxes are doing. We may need one of Mark's server guys if those things don't boot up."

"We might."

They walked back into the living area, where Celeste and Angela were busy setting out office supplies on the dining room table, which had been pushed up against the far wall with the chairs arranged around the three accessible sides.

A stack of lined yellow pads, and island logo pens, and file folders, and a big, heavy package of white copier paper to go with the all in one printer copier that was sitting on the floor nearby.

"We brought some of these." Elvis reached into the case and removed two desk phones. "Not sure what we can do with em though." He regarded the devices. "Let's run some cable around to that table, huh? We can put them out there."

"Need some internet juice." Arthur concluded. "What I hear though, that ain't happening any time soon." He went over to the case and ducked down, reaching in and pulling out a spool of thin cabling. "I heard on the radio the place where all the circuits come in is all chewed up."

"We got our DB here." Elvis said. "We got that and the lappies. We can work."

"If these things do." Arthur started unrolling the cable. "Guess we'll find out."

****

Dar folded her arms over her chest and regarded the cabling plant. To one side, two of the island engineers stood, the door to the plant held in their hands as they watched her in expectant silence.

The large casing, they were standing near held a huge tangle of stiff, dusty coaxial cabling with labels mostly rubbed off that was connected into a central hub covered in cobwebs.

A lizard peeked out from behind one of the junctures, tilting its head at the unexpected light.

The minivan was parked nearby, its engine turned off, its doors slid open, and its windows rolled down.

It was hot, and Dar was suddenly aware of the sound of crickets, which had been missing. It distracted her focus, already not at its best since most of her brain was off somewhere imagining the many situations Kerry could have gotten herself into by now.

Kerry was, she well knew, a sensible, thoughtful person who had a good core of common sense and didn't lightly take unconsidered chances. Of the two of them, she was the one who was apt to want to stop, and think, and discuss before doing something.

So, some dude with an airboat stops by. Dar really only had her own self to blame for it, because after all who had come up with the bright idea of finding an airboat? Had she not told Kerry, in fact, that was exactly what she needed to find?

Why yes, she had. She'd even told her where she'd most likely find one, but she had thought, not unreasonably, that Kerry would have gone with Mark to some place like Tigertails and hired them.

Not hook up with some rando by herself.

Her immediate instinct was to head off to the mainland and go find out. It was very difficult to look at the tangle of coaxial cabling and make her brain try to engineer this whole thing about internet that she now no longer cared about.

Logic alone held her there. The fact that while she could get on the Dixie and run over to the shore, once there, she had no way to get anywhere unless she called Mark back over and she wanted him to stay where he was in case Kerry came back there.

Even if she was able to obtain a vehicle, Kerry was now out on an airboat, which meant she was going places neither Mark on his motorcycle nor she in a typical car could follow.

She needed either an amphibious truck, or an airboat herself. Where was the nearest.... She glanced up at Sam, who was standing by. "Anyone out here have a jet ski?"

"Um." Sam stared at her, then at the cable, obviously trying to put her question together with the problem they were reviewing. "Uh... I mean sure I guess some of the residents do... I think... is it Chambers? Has one he keeps on the back of his boat."

John came up behind her. "So, what's the plan?" he said. "Boy were you right. We got bites so fast it's nuts. We're gonna make a mint."

Dar cleared her throat. She briefly closed her eyes and forced her mind to focus on the question. "So, this cabling goes from here out to all the camera sites," she said. "Problem is it's all coax." She studied the panel. "With converters on both ends we can make it carry IP."

"Do we have that?"

Sam cleared his throat. "Well, like I was telling Dar here. We had this project we were going to do to make these cameras all be internet cameras?" He looked from one to the other. "Anyway, we had this bunch of stuff sent over but the company who we contracted to do it flaked out."

Dar eyed him. "That seems to happen a lot."

"Cheapest bid," Sam acknowledged, with a half shrug. "So, we got all this stuff in the warehouse, and it's been sitting there for months. Maybe you can use some of it?" He eyed John. "My boss is gonna wanna get money for that though," He said. "That stuff wasn't cheap."

"Well..." John hesitated. "We didn't plan on any of that."

"Add the cost of each of them into the cost of the package," Dar said, in a dismissive tone, before anyone could say anything. "Individually it's peanuts." She exhaled. "Okay let's look at what that is, and I'll see if it'll do what we need. Then I need to get over to my office and pick up some gear to put in the middle of it."

John nodded. "Sounds good," he said. "Or, well, it sounds like at least there's a chance it'll work. Let's go look at the stuff—but I got one question. Who's going to go connect up the ends on the far side?"

"You," Dar said. "Move." She pointed to the cart. "I need to get this done. I've got other things to take care of I gotta get to." She pulled out her phone and dialed a number, it rang but wasn't answered.

****

The sound of the engine made speaking difficult, and so they had all gone silent as the airboat cruised along the flooded roadway heading north.

Kerry could see on the horizon, where she thought they had come from. She was already thinking ahead to what she would do and what she would say once they arrived back at the staging area.

Would the group she'd been with still be there? If they weren't, what would her strategy be? Just find the first person she could and get them to help?

Maybe do that anyway, and not waste time looking for the crew from Alabama? It should be straightforward enough, since after all she was bringing Tomas to them, not asking them to go find him. That was it. She would search out the first soldier she saw, and then, only if that didn't pan out would she try to find the others.

She nodded a little to herself, satisfied with this internal dialog. It was a habit of hers, making up little scenarios in her head and working out how she'd deal with them so when she was in the moment, she had a plan.

Totally opposite of what Dar did. Kerry smiled briefly. Dar just dealt with everything in the moment, and seldom made an attempt to prepare at all, content to allow her experience and intelligence to produce whatever it did.

So now, she cleared her throat a little, holding onto the rickety seat with one hand and wished the ride was over. And poor Tomas, whose face was white as a sheet and was in a cold sweat, was getting the attention he needed.

Kerry felt helpless, despite knowing she was literally doing all she could to get him where he needed to be. She kept going back to thinking about if she should have tried to contact someone or do something to make it happen faster.

Could she? Tomas was just one of thousands who needed assistance. She glanced over at him, and at Maria, who sat on the deck and held his hand, her face reflecting utter worry and misery.

She exhaled. Well, they were almost there, so no point in thinking about it.

"Okay, hang on," Joe called out. "We're gonna turn east."

Mayte, who leaned against the cowl around the engine fan leaned forward and took hold of the kayak, her young face solemn but stolid. She looked up as Kerry knelt beside her and grabbed hold of the raft with one hand and the seat with the other.

"Go on, Joe." Kerry said. "We're hanging."

The airboat tilted and Kerry leaned back, her fingers wrapped tight around the rubber tie down on the edge of the kayak as gravity pulled against them. Her knees were braced on the slightly corrugated surface of the deck and for a moment she thought she felt things start to slide off.

"Hang on," she told Mayte.

"Si, I have it." Mayte took hold of the edge of the fan cowl with one hand and pulled alongside Kerry. "Thank you, Kerry. You are amazing."

They pulled the kayak back the inch or so it had slid and then the airboat completed its turn and they were heading up the street toward the staging area, toward the flooded field where she had first boarded the boat with Joe.

"Get you far as I can," Joe said, briefly. "Gonna pull up near that tree up there. Don't want to get stuck."

Kerry got to her feet. "I'm going to get off and go get some help," she told him "I don't' want to try dragging him off the deck. It's just going to make things worse."

"Gonna charge you for waiting then." Joe eyed her. "Just like a taxi, you know?"

Kerry looked right back at him, their eyes almost level, as she put her hands on her hips, one eyebrow hiking up. She drew in a breath, her body flexing with it, and then let her facial expression speak for her.

Finally, he smiled just a little. "Just kidding, Sergeant Major," he said. "Just don't take too long cause I gotta go find me some more suckers, y'know?"

"If these guys are smart, they'll hook up with you once I talk to them," Kerry said. "But believe me I'm not going to waste a minute getting people over here to help him. He's really in pain."

Joe nodded. "That leg's a bitch." He throttled down the engine as they approached a tree laying sideways across the road, its branches extending out. "G'wan." He reversed the clutch, and the airboat slowed abruptly cutting the breeze to nothing as the boat bumped up against one of the branches.

"Okay." Kerry went to the front and jumped off, back into the water. "I'm going to go get some help. You guys stay here." She sloshed through the warm, murky water and got around the edge of the boat. "Hang in there, Tomas, I'll bring back a medic."

"Kerrisita," Maria said. "Should you go like that? Mayte or I should—"

"Nah." Kerry smiled easily. "It'll help me get attention fast. Don't' worry about it," she assured them, with more self-confidence than she actually possessed. "Be right back." She turned and evaded the branches of the fallen tree and started up to where the road emerged from the floodwaters.

There was a long, awkward pause. Then Joe went to the box and removed a rope, going over to tie the edge of the airboat to one of the branches. He glanced over his shoulder. "So...is she a friend of yours?"

"Kerrisita is our boss," Maria said.

"But she is also a good friend," Mayte added, after a pause. "And very smart."

"She's your boss," Joe repeated. He folded his arms over his chest.

"What do you all do? Are you like... a wilderness trek adventure tour seller or something? Or real estate or." He glanced over where Kerry had just disappeared. "Or a gym?"

"No," Mayte said. "We do computers."

His dark eyebrows drew sharply together, and he stared at her. "Say what?"

"We do computers," Mayte repeated. "We do programs and make things with computers and things like that." She got up and reached into the back pocket of her jeans and removed a slim billfold. She took out a somewhat soggy card and handed it to him. "That is us."

Joe took the card and looked at it. Then he handed it back. "Well." He half shrugged. "Guess everyone always needs computers, huh?" He sat down on the edge of his seat and looked at them. "But I ain't never had a boss like that, tell you what."

****

Dar eased her head around the palm fronds, their spikes catching her hair as she tried to avoid having them poke her in the eye.

Most people would not have suspected that palm trees, those elegant and well-known landmarks of the tropics actually had three-to-four-inch spikes on their floofy looking fronds and were a bit of a metaphor for the often creepy danger that rode under Miami's flashy and beach filled surface.

Dar had gotten one right through the center of her hand once, while trying to retrieve a likely looking coconut to open. Put her off the damn things for a long time.

Set in the crown of the palm tree, in the center of where the fronds all met, was a casing carefully hidden inside a covering of palm trunk colored plastic that she cautiously poked a screwdriver into the base of. She inserted the blade of the driver into a small slot and then twisted it.

The casing didn't budge. With a sigh, she left the screwdriver in place and retrieved a pocketknife from her cargo shorts and opened its blade up one-handed. She eased closer to use it to pry along the place where the base met the covering.

Inside the casing, behind the plastic, she saw a camera inside. She pried a little harder and heard a cracking sound, and then the top tilted up as the screwdriver fell out of place and tumbled down the length of the palm tree. "Crap."

She hastily stabbed the knife into the tree bark and pushed open the casing to expose the camera inside. It was covered in cobwebs, and the lens was cracked. Dar examined it for a moment, and then reached in and yanked it free of its housing.

It came away with such ease it nearly made her reel back off the ladder and she grabbed hastily at the palm fronds to keep from falling.

After her balance stabilized, she inspected the back of the camera. She put it down and then removed a piece of gear from her thigh pocket. She turned the camera around to look at the connections. "Seems simple enough."

She twisted the connector off the back of the camera and connected the cable into the device instead. Then she took the small jumper and put it where the original cable had been. It fit. But would it work? With a slight shrug, Dar climbed down the ladder to where a roll of cable was and sat down on it.

She unrolled a length of the cable and removed another tool from another pocket. She set it down again when she sighed, and looked up to see where she'd left her knife sticking in the bark. "Damn it." She got back up, climbed back up the ladder, yanked the knife out of the bark and got back down again.

Dar used the knife to strip the end of the cable, then closed it and put it in her pocket before she maneuvered the ends of the bare, thin, copper strands into a plastic connector. She muttered under her breath as she sorted the colors.

She used the tool to crimp the connector around the cable and then stood up, looping the cable and then wedging the loop in place in one of the jagged trunk husks that surrounded the palm. With a satisfied nod, she turned the spool of cable on its side and kicked it toward the cottage and watched the cable unroll as she walked behind it.

This might get them at least some access. How useful she had no idea. She walked up the steps, lifted the spool up, and rolled it across the porch until it bumped up against the outside of the building.

First things first. Might as well see what damage the servers had taken, to see if any of this was even worth her time.

Dar pushed open the door and entered the cottage, surprised to hear the distinct sounds of both server fans and keyboard clicking. "It come up?" She asked, in surprise. "All of them? Or just… what's the deal?"

"Uh huh." Arthur sat on the couch, legs extended, his laptop on his lap with a cable extended from it over to the case. "Auth and services are up, and the database is running an internal self-check."

"Huh." Dar planted her hands on her hips. "Nice."

On the ground in front of the server case was a monitor and a keyboard on the floor, their cables draped behind them.

"Your pop brought that over from your place." Elvis entered the room with his own laptop, a coil of ethernet cable in his other hand. "I got everything up to console and put the encryption keys in, so they'd boot."

Another cable ran across the floor to the table against the window, where Angela was seated using another laptop, pecking at the keys. A phone was in front of her, and it too was cabled to the switch mounted in the bottom of the rack. "The note system is working," she said to Dar. "I'm trying to keep track of everything for Ms. Maria."

"Unreal everything survived," Dar muttered. "Guess we had to have some luck, huh?"

"Checking the repository," Arthur said, briefly. "Problem's going to be we can't synch it out to anything. I mean, the build stuff is all here, and we can work local like you said, but man it feels weird not to be able to look stuff up."

"I'm working on that, matter of fact," Dar said. "I gotta run back to the office and grab a router and see if I can get something going. We need anything else here? I'm gonna grab the spare switch there too."

Both Arthur and Elvis looked up at her with interest. "Yeah?" Elvis sat down in one of the plush chairs on the far side of the living room. He put down his laptop and then stood back up to run the cable back across the floor toward the rack. "I think we're okay for now, for gear."

"Yeah," Dar paused. "So, since you all have this well in hand, let me go grab the boat and head back over. "Good job, people," she added. "We're gonna get there."

"Would you like me to take the cart for you over to the marina?" Celeste asked, a touch diffidently. "Your parents have the other one and they were going to get something." She had been organizing the pads and supplies on the table.

"I would." Dar patted her pockets. "Matter of fact, c'mon with me, I could use a hand carrying stuff out."

Celeste smiled in response. "Yes, ma'am."

Chapter Eight

Kerry was glad enough to get out onto dry land again and she made quick progress down the road toward the gates of the staging facility. She now had the sun warm on her back and her skin felt tight and a bit tender. She suspected aloe was somewhere in her future. Which was fine. If that was the most she got scolded for by Dar, along with the aloe, she'd take it.

Not much had happened since she'd been there last. There were more trucks parked in the lot, and two trucks pulled satellite rigs behind them. Now that the sun was bent westward, at least the heat was dissipating a little bit and a breeze had come up, with a welcome stirring of the humid air.

She was spotted as she cleared the last downed tree and one of the gate guards came out around the gate, one hand resting on his sidearm as she continued to approach.

Kerry felt a moment of wry irritation. C'mon, dude. How dangerous do I really look here in cargo pants and my underwear?

That thought seemed to occur to the guard as well, as he dropped his hand down to his thigh and then held up his other hand palm out toward her. "Ma'am?" He asked, in a questioning tone. "Are you all right? What's wrong?"

"Hi," Kerry said, in a brisk tone. "I have some friends back there behind the turn in the road, where it's still flooded. One of them has a badly broken leg. I need some help." She stopped a few feet short of him. "Can you help me, please?"

He reacted immediately to the entreaty in her tone. "Oh yes... oh yes, ma'am, absolutely." He turned and waved at the gate. "Need a medic!" He yelled, then turned back to her. "Would you... ah... "

"I'd love a T-shirt if you have one, and a cup of coffee," Kerry said. "But first off, I need to get my friend helped." She pulled her phone out of her pocket. "And let me see if I can get hold of some people while that's coming."

Three soldiers came running out of the gates, one of them with a kit slung over one shoulder. "What's the... oh, are you hurt, ma'am?" The medic in the lead asked her. "I see you're a little sunburned... you got some heat stroke?"

"No," Kerry said. "Back there, I have a friend who's got a broken leg. He got hurt in his house. He needs help very badly." She turned and waved them on. "I think you're going to need a stretcher."

The guard ran back to the guard station and stepped inside. Now he came back out and came trotting back over to her. "Here you go, ma'am," he said. "Can't help with coffee, but I had a shirt in the shack there." He held out his hand with a mottled green cotton wad of fabric. "Probably big on ya but it'll get ya out of the sun at least."

"I'll get a stretcher," the second medic said. "Go on and see what we got here, Jase. It's good, at least we can help someone instead of just hanging around here doin nothing."

"Yeah, got ya," Jase the medic answered. "Show me where we're goin, ma'am. We'll get it taken care of."

Kerry pulled the shirt over her head. It smelled of sun and bleach and a little bit of machine oil and she totally could not have cared less. "Thank you very much," she told the guard. "Let's go." She turned and headed back along the road, with the other two medics at her heels. "Really glad to see you guys."

"Glad you found us," the medic with the case said. "Where'd they get hurt?"

"Sweetwater," Kerry said. "Their house is flooded up to the second floor."

"We saw pictures," the other medic said. "We asked when we were going down there, but they don't' have no place set up for us yet." He half leaned over with the weight of the medical kit in one hand. "Damn it's hot."

"It is." Kerry led the way into the water and toward the tree. "Hang on guys! We're coming!"

"Feel bad for folks, y'know?" the medic said. "Seen some bad stuff down in the city."

They splashed around the tree and came within view of the airboat.

"Hey look at that!" The second medic said. "That's the ticket, man. That's what we need." He had dark skin and short, buzz cut hair. "More of those, right? C'mon let's go check that out."

Both medics now outpaced Kerry and the one with the kit set it down on the edge of the boat and went to work, focused on Tomas. "Easy man, we'll take care of you," the first medic told him. "What's your name?" He stayed in the hip deep water while the second medic climbed up onto the deck. "Excuse me, ma'am"

Maria slid back out of his way. "Gracias, gracias. Thank you so much for coming," she said. "He feels so bad with it." She watched the medics with an expression of relief.

"We'll take care of him, don't worry," Jase reassured her. "I been deployed twice. I know what to do here." He ripped open packages while the second medic put on a stethoscope and started rinsing Tomas' leg off with sterile water. "Let's get all that dirt offa there."

Joe came over to the edge of the boat next to Kerry. "Fast." He nodded at her approvingly. "Even got you a shirt. Nice work, Sergeant Major. Wasn't even ten minutes." He eyed her. "Ready to pay me?" He asked. "I got places to go, y'know? Want to get back to my place before it gets dark."

Kerry unbuttoned the back pocket of her cargo pants and pulled out a sheaf of folded bills. She sorted through them and kept half, then handed him the other half. "There ya go. "I'll be glad to see home myself tonight."

With a look of patent disbelief, Joe took the bills, counted them quickly, then folded them and put them into the front pocket of his jeans. "You actually were walking around with a wad of cash in your pocket? Are you for real? Do you know what dudes do finding chicks like that?"

Kerry folded her arms. "So why didn't you?" She finally asked. "I told you I had cash."

Joe looked at her in silence for a very long moment. "Did you want me to?" He asked, finally, in a doubtful yet puzzled tone. "You don't seem like that kind of weirdo."

"No." Kerry smiled faintly. "I just took a chance. You seemed like a stand-up guy. I work with people a lot. You get to recognize what's in their head."

He folded his arms, a lopsided smile appearing on his face. "You are kinda weird," he said. "But I seen worse I guess."

It had been a chance. Kerry acknowledged it. But standing here, seeing Tomas getting care, she felt it had been a worthwhile chance because it had the outcome she'd wanted it to. "I wanted to get help for my friends." She added, almost as an afterthought. "And you had exactly what I needed."

Would Dar have done it?

Or would Dar have just bought the damn airboat from him and drove it herself?

"Well, If you're a weirdo, at least you got cash," Joe finally said. "So, I guess it worked out okay."

Kerry smiled. "Win win?" She said, looking up at Joe. "You could stick around. I bet these guys could find something for you to do." She leaned closer and lowered her voice. "And those buildings have air-conditioning."

"Nah." Joe shook his head slightly. "They had their chance. I'm gonna go back around where that house was. I bet some of them folks there'll pay me."

"Be careful they don't try to take your boat," Kerry said, in a serious tone.

"You didn't like their heads?" Joe eyed her. "I should take you back out to the swamp. My mama'd like you, she's into all that stuff."

"Like I said." Kerry glanced at the small crowd. "You get to know what people's intent is. Just be careful."

"Huh."

"Okay," the dark-skinned medic said. "Got that splint on you, sir, and we're gonna lift you up and get you on our stretcher here. Then we'll take you inside. We got a triage room set up." He motioned to the other medic. "This here raft, that was a great idea."

"My daughter," Tomas said, proudly, though somewhat faintly, gesturing at Mayte. "And too, la jefa, Kerry."

Both medics turned to look at Kerry.

The sound of splashing interrupted them, and Kerry turned her head to see several bodies coming around the fallen tree, and after a blink they became slightly familiar to her. "Billy!" She called out, recognizing the figure in the lead. "Hey!"

"Hey yeah! There ya are!" Billy came plowing through the water. "You found you an airboat!" He said. "These your buddies? You were looking for?" He pointed at the deck. "Hi, there you all."

The others behind him came over, two of them going to where the medics were getting ready to shift Tomas over to the stretcher. "What happ... oh man look at his leg," one of them said. "Easy now there buddy. We'll get you to the clinic."

"Captain was looking for you. We wondered where you went off to," Billy said. "Should have figured you got it done." He had taken off his camo overshirt and was just in a T-shirt, as they all were, and sweat stained from neck to waist, his pants liberally mud spattered and dark gray.

Joe watched this in silence.

"Thanks," Kerry said. "Billy, this is Joe. It's his airboat." She indicated the vehicle. "Joe, this is Billy from Alabama. I bumped into him out where the flooding was. His squad gave me a ride back here."

"Hey, man." Billy held a hand out. "This your rig huh? You hunt with it?"

"Yeah." Joe eyed him with some suspicion. "You hunt?"

"Sure." Billy smiled easily. "I got me a flat bottom, and just before we came out here, I was catfishing off it," he said. "This is nice. Can I come up there?"

Joe thawed visibly. "Sure." He took a step back to allow Billy to climb onboard. "Watch out for the stick."

One of the other guard came over to stand next to Kerry, the short woman who had been gathering papers in the tent. "Some guy came looking for you," she said. "So, we were trying to figure out where you went, then the gate said you went off with that guy."

"Guy on a motorcycle?" Kerry asked. "The guy who showed up?"

The woman nodded. "You know him I guess," she said. "Sweet bike."

"He works for me." Kerry felt relieved. "I was hoping he'd show up here. Now I can get back to my office before a whole posse shows up looking for me in an M1 tank." She pulled out her phone and dialed Mark's number, regarding the phone as it rang and rang but wasn't answered. "Jesus these things are worthless."

"They are," the woman agreed. She took a step back and tugged Kerry's shirt. "Let's get out of their way, got enough people there picking that guy up."

Kerry put the phone back in her pocket. "He's probably inside the building." She moved back to allow the gang to gently get Tomas situated on the stretcher. "Stupid things made to be used in hurricanes that don't work inside or in the rain... Jesus!"

The woman laughed. "Yeah. I think he was with the technical people or something I saw him going into one of the kit rooms with a cable or a piece of gear."

"Definitely Mark if I had any doubt at all." Kerry chuckled. "Glad he's here."

The woman regarded the crowd around the stretcher. "Family?" She asked Kerry finally, in a mild tone.

"No, the two ladies work for my company," Kerry said. "Hey, guys, Mark's here," she called out. "He's over where we're heading to."

Mayte looked up as they got off the deck, the stretcher carried by four of the guard as the medics packed up their kit. "Here?" She looked around. "That is so great. We are all almost together."

"Coming close." Kerry turned. "Joe, you sure you don't' want to stick around? I bet Billy can introduce you to his captain, who'd love to talk to you about your boat. Right, Billy?"

"For sure," Billy agreed immediately. "C'mon, Joey. Let's go get you a drink and we can talk to the cap. We were looking for something like that out there, like Kerry told us to. We just didn't have a way to find ya."

"We can pull this in," two of the remaining guard said. "Will ya give us a ride later?"

Joe paused, then nodded. "Sure," he said. "So far I done well out of hanging with the Sergeant Major here. Coffee sounds good." He locked the engine and joined them as they waited for the stretcher to pass ahead of them, and then trooped after. "Leave it tied here," he told the guards. "Don't want to scrape the bottom. I took the key. Needs some gas anyhow."

"We got that," Billy said. "Whole tanker full."

"Sweet."

****

Dar set the sat phone on the flying bridge console, reflecting again on how frustrating the device was. Just as she thought that, though, it rang, and she picked it up and answered it. "Yeah?"

"Dar!"

"Hey, Colleen." Dar was disappointed. "What's up?" She asked. "Everyone doing all right up there?"

"Can hardly hear ya," their finance director said. "Are you on the boat again?"

"Headed back over to the office. I'm working on getting us back online," Dar said. "How's it there?"

"Well, that's why I'm calling. I tried calling Kerry first, no answer."

"Long story," Dar said. "She's trying to help out Maria and Mayte. So's Mark. They found Zoe."

"Righto, yep I heard that. Well here's the thing—we got the phones working and switched on the lines from Miami, and let me tell you, it's been... well, I hired two people on the spot to just sit here at a table answering the lines and taking notes."

"Jesus."

"He called too, dontcha know?" Colleen said. "Wanted to know about some circuit you promised him for yesterday."

Dar had to chuckle a little, however wryly. "What in the hell do these people expect? They not watching the news?" She sighed. "I'm doing everything I can." She looked around at the waterway. "I'm literally sitting here trying to figure out where to steal a truck to go get things moving. Gimme a break."

"Sure. That's what we're telling everyone who's calling but some of them don't want that from me and want to talk to either one of you. Can I give the nabobs, you know who I mean, this number?" Colleen said. "It's a handful. Probably five or six."

"Government?" Dar guessed. "We delivered our last checkpoint to them before the storm hit."

"And they paid for it," Colleen said. "I just ran the reports. Their payment hit the account so that's good news at least. But they've been the hottest trying to get you, said something about coming to find you themselves."

"Like we need more random military showing up here." Dar sighed. "Yeah, give them this number. No guarantee it'll work, but it's all we got for now. In maybe... "She studied the horizon, adjusting the throttles to send the Dixie along the coastline. "Maybe two or three hours I might have more access. Might."

"And we've got a ton of calls coming in," Colleen said. "Can we do this, can we do that, this emergency, that emergency, you know how it goes. If we could answer some of them, we can triple our budgets for the year."

"Colleen."

"What do you want? I am the financial person around here." Colleen sounded unrepentant. "People standing at the door with money in their hands I have to tell you about," she said. "And that lawyer was looking for you. Said it was something important."

"Richard?"

"We have more than one?"

Dar chuckled again. "Okay. Yeah, sure, give out this number to everyone. What the hell."

"Thank you, m'dear," Colleen said. "I will do that but will let them know it's not a definite connection. Let me know what the status is with the gals, would you? People here are asking. Everyone who called from the staff down there I told to drive up here. I've got some additional space."

"Thanks, Colleen," Dar said. "We'll get through this. I'll let you know soon as I hear from Kerry."

"Sure. And let me know what to tell Jesus about his circuit," Colleen said. "Something about Mary and Instagram was it?"

"Bye." Dar hung up, still laughing.

****

Carlos was waiting on shore when Dar nudged the bow of the Dixie into the sailing club's dock. The somewhat ramshackle pier they'd built and then almost destroyed had been bolstered, and, with doors and pieces of wood now presented a reasonably sturdy ramp.

"There's a rope on the front there," Dar told Celeste. "Toss it to Carlos. I don't want to hit that thing again."

"Sure." Celeste climbed down the ladder to the deck and moved quickly along the side of the boat to the lines coiled on the bow.

"Hey, boss." Carlos walked down the ramp and caught the rope as it was thrown to him. "Looks good, huh?" He gestured at the dock.

"Nice job." Dar cut the engines and let the Dixie settle against the dock. "Where'd you get all that wood?"

"Came off the windows." Carlos finished tying up the lines. "We figured we might as well use it, and Arthur's dad brought over those telephone poles from down the road."

Dar climbed down and then stepped over from the boat to the dock, surprised at the sturdy feel of the platform. "Feels pretty good. I gotta grab some gear from the storeroom. Mark's out at Southcom."

Carlos nodded. "He called me before. He said Kerry found some boat or something?"

"Or something," Dar said wryly. "I'm hoping the both of them get back there in one piece." She led the way up the ramp to the shore. The sailing club was still deserted and in a shamble, and none of the properties along the shore showed any life either.

They crossed the road and went up the walk to the office, and Dar saw all the windows flung wide open, furniture that had been soaked by the rain out in the yard drying in the sun. "You guys are really kicking ass."

Carlos smiled. "Wasn't just me and my buds," he said. "There's like a two-dozen people here now."

Dar eyed him. "Our people?"

"Our people, your people, some of the people from the café... randos... we're like the community center," Carlos said. "Everyone brought over stuff to share out, and stuff that was in freezers. We figured we might as well grill it before it goes bad."

"Good point."

Inside the office, it was hot, but with the windows open and the evening breeze coming onshore it wasn't as stifling as it had been. Dar heard voices, and the sound of a radio playing news. The inner doors to the courtyard in the middle of the square building were all open and a light gust of wind brought the scent of charcoal inside.

"So, what is it you need?" Carlos asked. "I coulda got it ready for ya."

"Not sure what we had in storage. I know Mark sent out a bunch of gear ahead of the storm," Dar said. "I need some switches and a router. Hope one of them got left."

She glanced outside as they walked along the hallway and then paused and stopped. "Huh." She went and stuck her head out the door. "Hey, people."

There were a dozen figures outside. The owners of the café down the street were there, standing next to a small wagon full of boxes. Celeste's colleague Jerry was loading charcoal into the grill, and two more people from ILS, one of the accounting admins and a cleaning supervisor were there, getting hot dogs set up to grill.

Carlos' two buddies were wrestling a table into place. Two of their LAN technicians were carrying boxes over to the picnic area, and one of Colleen's data entry clerks was there, opening a bag of chips.

Everyone turned at her voice. Celeste squeezed out from behind her and went over to the two newcomers, greeting them as they stood there a little uncertainly as they watched Dar approach.

The café owner came over. "Hello there, Dar. Thought we'd empty out the freezer. Carol said she saw you guys were down here. Not much else is going on. Most everything else down here's empty except Charline at the bar."

"The shack?" Dar asked, glancing past him as though she could see the little dive bar from where they were, which she could not. "She come down and open up, Dan?"

"Sure. Whiskey doesn't go bad," Dan said, in a practical tone. "Only crowd in town's down there. I left a big box of muffins with her. Figure they gotta soak it up with something." He observed Jerry now lighting the grill. "How'd you do out on the island?"

"Fine," Dar said. "Had a lot of surge come over, but it's got good drainage. House is fine. You?"

"Tree's down in the yard and we lost part of the roof over the living room." Dan shook his head a bit. "Seen pictures of out west. Don't make sense, does it? You live right on the beach, don't you? "

"We do," Dar said. "But there's seawalls and everything's two layers of concrete and all that. Went over pretty fast, and we've got generators out there."

Dan nodded. "We heard on the news," he said. "If I were you, I'd be glad it's on an island. I already heard of looting and whatnot going on down here, and that'd be a big old target. Is it true you even got a stock of gas? Stations here are hard up with everyone trying to fill their generators."

"Belcher's right out there," Dar said. "So yeah."

"We got us a generator, and some gas," Dar said, "but we figured we'd leave it for tonight and run some lights off it."

Carlos returned. "Dar, those cops came back before. We gave em some burgers."

Dar pondered that briefly and wondered if she should just take all the staff on the boat and back to the island with her. "I don't know if I want to leave you all out here."

Dan nodded. "Gets dark around here at night with no power. I told Charline to shut herself down once the sun's gone."

"We'll be fine," Carlos said. "We got my buds, and four guys who know pops said they'd be here around sundown and they didn't look like they were anyone to mess around with."

Dar still felt a little doubtful. She put her hands in her pockets and looked around at the middle section. The debris and fallen branches had been moved out of it, and the area tided up. Near one side, Scott's camper-van squatted stolidly, it's exterior slightly dented but otherwise intact.

Carlos seemed to read her thoughts. "Honest, boss. We're good. We had the windows open up on the second level, and all the doors and stuff locked down here. Nobody bothered us."

"Hey, Manuel." She deferred the thoughts as the maintenance supervisor from ILS came over. "How are you?"

He was a middle-aged man, in worn jeans and a guayabera, wearing scuffed leather cowboy boots and a bandana wrapped around his head to soak up the sweat. "Buenos Dias, Dar," he said. "It's so nice to see you. I came over to see if Maria was here, my wife was worried about her and Mayte."

Dar exhaled. "Yeah, we're worried too. Kerry and Mark are out in West Miami trying to find them," she said. "I'm hoping we hear from them soon." She glanced past him. "Hey, Sandy. You hear from Duks?"

The admin, who Dar had last seen before she'd left ILS came shyly forward. "Hi, Ms. Roberts." she said. "I have not heard from him, no. He had gone to Texas last week. But when Manuel said he was going to come here, I thought I would come too. I hope you don't mind."

"Nah," Dar said. "We'll share what we got. You're more than welcome to hang out."

"More people from the old place?" Carlos grinned briefly. "Hey, the more the merrier. How's the servers coming?"

Dar dragged her attention back to the task at hand. "We got them up," she said. "The kids are working on them, but we need comms."

A ragged cheer rose, from the watchers who had all edged closer to listen to her.

One of the two LAN techs came out with a box on his shoulder and put it down on the picnic table. "Arthur and El?" He asked. "Sweet."

Dar nodded. "So now I need to get some gear. I hooked up with some guys and a satellite over on the island," she said. "Colleen got the main phones forwarded to the cloud lines they're using and they're getting swamped with calls."

"Our customers?" the other LAN tech asked.

"Our customers and apparently a bunch of folks who want to be our customers," Dar said. "They're gonna forward the really annoying ones to me."

"Sweet," Carlos said. "With all the broken crap around, figures they want you to go fix it, right?"

Dar sighed and put her hands on her hips. "I think we need to get fixed first," she said. "We can't even talk to each other reliably. Not sure I want to deal with trying to sort out everyone else's problems."

Carlos scratched his stubbled jaw thoughtfully. "Probably be some good money in it."

"That's what Colleen said." Dar glanced around. "Hey, Bill. You got a minute? I need something from the storage room."

"Sure." Bill came over at once. "Whacha looking for, boss?" He dusted his hands off on his jeans. "We didn't pack enough gear with the box for ya? I put what Mark said to in there."

"Didn't figure I'd need a big router," Dar said. "We got anything here left?"

"Let me go check," Bill said. "C'mon, Ray. I saw some boxes in the back of the telecom room. Maybe one of them's a router." The two techs trotted off, one of them pulling a flashlight out from his back pocket.

Dar's phone rang. "Hang on." She pulled it out and glanced at it, feeling a prickle of relief. "Ker?" she said. "That you?"

"Hey, hon."

Kerry's voice was full of satellite artifacts, but Dar couldn't have cared less. She moved out into the open in the center of the space. "Where are you? You okay?"

"I found Maria," Kerry said. "She and Mayte and Tomas were in their house, Tomas has a broken leg. They're flooded out."

"Stop," Dar said.

"What?"

"Where are you, and are you okay?" Dar asked again. "Mark told me you went off somewhere and it scared the crap out of me."

There was a very brief pause, and a faint sound that might have been a tiny laugh. "Sorry, sweetheart," Kerry said. "I'm fine. We're at Southcom. My airboat for hire got us back here and the National Guard just carried Tomas into their triage room. Mark's here too."

"Okay." Dar relaxed a little, then paused. "You hired an airboat in the middle of Doral?"

"I hired an airboat owner that happened to show up here at the base," Kerry said. "He was being hassled by the guard, so I took advantage of them not knowing what the hell an airboat was and got it done."

"Ker."

"Honey, I learned my end justifies the means from you," Kerry said, in a firm, yet kind tone. "So don't even," she added. "Anyway, the whole first floor of their house was flooded, Dar. I think it's going to be a big loss."

"Poor Maria," Dar said, after a moment. "She doing okay? I do care about her, just not as much as I do about you. You know?"

"I know," Kerry said. "But they really needed help, Dar. I had to go."

"I would have too," Dar admitted. "I'm glad you found them."

"I know. I was trying to decide if you would have dealt with the guy or just bought the boat," Kerry told her.

"Would have depended on the attitude."

"His or yours?" Kerry said, with a slight chuckle. "But at least they're not trapped in their house anymore," she said. "How's it going there?"

"How's it going here." Dar regarded the gathering crowd around the grill as the sun dipped past the buildings and threw the area into shadow. "It's okay. We got the servers up. Now I'm looking for a router." She kicked a bit of grass with her boot. "Colleen said a bunch of people are trying to call us."

"I bet they are." Kerry sorted through the information. "Why are you looking for a router? I thought you had the gear packed in the case?"

"Long story," Dar said. "So, you coming back here? I'll wait for you."

"Yeah. Let me go see what's going on with Tomas, and what the plan is. I'm hoping they're going to take him over to Jackson or Baptist," Kerry said. "Then me and Mark'll head over, assuming I can find Mark."

"What?"

"He's fixing things somewhere in this fifties bunker," Kerry said. "I can see his bike from where I am, so I know he's around. Is Colleen doing okay up there?"

"Fine," Dar said. "Said a lot of people are calling looking for help. She gave some of the government people this sat phone number in case they wanted to call, but no one has yet." She paused and considered. "Or they did, and the stupid thing didn't work."

"Yeah, frustrating. Mayte's really pissed off about these phones," Kerry said. "Okay, let me go see what the deal is, and find Mark, and get over there. I can tell you I cannot wait to see our shower."

Dar smiled. "Can't wait to see you," She remarked casually. "And you can help me connect our ritzy cottage full of nerds into a palm tree when we get back."

"What?"

"Long story."

"Okay, hon." Kerry chuckled. "Talk to you in a bit."

"Mm." Dar grunted a response but closed the phone and regarded it briefly before she shoved it into her pocket and turned to check out the courtyard again. The sounds and the smells washed over her. She exhaled, and the tension leached out of her body, allowing her to enjoy the slight breeze that had come with the end of the day. It brought the scent of the bay to her.

In the distance she heard hammering. At the very edge of her awareness, a siren echoed softly, and the sound of a helicopter.

She walked back over to the barbeque. "Good news," she told the assembled. "Kerry found Maria and Mayte."

"Awesome!" Carlos responded instantly. "They okay?"

"Oh, that's great!" Celeste echoed him. "Is their house all right?"

"Tomas, her husband got hurt and the house is a mess," Dar said. "But Kerry got them out of there and they're at the National Guard assembly point in Doral. She's getting them medical help." Broken leg, apparently."

"Oh wow," Carlos murmured. "Good thing she found them, huh?" He said. "Figured Kerry would get it done. She does not mess around."

"True." Dar smiled briefly.

"That sucks about the house," Don said. "She lives out near Sweetwater, doesn't she?"

Dar nodded. She remembered Maria's house. It was a two-level stucco with a barrel tile roof. Every bit of the inside was carefully and proudly arranged to display to the family and friends they loved to entertain there. Tomas, she recalled, played the guitar and in the echo of her memory, she could hear him playing a Spanish tune through the sound of Spanish language with the scent of saffron all around.

Don shook his head. "I saw the helicopter shots out there. They don't think it's going to drain out for days and days."

"Well," Dar said. "They're in good hands now. Ker's going to make sure they're okay, then head back here."

"Glad that all got worked out. I was kinda worried about those guys going out there," Carlos told Dar, in an undertone. "Especially since its late."

"Yeah, me too," Dar said.

Bill came out of the building with another box on his shoulder. He brought it over to Dar. "This what you need, boss?" He upended the box on the table and opened it up to allow her to peer inside. "This is the only thing that wasn't a switch in the room."

Dar reached in to ease the piece of equipment out and inspected it. "Nope." She sighed. "I was afraid of that. I think we sent the two I thought we had in the bus with the tech team to keep them dry." She drummed her fingers on the useless equipment. "This is a phone gateway. Wrong code."

"Oh," Celeste said, her expression clearing. "I remember now where I'd seen those kind of machines. In the closet on the bottom floor of the office. I remember you being in there one time, Ms. Roberts."

She looked at Dar, who gazed at her with a thoughtful expression, one dark eyebrow slightly lifted. "Right?"

"Right," Dar said, slowly. "That's exactly the piece of equipment I need. One of the big platinum colored ones in that room, matter of fact."

"Any place around we can get one? Or get the guys to bring the one up state back?" Carlos suggested. "Probably not something you can get in BestBuy, huh?"

"No," Dar said. "Definitely not in BestBuy." She pondered. "Wonder if they have any over where Kerry and Mark are. Government building has to have something there. "Maybe we could borrow one." She took out her phone again. "Get the burgers going. Maybe we can swap them for hardware."

****

The sun was setting in the west, and cast long shadows down along the street that Southcom was situated on. The day's oppressive heat finally lifted a little as a light breeze stirred the shredded branches and leaves and fluttered the flags on their poles outside.

Kerry walked across the staging yard from the gate where she'd gone to get a satellite signal. As she dodged between the trucks and headed toward the door to the building, she replayed the conversation she'd just had in her head, glad at the very least she'd been able to have it.

Would have been better, she thought, in person. She wanted a hug, and she suspected Dar did as well. The worry in Dar's tone and relief had been palpable. But she felt a lot better for having spoken to her, and savored the raw, blunt honesty that was Dar at her most transparent.

She paused outside a moment to just stop and think about it, closing her eyes and imagining having Dar here with her. She could almost hear her voice and feel her casual touch, and her entire body relaxed, and the tension eased out of her.

It felt good, even though it was all in her head. She mentally reached out and imagined a hug between them and convinced herself she heard the low chuckle of Dar's response. The gentle scratch of Dar's fingertips on the back of her neck.

So real, it made her nape prickle. She opened her eyes and shook her head a bit to clear the images out of it. "Well. That was interesting."

She trotted up the steps and entered the building and walked past the wide, long desk that was surrounded by people in uniform. In the distance, she could hear the once pervasive and now rather odd sound of a phone ringing.

"Kerry!"

Kerry stopped and turned around, as Captain Dodge caught her up. "Oh, hi," she greeted him.

"My goodness, you all gave us a scare," He said. "Betty told me you found your friends." He indicated a nearby set of doors. "Buy you a cup?"

Kerry really didn't want to engage. She wanted to find the triage center and find out what was going on with Tomas. However. "Sure." She followed him into the mess. "Maybe you could help me find where they took them after we catch up?"

"Sure." He led the way over to a table with large commercial coffee dispensers and stacks of Styrofoam cups. "So, Betty said you found you one of them boats?" He glanced over his shoulder at her. "How'd that happen?"

"He found us actually. He was talking to the gate guards when I went outside to use my phone." Kerry took the cup of steaming coffee and moved aside to add some creamer to it. The air inside the building was chilly, a little shocking after spending the prior few hours in the steamy heat, and she was glad to take a sip of the hot beverage. "He was looking for someone to hire him. So, I did."

The captain shook his head and chuckled.

"The gate guards didn't know what he had to offer. They wanted to kick him out. So, I was lucky I was in the right place at the right time." She followed the captain over to a small metal table. "And I had cash."

Now the captain chuckled again. "Local boy?" He asked.

"Yeah, Kerry said. "He uses the boat for hunting. He lives on the other side of 27 I think. So, how's it going here?"

The captain sniffed reflectively. "It's a mess," he admitted, with appealing candor. "For all the prep we thought we did, we did it for the wrong stuff. You know?"

"I know," Kerry said. "Happens all the time in technology. You work up a solution to a problem and then the problem changes out from under you." She paused. "You know, over near Tamiami Trail, there are probably a lot of people like Joe who have airboats. Why not go hire them?"

"Hire the boats?"

"Hire the people," Kerry said. "That was the problem, you know. I think the guys at the gate felt like Joe should have volunteered to help. It's been my experience that people would rather make money." She took another sip of her coffee. "Know what I mean?"

Dodge regarded her thoughtfully. "We don't carry around cash," he said. "And I don't think we'd be wanting to get into it with the locals, if y'know what I mean. Now you want to go find your friends. You need a ride somewhere?" We're gonna go over to get the airport rolling."

"To get supplies in, yeah, I heard that on the radio this morning," Kerry said.

"To get the president in," Dodge replied, in a deadpan tone. "But we're hoping he's bringing some water and suchlike along too."

They got up, and Kerry carried her coffee cup along as she followed the captain out the door of the mess and down the depressingly carpeted hallway. The smell of machine oil was ever more pungent, and Kerry felt a headache coming on.

It was a long day. She was tired, and sunburned, and aware that there were things needing her attention that were stacking up.

She wanted a hot shower, and a bowl of hot, spicy Thai soup, and Dar.

Dodge turned right and went down another hallway, this one full of boxes and rolling cases. They were all in dark gray mottled colors, all with indecipherable stickers and duct tape residue all over them

Dodge jerked his head at the cases. "Like a damn traveling circus."

"Like a traveling band, actually," Kerry said. "Reminds me of a concert I went to last year. They were in a hotel we were staying at and saw them unloading."

He chuckled.

They continued down the corridor and Kerry heard the sounds of work going on around her. As she passed one set of flung open double doors the smell changed from machinery to electronics, and she glanced inside then halted as her name was called out.

Ah. Kerry turned around and went back. "Hold on," she said. "Think I just found my guy with a bike." She poked her head inside the room just as Mark got up from the floor where he'd been sitting. "Hey!" She greeted him. "What's up?"

"Hey!" He looked relieved to see her. "Man am I glad you got back here."

"So's Dar," Kerry said. She exchanged a knowing, wry look with him. "What are you doing?" She looked past him at the encased server, its side cover off and insides exposed.

Dodge came in behind her. "You know this guy? Oh, wait a second now... I remember you." He looked at Mark with some interest. "How'd you get all in here?" He put his hands on his hips.

"Long story," Mark said. "I was just doing these guys a favor while I was waiting on the boss lady here to get back."

Kerry chuckled dryly. "What happened?" She indicated the server.

"Plugged a one ten into two twenty," Mark said, succinctly. "I just swapped their power supplies out. You find them?"

"I did. Tomas has a broken leg. I brought them all back here," Kerry said. "I want to go see how they're doing, then we can head to the office. Dar's there, something about needing a router, and getting our gear online. You done?"

"Done," Mark said. "I told them to boot it up and see if it comes online." He closed a pocket tool and put it back into his pocket. "Where'd you get the T?" He followed Kerry as they went out the door again and continued down the hall.

"Long story," Kerry said. She scrubbed her fingers through her pale hair, and wished for that shower.

Dodge led them out a door into the growing twilight, where the heat had finally moderated and a breeze coming between the buildings blew over them. There was a short, neatly trimmed sidewalk between the buildings, and at the other end of that was another anonymous door.

"Should be in here." Their escort swiped his badge on the reader and the door unlocked, and then they were inside a large, high ceilinged space full of warehouse style ambiance and many different areas being staged for action.

On the far side there was a section blocked off with high, pale sheeted walls that were bordered with rolling cases that had liberally splashed on them a white square and red cross symbol.

Over the top of the sheets wide tubes were snaked, that led to a truck nearby with a large pumping system on a flatbed thrumming with engine noise. "Air scrubber," Dodge supplied, raising his voice to be heard. "That gang over there's mine," he said. "They usually stage choppers in here."

"Where'd they put them?" Mark asked. "They'd be freaking useful."

Dodge glanced at him. "Flew them out ahead of the storm. Didn't want to risk trashing em." He went to the edge of the white sheeted area and stopped in front of a desk. "Jackson, you got the list of folks in there?" He held out his hand.

"Sir." The man behind the desk handed over a clipboard. "Got like six of em now. Three people just drove on up in an old car just now."

"Gonna get worse from here."

Kerry saw an opportunity and she slid past him and motioned Mark after her as she went inside the medical area. looking around at the beds and stretchers. The hanging dividers mocked up an approximation of a hospital emergency ward, and it was hard to see past all the sheeting.

"Over there, Ker." Mark clasped her elbow and moved in the direction of a portable monitoring desk, set up against one flexible wall. "I see Mayte." He stopped to let a uniformed man push a cart with bandages on it past them. "We giving that guy the slip?"

Kerry suppressed a smile. "He's busy," She said. "I'm sure he's glad to be rid of us." She led the way over to the sheeted off area around a bed. "Hey, guys."

Mayte and Maria turned around and spotted her. "Oh! Kerry! We are glad you are here." She glanced past her. "And here is Mark!"

Mark poked his head around Kerry's shoulder. "Heya." He waved at them. "How's it going?"

Tomas was lying on a padded and adjustable medical stretcher. Two medics leaned over him, and tubes from two different IV bags already attached to his arms. His leg was stretched out and covered in bandages, and a splint had been applied.

His eyes were closed, but his face looked more relaxed than it had since Kerry had seen him yet today. "They give him some painkillers?"

"Si," Mayte said. "But they think we should go to the hospital. "They are finding out how to bring him there," she explained. "They told us it was a very good thing you found us."

"Si," Maria echoed her. "They said that, Kerrisita. They have already given Tomas some medicines to make him feel better for now. You see? He is not so pale anymore." She looked back over at Thomas, an expression of tired relief on her face.

Kerry took a pause for a moment of internal bemusement, as she sought for a way to defer the praise, and then wondered why she'd want to.

Was it embarrassing, a little? To be branded as some half-baked hero? Kerry thought about what she'd done, then shook her head just slightly. No, nothing really heroic here. She just took advantage of the circumstances she'd found, and being lucky.

"Good job, boss." Mark casually clapped her on the shoulder. "I told Barb this morning if I was ever up the creek, I'd want you and Dar coming after me," he said. "You just don't stop," he clarified, as everyone looked at him in some surprise. "You know?"

Kerry managed a brief grin. "C'mon, guys," she said. "I knew you were out there, and I saw the flooding. What was I supposed to do? Of course I had to come find you. You guys are family to us."

One of the hanging dividers moved aside and a bespectacled man in a khaki shirt and dark blue slacks entered. "Okay, we've got a transport all set up for you folks over to Jackson, but I'm gonna warn you, there's gonna be a wait over there. It's kind crazy right now."

Maria nodded. "I am sure many people are hurt."

"That, and they had some issues with their emergency generators. So, they've got limited intake ability," the man said. "So, you'll just have to be patient."

"Any option other than Jackson?" Kerry asked.

The man glanced at her, glanced at Tomas, and then back at her. "It's the public option, ma'am," he said, after a brief pause. "They're a good trauma hospital."

"They're the only trauma hospital," Mark said. "My uncle works there."

Kerry walked over to the administrator, her hands in her pockets. "How about Baptist? I'd really like to get them taken care of." She watched his face as he hesitated, looking around with a touch of embarrassment. "I'll guarantee the cost," she added, almost as an afterthought.

He gave her a look, as though taking in her disheveled appearance in some doubt.

Kerry smiled at him. "Don't worry. I'm good for it. Just get it set up and let me worry about getting them admitted. I'd do it myself, but all I got here is a motorcycle and we're not gonna fit." She kept her tone gentle and friendly, and he visibly thawed.

"Okay, ma'am," he said. "Let me tell the driver and we'll get you folks going. I'll be right back." He took himself and his clipboard and disappeared back behind the flap.

The medic who was adjusting Tomas' IV glanced over her shoulder at Kerry. "That was a blessing you just did," she said, bluntly. "I was over at Jackson about an hour past and it's a mess."

"Kerrisita," Maria protested. She got up from the bedside chair and came over. "It is okay now; we could wait for this. We did not bring our cards and things out with us from the house."

Kerry shushed her. "C'mon. Let's get this done. Mark, you can follow us, and we can go on from there," she said. "It'll be a longer drive but end up less time."

"Righto, boss." Mark wasn't fazed. "Just let's get going before they find more stuff for me to mess with. I thought they were thinking of inducting me and it's really not my scene."

Kerry glanced past the hanging partition, where a truck was driving in with flashing lights. "Yeah." She stepped back to let the medics raise the stretcher Tomas was on. "Just glad Dar's not here. We'd be hip deep in something by now."

"True that."

****

"Put that other torch over here." Carlos' voice sounded out of the darkness, and a moment later Dar heard the sound of a lighter being clicked, and then saw the kindling of a tiki torch being lit nearby. "Yeah, that's it."

The central space inside the building's structure was full of firelight and shadows, and the scent of grilling. Dar was seated on one of the picnic tables a little in the open. She listened to the chatter around her as the now round dozen residents of the building settled down with paper plates.

She was no closer to finding a router she could readily use. The voice gateway had been loaded onto the Dixie along with a box of spare internal parts and she had a half-formed plan of what she was going to try with them when she got back there and had a little access to download some router code.

"We might have the image for that release train on the disk." Bill came over and sat next to her, his plate full of very recently grilled steak. He set down the plate and took a drink from a bottle clipped to his belt. "But I dunno. I think that box was for those guys down in Kendall."

"The school?"

Bill nodded. "I had it on my list of setups but not until next week. Their building ain't scheduled to be done before then."He picked up a piece of steak in his fingers and bit into it, chewing thoughtfully. "Wonder how they made out? That thing was just getting drywall when we were down there last."

Dar thought about that. It was a small technology school, who'd contracted them to put in systems for their inaugural class scheduled for September.

Would they even still be around? Or was all that gear they'd purchased now just a big, useless expense? She exhaled. No real idea what any of their customers were going to end up, at least here locally. Maybe they really needed to think about all those people calling Colleen.

Carlos appeared next to her with a paper plate. "Steak, Dar?" "We got those loaves of Cuban bread from Don and they toasted up pretty good."

Dar took the plate. "Thanks. Smells great." She compressed the sandwich between her fingers, two pieces of grilled bread cut from the loaf, with the steak slapped between them, the scent of mojo and pepper, and the sharp tang of lemon rising from it.

She took a bite and chewed slowly.

Around them, it was very dark and the sound of sirens had blossomed. Carlos and his buddies had closed the back gates to the maintenance area, and just a few minutes ago two tall, burly men showed up with automatic rifles slung casually over their shoulders.

They were dressed in worn camo, and combat boots, maybe in their mid-forties. They accepted plates of steak with brief, appreciative grins.

Dar had no idea what their names were. Soon, she would get up and introduce herself and find out, since the small bit of information they had supplied was that they were buddies of Andy's.

She suspected the smell of the grilling might draw in people in the area, maybe some of the police, the National Guard. Or maybe the transients who lived on the streets, and the men and women who had been seen looting. In the darkness it was hard to say what was going to happen and so she was glad they were here.

The steak sandwich was hot, and tasty, and she was glad the bread absorbed the juice from it as she ate it, listening to the rumbling thrum and catching the scent of the burning oil in the torches that served a dual purpose.

Light, of course. But they were also full of citronella, a deeply pungent scent that drove off the mosquitoes that were already breeding in the thousands and thousands of pools and flooded areas all around them. They'd gotten rid of any buckets and basins of floodwater around the office, but she knew the buzzing whine of the insects would soon start to be heard. It reminded her, in fact, to take a jug of the citronella. She finished her sandwich, folded her paper plate into quarters and slid it into the plastic garbage bag before setting off to do just that.

She walked through the shadows and into the office, where the generator was now providing power to two lamps near the reception desk. It made the desk, the small kitchen and the conference room reasonably visible, but the long hallways and the stairs were thrown into darkness.

Dar walked up the stairs to the second level. It was stuffy and warm, and she paused a moment to let her eyes adjust to the dimness. She stood quietly before moving down the hallway and into the storage room near the end of it.

With the door open, she found there was enough dim light for her to see the outline of the shelves, and she went to the back shelf and picked up one of the containers of oil. She turned to face the door just as a large figure filled it and blocked her passage.

Dar stiffened and got a grip on the gallon of oil, getting her balance up over the balls of her feet as she drew in breath to challenge the intruder.

"Hey, hey!" the figure said and held its hands out. "Sorry about that, ma'am. It's Buddy. I'm a friend of your pa's."

Dar saw the outline of gray light behind him and relaxed. "Not funny."

"No, sorry," he said. "I just wanted to intro myself and Tucker to ya. Thought you might need some help to carry stuff." He backed out into the hallway as Dar moved forward and then emerged after him. "Didn't mean to startle ya."

"No problem," Dar said. "Thanks for stopping by. I get a little worried leaving these guys alone here."

"Well you should," Buddy said, blinking at her in a relaxed kind of way. He stood there in the darkness, apparently comfortable with the shadows. "There's some unfriendlies around here," He said, after a pause. "They know you got computers and stuff here, you know?"

"We sent most of it upstate in a bus," Dar said. "Except the servers that I sent to my house."

Buddy chuckled. "Heard that. But they don't know it. Figure they come in to look round, see if there's stuff they can take and sell."

Dar glanced around. "Really no."

"But you got food and stuff. Andy knows the noise and the light and fire, and all will bring em in," he said. "Got two more of our pals around here too. They're doing a roam around."

Dar studied him, his square, cropped hair profile visible to her. "Goes south fast, huh?" She asked, after a pause. "The people to jackass ratio?"

Buddy smiled, a surprisingly sweet expression on his face. "Never north. Don't take much to show it. Saw me a dozen fellas just before sundown hassling up some folks who were trying to get in to see their store, see what's left of it."

Dar thought about that. "Yeah, I noticed all the cops disappeared before it got dark."

Buddy nodded. "Don't blame them, you know? They told ev'rybody to stay in after dark, put that curfew up, try to keep people out of trouble. Ain't got enough of them to guard everywhere." He shifted the gun hanging over his shoulder a little. "Always pays to be ready to roll your own. You know?"

"Yeah. I kinda do." Dar now also smiled. "It's not deadly, but we're always ready to get things done for ourselves here too."

He nodded. "I seen your boys there putting in that dock. Who does that?" He laughed a little. "Who does that? People who got to get things done, using what they got, like boats. That's who does that." He glanced around. "That's what I told Andy before. He taught you good."

Dar's lips twitched a little. "I'm sure he appreciated that," she said. "Thanks for helping us out by the way. I do like having you all around here. Makes me feel better about the place."

He smiled again. "You going somewhere with that?" He asked, indicating the jug.

"Back to the boat," Dar said. "I'm going to need to put a few torches in my backyard once I get back there." She started down the hallway. "Didn't want to forget it. "

She got to the stairs where it was lighter and descended into the pool of lamps at the bottom. "Hope that generator lasts all night."

"We got some gas in my truck," Buddy said. "Mind if I walk with you to the water with that?" His tone was mild and studiously polite. "Just in case?"

Dar hesitated.

"I figure you could deal with stuff. But no need to take a chance when you don't need to, and two's insurance," Buddy added, placidly. In the light, she saw there were scars on his face, and on the hand resting casually on the top of the gun there was a missing finger.

"Sure." Dar indicated the door. "Let's go." She led the way out the door to the building and they walked together down the dark sidewalk and then onto the path that would take them around the side of the building toward the water.

****

Kerry glanced around the emergency waiting room at the hospital, which was mostly empty. Tomas had been taken into the triage area in the back and Maria went with him. She, Mark and Mayte took over one corner of the room, three chairs and a small table against one wall.

On the table there were three cups, all gently steaming from the beverage station just to the left of them. They had a choice of coffee or tea, and a worker had replaced the coffee dispenser just after they'd arrived so at least they were comfortingly fresh.

Powdered cream though. Kerry avoided it and sipped her coffee in its pretty much natural state.

Mark returned from the vending machine, and now he opened his hands and put his booty down on the table. "You figure a hospital would have something better, but there ya go."

Three O'Henry bars, three packages of peanut butter crackers, three bags of sun chips. "Hey, they have sun chips," Kerry said. "It could be worse. "

"Could be. It took my credit card. I don't have any small bills on me." Mark picked up a candy bar and stripped the plastic covering off it. "Only some twenties I got out of the ATM before the storm."

"Me too." Kerry picked up the bag of sun chips. "But, I'm glad we're here."

"Yes, Mama is very glad," Mayte said as she retrieved a package of chips for herself. "I hope they finish soon though, I am very tired. I did not sleep at all last night. It was so scary, and I was so worried about Papa."

"Hear that," Mark said, stifling a yawn. "Who could sleep in all the craziness?" He glanced around the room. "It shouldn't take too long, right? Not too many people in here."

There were about three others, one older man reading a magazine, dressed in neatly pressed slacks and a short-sleeved dress shirt, and two women, one younger one older, the older of whom was knitting something held on top of a bag.

Occasionally, they gave their small group sideways looks and Kerry felt she wasn't imagining that the looks were more than a little judgmental.

It was cool inside, and it smelled like a hospital, that mixture of disinfectant and wax. Kerry felt tired herself, her body sore and slightly uncomfortable with sunburn, conscious of the mud-stained pants she wore and the worn borrowed T-shirt.

Mayte was in a T-shirt and jeans, the lower half of her legs with a stained ring of debris and partially dry sneakers.

Kerry munched on her sun chips in quiet reflection. "I'm going to finish this and go outside and see if I can try Dar again," she said. "Let her know what's going on. "

"Surprised she's not here already," Mark said. "Oh wait, she doesn't know we're coming here to Baptist does she."

"She might figure we'd have come here," Kerry said, in a reflective tone. "And I know there's a bunch of people there at the office who have cars, so they'd ride her out here. I feel bad knowing she's waiting on us though."

"She doesn't care," Mark said. "About waiting, I mean," he added after both women looked at him in surprise. "You know."

"No, well..." Kerry cleared her throat a little. She was spared the further elaboration as one of the hospital workers came out and looked around, and those in the waiting room looked up and back at her in question.

Kerry hoped the woman was looking for them, and she watched the body language as she turned and headed in their direction. "Ah."

The woman came up to them. Mayte stood up. "How is my papa?" She asked at once. "Is he feeling okay?"

"You must be Mayte," the woman said. "Hello, my name is Rita, and I'm a hospital admitting manager." She glanced at Kerry and Mark in question. "Are you relatives?"

Mark looked at Kerry, one of his dark eyebrows lifting a little.

"My name's Kerry Roberts," Kerry said. "I'm the co-owner of the business that Mayte and her mother work for. This is Mark Polenti, he's a director of our company. How is Tomas doing?"

The administrator eyed her thoughtfully. "Okay, well, he has a badly broken leg as I think you all know," she said. "And he's got an infection, probably from the storm water."

Kerry nodded. "We had to get him out of his house. It was flooded."

"So, we'd like to get him admitted," the woman concluded.

Kerry sat back in her chair, crossing her ankles and folding her arms. "I'm glad to hear that." She could see the hesitation in the woman's attitude. "Baptist is in network for us."

The woman's attitude brightened at once. "Well, I'm glad to hear that. There didn't seem to be any... ah... "She glanced around. "How about we go talk in my office? Maybe I could get some clarifying details from you, given you probably know them."

Kerry stood up. "Why don't you guys stay here and finish your chips?" She suggested. "I've got our policy number and all that with me."

Mark looked relieved. Mayte a bit uncertain.

Kerry just smiled and gestured for the woman to guide them as she followed her across the waiting room. The woman paused to swipe her badge on a lock and then passed inside, holding the door for Kerry to follow her in.

They walked down a hallway that didn't seem too busy, given all the circumstances. The woman led the way to a small office and went inside. "Thank you for understanding," she said, as she closed the door behind Kerry and went behind her desk. "The patient wasn't sure what his situation was, and his wife is a little upset."

Kerry sat down and kept her tone mild. "Easier to talk to someone not related."

"Exactly," the administrator said, with a nod. "It's not that we wouldn't have taken care of him regardless." She gave Kerry a direct look. "Let's not have any misunderstanding. We're a hospital."

Kerry nodded. "But you're not the public option," she said. "I get it."

"Yes. We're expecting a lot of patients to start hitting us, and we know we'll get our share of... "She hesitated. "Anyway, they told us to push back as long as we could back to Jackson."

"That's why I had Tomas sent here," Kerry said, calmly. "Because I knew he was covered, and he'd get good care right away. We pay a lot for our medical insurance. We care about our people and I don't personally trust the government's charity."

The woman studied her for a minute, then she smiled. "Thanks for the honesty, Ms. Roberts," she said. "So let me get the details, and we'll get Tomas admitted so we can care for him. He wasn't sure he was... or, well, I think he was a little embarrassed to be covered under his wife's insurance," she said. "It's a... well it's an old fashioned attitude, I suppose."

Kerry pulled her wallet out from her back pocket and removed a card from it and handed it over to her. "There's the details," she said, then removed a second card and put it down. "And if they deny anything, put it on that."

The woman's expression went from satisfied to a subtle, obvious appreciation. "You have some truly fortunate employees." she said. "I'll let the doctor know." She smiled at Kerry. "Would you like a cappuccino?" She paused a finger on her intercom button. "It's been a long day."

"Sure." Kerry folded her arms, her brief smile acknowledging the irony. "It certainly has been a long day."

"How about a shower, and a pair of scrubs?"

****

It was dark near the water. They walked in silence side by side across the walk and through the destruction that was left behind the storm at the sailing club.

Dar heard the water, waves pushing up against the seawall and making the Dixie rock in her mooring, the boat's white hull visible against the darkness of the sea.

The moon was fitfully present, zipping behind clouds that were strung out across the sky, the horizon dark with them. "Rain," Buddy said, briefly.

"Like we need it." Dar could smell it on the wind though, and the breeze that ruffled her hair felt damp. She led the way down the steps to the dock and looked both ways before she walked out onto the makeshift platform the team had assembled.

"You walk like Andy," Buddy said, as he followed in her footsteps. "That little rocky bounce."

She did, she knew. She'd been told before, but she wasn't entirely sure why other than she knew she shared her father's tall, lanky build, the long bones in their arms and legs giving them a similar profile. "Always have," she said briefly.

They approached the boat, and Dar reached out to take hold of the railing. "Careful. She's really moving."

Buddy chuckled.

"Yeah, sorry." Dar stepped onboard as the boat rocked toward her and went with the motion. "I forget sometimes who the hell I'm talking to." She walked along the back deck and opened the gear box. "Here, give me the oil."

He handed over the jug. "You all thinking of heading out before it rains?"

"Not without Kerry." Dar closed the box and turned. "Speaking of, let me try my phone." She sat down on the back wall and removed the sat phone from her pocket. Buddy sat down in one of the deck chairs and extended his legs, crossing them at the ankles.

Dar dialed Kerry's sat phone number and listened to it ring, almost ready to hang up when it surprised her by being answered. "Hey."

"Hey!" Kerry sounded a bit out of breath. "Sorry I kind of thought you were trying to call me so I ran outside."

Dar's eyebrows knotted. "Um..."

"Just one of those feelings. We're at Baptist." Kerry exhaled and then the sounds of the background faded a little. "Let me get away from the emergency entrance. Three ambulances just pulled up."

"Ah huh."

"But Mark followed us on his bike, and we're almost done," Kerry said. "I got Tomas admitted here, and they're about to move him to a hospital room."

"Great," Dar said. "So, you'll be heading back here soon?"

"We will," Kerry said. "What's going on there?"

"I'm on the boat. It's going to rain," Dar said. "The gang is kinda hunkering down." She paused. "What's Maria and Mayte going to do?"

"I got them space in the residential hotel next to the hospital. They share the generators, and they use the rooms to house the doctors that work there," Kerry said. "All good."

"Rock star." Dar smiled.

"Well, hon," Kerry said. "It comes down to cash, you know? It's kinda gross to say it, but if I hadn't been here with my WASP privilege and my credit card, they'd still be... I don't know where." The frown was audible in her voice. "I don't regret it but damn it, why does it have to come down to that?"

"They'd still be in their house," Dar said. "Probably in real trouble if you hadn't been there."

"I know." Kerry sighed. "Anyway, I'm going to run back inside and see if they have him moved." Behind her voice there was a low rumble. "Ugh."

Dar heard the same far-off sound in her own ears. "Try to get out of there before the rain starts. With that and no lights that's not going to be a fun ride, and neither's taking the boat back across the channel."

"Did you find a router?" Kerry asked. "For the palm tree, or whatever it is that's going on there?"

"No. Well..." Dar half turned and looked across the bay, whose surface was ruffling with choppy whitecaps. "I found something I can maybe hack and use. We sent all our spare up with the bus," she said. "I'm guessing those satellite guys are standing outside the cottage wondering where the hell I am."

Kerry sniffed reflectively. "So, what... you mean, we have the servers up, and you found those guys out there with a satellite? To get that connected?"

"Something like that. They were trying to demo it, and... anyway. I told them I could rig up something to let them sell it to the whole island if they let me hook up the stack," Dar said. "We've got commits for this Friday. The guys were working on the code."

A softly echoing voice, and the sound of a siren came through the phone as Kerry thought, and Dar let the silence lengthen between them. The wind freshened, and it fluttered the fabric of her tank top against her, brushing her shoulders with a damp pressure.

Damn she wished the day was over.

"Why not go back over there and hook that up?" Kerry suggested after another long moment. "Then come back? I can only imagine a thousand antsy rich nitwits dancing on the dock waiting on being able to post their house pictures."

"Screw them."

"And our guys trying to do updates," Kerry said. "And you'll get something done, and not just be pacing around cursing under your breath at me."

Dar drew a breath to protest, then just chuckled a little.

"G'wan, hon. It'll give you something to do while we finish up here. Then I'll wait for the storm to come over before we head back. Safer for everyone," she said, in a gentle, practical tone. "They've offered me coffee, a shower, and a pair of surgical scrubs here. I'm fine."

About to protest, the tone made Dar pause and consider, probing the idea and realizing it quite appealed to her. "Damn good idea," she admitted. "All right, I'll head back and see what I can do for the link. Make sure you and Mark aren't going to be rolling around in sideways rain."

"We will," Kerry assured her. "Talk to you soon."

"Mm." Dar closed the phone. Then she turned to Buddy who was still parked in the back deck chair, observing the land side approach to the boat. "Wanna go for a ride?"

Buddy eyed her with interest. "In this?"

Dar nodded.

"Psh. Sure." He grinned briefly. "Want me to untie your lines?"

"Yeah." Dar slid the phone into her pocket and climbed up the ladder to the flying bridge and pulled the starter fob for the boat out. She slid it in place and pressed the starter button and heard the reassuring sound of the big diesels rumbling to life under the deck.

The boat started to drift back from the dock and a moment later Buddy climbed up to come stand by the bridge, one hand on the railing and the other resting on his machine gun. "Let'r go," he said. "Nothing like feeling the water under ya."

Dar settled into place behind the controls and let the boat move with the current, gently swinging the bow around and nudging the engines into gear. "That's true," she said, easing the Dixie away from the shore and sending her out into the bay.

The channel buoys were rocking in the chop, and a spatter of rain started impacting the Plexiglas shield around the bridge as she increased speed and the boat moved from a slow wallow into crisp motion, the bow cutting through the waves.

She flicked on the running lights, but kept the spotlights off, letting her eyes adjust to the darkness that stretched on either side of them now, the coastline that would, and should, be brilliant with illumination dark and anonymous.

Ahead she saw the edge of the bay islands, equally dark, and far off, the lonely string of emergency lights that outlined the bridge over to the port. Only on the far northeastern edge of her vision was a blur of light on the horizon that was the Coast Guard base, and the place she lived.

"Know what I like?" Buddy asked, after ten minutes of utter silence.

"What?"

"Boat captain who knows what's up." He went over and sat down in the other console chair, relaxing as they sped across the water. "Andy said you got him that big old thing he has."

Dar considered that, adjusting the throttle a little. "I had some cash come to me, and figured it'd be better put to let him get what he wanted with it." She reflected. "Found money, you know?"

Buddy nodded his head in a steady, continuous, positive way. "He put in time. Good to see things come to him," he said. "Scales came right on that one for a change."

Chapter Nine

"Here." Kerry's new friend the hospital administrator gave her a handful of fabric and a bottle. "it's what we use to have patients scrub up for surgery, so it doesn't smell fancy, but it gets the job done." She pointed toward a door. "Shower's in there. I'd get to it quick. I just saw another couple of flashing lights outside."

Just the shower would have been great, but Kerry took the offered supplies and ducked into the room indicated, which was a large, square space with tiled floors and a drain on one side.

A showerhead and spray were fixed to the wall over the drain, and a curtain could be pulled around it, and on the other side of that was a toilet and sink.

Spare and utilitarian and blessed as all heck. Kerry got out of her borrowed shirt and mud caked pants and grimaced a little at her sunburned reflection. She set the stack of cloth near the sink and took the bottle over to the shower, turning it on and waiting for it to go from cool to lukewarm.

The soap – smelled like... Kerry sniffed it. It smelled like weak dish washer detergent. Not overwhelmingly antiseptic, but it produced a small lather and left behind a feeling of clean and really what more could she ask for? It reminded her of the biodegradable soap they'd taken with them on their rafting adventure.

And, given the who knows what she'd been wading around in all day, the fact it was a hospital scrub was probably not that bad a thing. Kerry shut the thought out, and applied soap, as the water warmed to a temperature enough to relax her.

On the other side of the door she heard activity, so she quickly washed the gunk off her skin, turned off the water and shook herself before she went over to the sink and retrieved the slightly stiff linen towel she'd been given.

She already felt a thousand times better, even given the sunburn as she gingerly patted her skin dry. She dressed in the scrubs, and then, feeling a prickle of memory, glanced at her reflection as she remembered the last time she'd been in anything like them.

She studied the eyes in the mirror, and it felt like ten lifetimes ago. She'd changed so much from that overwhelmed young woman it was hard to even remember what had been in her head then, aside from that moment of profound and utter relief when Dar came through that door.

After she'd about conked her with a chair. She'd been mad and scared and truthfully in a panic right up until that moment and then almost unable to stand as all that adrenaline vanished in a puff of relief at the efficiency of Dar's reflexes.

She hadn't expected a rescue. In the darkest part of that day it had occurred to her that having her locked away might end up being a relief to Dar. That she was a complication that after the first excitement of their relationship might become unwanted.

That had then just gotten her angry and the anger had gotten her past the fear and then all she'd wanted more than anything was to whack the superior expression off that damn nurses face and somehow get out of there, get to a phone to call a taxi, believing at that moment all she had to depend on was herself.

She'd grown up a little, right then, in a screw the family I'm my own person sort of way. So, she'd figured it was up to her to get herself out of the mess she was in.

Kerry smiled a little. She just hadn't known Dar well enough yet to assume she'd show up there, or to understand that the one thing she really could depend on no matter what was on her new lover's ability to find a way to solve a problem. Her focus on a goal was one big ass train going straight downhill and you better be on the train or get out of the way.

So, of course, Dar had flown in a military jet across the country and broken into a hospital to find her. When you said it in your head it was so damn unlikely. When she thought about it even now it seemed outlandish. And yet, if you reviewed the individual steps and choices Dar had made, given what her options were and who she knew, it all made logical sense and so, of course.

Computers had told Dar where she was because of course they had. Circumstance had put her in the presence of a fighter pilot who liked her just at the right time. Luck had provided a reason for the hospital to desperately want her there, just like luck had provided Joe and his boat to Kerry when she'd really wanted them.

Just like random guys with portable satellites showed up when Dar needed them to. Kerry smiled. Luck. Or whatever. She had once told Dar she'd suspected she'd long-term paid off Murphy, because while the damndest things happened to them, the damndest things resolved them.

Dar had just chortled under her breath.

Kerry ran the plastic comb through her hair and folded her clothes, then put them in the plastic pull string bag she'd been given for that purpose. She pulled on the nubby bottomed socks and picked up her things and then glanced around out of habit to make sure she hadn't left anything.

Mark was camping in their chosen corner, a new supply of vending items on the table in front of him. He waved at her as she came over and sat down. The room was fuller now, about half of the chairs had people in them. "Yo," he greeted her.

"Hey." Kerry unslung her bag and put it down on the chair next to her. "Buh, that feels better." She ran her fingers through her drying, short cut hair. "Whoof."

"Yeah, until people start coming over and asking you stuff cause you look like you work here," Mark said, unruffled. "Because you do."

"I know." Kerry leaned back in the chair. "But I don't care. It's worth it. Jesus it feels so good not to smell like swamp." She hiked one nubby socked foot up and put it on her knee. "Maria and Mayte go upstairs?"

"Yeah," Mark said. "They came out and said they were moving Tomas. I told them to go and do whatever they needed to, and we were going to hang here until it stopped raining." He had a laptop out and was pecking into it. "You talk to the boss?"

"I did. I told her to go home." Kerry studied the choices of junk food with some interest. "She sounded antsy. You know Dar."

Mark nodded. "I called Barbara. She's cool. A bunch of our neighbors got together and they're grilling under a tarp they put up. And Marco, my back neighbor has a big ass generator going." He continued to type into his keyboard. "I'm fine to be out here long as I don't' end up sleeping in air-con. That I can't cop to."

Kerry chuckled softly.

"I heard samba in the background. Leave it to the Brazilians to start a party," Mark continued. "I told her to save me some churrasco."

Kerry paused and looked at him. "You called her?" She asked, in a puzzled tone. "Did you leave a sat phone out there?"

"Landline," Mark said. "Had to almost fistfight the ATT guy who came by and wanted to swap it out for fiber and VOIP. Told him don't touch my fucking POTS or I'd run his ass over with my Harley." He shook his head. "LECS."

"Dar once told me, LECS lie like fish." Kerry leaned over and snagged a package of peanut butter crackers. "I had no idea on earth what she was talking about until the first time I had to drop managed service into a customer's facility."

"Uh huh."

"Then I got it, but I was like, where the hell did she get that saying from?" Kerry opened the package and took out one of the crackers, a round item with slightly crumbly, certainly unfresh, peanut flavored filling between its surfaces. "So, I went down the uncle of all Internet ratholes and finally decided what she meant was they were bad liars as in, she could see right through them."

"Uh huh."

The door that led into the inner corridors of the hospital opened and Mayte appeared. She hurried over to them. She looked relieved, and much happier. "Oh, Kerry, that is so cute," she said. "It's so nice they gave you those things."

Kerry just smiled past the irony. "How's your dad doing? He get all settled upstairs?"

"Yes." Mayte nodded. "They are taking such good care of him. Mama is so happy he feels better," she said. "We are going to go now to the place next door and take a rest. So terrible today."

"You go do that," Kerry said. "We're just waiting for it to stop raining. I'm glad you guys are in a better place for sure. I feel like it's okay to go home now."

"Kerry, you are so kind." Mayte looked at her with an overwhelmingly grateful look. "I don't know what will happen tomorrow, but at least tonight we will sleep." The young woman looked as exhausted as that made her sound and she reached over to pick up a Hershey bar. "If it's okay I will take this for a snack."

"Hang in there mighty, Mayte," Mark said. "You guys'll get through this. We got ya." He closed the lid on his laptop and stood up. "I'm gonna get some coffee before that machine runs out. You want, poquito, boss?"

"I do," Kerry said. "And he's right," She told Mayte as Mark went over to the vending area. "We'll all get through this." She patted her arm. "Go on and get some rest and tell your mom I said she should go too. Don't worry about us."

"Okay." Mayte smiled, at last. "We will try to call you tomorrow and tell you what is happening." She got up and slid the chocolate bar into her shirt pocket. "Good night."

"Night." Kerry waved at her, and watched her go, disappearing into the swinging doors that led into the inner part of the hospital.

Outside the rain was coming down in earnest, a sheet of white blocking the view out the window of the entrance and the parking lot, past the overhang that Mark had parked his bike under. Kerry took another cracker out of her package and nibbled on it, wishing she, too, was at the end of her day.

****

Dar had her rain jacket on, its softly rubberized length coming down halfway to her knees, its surface beaded with water that was a mixture of fresh and salt, as they had plowed through a wind driven spray coming around the south side of the island.

On the near side dock, against the seawall, a marina dockhand was waiting for her in a bright yellow slicker as she came in behind her parent's boat into the second parallel slip.

Buddy climbed down and was on the back deck, his machine gun stowed inside the gear box and a hooded windbreaker protecting him from the rain. He had their aft line in one hand as he waited, the low rumble of the engines muted.

Dar eased against the pylons, bringing the Dixie to rest against the rubber bumper. She kept the boat in place as Jerry tossed the line to the dockhand and he tied them up to the cleat. Then she cut the engines and shut the controls down.

She climbed down the ladder. "Hey, Pitar."

"Evening, Ms. Roberts," the dockhand greeted her. "Welcome back."

Buddy wrestled the router box out of the cabin, shifted it up to his shoulder and stepped up onto the sidewall. "Look out there, buddy," he warned Pitar, who moved out of the way as he stepped over to the dock. "This thing's a boat anchor."

"They're heavy." Dar retrieved the gallon of citronella and followed him off. "Pitar, can you fill her please?"

"Sure," the dockhand agreed amiably.

"I radioed ahead and asked them to meet us," Dar told Buddy. She indicated the rain-washed landscape. "There's a road back there, somewhere."

"Nice."

They made their way up the dock and past the ruined marina building to find Arthur behind the wheel of their golf cart. He had the plastic sides rolled down and turned on the cart lights as they came into view.

"Yo," he greeted them as Buddy got the box into the back seat and Dar slid into the front. "People are seriously looking for you," Arthur said. "They been by our little crib a dozen times."

"I bet," Dar said. "Go by my place, then the cottage. I need to get a PROM programmer and my toolkit." She blinked the raindrops out of her eyes. "How's it going here?"

"I like this place," Arthur said, as he turned the cart and sent it barreling along the path, weaving in and around several other parked carts and piles of debris. "People come by sort of rando and give you cupcakes." He leaned forward to see better. "We were just working on that database parse."

"Buddy, this is Arthur," Dar belatedly made introductions. "He's one of our programmers. Buddy's a friend of my dad's."

"Hey." Arthur looked in the small, silvered plastic mirror.

"Yo," Buddy responded, his muscular arm draped over the router box. "Sup?"

There was debris in the road that Arthur kept running over, the rain and the infrequent emergency streetlights keeping him from really seeing where he was going.

"Stop," Dar said, after one jarring bounce nearly shook the router box off the seat, Buddy scrabbling after it. She waited for the cart to halt. "Trade places." She got out of the cart and went around the front of it, passing Arthur who obediently settled into the passenger seat.

Dar got behind the wheel and started the cart forward, focusing intently on the path as she steered the cart around the branches and other debris scattered across it. She knew the way better, of course, but there was also enough filtered light for her to see the larger items and not drive over them.

They came around the west side of the island and joined the main road that would take them past the ferry landing and around to where their condo was. As they passed the ramp there was yet more light and round the clock work being done.

Pressure, she was sure, from the residents who wanted a way off the island. She had to admit she'd appreciate having that herself, as having her truck handy when Kerry was in need of a pickup would be a big bonus. The rain slacked a little, and she could see the flare of a welding torch.

A rumble of thunder sounded. Dar ignored it as she drove through the entrance to where they lived and pitched down the ramp to the garage.

"Flood in here?" Buddy asked, looking around with interest. "See that door's all cattywumpus."

Dar drove inside. "It drained through here, but the door was stuck with the pressure outside." She parked the cart, got out and walked across the garage and past both her truck and Kerry's car to the storage cabinets on the inside wall. "My father and I got it out of the way."

Buddy got out and roamed around the space, inspecting the drains in the concrete floor and the foundation. "Solid," he said, somebody knew what they were at here."

Dar opened the storage cabinet and lifted a case up and put it on the floor then opened a deep drawer and removed a second case. She picked up both and carried them back to the cart.

"That box what those guys need?" Arthur asked, pointing behind him at the router. "They said you were getting something."

"Not really." Dar regarded her choices reflectively. "It's the right thing, but the wrong kind of thing," she said. "Like it is, I can't use it for what they need it for."

Arthur looked at her with interest. "You gonna fix it?"

Dar glanced up, with a faint grin. "I'm going to hack it," she said. "Void every warrantee this hundred-thousand-dollar useless piece of iron ever had." She went back to the cabinet and picked up a magnifying mirror and light and closed the doors.

"Oh, sweet," Arthur said, with enthusiasm. "Pirate class with Dar. I'm in!"

Buddy went back and got into the cart as Dar resumed her seat behind the wheel. "Hundred thousand in that box? I almost dropped it in the water coming off the boat." He studied the item with a bit more respect as they backed up out of the garage and the rain slammed around them. "But then again," he said, "they got toilet seats they pay that for where I been."

Dar chuckled a little, triggering the door to close as she got up and out of the ramp, and swung the cart around to head for the cottage.

****

Mark came back over to where Kerry was seated, flipping through a year-old People magazine. "You know what just occurred to me?"

"That we're going to break curfew when we do finally get out of here?" Kerry said without looking up.

"No."

"That Snickers and peanut butter crackers are kind of craptastic for dinner?"

Mark sat back down. "I want a cheeseburger," he said. "I can't cruise around on a Hershey bar anymore."

Kerry tossed the magazine on the table and shifted in her chair. "They must have a cafeteria in here somewhere. Want to go find it?" She suggested. "It's probably a bad cafeteria but maybe they'll have French fries."

"I'm down," Mark said.

****

It had in fact stopped raining by the time they went back to the emergency room and stuck their heads outside the sliding doors that were the entrance.

Outside, the halon lights outlined trees moving in a rustling breeze, but the sheets of rain were gone. Kerry took a step outside and looked up, she could see brief patches of night sky between the clouds.

"Make a run for it?" Mark suggested. "Guy at the desk said it's gonna rain again later."

"Make a run for it." Kerry slipped her string bag on her back and followed Mark outside.

She'd resumed her hiking boots and having eaten her budding headache was subsiding and she settled the riding helmet on her head feeling nothing much more than anticipation of the ending of the day.

"Let's get to the office," She said. "I'll call Dar from there." She looked forward to checking in with the staff, maybe sharing a cup of spiked coffee with them while she waited for her marine pickup. "Worse comes to worse we can hang out there if it starts raining again."

"Sounds like a plan." Mark started up the engine on the motorcycle and gunned it a little, the loud and distinct rumble filling the overhang. "Long night for those people back there." He adjusted his microphone. "Feel bad for those kids."

"Yeah," Kerry said. "Seems like they're in there a long time." She wondered silently what the holdup was and hoped it was just that more urgently ill people were being taken first. "Probably good for me to get out of there before I start trying to fix all of them."

"You said it, I didn't."

She took hold of Mark as the bike started to move, and then they were out from under the overhang and on their way.

The rain had freshened the air, and it seemed a bit cooler, but the roads were now filled with puddles and Mark had to take great care in navigating slowly through them. Once they were away from the hospital grounds, the lights were also out, making it all the chancier.

"I'm gonna get up on the highway soon as I can," Mark said, into her ear. "Less water." He waited at a dark stop light, edging into the intersection and watching both ways before he moved out and turned left. "Two blocks east and we can get onto a main road."

"Sounds like a plan," Kerry said. A bit of movement caught her attention and she looked to her right as they went through an intersection.

Down the side road, she saw shadows in motion. "Ah."

Mark gunned the engine and they went through the intersection at speed, getting past the side street and weaving between two large puddles caught in the bike's headlamp. "Hang on," he warned. "Some stuff up ahead."

Kerry shifted so she could see over his shoulder, and squinted, trying to determine what it was the headlight was reflecting back at them. "It's... I think it's a truck stuck," she said. "It's blocking the road... yeah."

A panel truck, its hazard lights flashing dimly, water up to its fenders. Beyond that they could see a tree in the road.

"Yeah." Mark glanced to either side of them. "I gotta go around. Hang on."

He turned right at the next corner and slowed, the water coming up over the bottoms of his wheels as they went along a side street, the sound of the motorcycle loud in the surrounding darkness.

****

The large dining room table had been moved to the back of the living room of the cottage and covered with a flattened cardboard box.

On top of the box, next to cans of soda and a silver bowl full of candy bars, was a disassembled voice router.

Its top case was on the floor under the table, and it's insides glinting in the light from the chandelier. The cards and chips inside it reflected gold and silver and surprisingly pretty.

Dar was seated on a stool next to the end of the table, her laptop still closed on the corner edge of it, while she set up a selection of tools and a small monitor.

Arthur glanced out the window as he came back in the room. "Here they come again." He flopped down on the couch and picked up his laptop. "Like thirty minutes is going to make something change."

"It might." Dar finished laying out her cables, routing them across the table and off the back edge down to the power strip on the floor. She used the twist ties they had been coiled with to make the lines neat and tidy in automatic motions.

She didn't look up as the door opened. She focused instead on plugging in the firmware burner and then check that it's LED came on.

It had been a long while since she'd had to use it. Dar dusted her hands off and straightened up on her stool and hoped she remembered enough of the process not to irretrievably blow something up. "Now what?" She asked. "I told you this was going to take some time."

"I know," John said. "It's just if I'm in here they won't come after me asking when it's going to be ready." He picked up a can of soda and took a seat on one of the rolling cases. "Couple of those guys are getting kinda hooty."

"They do get that way." Dar opened her laptop and pecked at the keyboard for a moment. "Kinda what have you done for me lately jackass of the week."

John chuckled a little. "Alex is over at that mansion place trying to buy em drinks and keep em calm." He opened the soda can and took a drink from the can. "At least I told him, if we have to be stuck someplace, this isn't bad."

"Right?" Arthur said, from his couch. "Hey El – you got a copy of that compiler?"

"I have it," Dar muttered. "I'll copy it to the utility directory."

John sipped on his soda for a few moments in silence. Then he got up and came over to look at what Dar was doing. "Using that coax plant was a pretty slick idea," he said. "Specially with those guys having those gizmos."

"Thanks. We just got lucky on that one." Dar moved over a little to inspect the inside of the router. "This was the closest thing I had to what we need," she said. "But it's not that close."

She opened her laptop and connected it to the ethernet cable draped between the Coke cans, then connected a USB cable from the laptop to the router and turned it on.

"Holy crap." John stared at the thing emitting a surprisingly loud roar. "Sounds like—"

"An airplane taking off. Yeah," Dar said. "It'll settle down after a while." She started up a terminal screen and watched the gear boot up. "You get everyone signed up?"

John snorted briefly. "You kidding?" After a moment, he got up and walked over to the rack full of gear and examined it, as he sipped his soda.

The door opened again and Ceci entered. "Hi, there."

"Hey, Mrs. R," Elvis said as he came into the room. He sat down cross-legged in front of the server stack. He picked up his laptop and put it on his lap.

Ceci made her way over to where Dar was seated. "Your father wanted me to tell you he's on his way back here with Celeste, and a bunch of guys you were supposed to give a ride back here for Jack," she said. "He had to go out and make one last run to the Coast Guard station."

"Oh crap that's right," Dar said, after a brief pause. "I forgot all about them."

Ceci nodded. "He figured," she said. "He stopped by the office to drop Buddy off, and found those guys waiting. Said he felt like a Metrobus."

Dar paused and picked up a small set of alligator clips. "No sign of

Mark and Kerry, I take it?"

"Not that he said, no," Ceci said. "They probably did the smart thing and just camped out at the hospital. That's a long, dark haul to make in the postapocalyptic wilds of West Miami." She spotted the bowl of candy and selected a Jolly Rancher. "Anyway, they got the generator going out there and he said three more folks turned up so it's quite the party."

"More of our employees?" Dar asked.

"He didn't say," her mother responded. "Could be a few of our lot, could be some of your ex-employees, could be more of his special forces friends, could be the cops. Hard to tell what we'll find when we get there tomorrow," she said. "Could be some random political types looking for handouts."

"Could be." Dar focused her attention to the laptop, as the router quieted down and lines of code spilled across the screen. "Anyway, with that many out there I can't just bring them all here. Not enough space."

"Were you thinking of that?" Ceci asked. "As in, we haven't pissed off enough people here?"

Dar paused and looked up, regarding her mother with intent focus.

Ceci waited, remembering that look from their joint past. Now though, she understood there was an utter lack of impatience or malice in it, and she finally realized sometime in the last year that the attention was more positive than negative.

"Just feels off, to leave them out there," Dar finally said. "In the dark, with all those empty streets around them. I know Dad has his friends there watching out, and I know they all volunteered, but still."

Ceci nodded. "And here we are in the center of all the nitwit jerktard stuffiness in the Northern Hemisphere," she said. "I want to share it with every vagrant in downtown Miami."

Dar chuckled.

"I do," Ceci repeated. "I grew up with people that had more money than sense, Dar. It's what struck me so forcefully about your father, when I met him. He had far more sense than money. I had no idea, scatterbrained young nitwit that I was, how rare that really is."

Dar smiled. "Some of these people are not that bad."

"A lot of them are," Ceci said, unrepentantly. "Unlike you, I actually talk to them." She glanced around at the inside of the cottage. "But y'know what?" She looked back at Dar. "I'm glad you grew up not giving a damn about money."

Dar considered that, thinking back to her childhood. "Yeah," she said briefly. "I didn't care."

"You didn't."

She hadn't. She remembered happiness being a sticky twilight, breathing in the scent of just past rain and sneezing out a gnat. "Kerry always tells me I won the early life lottery," she commented in a casual tone. "She'd have traded her childhood for mine in a heartbeat."

Ceci wasn't entirely sure what to say about that, but it sounded positive and so she issued an encouraging grunt. "All in all, I think we all ended up all right. I mean... She circled her finger to indicate their surroundings. "We're here."

"We are." Dar studied the router, now humming softly as the lines of text stopped scrolling and went still, the cursor blinking there, waiting for her. "So, before I haul half of downtown Miami out here, let me try and make this work so no one'll notice."

Ceci took that for the dismissal it was and perched herself on a stool where she could lean against the wall and watch what Dar was doing from a slight distance.

****

Mark stopped the bike again, and they were in a crossroads with water spreading in either direction away from them. Ahead of them was murky darkness, downed limbs, and in the distance, a brief glimmer of flashlights. "This is a mess."

"It's a mess," Kerry agreed. "Go back the way we came? Maybe go out west and then north?"

"Let me try that street up there." Mark pointed ahead of them. "It doesn't look that deep."

"In the movies those are famous last words." Kerry felt the bike start to move, and they made their way through the water at a slow speed, the engine rumbling softly. Mark had wrapped his exhaust pipe with an extender, so the end was elevated, but by his boots the flood was sloshing dangerously close to the spark plugs. "Kind of like—what could possibly go wrong?—"

"Hurr hurr. Don't invoke the screwball fairies." He gunned it a little, and they swerved through the impenetrably dark water, sending a ripple outward ahead of them that disappeared in the headlamp.

"Stay near the center island," Kerry said.

"Yeah," Mark muttered. "Hang on."

The wash of the lamp picked up a little of the path, and as they went past a stop sign and into the next intersection, Mark abruptly came to a halt. "Oh crap."

One of the poles that supported the streetlight on the corner was down in the street, blocking their way. Its concrete bulk sprawled diagonally across the intersection, only the top visible.

"That sucks." Mark released an exasperated sigh. "If we could get past this, we can get to that next street there, and it's just a half block to the onramp of the freeway."

Kerry looked to the right, where the base of the pole was completely submerged in deep water, that extended into the darkness and people's yards, covering the backs of cars that were just visible to her. To the left, she saw a tree down. Just past that, there was some motion in the darkness.

She looked behind them. On the edge of the road was a bus shelter. "Hey," she said. "If we took that bench and put it over there, could you ride the bike over it?"

Mark took off his helmet and turned around to look where she was pointing. "That thing probably weighs a ton," he said. "I guess we could try to drag it?" He looked and sounded doubtful. "Could I get the bike over it? Crap I don't know."

"Got a better idea?"

Mark looked around them in the darkness. He lifted his hands and they got off the bike and sloshed through the flooded street over to the shelter, which was skewed sideways, and half collapsed. It was aluminum, but beneath it was a bench made of wooden slats and concrete supports. It was cocked to one side and jutted into the street.

Kerry pushed aside one of the aluminum walls, and it bent crazily under her touch, the plastic shield that formed its protective surface cracked and separated. It moved as she pushed it though, and Mark stepped around behind her and put his hip against the back of the bench, leaning his bodyweight against it.

Grudgingly, it shifted. "Gonna take a while." Mark gave it another shove.

"Let me help." Kerry went to stand next to him and together they pushed against the end of the bench. When it moved its length, they went to the other side and got that into motion.

Kerry felt the debris and rocks under her boots, and was grateful she had them on, as the dank water soaked into the scrubs and leeched up past her knees. "Wish I had jeans on."

Mark, who did, remained wisely silent. They wrestled the bench across two lanes of the roadway and approached the crossroad, the water shallower as they neared where the bike had been left standing. "Know what?"

Kerry leaned against the end of the bench. "What?"

"Still need a ramp," Mark said, in an apologetic tone. "On both ends."

Kerry stopped, and regarded the bench. "That's what we'll use this back for." She tapped it. "Rip it off, put it on one side, get the bike up onto the bench, over the post, and then take it and put it on the other side and get it back down."

Mark looked thoughtfully at the back of the bench.

"You do have a wrench in that kit somewhere, right?" Kerry eyed him. "Cause these boards are bolted onto this thing." She touched the back of the bench, her fingertips running over the indented bolt that held the boards to the backing.

Mark pulled a small flashlight from his jacket pocket and turned it on, shining it on the bolt. "Might as well check before we waste our time," he commented and crouched to measure the bolt against his knuckle. "Hang on." He turned and made his way across the drowned island to where the motorcycle was parked.

Kerry was glad enough to take a little rest until the moon came out from behind the clouds and reflected off a pair of eyes not that far off.

She stopped and stared. "Oh crap." She let out a yell. "Mark, there's an alligator here!" Without thinking further, she climbed up onto the bench and kept the yellow eyes, drifting closer, in view. "Shit."

Behind her, she heard the sounds of boots hauling through the water and a moment later Mark was up on the bench with her. "Where?" He swung a large wrench in his hand. "Where is it?"

Kerry grabbed the flashlight from him and shone it out into the gloom. "It was right there." She pointed at the spot, which was now empty of staring yellow eyes but not of a ripple of motion. "I sure as hell wasn't thinking about alligators in all this."

"Florida," Mark said. "Let's get this over there. I got a wrench." He held up the tool. "It's adjustable. Should work."

They both watched the water intently in silence for a minute, as Kerry played the flashlight's beam across the surface. The water ripple settled and became still and then all they could hear was far off sirens and then the sound of mosquitoes.

"Right." Kerry got down. "Let's get this over with before it comes back and decides to see if we're a good snack."

"We're kinda big for them." Mark climbed down as well and they both shoved the bench into the crossroads, the water a bit shallower as they got it into place with one end against the concrete pole lying in the road.

"Our feet aren't." Kerry turned and started messing with the flashlight again. "You wrench, I'll keep watch." She stepped up onto the concrete pole and walked along it, relieved to have her body parts up and away from any hidden alligator jaws.

The pole was square, and around eighteen inches wide on all sides, and she was comfortable moving along it until she reached where it had cracked and part of it went off at a rightish angle and disappeared into the murky depths.

"Woot." Mark knelt on the bench and leaned over the top of it, feeling the bolt with his fingers as he fitted the wrench into place and adjusted it. "Let's hope they haven't painted over this a dozen times." He braced his weight against the wrench and hauled on it. "Crap."

Kerry half turned and flashed the light back at him. "What?"

"Probably put this in place with a pneumatic gun." Mark straddled the top of the bench and braced one boot on the stanchion, trapping the wrench against it with his knee while he wiped his hands and then took a better grip on the tool.

"Probably." Kerry returned her attention to the swamp around them. "Be careful."

"Be something," Mark muttered. "My old man would be laughing his ass off at me."

Kerry inspected some motion in the water a little way away, squinting as she thought she saw something poke up above the surface.

Eyeball?

"For what?" She asked, belatedly.

"Using this wrench." Mark grunted. "Social climbing jackass with a wood pole up his behind."

Kerry decided the lump wasn't, in fact an eyeball and continued her scanning. "Well, I sympathize," she responded. "I know what that's like, but I wouldn't have heard about this from my father because his head would have exploded long before with all the shenanigans I get into."

A loud crack sounded, and she turned hastily, to see Mark tumble off the bench backward, the wrench waving in one hand. "Mark!" She raced back over to the bench, but not in time to grab him before he splashed into the water.

"Ugh." He got to his knees dripping. "Well, it moved." He stood up and shook himself, then went back to the bolt. "Maybe you were right. We should have gone back."

Kerry stuffed the flashlight into her pocket. "I'll help. C'mon." She went over and took the wrench as he removed the bolt he'd already loosened, and got the tool attached to the bolt on the other side of the spar. "Counterclockwise, right?"

"Counterclockwise is left." Mark said, as he worked the nut off the bolt.

Kerry got her shoulder up under the wrench and pushed away from the ground, using the strength of her legs as she straightened them. The bolt grudgingly gave way with much less theatrics than the other had with Mark, and she quickly twisted the nut off.

Mark took the wrench to work on the bottom bolt on his side. "Didn't mean to get all literal on you," he said, after a moment. "With the directions."

Kerry chuckled dryly. "You forget who I live with." She dusted her hands off, and then knocked the board loose from the back of the bench and lifted it clear. She then carried it over to where the pole was submerged.

She wedged it into the mud under the water and propped the end on the pole. She returned to the bench to help with the second, but Mark had worked out the twisting and already had the board free. He stepped over the pole to put the board in place next to the first.

"Okay." He studied their work. "I'm gonna walk it up and onto that thing." He indicated the bench. "Grab the boards when it's on there?"

"Got it," Kerry said. "I'll hold this end down while you're doing that." She glanced at the bike. "Think this is going to work?"

"Hope it does," Mark said. "I lay this thing down, it's gonna hurt."

Kerry sighed and stood by, waiting for him to start up the bike and move it up the makeshift ramp. "No matter what happens, let's not tell anyone about this, huh?"

Mark chuckled wryly and put the bike in low gear, cautiously releasing the hand brake and making it creep upward. "No problem, poquito boss. Noooo problem."

****

"Any luck?" John had the sense to stay at a distance, hands behind his back, rocking up and down a little on his heels. "It's getting kinda late," He added, in an apologetic tone.

"Dude, shut up," Arthur said, without looking at him, his hands holding two very thin wires in place as Dar studied the circuit board, a soldering iron held lightly in one hand. "You're watching brain surgery."

Dar smiled briefly, then leaned over the router and lowered the iron, gently feeding in solder with her other hand and she laid down a new path across the glittering circuits.

Elvis was seated on the couch with his laptop somewhat forgotten in his lap, watching with interest.

Ceci was perched on her stool behind the table, content to observe.

This wasn't ever something she'd seen Dar do. The programming part, yes. Endless typing on keyboards and drawing diagrams with branches and boxes on them, yes. This? No. She knew better than to ask questions though, more so than hapless John.

"Okay." Dar pulled her hands back and then put the soldering iron down on its holder, pausing to regard the solder on the board and then reaching back and plugging the power cable into its socket. "Let's see what that did." She listened to the airplane sound of the router for a moment and then moved around from behind the table and headed for the door.

"Where are you going?" John glanced at the router. "Is it done?"

"Going to make a phone call." Dar brushed past him and out the door before he could ask anything else. She closed the door behind her as she walked away from the cottage and into the open space beyond. She was about to open her phone to call when it rang.

She answered it. "Hey."

"Ugh."

Dar grimaced. "What's up?"

"So, we left the hospital," Kerry said. "And we made it onto the highway, and we made it all the way down here to US 1 and we got to UM."

"Okay," Dar said. "And?"

"And there's a roadblock," Kerry said. "They won't let us down into Coconut Grove. They say it's too dangerous."

Dar looked around. "So, what are they suggesting you do?" She asked. "Go back to Baptist? Did you explain where you're trying to go?"

"Oh yes," Kerry said. "If they weren't convinced I was nuts before that, they are now. I told them there were a dozen people camping at our commercial office near the waterfront and we were going to get picked up from there by a motor yacht."

"It's true," Dar said, in a reasonable tone. "Not sure why they think you'd lie about that."

"Honey." Kerry sighed. "It's late, and these guys are not in a really reasonable mood."

"Well, can't help that I guess." Dar closed her eyes and searched her memory. "Okay. So, what direction will they let you go?"

"What do you mean?"

One of Dar's blue eyes opened up. "Kerry, they aren't expecting you to stay there at the roadblock. They won't let you go to the office, where will they let you go?"

"Oh." Kerry fell briefly silent. "Well, I don't know. I didn't ask him that," She admitted. "I was just pissed off, so I just walked away and came over here to call you."

"Okay. So, see if they'll let you go south on US 1, and then turn and go east on Hardee," Dar said. "Go as far east as you can, and you'll eventually run into the coast. Once you do that, call me and I'll be heading over there to pick you guys up."

Kerry's eyebrows contracted. "Just... anywhere?"

"Hon, I have no idea what the coastline looks like out there," Dar said. "Find someplace you think I can get the Dixie into. Or, like you suggested, go back out west and hang out at Baptist until the morning. Could be they've got the ramp fixed by then and I can get the truck off."

It would be safer, Kerry acknowledged, for them to just go back and wait for daylight. Safer for her and Mark, and safer for Dar, who wouldn't have to pilot the Dixie over in unknown area. She considered a moment longer, then remembered the flooding and the bus bench. Or would it?

Mark was seated on the bike, arms folded on the handlebars. "What's the boss saying?"

"Wants us to go east and find a spot to have her pick us up," Kerry said. "Or go back where we were."

Mark eyed her thoughtfully. "Go east where? Hardee?" He asked. "That's how I come to work. We can actually pick up Main past Douglas and get closer to the office." He glanced at the police, who were drinking coffee nearby, having decided they were mostly harmless.

"Unless there's another roadblock," Kerry said.

"Bet there isn't," Mark said. "They won't watch every street." He straightened up. "Going up US 1 woulda been easier, but we can still get there. Good deal."

"Okay," Kerry said. "Dar, we're going to try to go east. I'll call you when we get somewhere useful."

"Okay. Be careful," Dar said. "I'm gonna try to wrap up here."

Kerry hung up the phone and went over to the bike, resuming her place on the back of it. "Let's give it a try," she said. "Damn it I wish I'd brought that shotgun. It feels like we're so exposed on this thing."

Mark started the bike and gave her a look over his shoulder. "No offense, I'm kinda glad I don't have that up behind my ear." He gave the police a genial wave and turned the bike around and headed back south along US 1.

The cops waved back, visibly contented that their jobs had been successfully done.

****

Dar put the sat phone into her pocket and went back into the cottage. In her short absence her father had arrived and stood near the table and peered over Arthur's shoulder at the inside of the router.

"Lo," he greeted Dar.

"How's Kerry doing?" Ceci asked, from her perch in the corner.

"She and Mark got stopped by a roadblock. They're trying a different path," Dar said. She walked to the table and looked down at her laptop. It was mostly black screen and she reviewed the writing on it. "I'm going to have to go over there and grab them from the coast."

"Better ah do that," Andy said. "That there bike ain't' gonna fit on the back deck of yours. Got a ramp thing fit out for gear by ours."

"On your boat?" Dar glanced up at him.

"Yeap. Moving stuff," Andy said. "Where they trying to get?"

"Not sure. They're south of UM. They're going east and then they're gonna call me." Dar typed into the keyboard and reviewed the results. "Well. That's a step forward."

Arthur looked at the screen. "Is that the bus?" He asked, pointing at a set of cryptic readouts. "There?"

"Yeah." Dar reviewed the inside of the router. "Now those ports can talk to these ports and all I have to do is hack the operating system and recompile it to make it happen." She sat down and started typing. "Won't be line rate, but it won't matter."

"Wicked," Arthur said. "I'm going to go set up the repository to sync." He went back to the couch, picked up his laptop and put his sock covered feet on the ornate coffee table in front of it.

The door opened again, and a large man entered. "Where the hell... there you are you little bastard."

John stood up from where he'd been sitting in the corner. "Oh, Ricardo. Hi," he said. "We're making progress here and I—"

The big man walked over and grabbed John by the front of his shirt and yanked him upright. He was tall and well built, with a thick, muscular neck and frame that advertised many hours spent in a gym and the potential of a drawer full of Speedos.

"Oh, lord," Andrew muttered under his breath. "Ah done ask you, is this all needed right now?"

"I told you I am done with your bullshit!" Ricardo yelled, shaking him. "You promised me a connection! Where is it?"

Andrew headed toward the two of them, while Arthur and Elvis stood up uncertainly, glancing at Dar for direction.

Dar finished typing and stood up herself, sucking in a breath. "Hey!" She let out a short, sharp bellow. "Stop that, ya peanut brained git!"

Ricardo turned and stared at her. "You talking to me? Who the fuck are you?"

"Who the fuck are you?" Dar yelled right back at him. "I rented this place and didn't give you permission to walk your ass inside it."

John reached up to uncurl his fingers off his shirt front. "That's the person who's trying to get this thing to work, Ricardo," he said. "I wouldn't piss her off if I were you."

Ricardo released him and shoved him backward, then he turned and headed in Dar's direction only to find himself blocked by Andrew's tall form in a sudden, yet very deliberate motion.

"Get out of my way," he said, in an irritated voice. He stopped when Andrew ducked his head a little to stare him in the eye.

"Ah do not care for people yelling at mah child," Andrew said, in a very mild tone. "Ya'll will adjust your attitude, or ah will escort you out the door." He folded his hands in front of him and stood quietly, his body filling the gap between the chairs and the table.

"That a threat?"

"Statement of purpose," Ceci said from her corner. "You'll get a lot more out of this crowd with honey than with bullshit. Just saying." She had her fingers interlaced around her knee and she regarded Ricardo with a bland expression. "Over the top macho ain't gonna get you much either, since he's a retired Navy Seal and she's gay."

Ricardo stared past Andrew's elbow at her.

"And I'm a pagan priestess," Ceci said, with a smile. "Whadda you got, Mr. 305 and a half?"

"Thanks, Dad." Dar went back to her seat and continued pecking at her keyboard. "Thanks, Mom." She regarded the results and sniffed reflectively. "We should put the table against that door."

Ricardo now watched them all with a faint wariness. He took a step backward. "Who are you people?" He fell back on his original question. "You some shyster like this guy?"

"We're the Troublemakers," Ceci responded. "Cecilia and Andrew. The little tyke at the table over there is our daughter Dar. We live here."

"Okay." Ricardo drew the word out a little. "Ricardo Montaluco. I also live here. I just moved here last month and now this happened. My business relies on being able to get online, understand?"

"Got it," Dar said and started the router again. "Like everyone else. Believe me buddy, I'm doing what I can to get this going."

Ceci cleared her throat. "Look, Dar's doing some scientific mish mash thingamabob there to get this dude's random moneymaker to give everyone a link to the Internet. If you can't help them do that, leave it alone. Being an asshole is not going to speed up the process."

"She's right." Dar watched the device boot up. "If being an asshole sped up this process it'd have been done for an hour already because I would have tried that already." She glanced over at him. "So, unless you're a Cisco asic design engineer and can do this better than I can, go find something useful to do."

She went back to the laptop and sat down and called up another screen.

For a long moment, Ricardo looked from one to the other of them, his face expressionless. "All right," He finally said, in an abrupt sort of way. "You like empanadas? My wife just finished making some of those and some pandebono."

"Yum." Dar didn't look up from her keyboard. "Columbian?"

"From Bogota," Ricardo confirmed. "Send me one of these boys, we'll bring them back."

"I'll go." Elvis stood up and stretched. "My knees are killing me anyway," he said. "I could use a walkabout." He followed Ricardo out the door and after a moment, John ran after them.

"That went a lot better than I expected," Ceci remarked. "Totally wingbat direction, but hey. I'll take it."

"Lord." Andrew exhaled, shaking his head and returned his attention to the router on the table. "Ah do not know why folks can't start off reasonable and end up jackass stead of t'other way round."

Dar chuckled shortly. "Okay," she said. "Now let me get that image off the repository. Arthur plug me back in, wouldja?"

****

Mark slowed down as they got to an intersection and turned left across oncoming traffic, which thankfully was light. "Here's Cabellero, and the next corner there is Hardee," He said into the microphone in his helmet. "Let's see where this gets us."

They moved along the road, which quickly moved from commercial once they were a few blocks off the main US 1 roadway and into residential. "Oh boy," Mark muttered. "Trees."

Lots of them. Mark throttled down and moved ahead cautiously, as the roadway ahead showed full of debris. On either side were houses, but here, at least, the flooding, if there had been any, seemed to have receded. There were trees down across the yards and roadways, but some had already been dragged aside, and they made slow but steady progress.

Around them the sound of generators was significant. Through the branches and debris there was flashes of light, and in some cases, the house windows showed lit from within.

Twice, they passed groups of people in a yard, and in many places, the dim lights showed the blue of tarps in place over damaged roofs.

The houses on either side were of good size, and Kerry noted the cars they were driving past were newer models, with a lot of SUV's and sedans. "Nice area," She said.

"Barb and I looked here," Mark said. "We actually found a place down off Douglas, but we decided to wait until after hurricane season to see about buying. Glad we did, now."

"No kidding," Kerry muttered.

"Gonna go by there in daylight. Maybe if they took a lot of damage, we'll get a deal."

"Well, that's one way to look at it." Kerry chuckled a little. "Okay what's that up there?"

"Roundabout," Mark said. "I'm gonna go across the middle of it."

They got through the intersection then went along another several blocks, until they came to a T shaped crossroads that had a wall along one side. "Left, huh?" Kerry suggested. "Will that take us down closer to the office?"

"Should. I think this... it's hard to tell in the dark," Mark said, a little uncertainly. "Street signs are missing." He proceeded north along the wall. "I think I usually turned the street before this. It's not... well, it's going the right direction anyway."

It was very dark now, the roadway lined on both sides with trees. "Yeah, here's Douglas," Mark said, with a tone of relief. "Yeah here we go. Now we've just got to get up to Main, and then take Main down to the office."

That seemed the best plan. Kerry nodded. "Yeah, that's the ticket. Better for us to catch a ride from someplace we already know, and we've got people there," she said. "Maybe we'll just crash there. It's getting late."

"Makes sense. Got people, and food, and guys with guns there," Mark said, as, a few minutes later they reached a stretch of the road that was clear of debris. "There's Main up there." He sped up and headed for the corner, the light of the bike showing at last a clear path.

****

Andrew returned to the cottage via the back door. "Storm's hitting right up the Potomac," he announced. "Figure maybe a Category three." He stepped aside and held the door open, allowing a gust of warm, wet air to enter. "Them people are all fussed up there."

"Good," Dar said absently. "Keep them all from calling me." She glanced up, as a low rumble of thunder made itself heard. "Crap. Again?" She frowned. "I thought high pressure was supposed to come in after one of those things."

Ceci came in and pushed back the hood of a violently purple rain jacket. "Just was over at the mansion. Weather's being sucked up in back of Bob," she said. "Expecting a couple inches of rain, like anyone needs that right now," she said. "Extending that long front that's pulling it up the coast."

"What a mess." Dar looked down to check her watch. "And if it's raining those damn phones won't work either." She got up. "Give me that long cable there, Arthur. Let's see if this thing'll do anything useful before I have to head out again."

Arthur went over and picked up a coil of cable laying inside the door to the pool area. The door itself was cracked open to allow the cable to enter, and at the other end of it was John's minivan, parked on the coral deck. He came over to the table, uncoiling the cable as he went and laid it down between the couch and the table. "We should tape that."

"Let's see if it works first." Dar typed in a configuration and studied the results. "Then worry about taping it."

Arthur handed her the end of the cable and she plugged it into one of the ports she'd hijacked. The router considered the cable for a short period, then acknowledged what its purpose was meant for and enabled itself. Dar watched the counters increment, watching for errors.

Then she changed screens and went over to unplug her laptop from their rack and then walk back over to plug the end into another port on the router.

That port came up rather more quickly, and Dar cleared her screen and then refreshed it, watching the configuration change.

She checked the router's logs.

Then she opened up a browser and waited, agreeably surprised when it brought up a website. "Huh."

"Working?" Arthur asked, with interest.

Dar picked up her laptop and turned it around to display the screen. "Something's working." She felt a sense of relief, and then put the laptop back down. "Now, before everyone comes back, let's get some work done." She disconnected the second port from her laptop and then reversed her steps and plugged the cable back into the rack. "Let me reset the routing."

She went back to the router and then opened a session from it to the rack, and started typing.

"Rockstar," Arthur said. "That's like some deeply underground hackity hackstar there, chief."

Dar chuckled softly under her breath. "That was easier than doing it in a submarine tell you that."

Arthur paused and looked at her, as though trying to judge the relative mock level of the statement. Then he just shook his head. "I think I hear a cart outside." He got up and went to the front door, unlocking it and cautiously letting it open, keeping one foot behind it to block it if needed. "Oh, hey." He then stepped back and opened the door, as Elvis entered carrying a large, foil container.

"Keep it open," Elvis said, as he moved across the floor and went into the kitchen with the container. "I think that guy's like a restaurant owner or something."

Ricardo was back, with John at his heels. He carried a drink container and a stack of cups, and John had a stack of plates and another foil covered dish. "Okay," Ricardo said. "So, we got what I promised here, now what about you?" He set the container down on the table. "That's some hot chocolate."

He jerked his jaw at Dar in an aggressive way. "Hey?" He said. "You delivering the goods or what?"

Abruptly a rapid sequence of beeps cut through the room, odd and discordant and from multiple sources, including the two laptops sitting on the coffee table. A rapidly incrementing series of chimes and blurps filled the room along with strident bongs coming from the rack.

It made Andy jump, and he quickly looked from one machine to the other, before he turned to look over at Dar in question. "Hey, Dardar. What all's that?"

"What the hell?" Elvis came in from the kitchen with a double handful of empanadas. "What is that noise?"

Arthur was already diving past him to the couch. "Dingdongs. That's the mail server," he said. "Dar got it working. It's up. That's our mail coming in. It's synching." He squirmed forward and pulled his laptop over. "Lemme turn the freaking sound off before it makes me deaf."

Dar finished typing the last few characters of something she was doing and hit enter. "Spoiler alert," she said blandly. "It's working."

She turned to regard Ricardo. "Congratulations. Your bringing the grub did the trick. Good job." She left her keyboard and went to the front window, that was also cracked open to allow the input of the cable from the palm tree to enter.

"Wait... you're serious?" John rushed past to the back door and stuck his head out of it. "Hey! Alex! Alex!" He yelled out the open portal. "Hey!" He squirmed out the patio door and disappeared into the rain. "Alex!!"

Dar snaked the cable over to the router and plugged it into one final port on the back of it, then she went around to her laptop and made a final configuration change. "Okay," she said. "It's done. Dad, you ready to head out to the mainland?"

"That's it?" Ceci said. "Really? What's actually going on?" She made a gesture around the room. "With all the digital music bombs?"

"One of the servers in that case is our mail server," Dar explained. "I wrote it. When it saw the internet, it lifted its electronic hand up and said Yo, here I am. Send it. As in, all the mail that's been waiting for us since it all went down after the storm." She gestured at her laptop, which was still dinging like mad. "I use a caching service, so I don't have to change the MX records."

Ceci regarded her. "Sure." She nodded firmly. "Absolutely, of course you do. That makes all the sense."

Ricardo had a radio strapped to his waist and he talked into a headset and mouthpiece attached to one ear. "That's what I said, idiot. Plug in that cable and get to fucking work!" He turned to them. "Thanks," he said. "That was worth the food. I'll be back. I want to talk to you people about something." He left in a rush, slamming the front door behind him.

"Can't wait." Dar felt an almost giddy sense of relief. Not so much that she'd made the router work, but that the task was done and now she could focus all her attention on getting Kerry home. "Let's get out of here before the bastard figures out he's got a quarter point nothing bandwidth and wants me to change the laws of physics."

The sound of the rain outside felt like it was drumming on the back of her head, as she thought about the roads, and the dark, and the possibilities, and finished up her typing, already thinking ahead to the boat, and the trip and the water.

She turned off the sound on the laptop, having no intention at all at opening up the mail screen and looking at it.

Elvis came over to Dar with a plate and handed it to her. "These are pretty good," he said. "I'm not sure they're worth the internet, but it's better than that chicken they had in the big place tonight."

Dar picked up one of the pastries and took a bite. Her eyebrows lifted. "Mm." She made a noise of surprised approval. "That is good."

"All right." Andrew stuck his head in the kitchen. "We all's going around," he announced. "Ain't gonna be long out there I figure."

"Be careful," Ceci said. She went to the foil case. "Here, take one of these. It's almost hamburgerish." She offered Andy a caramel colored pastry. "I don't know what that jackass does, but whoever cooked these knew their business."

Andy took the item and cautiously took a bite of it, chewing warily. "That's some good," he said. "Gimme another one of them."

"Here, wait." Ceci fished inside the pantry. "Morons have a little picnic basket in here. We might as well use it." She filled up the basket with some of the treats, and a few napkins, and handed it to him. "Here. Dar probably expended a couple grands worth of brain cells on that gizmo we should enjoy the pay for it."

****

"This is a mess," Mark said, huddled against a half knocked over tree. "Fuckin rain."

Kerry had her arms folded over her chest, wet through. She leaned against the tree trunk herself, a rivulet of rain running down off her nose. "Glad it's summer," she said. "At least it's warm rain."

Mark exhaled, leaning his head against a cracked branch.

Kerry regarded the rain, which was barely visible in the pitch darkness, except as a vague, dense motion ahead of them. The tree was against a coral rock wall that ran alongside the road, dark and equally anonymous, it's surface scuffed and in places darkened with moss.

A rumble of thunder rolled overhead, and then, sudden and startling, a blast of lightning that outlined the street in violent silver.

"Shit." Mark eyed the clouds. "Maybe we should get away from this tree."

"And go where?" Kerry asked.

Mark just made a face, acknowledging the dilemma.

Lightning flared again, and Kerry caught sight, a distance away, of a gate in the wall. "Let's see if we can get in there," she suggested. "Maybe there's an overhang we can get under." She ducked out from under the tree and into the rain, holding one arm above her head.

Mark looked doubtful, but he pushed his motorcycle out into the road and followed her, grimacing as the rain hit him full force. "Maybe we were better off where we were," he muttered, but kept pushing, through a growing flow of water that was coming up over his boots.

He couldn't even tell what road they were on anymore. A turn off he'd though would lead them to Main Highway and the office had ended up dodging unexpectedly east, and they had ended up on this turn off with the wall on one side, and nothing but trees on the other.

No idea where they were. He thought they were going north now, but whether it was the rain or the dark he couldn't for the life of him remember seeing this route before. Maybe it was all the fallen trees? Without any lights and nothing to use for a directional beacon it was dark and creepy as hell.

Mark exhaled. It was scary. He was scared, and tired, and seriously regretting leaving Baptist where at least there it was cool and dry, and they had coffee. He felt his nape hairs lift and ducked his head as another lightning flash outlined the clouds.

Kerry was moving steadily ahead of him, a greenish white blur in the rain and then a moment later, the world lit up again with lightning. He saw the gate she'd spotted, and as the thunder rumbled loudly overhead, they turned to the right toward it.

It was an old gate, wrought iron, two halves that came together in the center and were wrapped with a stout chain, and as they came up next to it, a very visible lock. "Crap." Mark parked the bike and took out his flashlight. He turned it on and playing it on the lock. "We could maybe tie the bike to this and yank it open." He looked over his shoulder. "Not much runway."

The gate was at the corner of a bend in the road, and right across from it was a huge Ficus tree uprooted and sprawled across the road, blocking it.

Kerry took a step back. "We could climb over this," she said. "But that's abandoning your bike and I'm guessing you don't want to do that."

"Not unless I got no choice," Mark said. "These things are expensive, Ker."

"Yeah, I know." Kerry went to the other side of the gate where she'd spotted an indentation. "Hang on let me…" She paused. "Oh, wait now here's something."

Mark sloshed over to her. "What is … oh. Well, that's not really big enough for both of us." He looked at the small alcove. "You want to just hang out in there…" He paused. "I mean, no sense in both of us standing out in the rain."

"There's a smaller gate in here. Let me see your light." Kerry held her hand out behind her, and when Mark gave over the flash, she brought it around in front of her to look at something set into the wall. "Hang on… this isn't locked." She rattled something and then took a step back into the rain. "Ah hah."

Mark peered over her shoulder. "Oh," he said. "I might be able to get the bike through that but… "He looked past the open small gate. "Is there a point? This looks like a park." He took a step back and regarded the gates, looking at either side of them. "No plaque, but maybe one of the old private ones down here."

Kerry shrugged. "Better than nothing? Maybe there'll be a shelter we can hang out under. Like… you know, where a barbeque might be or something. And if this is going along the coast, and we can get near the water, I can call Dar for a pickup soon as it stops raining."

Thunder rumbled over their heads. "Sounds good to me," Mark said. "Let me get the bike before it floats away." He went back into the rain and got the bike up off its kickstand and pushed it over to the alcove. He angled the handlebars as Kerry pushed the gate all the way open and held it for him.

It was a tight squeeze, but he shoved the motorcycle through the gate and kicked it closed behind him as Kerry got out of the way. "Lead on."

Kerry held the flashlight and moved across the water-covered ground to where there was a gravel outline in front of the big gates. "Over here," she called back, and then started forward along the outline of the roadway.

A blast of lightning gave her a quick look at the path ahead, and she saw lots of trees. Some were lying down across their path. She thought she saw what looked like a square structure to the left farther on though, and she hastened toward it as the rain started to come down even harder.

The wind came up and blew hard against her, almost stopping her in her tracks and she paused. "I think we're heading toward the water."

"Don't walk into it," Mark warned. "The water I mean. Feels like Bob turned around and came back."

Kerry inhaled. Was that possible? Hurricanes were at the very least, fickle. But she didn't think any of the potential scenarios had included that one in it, and surely Dar would have said something if it had. She took a breath of air again. "I can smell saltwater."

Mark sniffed. "I just smell rain." He shrugged. "But I'm a native. It just smells like air to me."

Ah, yes. Kerry wiped the rain out of her eye and then she pointed. "I thought I saw a building over there. Let's try that." She took hold of one of the handlebars and helped Mark push, glad at least they had relatively solid gravel under their boots. "Watch out for that block there... not sure what that is."

"No telling," Mark said. "Hibachi maybe. We could see some home-less or something in here." He glanced around. "Now I do wish you'd brought that gun with ya. Since we're trespassing and all that stuff."

"Hopefully everyone's inside hiding from the rain." Kerry held the flashlight with her other hand, and they put their heads down and just moved as fast as they could, the thunder and lightning worsening. "And if not, maybe they'll take pity on us."

The square structure loomed up in front of them, and to their relief it had a covered porch. They got the bike up onto the raised concrete pad and both of them relaxed at the same time at the abrupt end of the deluge. Mark went over to the door and tried it cautiously. "What do you think?"

"What do I think?" Kerry came over with the light and turned the knob, pushing against the door as it grudgingly opened. "I think it's better than nothing." She drew in a breath, and found it full of the smell of wood and gasoline, and the rich scent of...

While she wasn't sure what it was, at least it wasn't that unpleasant. She stepped inside and shone the flashlight around, finding what appeared to be a garden shed. In one corner there were various grass cutting types of machinery, and lined up against the wall several cans of gasoline.

There were shelves on the opposite wall full of dusty cans and buckets, and in the back of the shed was a large square space with shoulder high walls. In front of that was a low bench. "Well." Kerry closed the door, shutting out the thunder of the rain. "It's empty and it's dry."

Mark nodded. "Good call, boss," he said. "We can wait it out here at least." He took off his riding jacket and hung it up on a nail in the wall. "Whoa that was nasty."

Kerry went over and sat down on the low bench. It was a relief to get out of the rain, despite the shelter's warm and stuffy atmosphere. "Maybe leave that door open," she said. "Get some air in here." She rubbed her nose in reflex, imagining the dusty air tickling it.

Mark went over and opened the door, blocking it with a bucket he found near the wall. "Hope the wind doesn't send the rain in here," he said. "I don't want to mess up whoever this is floor." He looked around the room. "Oh, hey wait a minute... I think I see something useful over there."

He walked over to the shelves and inspected their contents, as Kerry shone the light in that direction. "I think this is a... yeah." He worked at something and then light flared, outlining his dripping form. "A camping light," He said with some satisfaction. "My old man has a half dozen of these."

"Nice," Kerry said. "One of the oil ones? Yeah, I smell it." She shut the flashlight off to save its battery and extended her boots, letting her head rest against the wooden half wall. "Boy it's been a long day."

"No kidding." Mark sat down on a box and leaned his back against the wall of the shed. "Maybe we can get a nap in waiting for the rain."

Kerry closed her eyes. "Sounds great to me."

****

"This here's a big old mess," Andy said. "Ah swear."

"It's a mess," Dar agreed, with a sigh. "One step forward, two steps back. Been the story of my life this week." She studied the dock, deciding whether they should run for it, and get onboard and get moving.

She was thinking about Kerry. About where she was, and where hopefully she was sheltered, protected from the storm that was currently lashing the palm trees that had not fallen in the previous weather, but were now bending as though Bob had, in fact, turned back on himself.

"Wall." Andy said, after a long pause, where they both regarded the marina in silence.

"Let me see how far I can get out there." Dar turned on the cart and took a bumpy path across downed limbs past piles of rubble down to the lower level of the marina. The dock was narrow, but she maneuvered slowly past the half-sunk boats toward the far end.

Tied up alongside, both the Dixie and her parents' boat were rocking in the choppy wake, rain sheeting off their fiberglass hulls.

Dar parked the cart near the wall, and for a moment the thunder softened a little, as they were in a bit of shelter. "You get that thing started. I'll untie us?"

Andrew looked at her, one of his grizzled eyebrows hiking up. "How bout you steer," he said. "Figure we'll get on out of here faster with all that mess." He indicated the wrack filled marina. "I done close to poked a hole in that thing last time I parked it."

Dar smiled, silently accepting the unspoken compliment. "Sure." She took the fob and stuck it in her pocket, then she unzipped the plastic and ducked out into the rain, grimacing a little as it lashed against her and she drew in a breath, half air and half mist.

Rich and pungent and a mixture of the ozone smell of the water falling and the sharp crispness of the nearby sea as she crossed the dock and reached out for the railing of the boat, stepping over and onto the wooden surface of the ramp clamped onto the deck.

She wasted no time in climbing up to the flying bridge, a little different from hers, a little newer, with a Plexiglas housing around it to keep the rain off that she gratefully ducked into.

Below, in the flickering light of the work lamps in motion she saw her father untie the bow, and then head to the aft as she settled behind the console and got the engines started. Dual inboards like hers, but almost twice the power, and she felt the rumbling difference transmitted to her through her feet on the deck.

She'd driven the bigger boat a few times before. It wasn't as maneuverable as the Dixie due to its greater size, but she tapped the throttles with confidence as they drifted away from the dock. Ahead of her, where the marina building had once stood she spotted one of the dockmasters, drawn out by the sound of the engines.

She lifted a hand up and waved at him, as he stood there in the rain, peering out from under his thick rubber hood. It was impossible to see his features but after a moment, as if in resignation, he lifted his hand and waved back, and then he turned and went back under the series of tarps that had been set up for shelter.

Andrew climbed up to join her and sat down in the second chair behind the console, folding his hands in his lap as he hooked his military boots on the stainless-steel footrest. "Ah do like this here night riding."

Dar gave him a quick, sideways glance as she gently eased the boat out backward, past the Dixie's berth. "This?" She indicated the rain with her elbow, her tone one of mild disbelief.

"Sure," he replied, amiably. "It's just wet. Least it's warm."

"That is true." Dar reached the open space in front of the marina entrance and swung the aft around, for a moment facing directly into the open gap. She shifted into forward and headed out into the channel. "I dunno. I'd rather just take a swim in the pool."

Andrew chuckled.

It was very dark as she turned out into the channel, relying on the markers and the depth sounder for a backup as they moved past the island and its halo of lights.

The headwind was fierce. Dar felt it shove against the hull and it thrummed the Plexiglas cowl behind which they were standing. She turned off the floodlights and left the running beams on only, letting her eyes adjust to the shadows as they left the island behind.

"Ya'll want you some night eyes?" Her father asked, after a minute or so.

"You have some?" Dar wasn't surprised, when he opened a drawer in the console and withdrew a set of goggles and handed them over to her. She slid them on one-handed and adjusted the fit. She blinked a few times as the world adjusted from grays to oddly outlined flashes and almost colors.

After a minute of that, Dar removed the goggles and handed them back. "Too weird. I'm fine." She resumed her attention to the channel. "Tide's coming out."

"C'n feel it," Andy said, as he put the goggles back in the drawer. "Figure they all made it to the office?"

"That's where I'm going to start," Dar said. "At least I can tie up there."

"C'n find us a truck."

"Find?"

****

There was a point, Kerry found, when you were so tired you really could sleep sitting up on a wooden bench in a stuffy shack, with only the random puff of damp air to cool you down.

Even dressed in sopping wet medical scrubs and wet   hiking boots.

Not entirely a deep or particularly restful sleep, one of napping, and waking and napping again, shifting a little to attain a bit more comfort or relieve a cramp, but now at least she wasn't' dripping water on the concrete floor.

In a moment of waking, she regarded the dim and flickering light that coated the inside of the shed in mellow gold. She heard the rumble of thunder from the outside and the pattering rattle of rain against the windows and the overhang.

Mark was curled up on a bag of... gardening soil? Mulch? Kerry could barely see it and figured it didn't matter any more than the provenance of her bench did. It had been a long day, and at least for now this little shed provided all the shelter they could have reasonably asked for given everything.

She let her eyes close again and listened to the rain outside. As long as she heard it, she knew they were in a holding pattern. There was no way for her to communicate, no way for her to let Dar know where she was, and no way for them to move on.

It gave her a sense of... a moment of lack of anxiety. An internal acknowledgement that it was okay to just sit here, under a solid roof and wait for the world outside to change so she could move on and do something else. The only worry she had was the worry of worry itself. She knew that out there, somewhere, Dar wondered where she was.

Was she still on the island? Waiting for the rain to stop? Kerry smiled. No. Rain was meaningless to Dar. Not rain, not dark, not rough or strange waters. The only thing that would prevent her from searching is the fact she had no idea where to go.

So probably, Dar had gone or was going to the office. Just like Kerry had intended on doing. Just like they'd discussed, so at least, there was a starting point. And when the rain stopped or the day came, whichever first, that's where they'd head.

Until then?

A soft sound made her open one eye, to see the sleek, wet form of a small animal scoot through the door and then stop, clearly not expecting to find other living creatures inside. She opened her other eye. "Hey there, little guy."

It was a cat. There was no collar on it, and it was covered in thick, muddy colored hair plastered all over its body, whose ultimate color she could only guess at.

With a sneeze, the cat shook itself and sat down. It shook its paws one at a time and sent tiny spatters of mud across the floor.

Kerry watched it, and after a minute the cat moved over to near the door, but enough inside to be out of the rain. It sat down again and then tucked its paws under it, watching her in return with inscrutable eyes.

Kerry closed her eyes again. If that was the… she paused in mid thought, as the sound of running footsteps drifted in on the breeze. Not that close, but not far away either. She sighed, opened her eyes and listened.

Near the door, the cat had also heard, and turned its round head, it's pointed ears twitching.

Someone, possibly, trying to get out of the rain just like they had. Kerry wondered if the faint light from their lamp would draw them over to the shed, or was the heavy downpour enough of an obscuring factor?

She reluctantly shook herself fully awake and stood up. The cat backed away from her warily and scooted into the empty square space behind where she'd been sitting. She went to the door and stuck her head out and looked past the bike parked against the wall to the open space beyond.

Trees and debris and a curtain of rain were all she could see. The footsteps had faded. Then motion caught her attention and she looked over toward the gates they'd entered from, and saw four or five moving bodies, and now those footsteps echoed. "Ah."

"What's up?" Mark scrambled to his feet and came up next to her. "What's going on?"

"People." Kerry pointed at them. They were running past between the trees but then, one of them looked over and saw the shed and the light and yelled out. "Ah, crap."

"Hey, probably just looking for shelter." Mark said, reasonably. "We got space in here sorta." He glanced around. "Well, maybe not."

Kerry took a step back and looked around the shed. She walked over and took down a hoe from one of the hooks then leaned against it. "Let's hope they're friendly."

"Why wouldn't they be?" Mark asked. "I mean, we're in a park."

"We're in something, behind a locked gate," Kerry reminded him. "Maybe it's a historical ground?"

"Huh." Mark opened the door all the way and squared himself into the entrance. "One way to find out. Hey!" He lifted his voice and gave the oncoming men a brief wave. "Hello?"

The nearest newcomer hauled up as he reached the overhang. "What the hell you doin in here, boy?"

Mark stood his ground. "Staying out of the rain. What does it look like?" He, perhaps consciously, deepened his tone, and braced his hands on either side of the doorframe. "The hell is your problem?"

"You're trespassing, is my problem." The man came up under the overhang. "This is private property." He was dressed in a rain slicker, dark green, and a pair of rubberized pants with rubber boots, and was tall and well built. His face was bearded.

His dress wasn't a uniform, but he had a large, long flashlight gripped in one hand and there was plenty of room in the rain jacket for a more deadly weapon.

Kerry figured a bit of dialog couldn't hurt. She came up behind Mark, still holding her hoe, and peered past his shoulder. "We didn't mean to," she said. "It was just washing us off our bike." She indicated the motorcycle. "Sorry about that."

The sudden intrusion of her lighter, female voice made him take a step back. His attitude visibly changed. "Well, how'd you get in here?" He asked, glancing at the bike. "Somebody called us, said they saw people up by the wall."

Two other men came up behind the first, all dressed in the green rubber raincoats. "John went to check the house, Robby. Make sure no one got in," One of them said. "All kinds of trash out in the streets you never know what you got here."

Robby, the tall, bearded man, made room for them to come in out of the rain behind him onto the porch and for a moment it was a silent, uncomfortable standoff.

"We came in the gate," Kerry provided, in a mild tone. "We were trying to ride back along the road and the rain was too hard."

The silence lengthened. "That's a nice bike," one of the other men commented, after it had gone on what seemed like a very long time.

"Thanks," Mark said. "Not great in the middle of this though." He indicated the rain. "We were just trying to get somewhere. The cops stopped us up near the U."

A fourth man came up. "All clear by the house," he reported. "Looks like it's just these folks."

"The gate was locked," Robby said, eyeing them doubtfully. "I had to unlock it to get in."

"Maybe we were just lucky," Kerry said. "It was open. I'm no locksmith." She smiled at him. "I run an IT shop."

Mark edged aside to let Kerry ease past him, seeming to realize that she presented a more sympathetic figure. Even in the middle of the night and the middle of a deluge, guys were guys and even in damp hospital scrubs, Kerry was an attractive woman.

Two of the men had flashlights on and the combined glow of them outlined the concrete porch as they pointed the beams down at the ground, after they briefly outlined Kerry's figure. The three that just arrived all looked at Robby, who was, apparently their leader.

"Yeah, okay," Robby said, after a pause. "I don't blame you none. I'd have tucked out of the rain if I could, too." He glanced around. "It's just people get in here, y'know? Homeless and all that and mess around with the place and the old man, he didn't cotton to that."

Old man. Kerry frowned suddenly. "Sorry to ask this," she said. "Would you mind telling me where we actually are? I'm not from around here," she added, as an aside. "I've never been this far south in the Grove area."

One of the others laughed a little bit. "No, you sure ain't. Where you from?" John asked. "You talk like a Northerner."

"Michigan," Kerry replied. "Little place called Saugatuck up on the lake."

They all clustered closer, to get out of the downpour. "Well, ma'am," Robby said. "You all are in a little place called Hunter's Point." He paused. "Sure you never heard of it," he added. "Figures in the history round here way back though."

Kerry blinked. "Hunter's Point," she repeated. "Are you kidding me?"

Robby looked surprised. "You have heard of it? Yeah, this is old man Hunter's place," he said. "He done passed, a bit ago, and we've been keeping it all tight like he'd want it. My dad used to keep the grounds here. Old man treated him right."

Kerry leaned back against the doorframe of the shed. "I've heard of it," she said. "It's really nice of you to keep an eye on it... for his... family? Someone was telling me now his daughter. Or maybe..."

"Yeah," Robby said, briefly. "Something like that. But I think he'd be all right with you all staying here in shelter. He wouldn't mind ya, not you being up from Michigan. He had him a place up there, off one of them lakes."

"Old man'd be all right with it," John agreed, in a quietly assured voice. "He'd a liked that there bike I tell ya." He took a step back and studied the Harley. "He woulda."

Robby nodded. "Stick here," he told them. "Lot of trees and stuff down and no lights." He motioned for the rest of them to leave. "We'll be back in the morning and open the gates up again so you can get out of here."

"Thanks." Kerry put her hands into her pockets, as she watched them leave, quickly disappearing into the curtain of rain that had turned the ground near the shed into a long stretch of racing water. "Well."

"Kinda jerky jerks," Mark commented. "I went to high school with guys like that. Guys on the football team who beat up nerds in the locker room." He leaned back against the doorframe. "Never saw the internet coming."

"No one really did back then. But hey, they liked your bike." Kerry turned and made her way back inside the shed, going to the center of the room and standing there in thoughtful silence.

Mark went back to his sack of garden matter and sat down. "Glad they chilled out." He sighed. "They liked my bike, but I think they liked you more." He chuckled. "Ma'am."

Kerry smiled. "Wonder what they would have said if I'd told them there is a slightly more than zero chance I actually half own this place." She looked around the inside of the shed, seeing it now with an odd shifting of perception.

"Say what?" Mark sat there, legs splayed, hands propped against the sacking. "This place?"

Kerry went over and sat down again on her bench. "You know we've been looking for a new house," she said. "Before the storm hit, Dar came over to look at a place called Hunter's Point, it was for sale." She looked around. "Has to be this place, right? Couldn't be two of them."

Mark continued to stare at her. "You guys bought this?" He seemed unable to process it. "Man, I've heard stories about this place my whole life. The whole thing with him refusing to use the property, and being a pissant to the county and holy crap? This? It's a historical something isn't it?"

"Something, yeah. Well. We tried to," Kerry said. "It was all happening before Bob came through. There was a bunch of legal stuff and I don't know if it all went through or what happened. Probably not, now that I think about it, but isn't it funny we ended up here?"

"That's wild."

"It is. Now I really wish it was morning so I could see the place." Kerry drummed her heels on the floor. "Dar said she thought I'd like it. She did. She said it was big enough for me to have a flock of sheep on the property."

"You want a flock of sheep?"

"No." Kerry chuckled. "I asked her if there was room for a garden."

"Huh." Mark shook his head a little. "That's crazy. But now I wish it was light too. I wanna see it."

Kerry checked her watch. "That and Dixie's coffee maker," she muttered. "C'mon sun."

"No freaking kidding."

Chapter Ten

They heard the office before they saw it, once Dar had shut down the engines and they were tied to the makeshift dock.

The sailing club was still in its woebegone state. It was obvious no one had done anything to it, no bit of debris had been moved, save the flotsam and jetsam they had used to create their footpath.

The building next door, a high-priced restaurant, had been swept clean by the storm surge and was equally abandoned. So when they heard the sounds of salsa music echoing out of the rainy darkness it was relatively simple to guess where it came from.

"What the world?" Andy finished tying up the boat and straightened up. He planted his hands on his hips.

Dar pulled her rain hood up. "Let's go find out." She was glad to have the gear on, despite the muggy heat as the rain drove against them. The choppy water rocked the boat against the pier and she ducked her head a little as they headed into the wind onto the shore.

They got onto the tree strewn pathway and climbed up through the debris on the back of the club. A broken shutter flapped in the wind, smacking against the concrete wall.

Past the club they climbed back down onto the roadway and then crossed the road between the shoreline and where the office was. Now, in conjunction with the music, they saw the low gleam of lamps inside the windows on the lower floor.

Dar searched the front of the building as they approached the doorway, disappointed when she didn't spot Mark's bike. "Damn it." She'd been hoping it was just the rain keeping them in radio silence. "They're probably under an overpass somewhere."

"With that bike? Something like it," Andrew said. "Shoulda set them up with a Humvee."

Dar eyed him. "We have any?"

They turned the corner and approached the front door, and then halted as a dark figure blocked their path, along with the sound of a gun being cocked.

"Yo, boy." Andy started forward again. "What're you all doing out heah?"

"Hey." The figure stepped back and pushed the door open for them. "Had some trouble before. Mick and Garvy are round the back." He lifted a hand. "Hey, there, ma'am. Got a little party going on inside."

"So I hear." Now in the reflection Dar recognized Buddy, tucked into a sheltered spot near the door with a large thermos nearby. "Carlos in there?"

"Big boy? Sure." Buddy settled back onto his perch, shifting his gun into the crook of his arm. "They'll be glad to see ya."

They entered the hallway and turned the corner and stopped in surprise at the crowd of people clustered around long folding tables. "What the heck?" Dar muttered. "Who are all these people?"

Andy stared past her. "Ah'm sure ah do not know."

Carlos spotted them. "Hey, guys!" He yelled a greeting over the music. "C'mon over!" He gestured to someone standing in the doorway to the small downstairs kitchen. "Hey, turn it down a little. The boss is here."

There were at least forty people in the hallway. There were big fans on either end of the long corridor and damp, cool air was being pulled in from outside and circulated around the folding tables that held all sorts of miscellaneous food and drink on them.

There was a hotpot, three coolers full of ice, a slow cooker, all with cables dangling over the side of the table and a long extension cord running down the hall and out the loading dock door. The music quieted a little, and now the sound of a generator was clearly heard from that direction.

Dar was halfway down the tables before she realized she did know some of the people. Aside from Carlos and his buddies, and Celeste's coworkers from ILS, two of Scott's old friends were there, and their landlord. The folks who she didn't know were looking at her with deep interest and Dar figured if she didn't know them, apparently, they knew about her.

"Hi," she offered a general greeting.

"Lo," Andrew added, from just behind her. "You all having a party?"

"Hey, Dar, hey Mr. R." Carlos was seated on a duct taped stool. He held a plastic cup of what looked like beer. "We got stuff left from the grill. Ya hungry?"

"No, we got some stuff back at the house," Dar said. "We got the internet up over there."

"Yeah?" Carlos said. "We heard from the cops they might have some cell service up here tomorrow, maybe tomorrow night."

Their landlord came over. "Hey, guys. Sorry about what happened before the storm."

"Ya'll should be," Andrew said, sternly. "This here's a responsibility you done had."

"Didn't even know it was happening." The young gay man shrugged a little bit. "Soon as I heard, I did what I could, but they said you already took care of it. And you did a great job! I saw some of those other places on the way in here. Holy moly."

"Still a lot of damage," Dar said. "The skylights all leaked."

He nodded. "Carlos told me when I got here. I went and looked," he said. "I'll have an appraiser come over. I have a guy who works with us."

"Hey, what's up with Kerry?" Carlos asked. "They making it down here? Must be if you guys are here. But that weather's crap."

Andrew circled the table and went over to two of his buddies, who were relaxing on a table near the end of the hallway.

"Glad those guys were here," Carlos said. moved over to stand next to

Dar. "We had about a dozen thug types come around when we were grilling. Said they were the neighborhood protection squad." He cleared his throat. "We put a guard on the front after that."

"Nice."

"Yeah they ran like crazy when big A's buds came around the corner with those machine guns. It was kinda funny, but it wouldn't have been, you know what I mean?" He glanced around at the crowd, most of whom had gone back to their casual conversation. "I don't mind a little scrapping, but it wasn't really the time or the place for it."

"No." Dar settled onto one of the stools near the wall. "So, what was their pitch? "She folded her arms over her chest. "I mean, what were they going to protect you from? A truck of their buddies?" She asked. "Or were they offering to sell you stuff they poached?"

"Said no cops were around, so we were sitting ducks," Carlos said. "I was just getting done saying hey, we just fed us some cops when the spooks came up behind me rattling their triggers. That one guy, Hank? He's a scary dude."

"Most of my father's friends are scary dudes," Dar admitted with a brief smile. "I've had them around so long I don't notice it anymore."

Carlos regarded her. "Your pop's a little scary," he said. "Come to that, boss, no offense but you're a little scary, so that don't surprise me you thinking that's normal." He glanced behind him. "But I think these guys are sort of enjoying this whole thing a little."

Dar studied the three men at the end of the table. "Yeah, could be." She exhaled. "Anyway, I was hoping Kerry and Mark would be back here by now. They got stuck at the checkpoint at the U about two hours ago."

"That's not that far." Carlos looked at his watch. "So, where the hell are they?"

"Wasn't raining then," Dar said. "Figure they're under some shelter waiting for it to stop." She pondered that. "But after what you just told me, now I'm wondering how many of those gangs are out there."

Carlos looked a little concerned. "If they were at the U two hours ago... man, that's only like fifteen minutes from here unless they ran into debris or that stuff. It's pretty dark out there too." He put down his cup. "Maybe we should go look for them."

"Yeah." Dar drew the word out slowly. "I was hoping they'd get the damn ramp fixed so I could bring the truck over, but they're not done yet."

Andrew came over. "Hey, Dardar? We got us a Humvee. Ya'll wanna go out and find them two?"

"You got a hummer?" Carlos looked impressed.

"Tch." Andy grunted. "None of that candy assed stuff, a real one."

A Humvee! "Absolutely." Dar felt a sense of relief. "I know roughly which way they were going to take. But I know Mark's not going to want to leave that bike."

"Got us a trailer hitched up'll take care of that." Andy clapped her on the shoulder. "Let's go. Hank was using it to haul his landscaping stuff round."

"Problem solved." Carlos said. "I'm gonna go see if those cops are out there still. Let them know we're looking for some people." He motioned one of his buddies over. "C'mon, let's go for a walk, get your Gore Tex on." He headed toward the door and reached for one of the large raincoats hanging on a door edge nearby.

"Lord. Wall, that can't do no harm anyhow." Andy pulled his hood up again as Hank came over and gave Dar a big grin, and a thumbs up. "C'mon, boy. Let's us go hunting round here."

Hank was a stocky man of middle height, and the distinctive scar of a cleft palate. His eyes were deep set and he had one earlobe stretched out with a round bone earring. "Yo, junior," he greeted Dar. "How's it?"

He had a lisp and a scar on his neck and there was a little crazy around the edges of his smile. Dar had known him since childhood. "Hey, Hank," she returned the greeting. "How are ya?"

"Having me some fun," Hank said, with a twinkle in his eye. He patted the stock of the automatic rifle slung over his shoulder. "Let's go find ya friends."

Dar was glad enough to follow her father and Hank out, moving from the faintly stuffy and slightly beer scented air inside back out into the rain, relieved to be doing something to find Kerry instead of just waiting around.

She shook her head and then looked up as an engine fired to see a camo painted Humvee parked in front of the office with an equipment trailer hitched up behind it. It was an older model, with some battered panels and bent fenders, and a ramming grid mounted on the front.

There was a machine gun on the roof, covered in a heavy tarp, and the exhausts were piped up with snorkels that tipped up over the roof of the vehicle.

"That'll do," Andy said, with satisfaction.

Hank was behind the wheel, warming up the engine. "Found it at an auction. Spent a year fixin it up. Ain't great on gas but pulls the hell out of my stuff and people leave it alone. I got a job to cut up some trees at Bayside tomorrow."

Dar got in the back behind the driver's seat, glancing up at the hatch that would allow someone to stand and fire the gun. "That thing have bullets?"

"Sure." Hank waited for Andy to slid into the passenger front seat and close the door. "Almost put a water cannon up there but it leaked all over the place. Pain in my ass." The floor of the truck was bare steel, dented and scuffed and now almost completely covered in mud.

"Nice," Dar complimented him and meant it.

He put the truck into gear. "Where're we going, junior?"

"Do not call her that." Andrew frowned.

"She don't care," Hank said. "Hey?"

"Head south on Main." Dar felt the vibration of the engine all the way through the frame of the military truck. Now that her eyes had adjusted, she saw the belted armament container under the gun, and tucked into slings behind both seats were handguns.

It was a little like being inside a Mad Max movie, only it was raining, and they were in Miami instead of some desert somewhere. She returned her attention to the machine gun. "They let you roam around with that up there?"

"Today? Sure." Hank started out along the road, running the Humvee over the road bumps with a jarring motion. "Don't usually. Scares the civs." He looked both ways. "Cops where I live know I'm crazy so they leave me alone."

Dar wasn't sure the National Guard or the cops would appreciate the blatant arms, regardless of what was going on around them. But as it was dark as the inside of a gorilla's butt and there were roaming gangs of curiously weenie racketeers, she supposed it would be all right.

The musty smell of canvas and gun oil called up memories of her childhood and she relaxed against the hard seat. She braced her boots on the floor as the truck rumbled through the dark streets and they got to the main street in the Grove. The eponymous Main.

"What'd them cops say?" Andy asked, after a few quiet moments.

Hank shrugged. "Came for food," he said. "Said they'd picked up a couple dozen looters and ran em up to the jail. They also ran out some dudes selling water for twenty bucks a jug." He slowed down as they came to an intersection with no lights and some surprising but light cross traffic. "Usual crap in this kinda thing."

The cars on the road were going along slowly, most had more than one person in them. "Sightseers," Hank commented. "Jackass."

"Maybe." Andy watched them move past. "Out looking for something that's sure."

"Maybe they're just enjoying the air-conditioning," Dar remarked dryly from the back seat. "Maybe we should close down the office and send all those people home," she added. "Are we idiots back there in the middle of a blacked-out city?"

"Think goin home's safer for em?" Andy glanced at her in the rearview mirror. "Don't think so, Dardar. Least they got folks around em and cops stopping by." He looked out the window as they passed a group of men huddled under an overhang. "Back in the back there, no tellin."

The group of men turned their heads and watched them go by, one of them pointing at the truck as they all took a step back more firmly against the building wall.

"That's probably true," Dar admitted. "Look at some of these streets. You can't even see a hundred feet through all the down trees and light poles." She knew there were houses back behind them, and once in a while she saw the brief glimpse of a lamp.

The rain increased, thundering on the roof of the Humvee, and a mist of it blew in the windows, dusting Dar's face with it. She blinked it out of her eyes and took in the richly mineral scent, licking some droplets of it off her lips. "Turn down along Monroe toward the water."

The Humvee went off the road and around the debris with relative ease, and through the rain they smelled the scent of newly cut wood.

"Somebody been through here with a chainsaw," Andrew said. "You think they went down here, Dar?"

"I told Kerry to get to the coast," Dar said, absently. "Find someplace with a dock I could get the Dixie into." She shifted and stuck her head out of the window, ignoring the rain. "There aren't that many places... most of that stretch past here is residential."

"Well, we can't get past this." Hank pulled the truck to a halt, as they came up on a huge Ficus tree, turned on its side and blocking the entire throughway. Someone had been working at it, there were chunks of it missing, but a backhoe was parked in the rain nearby, the cab covered in a tarp.

"They couldn't either," Dar said. "Let's try the next street."

"Could they all be tucked up near that school?" Andrew asked. "Maybe didn't get down this far."

"Could be," Dar said. "Might have tried coming down Hardee."

"Let's buzz by Sacred Heart first. They got that old fashioned carport thing," Hank suggested. "Maybe they went under that." He turned the truck around and went back up the road, turning back onto Main and continuing down into a heavy wash of rain.

****

She'd woken up too much. Kerry regarded the darkness outside, watching the rain fall through the partially opened door. Mark had fallen back to sleep, curled up on his sack full of mulch but the brief interaction they'd had with the erstwhile guardians of the property now had her mind going too much for her to sleep.

And she wished she had something to drink.

And she wished it would stop raining, so she could go outside and try to call Dar.

She tipped her head back and looked up at the ceiling of the shed. It was wooden, but even in the low light she could see the pale strips of hurricane strapping, and the walls were concrete block. No matter the condition of the rest of the property this, at least, had been built to current code.

The floor her boots were resting against was also concrete, and it had a slight decline to it, into the center where she could see the outline of a drain.

So they could wash the place down, she figured. But why would they want to do that in a garden shed? It's where she'd expect to find dirt, after all.

She got up off the bench and stretched her body out. Then she turned to study the space with a bit more curiosity. She put her hands on the half wall she'd been sitting against and looked over it into the square portion behind it.

It was concrete floored as well, the same faintly slanted surface and in the center of it, another drain. She looked down on the inside of the wall, surprised to find a bin fastened to the inside of it.

Agreeably glad to find a little something to engage her restless brain she walked around the half wall and into the other space. She went over to the bin and leaned closer to examine it. It was a thick plastic, and in the corner there was a second, this one with a hole in the bottom.

Kerry straightened up and frowned. She planted her hands on her hips and studied the bins. Then she turned around and looked at the rest of the space, realizing that there was another door in the outer wall, with a split top and bottom that could be swung outward.

It seemed well fastened, and not much used, but as she touched the surface she wondered, a faint flicker of memory from their recent vacation surfacing.

Was it a stable? She turned around in a circle and regarded the clean, silent space. There was room, she thought. Room enough for a horse to be kept in the square space and the bins maybe were where they kept its food. She looked at the second bin. Maybe kept its water in there.

A horse. Kerry regarded the door, then walked over to the half wall and realized there were eyebolts on both sides of the opening where something could have been strung up to block entrance into it and figured, yeah. A horse. But a horse in the middle of Coconut Grove?

Well. Kerry leaned on the half wall and looked at the rest of the space. Definitely full of gardening tools and implements there was no doubt of its purpose, but the cabinets and shelves that ringed the walls really could be used for anything.

Why not for a small stable? She smiled faintly and wondered if Dar had seen the little shack. The thought of a horse living there in the past would have interested her without a doubt. She thought back to the day Dar had visited the place and faintly shook her head. No, she hadn't mentioned it.

But then, why would they have spent time looking at a garden shed? On that day, with the storm bearing down on them and all that going on? Surely the broker had merely   mentioned it, maybe pointed at it as they made their way up to the house.

The house. Kerry looked off into the distance, wondering what condition the house was in, that they might be responsible for. Were they now obligated for a money pit the size of Biscayne Bay?

Along with everything else? She knew half their projects would be canceled. Who knows how many customers would back out, be wiped out, no longer calling, or making preparations they'd done for jobs now nothing but unfunded expense.

Now the thought that they'd gambled on buying property on the cusp of disaster seemed the most idiotic of things they could possibly have done.

Kerry sighed. Why hadn't they thought of that? About what would happen if they had to do things like rebuild the office. Or not have customers and they needed that funding to keep the company afloat while things got back together?

What if that stupid landlord ran out on them and they never heard from him again? What if they were left holding that bag? She thought about that for a moment. Well, what if that happened? They would just have to find some other place to park.

Just like they'd spun up out of nothing, maybe they'd have to do it again. Kerry went around the half wall and over to the door and pushed it all the way open and emerged onto the overhung porch.

It was still raining. But the incessant downpour seemed to have eased somewhat and she could see the path they had come up from the road on. The path continued on and curved along the trees and disappeared again into the darkness. She glanced at her watch. "Jesus. Is it only eleven?"

The darkness drew her, now that she knew where she was, and it was almost impossible for her not to emerge out into the rain and start exploring the property, as idiotic as she knew an idea that was.

There were a lot of trees. She sighed. So that wall they'd been driving along was part of the place too. Did that mean they'd be able to let the dogs roam at will all over? "Oh my God they'll love that." She spent a moment imagining their pets racing around.

It was obvious, too, that one thing they would have here was privacy. She turned and measured the distance to the outer wall, and then she shaded her eyes and tried to peer through the trees to where she assumed the house was. Real privacy.

Shutting their door gained them that where they lived now, but she was always conscious of their condo's shared construction no matter how well built the walls and this—Dar had been right. She could keep a flock of sheep to crop the grass here and no one would know.

They could, actually, keep a horse in the little stable.

Would Dar like that? Kerry knew there were horse ranches not that far away and wondered how difficult it would be to figure out how to buy one. And would it like living here?

Huh.

Kerry looked around at the expansive grounds. Now that she saw them it seemed impossible obtaining them could have happened so easily. She also acknowledged that these grandiose thoughts of buying horses and potential flocks of sheep were ridiculous.

But fun to think of. She folded her arms and leaned back against the wall of the shed. More entertaining than thinking of the whole company going down the tubes anyway.

She reluctantly turned and went back inside the shed and sat down on the bench. She leaned forward and rested her elbows on her knees and checked her watch, willing the time to pass faster.

Through the faint sounds of rain coming through the door, she then heard footsteps, coming her way.

****

"This here's a big old mess," Andy said. "Maybe them kids figured they weren't gonna get down this way and went on back."

"That would make sense," Dar agreed. They were standing outside the Humvee in their rain gear, where Main Highway met some of the feeder streets that angled off to the west and where a huge Ficus tree had collapsed to block the way in both directions.

And the streets going right angles to it were flooded, so deeply none of them thought a motorcycle would have been easily gotten through it.

A Ficus, and three light poles, and an overturned eighteen-wheel truck whose sides were gashed open and evidence around it that the gashes had been pried open further and items removed.

"Too bad," Hank said. "This was getting fun."

Dar wouldn't really characterize it quite that way. She tugged her hood up a bit more and looked around and tried to figure out what their next steps should be.

Go back to the office? That was probably the smartest thing to do.

But wait. She blinked and squinted a little, willing the gray shadows to resolve in the distance around the back of where the tree had emerged.

"What'cha looking at, Dardar?" Andy came up behind her and looked over her shoulder.

"Can we get through there?" She pointed at the corner of the road, where the tree's roots had come up and exposed a large hole. Behind it there seemed to be a bit of a gap. "Back in that corner there, between that concrete light pole and the bench?"

"Sure." Hank got back behind the wheel and started up the engine, while they scrambled in behind him. "Gonna be tough to make that turn with the trailer but we'll give 'er a try." He put the truck in gear and rumbled over the divider in the road, running right over a collapsed street sign.

Andy had his flashlight out and he focused it on the gap. "Got you a car blocking that on t'other side, ah can see it."

"Not fer long."

Dar debated closing her eyes, then she just grabbed hold of the rigid framework of her seat and looked sideways out the open window as the truck rammed through the gap she'd seen, the front bumper ripping apart one of the branches.

The truck tipped onto its side as they ran over the bench and she was glad of her grip as they almost went over enough to take on water through the window on Andy's side. He had one hand latched onto the gap where the gun was fastened and looked completely unfazed by motion.

They were over the bench in a moment and righted themselves, landing back upright with a jarring bang as they got through the open space and dragged the trailer behind them.

Dar resisted the impulse to look behind them, focusing on the path ahead instead as the front windshield repelled the rain and gave her a reasonable view. "No way they came through here."

"No way," Andy agreed, as they plowed into a deep flow of water and it sloshed over the floorboards. "Be up over the engine in that there thing."

They got through and ended up past the crossroads and found flooding in all directions. "Well. Damn." Dar sighed. "Let's see if it gets any better off to the west."

"Sure." Hank cheerfully put the truck into a lower gear, and they lurched forward. "Getting the inside washed fer free here. All good, y'all, all good."

There were no people around, not unreasonably. Between the rain and the flooding, and the residential streets, the opportunity for looting would be less lucrative. "Probably focused around that truck back there. Wonder what was in it?" Dar said.

"Beer," Andy responded. "Had it a Budweiser picture on it. Probl'y still half full I reckon."

Hank chuckled. "Hey, it's not that bad," he said. "You a beer fan, junior?"

"Not really," Dar answered absently. "Kerry's the alcohol expert in the house. I'll drink what's put in front of me." She watched the wake from the truck roll out in front of them. "But I've never really been a drinker." She glanced to her left. "Hang on, can we go down that way?"

Hank looked at her in the rearview. "East? You said go west."

"Yeah, I know. Let's just go down that way for a minute."

With a shrug, Hank turned the wheel and changed direction then ran the Humvee up and over the center island that was covered in water. "Hang on."

The street she'd spotted was overhung with trees and full of debris. But as they bumped up over the curb and down again and plowed through the flooded area. After a minute the water subsided. "Goin up a little."

Dar nodded. "Yeah, that's what I thought. Seemed like it was higher there."

"Big old mess." Andy fell back on his original complaint. "Lord it's gonna take an age to get this sorted out."

It was full of fallen branches and on either side, dark and abandoned houses with no sign of any life at all. Dar hoped that it was because their owners had prudently sheltered elsewhere.

The road angled a little to the northeast, and then out of the gloom the houses disappeared and with a faint curve they were going alongside a wall.

Andy shone his flashlight on it. It was at least eight feet tall, and old, coral construction that was no longer allowed. "Looks like the base of that there cabin of yours down south," he commented. "Lot of that down these parts from back when."

Dar stared at it for a minute. "Oh," she said, after a brief, surprised pause. "Crap this must be Hunters Point." She stuck her head out of the passenger side window into the rain. "Didn't realize we were…. Huh." The whole issue of the Point and the deal bubbled up in her memory. "No idea what happened with that."

Andrew was now also looking at it with far more interest. "Do tell."

Hank slowed his roll, looking through the front windshield at the barrier. "That the crazy guy place?"

"Yeap," Andy said. "Sure is." He regarded it. "Nice big old wall. Ah do like that."

"Ain't nobody down here for sure," Hank said. "You think maybe they… he looked down the wall. "No place to hunker down." He glanced at Andy, then at Dar. "Turn around?"

"There's some gates up ahead. Let's see if they're open." Dar leaned on the windowsill. "If they saw the flooding and turned down here, they might have gone in, especially if Kerry realized where she was."

"Yeap." Andy nodded in satisfaction. He turned to look at Hank, who looked at them with a puzzled expression. "Dar went and bought her the place."

"Tried to," Dar demurred. "No idea how that worked out. Richard never called me back before the storm hit."

Hank brought the truck to a halt. "Say what?" He said in a tone of utter disbelief. "Y'all bought Crazytown? For real?" He asked. "Didn't think the old man'd ever sell to nobody!"

"Died." Andy gave him a poke. "G'wan and drive ovah to them gates."

"Jesus P Fish." Hank shook his head and put the truck back into gear and gunned the engine. They trundled forward, the trailer bumped and clanked along behind them as the road went dry and the sound of the tires went from a slosh to an almost sizzle. "Ya'll are nuts."

****

"Gate's locked," Dar peered through them into the darkness. Despite the rain behind her she thought she heard voices ahead. "Dad, check that little door over there. That's how we got in when we were here."

Obligingly, Andrew pulled his hood up and went over to the side of the gates, turned on his flashlight and examined the other entrance.

"Get out the way, junior." Hank stood on the running board of the truck, his lights blaring past Dar to illuminate the area beyond the gates. "Ain but take a minute, knock those suckers down."

Dar looked at the chain. "How about breaking this?" She said. "If I do own this thing, I don't want to have to worry about replacing the damn gates."

Hank came over and examined it. "Oh yeah. No problem. Hang on." He went back to the front of the truck, where an industrial winch was bolted. He unlocked it and brought over a hook. "Gimme that."

Andrew came back. "Locked up over there, Dardar." He glanced at what Hank was doing. "That'll do," he added a moment later, as Hank clipped the hook into the chain wrapped around the gates and went back to the truck.

"You all get out the way there," Hank directed, as he closed his door. "That thing'll let loose and conk ya."

Dar and Andy obediently backed off and went over to the smaller entryway and waited out of the rain.

Dar peered through the iron grate in the smaller door and watched the shadows and glare of the headlights play out.

"Y'all think she's in there," Andy said, after a long moment of silence.

"I do," Dar said in a tone of calm certainty. "I'm not into any of that mental garbage but I know what this feels like," she admitted. "It's like a string pulling me."

Andy chuckled. "Ah don't know nothing about that, Dardar, but I can smell on the ground here that motorcycle likely came through." He indicated the small space. "Scuffed them up some leather and somesuch on the edge there."

Dar inhaled a little, now realizing she could smell the faintest hint of gasoline and oil. "Here?" She touched the mark on the wall.

"Yeap."

"Here we go!" Hank yelled from outside, and threw the Humvee into reverse, the trailer bumping up and over the median behind him. "Watch it! Gotta back up, it jammed the damn winch."

"Lord." Andy looked out at the truck as it pulled the cable taut and they heard the whine of the winch motor. "Wish we just had us a bolt cutter."

Dar started to chuckle then she turned as she heard a yell coming from inside the compound. "Uh oh." She turned and peered through the grate and saw dark, running bodies in motion, several heading for them. "Oh boy."

"Lord." Andy stepped out into the rain. "Hurry it up!" He circled fist in the air. "Got comp'ny!"

A group of the shadows split off and headed to the left. She heard more yells, the words in them cut off by the rain and the wind, but then a lighter tone cut through and she grabbed the smaller door and shook it hard and leaned back to pull against it with her weight as she recognized the sound.

It stayed firmly locked, and so she abandoned it, darting out into the rain and turned to regard the wall. Eight feet? Nine? Didn't matter.

She hiked up the sleeves on her jacket and took two long steps, crouching and then leaping up to catch the top of the concrete and coral surface. The top had a bit of an edge, and she gripped hard and hoped that it would hold and not send her flying back flat on her ass.

It held. She hauled herself upward and swung her body up onto the top of the wall with a grunt.

"Dar!" Andy yelled from behind her. "Hang on a... "

Too late. Dar was up and pressing her body over before the echo of her father's startled yell faded, adrenaline pumping through her as she let herself drop to the ground. She grimaced a little as the distance jarred her bones and nearly sent her sprawling in the sodden, slippery leaves.

She heard the crackling twang as the chain broke, and the roar of the truck's engine, but now she heard urgency in the yells and what she thought was the sound of a gun.

Then she took off running.

****

"Now what?" Kerry got up and got to the door. She heard more than one person running and the sound of an engine not that far off. "Mark!"

"Huh?" Mark's head jerked upright, and he blinked. "Wh... what's going on?"

"No idea," Kerry said. "Someone's... I think there's lights by the gates." She walked out of the shed and looked that way and saw headlights. "Yeah... not sure..."

Mark was at her shoulder. "What the hell's that all about?"

Now the footsteps headed in their direction and they saw a half dozen men running toward them. "Those guys are armed," Mark said. "Same guys as before?"

"No way to tell." Kerry took a step back into the shed and looked around. "Anything here to... huh."

"Yeah, I just came back down on wish you'd brought that gun." Mark retreated at her heels and closed the door behind him. "There's nothing but... oh, well, a bucket. Or that wheelbarrow."

"Or a hoe." Kerry took one off the wall and examined it. "Too bad it's not a scythe."

Mark looked at her. "You know how to use a scythe, boss?"

"Hell no." Kerry hefted the hoe in her hand. "I can barely use a potting shovel. But it sure sounds good." She handed him the hoe and took a rake for herself. They turned as the door was flung open and the rain came inside along with the thick, pungent scent of rubber. "Hey!"

"Get out!" The man, a stranger, yelled. "We got trouble here! Go on! Go up by the house! Fore you get hurt!"

"What's going on?" Kerry asked. "Is someone coming in the gates?"

"Get out!" The man came forward and two more came in after him. "Get hold of these people and get them up by the house. We don't got time to be arguing with them."

"Hey wait a minute," Mark protested, as two of them grabbed his arm, one taking the hoe out of his hands and tossing it in the corner. "Hey stop! Hold on, guys!"

The first one, tall and bearded, and drenched, went for Kerry. Instinctively, she took a step back and swung the rake across her body, whacking him in the hand with it. "Hey!" She let out a yell. "Stop it! Leave us alone!"

"You're gonna get hurt!" The man shook his hand, sucking in a breath. "Damn you, lady, we just want to get you someplace safe! We got some yahoos in a damn army truck breaking down the gates, now come on!" He dodged her rake and grabbed her arm, and without much effort hauled her up and over his shoulder. "John! Get him and let's go!"

Startled speechless, Kerry found herself half upside down, the breath knocked out of her. She scrabbled for a hold on the slick raincoat and dropped the rake. "Stop! Ow! Hold it! Let me down!"

"We should go with em, Ker." Mark held his hands up and hastened to the door. "Who knows what that all is."

"Mark," Kerry half growled under her breath. "What are the odds, if people showed up at the gates here, in an army truck that we don't know them?" She twisted as they went through the doorway and then they were in the rain and a rumble sounded overhead. "Stop It!"

Off in the distance she heard a high-pitched whine and the rumble of a heavy engine.

"They're breaking the gates!" A man's voice shouted nearby. "Get the shotgun! Hurry!"

"I'm goin up to the house!" The man carrying her yelled. "Those effing cops ain't worth shit. They're scared to come down here."

"Effing army truck with a machine gun I don't' blame them!" One of the men hauling Mark along bawled back. "Move, move! "C'mon! We gotta get under cover where we can hold em off!"

The man carrying Kerry started to run and then she was just hanging on for dear life as they threaded between heavy trees and over rough ground. She finally caught her breath. "Let me down so I can talk to those guys."

"Crazy woman!" The man said. "Just shut up and we'll be there in a minute."

He was traveling uphill now, and outpaced the two with Mark, going off on a side path. "Lemme get up onto the... oh crap someone's coming."

Kerry heard racing footsteps heading their way. "Oh boy."

"Shit," the man said. "C'mon, one more minute and I'll be there..."

Kerry couldn't see behind her and yet she didn't really need to. "Stop and let me down or we're both going to get hurt." She yanked on his hood. "Dude, stop!"

He ignored her, letting out a bellow. "John, I'm there! Go in the back!"

With a deep breath Kerry suddenly arched her body and yanked herself to one side as hard as she could. Then she caught her boot against a tree and shoved away from it with every ounce of effort she could muster and struggled to get herself free from his grip.

He was going uphill and lost his balance. "Shit!" He yelled, and with a truly heroic effort he twisted in midair and landed on the side Kerry wasn't on, releasing her to roll free and thump hard against a tree stump to one side of the path. "What in the hell you do that for you..."

He scrambled around and got to his feet and was hit by a freight train coming from the dark, from between the trees, traveling at speed that didn't even slow down an instant before it plowed into him, lifting his body up and sending it into a deep hollow between the trees full of mud and leaves.

He sprawled there, then there was the sound of an engine nearby and headlights outlined them in stark blue light. He looked up through it at the tall figure facing him with half clenched fists, dressed in rain gear that obscured all other detail.

"That's why I did that." Kerry pulled herself upright with one of the tree roots sticking out. "Oof."

Dar abandoned the seated man once she realized he was done resisting and went over to her, offering a hand up. "You okay?" she asked anxiously. She shoved her hood back, ignoring the rain. "Wow I'm glad to see you."

"Wow I'm glad to see you too." Kerry heaved a sigh of relief as she gave her a hug. "I was in that shed just wishing you'd show up and here you are."

Dar returned the hug, a smile creasing her face. "Glad we came out to find you."

The rest of the crowd caught up, and in a moment Mark was there, dusting off his shirt as he stepped up next to them. "Pops is here," he said. "Y' know, you were so right on about that, Ker," he added, in a matter of fact tone. "They do have a machine gun though. Not sure where that came from."

Dar's heartbeat settled down, and the goosebumps eased under her rain gear. Her body's adrenaline production waned and her knees began to shake. She was glad to have Kerry leaning against her and for a long moment she rested her chin on Kerry's head and gently scratched her back.

"Well, you know Dad. Doesn't surprise me," Kerry responded. "They're lucky that's all they had, and I was able to stop that big ox before they holed up in some bunker and we were under siege from my own family." She shook her head. "Make this night a lot longer than it's already been, and it's been at least two days already."

"All right, you boys just stand up over theah." Hank was behind him, and the sound of an automatic rifle being cocked was clearly heard. "Nobody don't touch nobody and we'll be just fine."

Andrew appeared from between the trees, a handgun in one hand, muzzle pointed skyward. "You kids all right? Boys here got some candy assed ideas they're police or something." He glared at the small crowd of now cowed guardians. "Running round here like that. Mah God."

"We're fine, Dad," Kerry answered for both of them.

The man who had been carrying Kerry hadn't gotten up. He was still on the ground, his arms propped behind him. "Who in hell are you people?" He finally asked. "You're trespassing on private property, you know that?"

"Are we?" Kerry looked up at Dar.

"Possibly," Dar responded. "Possibly not." She hunched her shoulders as the rain started coming down harder. "How about we go under some shelter and sort it all out." She pointed at the bulk of the building ahead of them, all flashes of concrete and shadows in the headlights.

"Scoot." Hank gestured with the muzzle of his gun at the dour looking men. "C'mon, c'mon. Don't make me itchy."

They made their way down a small set of steps and to a protected entrance, in awkward silence. Followed by the two armed veterans, then Mark, then last, Dar and Kerry still arm in arm.

"Found a place you can get the boat in, hon," Kerry said, as they stepped across an inset granite threshold and through a narrow passage. She felt Dar chuckle through her hold on her. "How crazy is it we ended up here?"

"For us? Not crazy at all."

****

The back entrance let them directly into a huge old-fashioned kitchen, with a long, weathered table in the middle and built in, old style wooden cabinets around the walls. There were several soapstone sinks and on one end of the kitchen, a cast iron wood burning stove.

There was evidence of recent habitation. There were stacks of water against the far wall, and several coolers were lined up next to them, along with some containers of powdered milk and sugar. On the counter near the stove was a large battery charger unit, and that had a single thing plugged into it, a coffeepot.

It had high ceilings. In her first somewhat startled, fragmented view of it, Kerry got a sense of space and age, and whitewashed walls. She smelled a hint of woodsmoke and stone and weathered wood. A halfhearted veneer of cleanser over the top of it.

The walls themselves had no adornment. There wasn't any sign of any personal touch in it. Just the big room and its anonymous history. Kerry was reminded of an old church she'd once toured, built from native rock and abandoned by its congregation. Solid and yet somewhat sad.

There was a battery lantern in the corner and after they all entered and filed in, one of the men turned the lamp up. They could finally all see each other in more than just silver splashed lightning and the headlamps of the Humvee.

It was an oddly assorted group. The guardians of the property were in their dark rain jackets, so alike they seemed almost a uniform, with rain pants and boots, They were all in their twenties or thirties, most bearded, all of them husky and athletic. They stared at the intruders with dour resentment.

Kerry was still in her now drenched scrubs and her hiking boots. She ran her fingers through her hair to halfheartedly sort it. She removed a sodden leaf from her neck and twirled it idly in her fingers before she put it into her pocket.

Mark had on his riding jacket, which he quickly stripped off now that they were inside and laid it over one of the benches near the wall. His shirt was spattered with rain and dirt underneath, it's pale khaki looked almost camouflage itself.

He turned and then went to stand behind Kerry. He pushed his glasses up onto his nose and then stuck his hands into his pockets in a stolid, understated support.

Dar wore her Helly Hansen poncho, with its hood pushed back, her dark hair wet and tangled and yet framing her angular features with stark precision.

Both Andy and Hank were in military raingear, in a dappled shadowy camo and stained, worn boots. The dimly golden light picking out the scars on their faces and glinting off the intent focus of their eyes.

Andy had put away his pistol, but Hank had his gun slung over his shoulder and cradled in both hands. He stood with his back against the wall near the door and watched them all, mostly in shadows this far from the lamp.

They all stared at each other, then Dar drew in and released a breath and took charge. She unzipped the throat fastening on her poncho and pulled it off, shaking the drops of rain off and then putting it on the bench next to Mark's jacket.

"All right," she said. "I'll start." She planted her hands on her hips.

"Hey wait a minute," John spoke up, cutting her off. "You were here the other day with the old man's grandkid." He studied her. "I saw you with her, and some other guy."

Dar nodded. "I was," she said. "My name's Dar Roberts." She paused. "This is my partner, Kerry." She indicated the shorter blonde woman at her side. "This is my father, Andrew, and our friends Hank and Mark." She angled her head in their direction. "Now who the hell are you?"

John watched her. "You buy this place?" He asked. "'Cause I know that little bitch wanted bad to sell it."

"Maybe," Kerry spoke up briefly.

"What does that mean?" He looked at her, then at Dar.

"Exactly what it sounds like. We might have. We signed the deal, and our lawyer was working on it, but then the storm hit, and I haven't heard from him yet," Dar said. "So yeah, maybe we... "She indicated Kerry and herself. "Own the place. Maybe we don't."

The guardians all looked at each other. "Shit," John said. "She really did it."

"Bitch," one of the others muttered softly under his breath. "He shoulda cut her out. He knew she'd sell soon as he was cold."

"So maybe you all are the ones trespassin," Andy said. "So, suppose you all speak up on who you are fore ah do call me some cops and have you hauled off on outta here."

"Cops won't come here," John said. "We called em when you were breaking the gates. Told us to fuck off."

"You all would be surprised what might show up here if we done the callin." Andy's tone was mild, and faintly humorous.

"Or we just shoot ya and dig a hole for ya," Hank suggested. "Got me a little bobcat I could use for it." He smiled at them with a gentle, dreamy expression on his face.

Kerry gently reached over and tugged Dar's sleeve. She jerked her head toward the door, and they walked together out of the kitchen and into the rear entranceway, leaving all the men to stand there watching each other.

"What's up?" Dar asked.

Kerry folded her arms and waited for Dar to half turn and focus on her. "These guys used to work for Mr. Hunter," She said. "We met them after Mark and I took shelter here when it was raining like crazy. We found that small gate open."

Dar nodded. "Okay... so... "She glanced behind them at the kitchen door. "What was all the running around over?"

"Well." Kerry cleared her throat gently. "Someone broke down their front gates with an armored truck. Until then they were just fine with us hanging out in their garden shed and we were just waiting for the rain to stop to call you."

"Ah."

"So maybe don't be so hard on them." Kerry bumped her head against Dar's arm. "I think they were his homies. They're kind of like Hunter's Point park rangers."

Dar laughed faintly. "Rangers?"

"They were trying to force us to safety. "Kerry said. "From you and Dad," she added. "And Hank."

Dar laughed a little harder, reaching up to cover her face with one hand. "Oh, Jesus."

"Of course, I knew it had to be you. Who else would know exactly where I was and show up in a Humvee?" Kerry said. "The minute they said it was an army truck I knew."

"It's Hank's gardening truck." Dar scrubbed her fingers through her wet hair. "It's got a trailer we figured we'd use to haul Mark's bike on. But anyway, I heard you yell and I..." She glanced past Kerry and then back to meet her eyes. "Didn't stop to think."

"No, but I'm glad," Kerry replied soberly. "Glad you guys came." She rested her head against Dar's shoulder. "I was sitting there really wanting you to be here and then you were." She let her eyes close a moment. "Good God I'm tired."

Dar kissed the top of her head, mud and leaves irrelevant. "Me too. Let's go wrap this up and go home."

****

"He called her Minnie." John was seated on a chair, his hands clasped together as he leaned his elbows on his knees. "Minneola, her whole name was. She was full blood Seminole."

They'd turned on the coffee pot and made some coffee, as the storm outside put down a curtain of rain so thick you couldn't see anything past it.

The guardians put what they had on the table, and they were all seated around it, working their way through some cake doughnuts and Fritos. Doug, the man who had carried Kerry, sat on a box near the stove.

"He was crazy about her." John picked up his cup and cradled it in his hands. "She knew how to do everything, y'know? She could cook, and make pretty shirts, just all kinds of stuff. My dad told me when he lived here, when he was a kid, she had a horse, and she would ride it all bareback and everything."

"Folks round here didn't much care for Indians back then," Doug said. "That's what the old man used to say. But he didn't care."

"Didn't care," John agreed. "My pop said he'd get a gun out and like to shoot anyone who had anything to say about her, little Minnie." He looked up at his unusual audience. "Sounds crazy."

"Not really," Kerry said, at the same time as Andy did. Hank laughed, giving the side of his gun a pat and the men in green raincoats just looked at each other uncomfortably. "Wonder how he felt about food fights," she added. "So far he sounds like a pretty good guy."

Mark chuckled at that, extending his legs out and crossing his ankles.

"Anyway, she gave him two boys and a girl," John continued. "They all grew up here. Old man had money... not really sure how he got some of it, but they always did all right. Kids grew up though and went off, didn't want to live here."

"Went to Colorado, one of them, and the other two to Cali," another of them said. "Left the old man and Minnie here by their selves in this big old place."

"He didn't care. He liked it," John said. "Told everyone else to get lost and leave them alone. Then Minnie got killed one night. She was just out near the water, watching some birds like she did sometimes and some drunk asshole in a big ass sailboat came past and shot her in the head."

Kerry's eyes widened. "What?" Her voice sharpened.

"Yeah, it was stupid," Doug said. "Just stupid. Bunch of jerks just bought them a boat and took it out in the bay and were shooting pelicans." He frowned. "Said she looked like a pelican, in her little shawl and all that, down by the water."

"Some bitch," Andy said. "Hope the law got them."

"Rich guys," John said. "Bought their way out of it. Paid the judge. You know how it is." He half shrugged. "People like that don't pay."

Kerry turned and looked at Dar who had straightened up and put her cup down on the table.

Thunder rolled over head, and lightning flashed outside.

"Anyway, old man was never the same after that," John said. "We felt bad, y'know? I always liked this place, we hung out here. Camped near the far wall down south on the edge of the property. We took care of things. You know, after work and all that."

"Old man treated us good," one of the others said. "We'd come sing carols for him on the holidays, like that. Then one night we came here, just near dark, and there were fire engines and I don't' know what else all over the place."

"Someone called the cops, I guess," John said. "He was lying on the ground, you know? Just fell down and died. Poor old guy. They took him off, then a few weeks later, she showed up waving some papers around talking crap about everything."

Kerry stood up and walked around in a circle, looking at the kitchen. "Why?" She asked. "It's a gorgeous property. There's nothing like it any-where around here."

John shrugged. "Found out she couldn't do nothing with it, I guess." He looked at her, then at Dar. "Ya'll know that, right?" There was a touch of malice in his tone. "You can't turn it into no hotel or nothin."

"They told us." Dar got up and looked around as well. "Last thing in the world I want to do is own a damn hotel."

"You want to go buy it anyhow?" Doug asked, in a puzzled tone. "Well, you all showed up in a car with a machine gun so maybe you're cra-zier than the old man was."

Dar walked to the doors in the back of the kitchen and pushed them open, swinging, heavy wooden doors covered in material that felt worn against her fingertips. "He wouldn't ever sell to anyone," she commented. "That's what you said, wasn't it, Dad?"

"Yeap," Andy said. "Gov'mint wanted to buy the place once ah heard bout it. Make it into a VA home or somethin. Wouldn't let em." He regarded the men, who had turned to look at him. "Probly woulda ended up something else anyhow, bein the gov'mint."

"Possht." Hank made a rude noise. "End up some tin bar jock strap's gym locker."

That seemed to go over well with the guardians. They exchanged glances, and faint smiles, and resettled themselves, their postures relaxing.

One of them got up and went to the coffee pot, the old-fashioned per-colator kind and triggered the dispenser into his cup. It sent the scent of slightly chicory scented steam into the room, and Doug went over to pick up two cookies, juggling them in one hand.

"Yeah, no, he sure enough didn't trust the government," Doug said. "Specially not the locals, not these days." He put a cookie into his mouth and bit down on it. "Scams, you know?"

"Yeap."

"Fought like nuts to get this place named historic, so no one else could do nothin with it." John nodded. "They just done that, maybe four months back." He paused thoughtfully. "Maybe that's why he kicked off finally. Figured it'd be okay after that."

"Coulda." Doug nodded. "Didn't want nobody to ruin it up." He looked sideways at them. "Fancy it up."

"Hope he liked cabling and wet dogs." Dar went through the door, letting it shut behind her as she walked down the long hall, emerging out into the large, long high-ceilinged space in the center of the house.

The kitchen was in the back of the house. The hallway had long lines of cabinets and then another set of doors that closed that all in from the space she was in now.

She heard the door open and close behind her, and waited, not bothering to turn to see who'd followed her out. "Damn storm," she said.

"Damn storm," Kerry echoed, coming to stand next to her. "Looks like it made it through though." She flicked on the flashlight she'd had hung around her wrist and shone it in all directions. "This place is huge."

"It is." Dar had her hands in her pockets, and she turned around in the circle. The lightning and gray skies from outside reflected through the windows, facing the water. They had survived the hurricane seemingly untouched. "Wonder if those guys boarded it up."

"Bet they did." Kerry walked toward front of the house that faced the water, the large space with its vaulted ceilings and bowed, full length windows. "Wow."

It was hard, really to absorb the sense of space inside the place. It was three floors, but they were high ceilinged and vast, full of angles and shadow. The lightning only added to the sense of presence and mystery. "Dar, we could play tennis in this room."

"Why would we play tennis? Neither of us like it," Dar asked, in a reasonable tone. "Handball maybe."

"Those ceilings are high enough for it." Kerry laughed a little bit. "Jesus."

"Are we crazy?" Dar asked. "This is twice the size of our whole office building. You and I could actually live in the Dixie. Why the hell did we even think this was a good idea?" She asked. "Did I think, since you never even saw it," she corrected herself.

"We've always been a little crazy." Kerry took a step forward and looked around. "But you know what, Dar? I think I like this place."

"Thought you would," Dar admitted. "When I walked in here in my head I just said, Kerry's going to love this." She put her hands in her pockets and rocked up and down on the balls of her feet.

"It's way too big, and the property's insane, and it's going to be so much work and it's so expensive and you know what? I still hope it went through." Kerry walked forward to look out the windows, imagining herself sitting there, watching the sunrise though them, having a cup of tea. "I want to live here with you."

"Do you?"

"I do." She turned to find Dar watching her, a gentle, charmed smile on her face. "I'd like to have met the old man, and Minnie." She walked back and held her hands out, which Dar reached out and grasped. "This place is amazing."

Dar lifted one of her hands up and kissed Kerry's knuckles in a movement of casual gallantry. "Timing sucks," she said. "We don't even know how many customers we're going to keep. We could end up half bankrupt. Or all bankrupt. Then what?"

Kerry studied her. "Then we sell your brain, a cell at a time," she said. "That should take care of that."

"Kerry."

Kerry chuckled. "Hon, I'm sorry. I'm just too tired right now to stress out. I just want to go home and get in bed with you. Hell, I'd settle for the Dixie's cabin right now." She paused, thoughtfully. "Hell, I'd settle for the window seat in your office."

"Not with that party going on, and unfortunately, we brought Dad's boat." Dar pulled her closer and wrapped her arms around her. "We figured we'd have to get Mark's bike aboard and he has a ramp on the back."

"A ramp?"

"I didn't ask, you shouldn't either."

"Should I ask about the machine gun?" Kerry wondered. "That was kinda radical even for him."

Dar chuckled softly. "It's real," she admitted. "There's a magazine of rounds in there under it."

"Of course, it's real. I assumed it was."

Kerry studied the inside of the big room, really finding no details other than a vague sense of pale walls, and a staircase moving up into the shadows. "Wish I could see more of what everything looks like," she murmured. "But I do like that kitchen. "It's so big, and that one corner is just right for that inside garden I've been wanting to try."

Dar nodded. "I liked this place because it's not a square box like all the other square boxes around here," she mused. "And the space and the trees. It smelled good. There's mangos around somewhere, and citrus," she added. "And boarded up or not, there's no water in here. He knew what he was doing when he built it."

"Well, we don't know that," Kerry said. "But I don't hear anything dripping." She reached around Dar and flashed her light along the floor in both directions. "Seems dry."

"And it had an awesome view," Dar said and looked over Kerry's shoulder, as lightning lit up the emptied pool, and the stained stone wall, and beyond it the algae streaked dock. "I bet we could end up petting a manatee out there before breakfast."

"I think I'd like to pet a manatee. Or at least, share my banana yogurt with one." Kerry leaned against her. "The dogs are going to love this place."

"Oh, yeah." Dar exhaled, in some contentment. "The structure of this place is solid. Who'd want to make a hotel out of it?" She wondered. "I liked the way it looked." As she said it, there was a faint creak around them as the downpour seemed to ease. "Sorta felt like a castle."

"Are these all stone floors?" Kerry looked down, examining the surface her boots were on. "As in actual stone? Not tile?"

"They are." Dar scuffed her toe on it. "Upper floors are hardwood," she said. "It's all real, old timey solid stuff."

"Which is going to be such a party to work around making this livable for us," Kerry said. "But kinda fun too, I think."

"Master bedrooms got the same view as this." Dar indicated the floor to ceiling windows. "We'll work it all out."

Kerry turned off her flashlight and closed her eyes. She felt Dar's breast move against her and the shift of her jaw as she pondered there in thoughtful silence. "Well, Dardar, should we say screw the rain, and just head back?" She suggested. "I get the feeling this isn't ending anytime soon."

"Yup." Dar patted her on the back. "Let's go and get this over with. I want a shower, and some hot milk and another day." She paused. "Did I tell you I got the internet up?"

Kerry silently laughed. "Oh, God. On second thought, let's just stay here. I don't want to see my email."

****

The kitchen door opened again and Dar and Kerry came back inside. "Not going to stop raining," Dar said. "We might as well stop waiting for it to."

"You all ready to get on outta here, Dardar?" Andy stood up, reading her body language without effort. "We can get that buggy backed on up. Figured your bike'd fit on the trailer." He added as an aside to Mark.

"You guys rock." Mark stood. "Yeah, riding in this'd be a nightmare. We heading to the office? I can crash in my office. I got a go bag in there I left just in case," he said. "Man, I'll be glad to park it for the night."

"We'll be back when we find out what the deal is with the place," Dar told the green clad men. "Did you board the windows up?"

John nodded. "My dad's in construction. We had plenty of wood."

They all looked at Dar with expressions and emotion she readily understood, having been a leader of people now for long enough. "Thank you," she said. "I'm sorry about all the chaos when we got here. We didn't mean for anyone to get hurt."

Kerry silently gave her a pat on the back.

Doug eyed her, then rubbed his chest. "Lady, I gotta tell you I haven't got hit like that since I was a linebacker in high school," he said. "We didn't mean anyone no harm. We thought you all were trouble."

Kerry grinned. "We are."

Dar smiled and draped one arm over Kerry's shoulders. "If you hang around and keep an eye on things, either way, we'll take care of you all. I can't imagine what those windows would have been like if you hadn't protected them," she said. "Probably won't know for a couple days what the deal is with the title."

Doug nodded. "We don't want nothing," he replied, unexpectedly. "We'll do it for him, until they chase us off." He smiled a little in obvious relief. Hope it works out though. I think the old man'd like you folks."

"Yeah." John started laughing. "He would. You'd be right on up his alley. Specially with that machine gun."

"Let's go," Andy said, pointing at the back door. "C'mon, Hank. Gonna have to untangle that cable. Think you dragged in a tree or something with ya." He followed Hank out the door, and they filed after him.

Doug pulled his hood up. "We'll help. Might as well end the night up the right way," he said, as the rest of the guardians quickly joined him. "Well, that sure didn't go where I thought it would," he added, with a faint shake of his head.

"Hell no." John went to hold the door. "Heeeeeeellllll no."

****

It was still raining when they got to the office, the upper windows showing dim glows of lanterns inside. They heard the sound of the generator rumbling softly over the rain hitting the street as Hank pulled the Humvee with its cargo of motorbike and passengers into the parking lot.

Kerry was seated in the middle of the back seat, leaning against Dar, her eyes closed. When they came to a halt, she opened one eye and looked through the front seats, past the string of bullets through the muddy window. "Home sweet home."

"Glad to see the place, gotta admit that," Mark said. "Shit, I'm tired."

Kerry, who'd gotten in a fifteen-minute nap, nodded. She waited for Dar to open the door and get out, and she scooted over and followed her up the sidewalk toward the front door.

It was quiet, and late, and yet there was still a guard at the door, who recognized them and passed them on. "Lo," Andy said. "They quiet down in there?"

"Yeah." The guard nodded. "I just been out here an hour. All them extras went on home. Just them that belongs in there now. That guy what owns the building said he'd be back tomorrow to talk with you all."

"Good." Andy held the door for them and then followed them inside as they moved into the stuffy shadow filled hallway that was now quite abandoned.

"Yeah, can't wait for what he has to say," Kerry grumbled. "Probably going to tell me he's going to let some cousin of his fix the place."

"Mm," Dar muttered under her breath.

A floorboard creaked over their head, and Andy glanced up to the top of the stairs where a solar charged lantern hung. He lifted his hand and the armed figure at the top of the steps waved back.

Dar moved into the central hallway and glanced down it. The strings of tables were still there, but they'd been tidied up. Things that were leftover were packed neatly away.

She was glad to see the cleanup. She went to the door to the central open space and put her head out to look around the rain drenched, but equally tidy, picnic tables.

Mark sighed. "I'm gonna go crash in my office," he said. "Don't even care of it's hot." He swung to the left and climbed up the steps to the second floor and exchanged a brief wave with the man on guard. "Hey, Pete."

"Yo," Pete said. "Glad they found you guys."

"Me too," Mark said. "I just want to park my ass on a chair and sack out."

"Heard ya." Pete smiled. "Gals put soap and all that in the shower room if you want," he said. "Water's not hot but this is Floooreida, and it ain't cold neither."

Mark chuckled and walked past him down the hall and into his office, which was dark and quiet and blessedly free of weird guys and rain. "I can shower in the morning," He muttered under his breath. "Been freaking showering all damn day long."

****

Kerry used the restroom and then wandered back into the central hall, where Dar stood, arms crossed, talking to Hank. "You up to driving home, hon?"

"Yeah, I'm fine." Dar had taken off her rain gear and pulled her hair back into a ponytail. "Dad's taking a look around," she explained. "I was just thanking Hank for coming out with us."

"Naw. It was fun." Hank produced a smile that was unrestrained and real. "Reminds me of old times, with your dad." He rocked up and down. "Didn't figure we'd end up ending up though where we done."

"No, well..." Dar shrugged a little bit. "We were all going in the same direction. Had to end up somewhere."

"I was surprised I was where I was." Kerry folded her arms over her chest. "When those guys told me it was Hunter's I was like... what the hell? But then I realized where it was and it sort of did make sense... did you realize where we were heading, Dar?"

Dar shook her head. "Didn't even think about it. But when I saw the wall there... "She hesitated. "I figured that kind of coincidence usually doesn't pass us up." She looked down the hallway, then back at Kerry, one eyebrow quirked a little bit.

Kerry looked back at her and tried to work out the expression on Dar's face, concluding that it was possible coincidence wasn't quite the word Dar meant.

"That place there is sweet. Hardwood hammock and all that stuff," Hank carried on, ignoring the silent communication.

"A what?" Kerry asked, putting the question away for later.

"Hardwood hammock," Hank said. "Old timey stuff from round here. Limestone wibbly wobbles and native trees and all that stuff." He nodded his head. "Got your holes and gullies and all that. Ferns, y'know?"

Kerry regarded him, as he strolled off, whistling a little under his breath. "I have to look that up," she said, after a brief pause. "Now that Thor, god of the internets has gotten that going back at the house." She gently elbowed Dar's ribs. "Is that hammock, as in Matheson Hammock?"

"Yeah, it is actually," Dar said, after pausing to think. "It's all about the limestone substructure of the area, and something called the Miami Rock Ridge."

"The only ridge I've seen in Miami is the Dade County landfill," Kerry said. "What kind of ridge are we talking about here?"

"Not that kind of ridge." Dar stifled a yawn. "I know where there are some near here. We can go see them the next time we head over to the new place."

Dar caught sight of Andy's tall figure coming down the hall. "Ready to go, Dad?" She called out. "Rain's not gonna get any better."

"Hell yes," he agreed. "C'mon." He walked past them to the reception- ist stand, and retrieved his raincoat, as both of them followed. "Done about had enough for one day in this here retirement." He shook his head. "Lord."

Dar put on her jacket and Kerry detoured into the conference room to grab a poncho she slid over her head. "Would have been nice to have this with me tonight." Kerry commented. "Jesus I'm tired of this damn weather. Didn't they say it was going to be clear after that damn thing hit?"

"Ran into that front." Dar responded, briefly. "No telling with these things."

Without looking back they went out the door and into the rain, Andy flicking on his flashlight as he led the way down the sidewalk and then turned to go around the side of the building.

Everything around seemed dark and empty. At this time of night Kerry expected it to be quiet, but still lit, always with a few people strolling along the street, or sitting at one of the cafes whose front porches were shadowed and full of debris.

The only light anywhere was the faint hint of amber glows from the windows of their own building, the flickers of candles and the generator run floodlight whose blue glare flickered from inside the open square of the building and lit the back loading dock.

Kerry reached out and took Dar's hand in hers and felt Dar's long fingers curl around hers.

They walked past their building and down the lane towards the sailing club and the water, feeling the rain beat against their backs driven by the offshore wind coming from the northwest. Past the debris still in the road, and the downed trees, and the sodden masses of garbage that stank.

She was glad of the wind then, driving past them, as they crossed the road and went through the parking lot of the club, climbing over two telephone poles lying over several cars and ducking under the power lines laying across everything, from the towers that had collapsed on either side of the building.

She could see the bay, and the white mass that was Andy's boat bobbling in the waves, and in the moment she was glad they were leaving the dark city behind and that soon, in maybe a half hour, maybe forty five minutes, she'd be able to stand in her own lit, cool home and be comfortable.

Like no one behind her could. Super glad that Dar hadn't taken her suggestion. She glanced at the inky black water on either side of the ramp, its surface full of sea wrack, and floating wooden debris.

"Careful there." Andy directed the light on the slick deck. "Aint no time to be swimming."

"Want to do me a favor?" Dar asked, as they edged along the makeshift ramp that extended out towards the boat.

"Pot of coffee?" Kerry reached out to grab the railing of the boat, as Andy crossed from the ramp to the deck, and she felt the boat move under his weight. "And I bet I can find some ice cream in there."

****

It had taken over an hour. The weather, and the uncertainty of navigating in the pitch darkness had made Dar cautious, and it was well after midnight when they came around the south side of the island and approached the entrance to the marina.

It was, as she had expected, quiet and empty of dockhands. But the work lights were on and it was a relief to be able to see clearly, and she gently nudged the big boat into its slip past her own against the outer seawall dock glad at least that the rain had slackened, if not stopped.

To her right on the console was a thermos and she picked it up and took a swallow of the strong coffee inside, then set it down before she let the boat drift lightly against the bolsters, waiting to see her father step off and take the ropes before she shut down the engines.

"We're tied." Kerry called up from the aft pylon.

Dar shut everything down and made her way down the ladder from the flying bridge, with one hand on the ladder and the other gripping the thermos, glad the steps had a roughened surface on them as rain dripped into her eyes.

She joined them on land and they made their way up the dock and along the side of the temporary marina tent, it's roof flapping in the wind and rain rolling off it's slanted surface.

Then they were at the cart, and this time Andy took the wheel, motioning Dar to get in behind him. "You done all the drivin today Dardar. Take me a turn."

Dar got in the back seat and extended her legs sideways as Kerry zipped the plastic shield down and they started off along the service path around the back of the destroyed marina building.

Everything here was also silent and seemingly abandoned, the difference was there were periodic lights along the road, some temporary, and through the trees real lights were seen from the buildings and townhouses that ringed the island.

"Is that a helicopter on the golf course?" Kerry commented.

"That's a helicopter on the golf course." Dar concluded. "I guess they managed to drain the damn thing." She regarded the outline. "Private."

"Them people live here, aint' surprising." Andy said.

"You live here, dad." Kerry reminded him. "And we do too for now."

"Aint' what I meant."

"Well." Dar shifted a little, half turning to watch the aircraft as they went by. "Maybe I should learn to fly one of those things. Hell of a lot faster to get around with then a couple of motor yachts." She looked at Kerry, who had turned around in the front seat to look at her. "What?" She asked. "If Alastair can fly a plane, I could."

"Too many damn trees for them things." Andy steered around a pile of debris in the road. "Too many trees, and too much wind, them pilots for the coast guard were saying."

"Yeah." Dar thought about what it had been like piloting the boat and imagined trying to do that in the air. "That's a point."

As they came around the curve in the road, they could see there was, despite the late hour, activity going on in the section of housing where they lived. "Now what?" Dar reversed her position, sliding to one side so she could see past Kerry. That the bunch next to ours?"

There were dozens of dark cars parked in the road along the wall that divided the homes from the road and the interior of the island including it's golf course. Two of them had been pulled up next to the entrance gates and there were figures standing around both, and on either side of the entrance bright floodlights were positioned, glaring out into the night.

Some of them heard the cart approaching and two men turned to look at them as Andy steered the cart, slowing it down before he turned into the opening that led into their section of the townhomes. "Cars got on here somehow. Figure maybe them ferries are running?"

"Hope so. That'd be great if we could take the truck off tomorrow." Dar said. "That makeshift dock back there is starting to fall apart. I could feel it when we were crossing before." She shifted back around as they arrived home, and the cart came to a halt.

The front lights were on, and as they got out and climbed up the slope from the parking area to the stairs the door opened and Ceci poked her head out. Spotting them, she emerged all the way and got the door closed before the barking dogs behind her could squeeze out. "Ah hah!"

"Lo." Andy waved, as they climbed up the steps. "Got a fuss going on ovah there?" He indicated the next section.

"Spooks." Ceci informed them. "I figure the governor's probably moving his cocker spaniel in." She added, in a wryly amused tone. "So how'd it all go?"

"Long ass day." Andy concluded, as they went inside, to be greeted by Mocha and Chino and thoroughly sniffed. "Get out the way, furballs."

"Do I want to know why you're wearing hospital scrubs?" Ceci asked Kerry, as she pulled off her poncho and left it hanging on the door to the closet set in the underside of the stairs. "Where the Samhain were you the whole day?"

"Long story." Kerry sighed, taking in a breath of the cold, dry air and savoring the chill of it against her skin. "It's been one of those days that were about a week long."

"Meet you in the shower?" Dar gave her a nudge. "I'll fill in the details."

Kerry didn't argue. She went into the ground floor master suite and into the large bathroom, already pulling the scrubs up over her head and ridding her body of their damp mustiness. She watched the cool air lift goosebumps on her skin, and went into the shower to turn it on.

She fancied she could still smell the antiseptic smell of the hospital soap and was happy to step under the hot water in it's drenching stream and pick up one of their sea sponges, putting some of their preferred wash on it and scrubbing her skin with it.

The heat picked up the scent of the soap and filled the shower with it and Kerry smiled, hearing over the sound of the shower Dar's voice as she moved in her direction. "Know what?" She asked, as her partner entered the room.

"You're glad we decided not to stay at the office." Dar stated amiably. "Cause I sure am." She joined Kerry in the shower and took over the sponge. "Yikes you did get sunburned."

"I did." Kerry agreed, contentedly washing the grit out of her hair. "Did I tell you I ended up losing my shirt escaping from a mob?" She said. "In that bag I had there's a national guard t-shirt I conned out of someone while Mark was fixing a database server."

Dar paused, and looked over Kerry's shoulder so they could make eye contact. "What and what now?"

"I told you this day was a week long." Kerry sighed. "Jesus."

"Save it for tomorrow." Dar put her arms around her as they stood under the drenching spray together. "We can go over it at breakfast."

Kery smiled, savoring the lack of rain, lack of heat, lack of confounding issues to deal with in this moment of utter comfort of the soul. "Tomorrow's another day." She agreed. "And no way can it be as crazy as today was."

About the Author

Melissa Good is a full time network engineer and part time writer who lives in Pembroke Pines, Florida with a handful of lizards and a dog. When not traveling for work, or participating in the usual chores she ejects several sets of clamoring voices onto a variety of keyboards and tries to entertain others with them to the best of her ability.

You can contact Melissa by email at: merwolf01@gmail.com

Visit her website: http://www.merwolf.com

Books by Melissa Good

Tropical Storm

From bestselling author Melissa Good comes a tale of heartache, longing, family strife, lust for love, and redemption. Tropical Storm took the lesbian reading world by storm when it was first written...now read this exciting revised "author's cut" edition.

Dar Roberts, corporate raider for a multi-national tech company, is cold, practical, and merciless. She does her job with razor-sharp accuracy. Friends are a luxury she cannot allow herself, and love is something she knows she'll never attain.

Kerry Stuart left Michigan for Florida in an attempt to get away from her domineering politician father and the constraints of the overly conservative life her family forced upon her. After college she worked her way into supervision at a small tech company, only to have it taken over by Dar Roberts' organization. Her association with Dar begins in disbelief, hatred, and disappointment, but when Dar unexpectedly hires Kerry as her work assistant, the dynamics of their relationship change. Over time, a bond begins to form.

But can Dar overcome years of habit and conditioning to open herself up to the uncertainty of love? And will Kerry escape from the clutches of her powerful father in order to live a better life?

Hurricane Watch

In this sequel to "Tropical Storm," Dar and Kerry are back and making their relationship permanent. But an ambitious new colleague threatens to divide them — and out them. He wants Dar's head and her job, and he's willing to use Kerry to do it. Can their home life survive the office power play?

Dar and Kerry are redefining themselves and their priorities to build a life and a family together. But with the scheming colleagues and old flames trying to drive them apart and bring them down, the two women must overcome fear, prejudice, and their own pasts to protect the company and each other. Does their relationship have enough trust to survive the storm?

Enter the lives of two captivating characters and their world that Melissa Good's thousands of fans already know and love. Your heart will be touched by the poignant realism of the story. Your senses and emotions will be electrified by the intensity of their problems. You will care about these characters before you get very far into the story.

Don't miss this exciting revised "author's cut" edition.

Eye of the Storm
(second edition)

Eye of the Storm picks up the story of Dar Roberts and Kerry Stuart a few months after the story Hurricane Watch ends. At first it looks like they are settling into their lives together but, as readers of this series have learned, life is never simple around Dar and Kerry. Surrounded by endless corporate intrigue, Dar experiences personal discoveries that force her to deal with issues that she had buried long ago and Kerry finally faces the consequences of her own actions. As always, they help each other through these personal challenges that, in the end, strengthen them as individuals and as a couple.

Red Sky at Morning
(second edition)

A connection others don't understand...
A love that won't be denied...
Danger they can sense but cannot see...

Dar Roberts was always ruthless and single-minded...until she met Kerry Stuart.

Kerry was oppressed by her family's wealth and politics. But Dar saved her from that. Now new dangers confront them from all sides. While traveling to Chicago, Kerry's plane is struck by lightning. Dar, in New York for a stockholders' meeting, senses Kerry is in trouble. They simultaneously experience feelings that are new, sensations that both are reluctant to admit when they are finally back together. Back in Miami, a cover-up of the worst kind, problems with the military, and unexpected betrayals will cause more danger. Can Kerry help as Dar has to examine her life and loyalties and call into question all she's believed in since childhood? Will their relationship deepen through it all? Or will it be destroyed?

This is the revised "author's cut edition." Some scenes were added such as: a shopping excursion downtown where Kerry buys leather; a flashback to Dar's first shopping trip to buy business attire – see how her clothing went from jeans and sweatshirts to power suits; and a mugging.

Don't miss this new edition.

Thicker Than Water

This sequel to Red Sky at Morning is the continuing saga of Dar Roberts and Kerry Stuart. It starts off with Kerry involved in the church group of girls. Kerry is forced to acknowledge her own feelings/experience toward/with her folks as she and Dar assist a teenager from the group who gets jailed because her parents tossed her out onto the streets when they find out she is gay. While trying to help the teenagers adjust to real world situations, Kerry gets the call concerning her father's health. Kerry flies to her family's side as her father dies, putting the family in crisis. Caught up in an international problem, Dar abandons the issue to go to Michigan, determined to support Kerry in the face of grief and hatred. Dar and Kerry face down Kerry's extended family with a little help from their own, and return home, where they decide to leave work and the world behind for a while for some time to themselves.

Terrors of the High Seas

After the stress of a long Navy project and Kerry's father's death, Dar and Kerry decide to take their first long vacation together. A cruise in the eastern Caribbean is just the nice, peaceful time they need – until they get involved in a family feud, an old murder, and come face to face with pirates as their vacation turns into a race to find the key to a decades old puzzle.

Tropical Convergence

There's trouble on the horizon for ILS when a rival challenges them head on, and their best weapons, Dar and Kerry, are distracted by life instead of focusing on the business. Add to that an old flame, and an aggressive entreprenaur throwing down the gauntlet and Dar at least is ready to throw in the towel. Is Kerry ready to follow suit, or will she decide to step out from behind Dar's shadow and step up to the challenges they both face?

This is the first part of the story formerly known as Moving Target.

Storm Surge, (Books 1 & 2)

Its fall. Dar and Kerry are traveling – Dar overseas to clinch a deal with their new ship owner partners in England, and Kerry on a reluctant visit home for her high school reunion. In the midst of corporate deals and personal conflict, their world goes unexpectedly out of control when an early morning spurt of unusual alarms turns out to be the beginning of a shocking nightmare neither expected.

Can they win the race against time to save their company and themselves?

Stormy Waters

As Kerry begins work on the cruise ship project, Dar is attempting to produce a program to stop the hackers she has been chasing through cyberspace. When it appears that one of their cruise ship project rivals is behind the attempts to gain access to their system, things get more stressful than ever. Add in an unrelenting reporter who stalks them for her own agenda, an employee who is being paid to steal data for a competitor, and Army intelligence becoming involved and Dar and Kerry feel more off balance than ever. As the situation heats up, they consider again whether they want to stay with ILS or strike out on their own, but they know they must first finish the ship project.

*** *This is the second part of the online story formerly known as Moving Target.* ***

Moving Target

Dar and Kerry both feel the cruise ship project seems off somehow, but they can't quite grasp what is wrong with the whole scenario. Things continue to go wrong and their competitors still look to be the culprits behind the problems.

Then new information leads them to discover a plot that everyone finds difficult to believe. Out of her comfort zone yet again, Dar refuses to lose and launches a new plan that will be a win-win, only to find another major twist thrown in her path. With everyone believing Dar can somehow win the day, can Dar and Kerry pull off another miracle finish? Do they want to?

Fans of this series should note that due to its length this story will be split into three novels. The determination of where to make that split was a joint decision between the author and the publisher.

See the title Tropical Convergence for further details on the first part and the title Stormy Waters for details on the second part.

Winds of Change (Books 1 & 2)

After 9/11 the world has changed and Dar and Kerry have decided to change along with it. They have an orderly plan to resign and finally take their long delayed travelling vacation. But as always fate intervenes and they find themselves caught in a web of conflicting demands and they have to make choices they never anticipated.

Southern Stars

At last, Dar and Kerry get to go on their long awaited and anticipated vacation in the Grand Canyon. They are looking forward to computer free time, beautiful scenery, and white water rapids. As always, though, life doesn't go smoothly and soon challenges are at hand.

Jess and Dev Series

Partners (Books 1 & 2)

After a massive volcanic eruption puts earth into nuclear winter, the planet is cloaked in clouds and no sun penetrates. Seas cover most of the land areas except high elevations which exist as islands where the remaining humans have learned to make do with much less. People survive on what they can take from the sea and with foodstuffs supplemented from an orbiting set of space stations.

Jess Drake is an agent for Interforce, a small and exclusive special forces organization that still possesses access to technology. Her job is to protect and serve the citizens of the American continent who are in conflict with those left on the European continent. The struggle for resources is brutal, and when a rogue agent nearly destroys everything, Interforce decides to trust no one. They send Jess a biologically-created agent who has been artificially devised and given knowledge using specialized brain programming techniques.

Instead of the mindless automaton one might expect, Biological Alternative NM-Dev-1 proves to be human and attractive. Against all odds, Jess and the new agent are swept into a relationship neither expected. Can they survive in these strange circumstances? And will they even be able to stay alive in this bleak new world?

Of Sea and Stars

Of Sea and Stars continues the saga of Interforce Agent Jess Drake and her Biological Alternative partner, NM-Dev-1, that began in Melissa Good's first two books in her Partners series.

This series chronicles what happens to human kind after a massive volcanic eruption puts earth into nuclear winter. The planet is cloaked in clouds and no sun penetrates. Seas cover most of the land areas except high elevations. These exist as islands where the remaining humans have learned to make do with much less. People survive on what they can take from the sea, and with foodstuffs supplemented from an orbiting set of space stations.

This new world is divided into two factions, and the struggle for resources between them is brutal, pitting one side against the other.

In Of Sea and Stars, Jess and Dev uncover a hidden cavern at Drakes Bay full of growing vegetables and fruit trees. There is evidence that the "other side" has been negotiating with Jess's brother, and with someone on the space station that created, Dev. This sends them on a quest into space to solve the mystery.

Bringing Stories Along the Queer Spectrum to Life

Visit us at our website: www.flashpointpublications.com